MAR 0 9 2015.

W9-CAJ-576

Praise for *New York Times* bestselling author Vicki Lewis Thompson

"*Cowboy Up* is a sexy joy ride, balanced with good-natured humor and Thompson's keen eye for detail. Another sizzling romance from the RT Reviewers' Choice award winner for best Blaze."

—*RT Book Reviews* on *Cowboy Up*

"Vicki Lewis Thompson has compiled a tale of this terrific family, along with their friends and employees, to keep you glued to the page and ending with that warm and loving feeling."

—*Fresh Fiction* on *Cowboys and Angels*

"Intensely romantic and hot enough to singe… her Sons of Chance series never fails to leave me worked up from all the heat, and then sighing with pleasure at the happy endings!"

—*We Read Romance* on *Riding High*

"If I had to use one word to describe *Ambushed!* it would be *charming*… Where the story shines and how it is elevated above others is the humor that is woven throughout."

—*Dear Author* on *Ambushed!*

"Thompson continues to do a great job with her popular Sons of Chance series by bringing the entire town of Shoshone and the Last Chance Ranch environment alive in this wonderfully engaging installment."

—*RT Book Reviews*, Top Pick, on *Wild at Heart*

Vicki Lewis Thompson's passion for travel has taken the *New York Times* bestselling author to Europe, Great Britain, the Greek Isles, Australia and New Zealand. She's visited across North America and has her eye on South America's rainforests. Africa, India and China beckon. But her first love is her home state of Arizona, with its deserts, mountains, sunsets and—last but not least—cowboys! The wide-open spaces and heroes on horseback influence everything she writes. Connect with her at vickilewisthompson.com, facebook.com/vickilewisthompson and twitter.com/vickilthompson.

New York Times Bestselling Author

Vicki Lewis Thompson

Should've Been a Cowboy
and
Cowboy Up

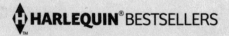

If you purchased this book without a cover you should be aware that this book is stolen property. It was reported as "unsold and destroyed" to the publisher, and neither the author nor the publisher has received any payment for this "stripped book."

Recycling programs
for this product may
not exist in your area.

ISBN-13: 978-0-373-40108-6

Should've Been a Cowboy and Cowboy Up
Copyright © 2015 by Harlequin Books S.A.

The publisher acknowledges the copyright holder
of the individual works as follows:

Should've Been a Cowboy
Copyright © 2011 by Vicki Lewis Thompson

Cowboy Up
Copyright © 2011 by Vicki Lewis Thompson

All rights reserved. Except for use in any review, the reproduction or utilization of this work in whole or in part in any form by any electronic, mechanical or other means, now known or hereinafter invented, including xerography, photocopying and recording, or in any information storage or retrieval system, is forbidden without the written permission of the publisher, Harlequin Enterprises Limited, 225 Duncan Mill Road, Don Mills, Ontario, Canada, M3B 3K9.

This is a work of fiction. Names, characters, places and incidents are either the product of the author's imagination or are used fictitiously, and any resemblance to actual persons, living or dead, business establishments, events or locales is entirely coincidental.

This edition published by arrangement with Harlequin Books S.A.

For questions and comments about the quality of this book, please contact us at CustomerService@Harlequin.com.

® and TM are trademarks of the publisher. Trademarks indicated with ® are registered in the United States Patent and Trademark Office, the Canadian Intellectual Property Office and in other countries.

Printed in U.S.A.

CONTENTS

SHOULD'VE BEEN
A COWBOY

For my editor Brenda Chin,
who gave me the opportunity to create a
multibook series about my favorite subject—cowboys.
A tip of the Stetson to you, Brenda!

Prologue

May 14, 1956, from the diary of Eleanor Chance

I LOVE GIVING birthday parties. And when your only child turns ten, well, today was a big day at the Last Chance Ranch. We had unseasonably warm weather in Jackson Hole, and after the kids left, tummies full of birthday cake and ice cream, Archie went to the barn and brought out Johnny's big present.

She's a beautiful little filly who looks exactly like the horse that the Lone Ranger's sidekick, Tonto, rides— white with bay patches. While most kids would want an all-white horse like the Lone Ranger's, Johnny loves Tonto's horse, Scout.

And so this filly will be named Scout, even though she's a girl. Everyone around here calls Scout a pinto, which is what Tonto's horse is, but she's actually a registered paint. That means she has pinto coloring, but she also has papers and can be bred later on.

She cost us a fair bit, but the money went to a good cause. One of our neighbors needed to sell this filly so he could pay for his wife's back operation. The operation was Ginny's last chance to avoid living in a wheel-chair, and I'm happy to say the surgery was a success.

That's what this ranch is about, giving people and animals one last chance. So everyone came out ahead on this deal. Besides, Archie says Scout is an investment as well as a birthday present for Johnny. Cattle ranching has been good to us, especially during the war when the army needed beef, but Archie thinks we should diversify, and for years he's dreamed of raising horses.

Scout's a dream come true for Johnny, who's begged us for a pinto from the moment he saw his first episode of *The Lone Ranger.* But Scout could be the beginning of Archie's dream, too. I sure hope so, because spending all that money on a registered paint was a gamble, even if it was for a good cause.

I keep reminding myself that Archie won the Last Chance in a card game nineteen years ago, and that's turned out pretty well. As Archie always says, "Chance men are lucky when it counts."

1

WHAT ROTTEN LUCK. Alex Keller ended the phone call, tucked his phone in his jeans pocket and nudged Doozie into a canter. He needed to get back to the ranch house and figure out what the hell to do now that the country band he'd hired wouldn't be showing up tomorrow. He couldn't expect to get a replacement at four o'clock on a Friday afternoon, which meant no live music for the open house. Damn.

The open house had been his idea. Two months ago, after accepting a job as the first-ever marketing director for the Last Chance, he'd proposed the event to increase the ranch's visibility and establish it as the premier place to buy registered paints. Technically he was up to the challenge. He held a degree in marketing, and although he'd spent most of his career as a high-profile DJ in Chicago, he'd also been instrumental in the radio station's marketing campaigns.

But this was his first event for the ranch, and he needed it to go well. The Chances were family now that Alex's sister Josie had married Jack Chance, so the ranch's bottom line had personal significance. The Chances weren't in immediate financial danger, but spring sales had been slow. Alex had been hired to fix that.

He'd saddled Doozie earlier that afternoon, figuring a ride might settle his nerves. Instead he'd ended up with a phone call that added to his growing list of problems. Most of the issues involved keeping the invited guests dry. Rain-filled clouds hovered on the horizon and only one of the three canopies he'd ordered had shown up. Now he had no band, either.

Live music would have gone a long way toward setting the tone for tomorrow's open house, even if it rained. Sure, he could rig up a sound system and use canned music and his DJ abilities, but it wouldn't have the same feel as live music, and he couldn't be stuck behind a microphone all day.

At this point on Friday afternoon, nothing could be done about either of those glitches. He'd spent all his life in Chicago and was used to its vast resources. If one band canceled, you hired another, and if one delivery of event canopies didn't work out, you went with a different company. Jackson Hole, Wyoming, was a whole other situation, and he was screwed.

He had to make this work, though. All three of the Chance brothers—Jack, Gabe, and Nick—had put their faith in him, and he'd do his damnedest. Everyone knew Alex Keller was a hard worker, especially his ex-wife, who'd wanted him to work less and play more.

Oh, well. Crystal was back in Chicago cavorting with her new boyfriend, and he was out here in God's country, working his butt off because that's who he was. And he couldn't complain. The ranch's location, west of a little town called Shoshone in the Jackson Hole region, was spectacular.

Following his divorce last summer, he'd left Chicago and found a combination DJ/marketing director position with a radio station in Jackson. But he'd spent more time out at the Last Chance than at his apartment in Jackson and had, to his surprise, gone country. When the offer came to work for the Chance brothers, he'd jumped at it.

Slowing Doozie to a trot as he approached the barn, he glanced over at the massive, two-story ranch house, a log structure that had grown as the family had grown. Its front windows faced north with a view of the state's scenic crown jewel—the perpetually snowcapped Tetons. The acreage was worth millions, and the family wanted to keep every square foot of it, which meant the Chances were land rich and cash poor.

From what Alex had heard, Jonathan Chance Sr. had been comfortable with that, but after his death, his three sons had taken stock of the situation. They'd decided on a more aggressive breeding and sales program for the ranch's registered paints to give the operation a bigger financial cushion.

Alex could see why. A ranch this size had a fair amount of overhead, including a payroll for several regular hands and a few seasonal ones, all of whom had to be housed and fed in addition to their wages. On top of that were maintenance and utility costs for the large ranch house, the bunkhouse, the heated barn and various other outbuildings.

Dismounting by the hitching post beside the barn, he answered a greeting from Emmett Sterling. The ranch foreman, a seasoned cowboy in his late fifties, paused on his way into the barn. "Want me to take care of her for you?"

"Thanks, but I'll do it." Alex had bonded with this

bay mare, who'd put up with his beginning riding mistakes without complaint. Doozie had arrived in Jackson Hole last summer about the same time Alex had. They'd both been in need of sanctuary, and the Last Chance had provided that.

Doozie wasn't a paint, so she couldn't be part of the breeding program, but she'd been allowed to stay, anyway. Alex thought it was appropriate that she'd been assigned to him, because he wasn't a cowboy, but he'd been allowed to stay, too. Doozie would never become a paint, but damned if Alex hadn't started to feel like a cowboy.

After settling Doozie in her stall with Hornswaggled, a goat who was her constant companion, Alex headed for the ranch house, where a cold bottle of Bud was calling his name. These days he drank beer instead of wine, just as he wore jeans instead of chinos.

A guy couldn't hang out in a living room with a wagon-wheel chandelier and Navajo rugs on the walls and keep wearing city-slicker clothes. The unwritten dress code for logging time in the cushy leather armchairs in front of the giant rock fireplace included faded jeans, boots and a Western shirt.

Alex had complied. The day he'd bought a Stetson and settled it on his head, he'd bid a permanent farewell to the Chicago city boy he used to be.

His boots echoed hollowly on the porch as he crossed to the large front door and pulled it open. No one was in the living room, which always smelled faintly of wood smoke even if the hearth was cold, like now. He turned left down a long hall. His route to the kitchen took him through the dining room with its four round tables that each sat eight people.

At this time of the afternoon the tables were empty,

but three hours ago the place had bustled with activity. The Chance brothers had continued their father's tradition of eating lunch with the hands so everyone could exchange information about ranch chores. Sarah, Jonathan's widow, usually joined the group, and now her three daughters-in-law were included, too.

When Alex heard Sarah's laughter coming from the kitchen, he knew she must be talking to the cook, Mary Lou Simms, who was as much a friend as an employee. Alex wished he weren't the bearer of bad news. He'd worked hard to make this event tomorrow successful, but now he wasn't sure it would be.

Sarah needed to know that, even if it spoiled her good mood. He could talk to the Chance brothers over dinner. Friday night was family night at the big house, a way to stay connected now that all three pairs of newlyweds lived on different sections of the ranch's vast acreage.

Taking a deep breath, Alex walked into the kitchen and found Mary Lou and Sarah pulling baby stuff out of a mail-order box. Gabe's wife, Morgan, was eight months pregnant, and soon-to-be grandma Sarah had obviously gone catalog shopping.

Sarah was the kind of woman who seemed ageless even though she'd let her hair go white. She wore it in a sleek bob, and her high cheekbones and flawless skin made her look years younger than she was. Her mother had been a runway model, and Sarah took after her.

Alex had heard that Mary Lou had been a blonde bombshell twenty years ago, but now she enjoyed her own excellent cooking and didn't seem to care about a few extra pounds or the state of her unruly gray hair.

Sarah glanced at Alex as he came into the kitchen. "What do you think?" She waved an impossibly tiny shirt in a red bandanna print. "Since Gabe and Morgan won't tell me if they're having a boy or a girl, I'm going with unisex clothes, which is probably better because they can be handed down."

"Cute." Alex hoped that was the appropriate response, because he'd never given much thought to baby clothes. Crystal had been fanatical about birth control during their years together, and he'd had no burning desire to be a father, especially after the marriage began to sour. Baby clothes were foreign objects to him. "Mind if I grab a beer?"

"Help yourself." She held up a one-piece deal that was supposed to look as if the baby wore jeans and a Western shirt, although it was printed on stretch terry. "Is this adorable or what?"

"Sure is!" Alex crossed to the refrigerator and opened it. Maybe once he'd wrapped his hand around a cold beer, he'd be able to find a gentle way to introduce some gloom and doom into this happy little baby scene.

Sarah was understandably excited about the impending arrival of her first grandchild. Alex had been the DJ for Morgan and Gabe's wedding reception last August, and Morgan had stated clearly then that she didn't plan to rush into motherhood. Yet within a couple of months she'd turned up preggers and was apparently thrilled about it.

Thoughts of Morgan's wedding always reminded Alex of Morgan's younger sister, Tyler, who had agreed to spend a memorable few hours in the hayloft with him following the reception. Alex couldn't smell fresh hay without remembering the feel of Tyler's soft, willing body and her muted cries of pleasure. They'd taken care not to make too much noise so they wouldn't draw any unwanted attention.

She'd left the next day, returning to her job as activities director for a luxury cruise line headquartered in L.A. She'd confessed that constant traveling didn't leave much room for relationships. Just as well, he'd told her. He was still recovering from his divorce.

True enough, but watching Tyler leave hadn't been easy. That night in the hayloft had been perfect, at least from his viewpoint. He'd tried to talk himself out of that assessment but hadn't quite succeeded.

He'd resisted the urge to ask Morgan about Tyler in the months that followed. He was pretty sure nobody knew that he and Tyler had spent the night together in the hayloft. The Chance family had been too preoccupied to notice, and Alex somehow doubted Tyler had confided in Morgan.

If she had, he would have seen it in Morgan's eyes or felt it in her treatment of him. So maybe the night had meant nothing more to Tyler than a champagne-flavored roll in the hay. Somehow he doubted it, though.

He'd sensed that she'd been as deeply affected as he'd been. Then again, she'd been his first since the divorce, so maybe his perception hadn't been accurate. In the following months he'd dated a couple of women from the Jackson Hole area, but they hadn't inspired the gut-level response he'd had to Tyler.

As Mary Lou and Sarah continued to coo over the baby clothes, Alex reached for the longneck. He'd curled his fingers around it when Morgan called out a greeting from the kitchen doorway. He hoped the baby clothes weren't supposed to be a surprise.

"Look who's here!" Morgan sounded breathless. "My

world-traveling sister just flew over from L.A. to surprise me!"

Alex straightened up so fast he banged his head on the
door of the refrigerator. Praying nobody had noticed, he
held his bottle of beer in a death grip and slowly closed
the refrigerator door. His heart hammered as he turned
to face the woman who'd played a prominent role in his
dreams for nearly ten months.

His memory hadn't done her justice. She was even
sexier than he'd remembered, with her ebony hair curling around her face and down the back of her turquoise
dress. Dark eyes that reflected her mother's Italian her-
itage met his. She seemed as shocked to see him as he
was to see her.

Although she looked nothing like Crystal, who was
blonde with Scandinavian ancestry, Alex couldn't help
noticing surface similarities to his ex-wife. Obviously
Tyler spent time and money on her hair, nails and clothes.

She wore a dress that revealed a little cleavage and
high-heeled sandals that showed off her pedicure. And
she smelled amazing, like a bouquet of peach-colored
roses. Although he'd fully embraced the country life, he'd
been a Chicago boy first, and all that careful grooming
still had the power to turn him on.

But it was more than that. One glance into those eyes
and he knew that what they'd shared in the hayloft had
been more than just sex. Whether they were prepared to
deal with it or not, they were emotionally involved. Still.

"Hey, Tyler." He managed what he hoped was a nonchalant smile. "How're you doing?"

TYLER HAD BEEN DOING just fine until she'd walked into
the Last Chance's kitchen and found Alex leaning into

the refrigerator, his tempting buns encased in well-worn jeans. She hadn't expected him to be at the ranch, and she certainly hadn't expected him to have transformed himself into a cowboy. Judging from his denim shirt, snug jeans and scuffed boots, that's exactly what he'd done.

Ten months ago he'd been a hottie who'd tempted her into one night of wild sex. She'd tried to convince herself it had been about superficial pleasure, but there was nothing superficial about the feelings flooding through her now. She'd had casual affairs. This didn't qualify.

And God, did he look good. Apparently Wyoming agreed with him. The cute city boy had been replaced with a ruggedly handsome man. The dark blond hair he'd worn short and preppy now touched his collar. His face was leaner, his gray eyes more piercing, his body more ripped than she remembered. In ten months he'd gone from hottie to hero.

And what they'd shared had definitely been more than just sex. This man had made wonderful love to her, and she wanted him to do it again. Her skin warmed and her heartbeat quickened at the memory of his caress, his kiss, his gentle words. The time they'd been apart shrank until she felt as if she'd lain naked with him only hours ago.

On that cool August morning she'd forced herself to leave without a backward glance, although she'd mentally glanced back more than she cared to admit. Now she had even more reason to avoid a relationship, but she wondered how on God's green earth she'd be able to resist him.

"Tyler, you remember Alex." Morgan seemed to think her sister's silence meant she needed prompting. "He was the DJ at our wedding reception."

"Right." Tyler smiled at him. "I thought you looked familiar."

He cleared his throat. "There was a lot going on that night."

Especially in the hayloft. "It was a memorable evening." Tyler forced her gaze away from his before someone figured out just how well she remembered the guy who'd played the music, the guy who had a really talented mouth, clever hands and a way of stealing a girl's heart when she wasn't looking.

"I adored my wedding." Morgan seemed oblivious to the undercurrents swirling between Tyler and Alex.

"The ceremony on horseback was certainly unique." Tyler focused all her attention on her hormonal and understandably self-centered sister, who looked as if she'd stuffed a basketball down the front of her green paisley dress. Morgan had a month to go before she delivered, which meant this would be a large baby, because she looked ready to give birth at any moment.

Anyone who saw dark-haired Tyler and redheaded Morgan and knew they were sisters would understand why their parents had decided to combine last names and create the O'Connelli surname to honor both the Irish and the Italian sides of the family. It had been a quirky solution from a certifiably quirky couple.

"And there was Jack's incredible toast at the reception," Sarah added. She'd managed to shove into the box whatever she'd been holding when they'd arrived. "I'll never forget that toast."

"Me neither." Morgan sighed. "The whole event was so romantic and happy that I think it helped bring Jack and Josie back together. Was that when they decided to have a double wedding with Nick and Dominique?"

"I think the four of them did come to that conclusion sometime during the reception." Sarah moved in front of the box sitting on the round oak table, as if wanting to block it from Morgan's view. "We were lucky to get their ceremony planned and completed before the first snow."

Tyler suspected the box was full of baby things. She had quite a few in her suitcase, too. She'd managed to finagle this short leave from work, knowing she'd be in the middle of the Mediterranean when the baby arrived.

She glanced at Sarah. "So how does it feel, having all three of your sons married?"

"Very empty nestish," Sarah said. "I hope you can stick around for a while. We have plenty of room upstairs now and I'd love the company."

"She might be happiest here," Morgan said. "I'd love to have her sleep at our house, but with the construction still in progress, and only the master bedroom finished, it's sort of—"

"Like camping out." Sarah laughed. "Tyler, you'll want to take one of the upstairs bedrooms and leave the newlyweds to their chaos. I told them all to wait and move when the houses were done, but all three couples insisted they wanted to rough it in their new digs. I've tried not to take it personally," she added with a grin.

"I can sleep wherever," Tyler said. *Except the hayloft.* "But if there's a room available upstairs, that sounds wonderful."

"Great." Sarah beamed at her. "How long can you stay?"

"I have to fly back next Wednesday."

"Wow." Sarah blinked. "That's hardly enough time to unpack."

"But at least she's here, which is totally awesome." Morgan's happy gaze met Tyler's.

"I had to see the new mommy-to-be." And her sister's enthusiasm made the effort so worthwhile. Alex's presence was a small complication she'd work through.

"Tyler about gave me a heart attack," Morgan said. "I didn't know she was coming until she called me from the L.A. airport and said she was on her way."

"I wasn't sure I could get off until the last minute, and I had to sign in blood that I'd be back on Wednesday."

Morgan regarded her sister with obvious pride. "That's because Tyler's the activities director for a *world cruise* that sails from L.A. a week from today. If she gets a good evaluation at the end of it, she's been promised a promotion to cruise director, which means she'll be the head honcho next time out. How cool is that?"

"Very cool." Sarah gazed at Tyler with obvious respect.

"Good for you, Tyler," Mary Lou added.

"Thanks. If I get this promotion, I'll be the youngest cruise director in the history of the company." Tyler found herself basking in Sarah's and Mary Lou's approval. Her parents, who claimed to care nothing for status or worldly goods, hadn't been particularly impressed by her rapid rise in the business. She hadn't thought she cared whether they were impressed or not, but maybe she did.

"That's terrific." Alex lifted his unopened beer bottle. "Can I get drinks for anyone? We should toast Tyler's success."

"Well, I don't have the promotion yet." But maybe it was good that the subject was on the table, so that Alex knew that she was still fully immersed in her career and excited about the next big step.

Or maybe he wouldn't care. Maybe he was over his ex and had hooked up with somebody from around here. All her worries about resisting him might be for nothing if he was otherwise occupied.

"I'd love a beer," Mary Lou said. "Move aside, Alex, and I'll see that we all get something cold to drink and happy-hour munchies. Sarah, I know you'll join me in a Friday-afternoon beer. Tyler, what will you have?"

"The same, thanks." Maybe a cold beer would settle her nerves. She'd expected she might see Alex while she was here, considering that he was Josie's brother and part of the extended Chance family. But she hadn't planned on running into him first thing out of the gate and immediately having to deal with her emotional reaction.

"Root beer for me, please," Morgan said.

"I know, honey," Mary Lou said. "I have it right here." She opened the refrigerator and began passing out bottles.

Sarah quietly removed the box from the table and tucked it out of sight before swinging into hostess mode. "Everybody have a seat. I'll get us some chips and dip. The rest of the gang will probably show up pretty soon, and if I know my boys, they'll be ready to toast the beginning of the weekend with a cold one."

Tyler chose a seat at the opposite side of the table from where Alex stood. She couldn't help sneaking glances at him, and every time she did, he was looking back. Not the usual behavior of a man who had a girlfriend.

He could still be unattached, and if so, she'd have to be very careful. As if her memories of his lovemaking weren't enough to make her heart race, he'd turned into every woman's fantasy—a broad-shouldered, lean-hipped, yummy cowboy. She wondered if he'd bought himself a Stetson.

In no time Mary Lou and Sarah had the impromptu party organized with drinks all around. Bowls of chips and several kinds of dip sat on the table along with a stack of napkins.

Sarah took a chair and raised her beer bottle. "Here's to your world cruise, Tyler, and the important promotion I'm sure will follow."

"Thank you." Tyler began to understand why Morgan loved being a part of this stable, loving family. Morgan, Tyler and their six siblings had lived a vagabond lifestyle, traveling the country in a psychedelic van with their New Age parents.

They'd spent a few months in Shoshone back when Morgan and Tyler were teenagers. For Tyler, it had just been one stop in their constant travels, but Morgan had loved it and had vowed to come back. Although Tyler had inherited her parents' wanderlust, Morgan had yearned for roots, and now she had them. Her baby would represent the fourth generation of Chances living on this ranch.

"I guess that means you can't be here when the baby's born," Mary Lou said.

"Exactly, which is why I came now. When that little tyke arrives, I'll be somewhere in the Mediterranean. On the way here from the airport I tried to talk Morgan into setting up Skype in the delivery room, but she wasn't buying it."

Morgan made a face. "Sorry, but I have this image of the entire crew of the *Sea Goddess* gathered around your computer watching me give birth. I'm even thinking of having the baby at the ranch, to keep the moment more private and special."

"You thought I'd invite people to see the birth on my laptop?"

"Well, maybe not, but—"

"Shoot, I'd put it up on the big screen in the movie theater!" As Morgan's eyes widened, Tyler nudged her in the ribs. "Gotcha."

"No, you didn't. I knew you were kidding."

"Did not. You should have seen your face. Are you really thinking of having a home birth?"

Morgan glanced at Sarah. "I'd like to."

"And Gabe and I are trying to talk her out of it," Sarah said. "Maybe if we were five minutes from the hospital, I wouldn't worry, but if something goes wrong, it's a long trek into Jackson."

"Nothing will go wrong," Morgan said. "My mom had all of us in the back of the family van."

"Yes, but dad said he always parked it next to the hospital." Tyler was inclined to agree with Gabe and Sarah on this one. She looked across the table to where Alex sat peeling the label off his beer bottle. Maybe he wasn't all that comfy discussing the birthing process.

Giving birth wasn't her top priority, either, but she found herself longing to hear him talk. During the reception last summer his voice had seduced her long before she'd suggested they share a bottle of champagne in the hayloft. "Ever seen a baby being born, Alex?"

He stopped peeling the label and looked at her with his intense gray eyes. "Can't say that I have. How about you?"

That voice, honed by years of radio work, gave her goose bumps. "Yes, and it's an awesome experience, so

I was hoping for a Skype's-eye view of my big sister's event." She was still curious about why he was at the ranch this afternoon. He seemed completely at home, as if he lived here, and yet she was sure he'd planned to rent a place in Jackson once he started his job there.

"So how are things at the radio station?" she asked.

"Oh, he left that job, Tyler," Morgan said. "He's the marketing director for the Last Chance now, and he lives out here."

Tyler could have used that information earlier, before she'd walked into the kitchen and been struck dumb by the incredible backside of Alex Keller. But Morgan would have no reason to tell her. Morgan didn't know about the night in the hayloft.

Alex leaned forward. "And speaking of my job, I've run into a couple of snags for tomorrow's event."

"What event?" Tyler had a feeling that Morgan had neglected to mention several important items during the drive from the Jackson airport. Tyler couldn't blame her, though. Morgan had spent the drive talking about her plans for the baby's room, assuming it was completed in time for Morgan to add the decorating touches she had in mind.

"I've set up an open house," Alex said. "I've had to operate under some tight time constraints, but I wanted to catch people at the beginning of the summer with the idea that if it goes well, we can do it again in August."

"It will go well," Sarah said. "We've invited everybody who might be a candidate for buying one of the Last Chance paints, and we should have a good turnout because June is when the summer tourist season gets rolling. We'll have tours of the barn, cutting-horse demonstrations, plenty of food—"

"Sounds great," Tyler said. "I'm not a prospective buyer, but I'm sure I'll enjoy all that, if I'm invited, that is."

Morgan touched her arm. "Of course you're invited! You're family!"

"Thanks." Tyler was surprised by how pleased she was to hear that. She loved her carefree life and didn't mind that *home* was a sparsely furnished efficiency apartment in L.A. with no live plants and a refrigerator that was usually empty. But she wouldn't mind borrowing the nurturing environment of the Last Chance for the next few days, providing she could control her urge to snuggle up with Alex.

Her fantasy man leaned back in his chair. "The thing is, I'd hoped to establish the mood with live music, but the country band I'd hired just canceled a half hour ago."

"What about Watkins?" Mary Lou set down her beer. "That cowhand plays a decent guitar if you could talk him into doing it."

"It's a thought, but that's not the only issue. I also ordered three event canopies because we're supposed to have some rain, but only one showed up. I'm a little worried that—"

"Say no more." Tyler leaped into the breach automatically, a learned response from handling this kind of crisis all the time on cruises. "It'll be fine. I'll help you figure out some alternatives." Belatedly she realized that her offer would throw her into direct contact with the man she'd decided to avoid for the duration of her visit.

Alex sat forward, hope in his eyes. "You will? That would be great." Then he seemed to catch himself. "Wait a minute. You're on vacation. You shouldn't have to—"

"Don't kid yourself," Morgan said. "She loves this

kind of thing. It's her job to coordinate all the onboard entertainment, so parties are her deal. I had to hold her back or she would have planned my entire wedding from her stateroom on the *Sea Goddess*."

"Then I accept." Alex blew out a breath. "I don't know what kind of magic you can work, but whatever it is, I'll take it."

Magic. That was the exact word she would use to describe the night they'd spent together in the hayloft. She was realistic enough to know how much she'd be tempted to make love with him again, but that was a really bad idea. Considering the emotional tug she felt every time he looked at her, they could end up in a no-win situation that would break both their hearts.

2

LOOKING INTO TYLER'S dark eyes, Alex imagined he could read her mind. She already regretted her decision to help him, but he wasn't about to let her off the hook. He needed her expertise.

If that meant they'd have to work together and deal with the heat that still simmered between them, so be it. He wasn't about to interfere with her world cruise and probable promotion. He'd tell her so once they were alone.

In fact, having a private moment to clear the air was a very good idea. "I don't want to rush you, but we don't have a lot of time to cook up those alternate plans. If you'd be willing to take a look at the outdoor setup before dinner, that would be great."

"Sure." She pushed back her chair. "Give me ten minutes to take my suitcase upstairs and change clothes."

Morgan stood and pressed a hand to the small of her back. "I'll go with you and help you get settled in."

"That's okay." Standing, too, Tyler wrapped an arm around Morgan's shoulders and gave her a quick hug. "No point in lugging baby whosit up those stairs."

Sarah's eyebrows arched. "So she hasn't told you whether it's a boy or girl, either? I thought she might have let it slip to her little sis, and then we could pry it out of you before you leave."

"I haven't told *anybody*." Morgan sat down again. "Gabe and I are the only ones who know, and it'll stay that way until July when the little kid makes an appearance."

"How about a name?" Mary Lou asked. "Have you picked one?"

Morgan nodded. "Yes, and I promise that you'll know immediately from the baby's name whether I had a boy or a girl."

Tyler sighed with obvious relief. "Thank God. As you noticed when some of us were here last summer, our parents conspired to give all of us unisex names."

"And I have to admit I had trouble keeping everyone straight during the wedding last year," Sarah said. "I'm sure I called you by your twin brother Regan's name at least twice."

"Don't feel bad about it. Regan and I had our names switched so many times in school it wasn't funny."

"I agree it was a nightmare while we were growing up," Morgan said. "But now, as a real-estate agent, my name works because it's easily recognizable. Still, I'm not doing that to my child."

"I'm glad." Tyler picked up her empty beer bottle and the napkin she'd used for her chips. "Anyway, let me scoot upstairs and get changed."

Mary Lou made a flapping motion with her hand. "Leave the bottle and napkin, sweetie. I'll take care of it."

"And I'll carry your suitcase upstairs." Alex pushed back his chair and stood.

"I can manage," Tyler said.

Alex gave her a smile. "It's the gentlemanly thing to do, and I'm the gentleman who's available." Hell, he probably shouldn't have said *that*. He'd blame all those years of being a glib DJ.

"Thank you, but it's a small suitcase, and I really can—"

"You don't know which room." He was determined to grab this chance to talk with her. "Where should I put her, Sarah?"

"Let me think." Sarah tapped her chin. "Maybe we should stick with the wing you're in, because we're having some problems with the pipes on the other side. I need to call a plumber, but I haven't done it yet. Gabe's room should be in decent shape."

"It was the last time we were up there packing his high school trophies," Morgan said. "I don't think the bed's made up, though."

Sarah started to rise. "Maybe I should come up there with you."

"Sit still." Alex wasn't giving up this opportunity to have a conversation with Tyler. "I know where the linen closet is. Tyler and I can handle it."

"Absolutely," Tyler said. "I'm perfectly capable of making a bed."

And lying in it? Alex was trying so hard to play it cool, but thinking of Tyler smoothing sheets over the bed she'd sleep in for several nights, a bed that would be in a room right across the hall from his, didn't help at all. He'd never shared a bed with her, but he had no trouble imagining how wonderful that would be. The hayloft had been earthy and exotic, but a good mattress had advantages, too.

At this point, he needed to decide how he felt about the possibility. Obviously, considering her career plans, it couldn't be more than a short-term experience. Was that a mistake? Maybe, but not a huge one unless they slipped up on birth control, and he wouldn't let that happen.

Still, an affair could be a small mistake in that both of them could get more involved than they wanted to be. He didn't know if he could jump into a temporary affair with her and jump back out with ease. And even if he could, what would be the point? When he was totally honest with himself, he had to admit that he craved what all three Chance men had found—a solid marriage that showed all the signs of lasting a lifetime.

He'd always wanted that, but he'd chosen the wrong woman the first time around. He didn't like making mistakes, and he wasn't about to make another one. That meant being careful with his heart. He wasn't convinced that Tyler didn't already own a piece of it.

She had a zest for life he'd admired from the moment she'd stepped onto the dance floor last summer. She'd been the one to suggest the romp in the hay, which had told him she wasn't some finicky city girl and she had self-confidence, besides. That night he'd also learned that she was an unselfish lover with a great sense of humor.

Being wanted by someone like Tyler had soothed his divorce-battered ego. But he wasn't feeling battered anymore, and she still had the power to make him ache with longing. He wasn't positive he could satisfy that longing without taking an emotional risk.

"We'd better get with the program," Tyler said.

What program? Alex made a mental U-turn so he could figure out what she was talking about. Oh, yeah. He was supposed to get her settled upstairs so she could go outside with him and make suggestions for the open house. His concentration was already whacked.

"I left my suitcase and purse out in the front hallway." Tyler looked at Sarah. "Thank you so much for putting me up for a few nights."

Sarah laughed. "I'm afraid Alex plans to make you earn your keep. Don't let him work you too hard."

"Actually you should worry about me working Alex too hard. He may regret asking for my help. I'm a slave driver when I get going."

Alex shook his head. "No worries. I admire dedication."

"Good. Me, too. We should make a good team."

And maybe that's all she had in mind. He could tell by her matter-of-fact tone that she wasn't flirting, not even a tiny bit. He should be relieved if she wasn't interested in getting chummy. Instead he felt the sting of disappointment.

He followed her out of the kitchen and through the empty dining room. Her hair bounced when she walked and her heels clicked on the hardwood floor. Her shoes were the kind that didn't make an appearance very often at the Last Chance, where boots were the norm.

Tyler's shoes consisted of an arrangement of black straps that left most of her foot bare. Her toes were shiny, as if they had clear polish on them, but the white part was brighter than a natural nail would be. Crystal used to get that kind of pedicure, and he vaguely remembered it was connected with a nationality. Maybe French.

He'd never thought of himself as having a thing about toes, but Tyler's French pedicure generated a definite response from his libido. He could imagine himself kissing his way down to her slender toes and running his tongue between each one. During the night they'd shared, they'd been too busy with some very satisfying basics and hadn't detoured into embellishments like sucking on toes.

Her shoes stirred his baser instincts, too. The heels were at least three inches, maybe closer to four. In Chicago they'd call them do-me shoes.

He wasn't sure what they'd be called in Wyoming, but the effect was the same on a guy no matter where a woman wore them. As Tyler's heels created a sensuous beat, Alex imagined backing her up against the nearest wall and wrapping her legs, sexy shoes and French pedicure included, around his waist. Her skirt would be easily bunched up, and if she still favored thongs, her panties would provide no challenge whatsoever.

"How long have you been living at the ranch?"

"Uh…" His brain wasn't functioning as efficiently as it might, considering a certain amount of blood had been routed elsewhere. "About three months, I guess."

"I thought you liked being a DJ."

"I did. I do. But as a DJ I work indoors, and that just seems like a waste in this kind of country. The marketing director job allows me to live on the ranch and spend a lot more time outside." Talking about something besides sex helped control his reaction to her. But every time he took a breath, he caught a whiff of her sweet perfume— part peach roses, part Tyler.

"The Jackson Hole area seems to have a strong effect on people. It sure captivated my sister. She loved it when we lived here years ago, and she loves it even more now."

"Yeah, she's talked about going to high school in Jackson." Alex paused to pick up Tyler's flowered suitcase and she grabbed her black leather purse before they headed up the winding staircase to the second floor. "So you didn't fall in love with the place?"

"We were only in Shoshone for about six months. I was thirteen and miserable because I had to wear hand-me-downs to school. I wasn't paying much attention to my surroundings."

"That's a tough age. I don't know if anybody's happy at thirteen." He was willing to bet she'd been a knock-out, though, even at thirteen and wearing hand-me-down clothes. "So what do you think of the area now?"

"It's beautiful. And Morgan's so happy here."

"So's my sister Josie. She came out on a skiing trip and made the decision to move. I wouldn't have discovered this place if she hadn't come here first."

"And now she's married to Jack. Were you the DJ for the reception then, too?"

"I was. They got married, along with Nick and Dominique, in early October." But there had been no Tyler O'Connelli on the dance floor that night, no woman stirring him up and tempting him with hayloft sex. "Like Sarah said, we barely beat the snow, but now all the Chance men are hitched."

"Wow." Tyler laughed. "Must be something in the water."

"Yeah, you might want to stick with bottled."

"No kidding. Does Josie still own the Spirits and Spurs bar in Shoshone?"

"She does." They reached the top of the stairs. "To your left." He gestured in that direction. "Now that Josie lives out on the ranch, she's not constantly at the bar, but she loves that place and I think she likes having her own income, too."

"I sure get that." Tyler's voice grew more animated.

"I would *never* be financially dependent on a man. My mother and father seem to have worked it out, but sometimes I wonder if she'd had her own money whether she might have vetoed some of his crazy ideas."

Alex filed that statement away as a valuable insight into Tyler's attitude. She wanted to maintain control over her life, and he admired that, too.

He paused beside the doorway into Gabe's room on the right side of the hall. "This is it. Home sweet home for the next five fun-filled nights." Probably shouldn't have said that, either, but it was cruise lingo and...okay, he *was* flirting, even if she wasn't.

She glanced up at him. "And where is your room?"

He pointed across the hall.

"Oh."

He put her suitcase on the floor. "Look, Tyler, that wasn't my idea. There are some plumbing issues in the other wing, like Sarah said."

"I know. I just—"

"You just wanted to pay a surprise visit to your sister," he said gently. "You didn't count on dealing with me, and you certainly didn't expect me to be sleeping across the hall."

"Right." Relief softened her dark eyes. "Thanks for understanding."

"Oh, I understand, all right. I'm as conflicted about this situation as you are."

"Because of your ex? Are you still—"

"Hell, no, I'm not still hung up on Crystal." He looked into her eyes and figured the truth would work as well as anything. "But I'm afraid I might get hung up on you."

Her pupils darkened and her full lips parted. Then

she glanced away, as if she wanted to cancel that involuntary reaction.

Too late. He'd seen desire flare in her eyes and it had created a predictable response in him. He hoped she wouldn't notice the bulge in his jeans. "Are you afraid you'll get hung up on me?"

Her breathing quickened, making the turquoise fabric covering her breasts quiver. A turquoise pendant nestled in her cleavage and silver-and-turquoise drop earrings peeked through her dark curls. Her outfit was sexy, but he knew that had nothing to do with him. She hadn't expected to see him today.

The dress, the shoes, the jewelry, the hair—they were an expression of Tyler's style and another reason he'd been attracted to her last August. From his position on the DJ platform he'd watched her rhythmic, undulating movements with increasing fascination. When she'd appeared with champagne and an invitation, he'd been a goner.

"I am afraid we'd become too involved." She gazed up at him. "When I saw you in the kitchen, I had instant recall of you and me in the hayloft."

"I always wondered if you told anybody about that."

"No. Did you?"

He shook his head. "We agreed it wasn't going anywhere, so talking about it seemed too much like adolescent bragging."

"I appreciate you keeping it quiet. I saw no point in telling anyone, either. We're consenting adults who wanted to have some harmless fun. End of story."

"Exactly." But it wasn't the end of the story. He knew it, and he suspected she did, too.

She hesitated. "I like you, Alex. I'm worried that if

we pick up where we left off, it could turn into more, and I'm leaving on Wednesday. That isn't going to change, no matter what happens between us."

"I know." He couldn't seem to stop looking into her eyes. The hayloft had been dark and he hadn't been able to see how beautiful they were—a deep, velvet brown that was almost black. "It might be better if we could just avoid each other."

"I screwed that up by offering to help you with your open house tomorrow. It was a reflex. I see a party in trouble and I'm all over it. Sorry."

"Don't be." He loved the way her lashes fluttered when she apologized. "I could tell you wanted to take that offer back, but I really could use some ideas, and I'm sure you've dealt with unexpected problems hundreds of times."

"You mean like a typhoon in the middle of a formal dinner dance?" Her full mouth curved and two tiny dimples appeared in her cheeks.

He smiled back. He'd forgotten about the dimples. "Yeah, like that. My lack of entertainment and my canopy issues must seem pretty small compared to what you've experienced."

"When it's your event, nothing is small. Listen, we'll work this out. Just because we're attracted to each other doesn't mean we have to act on it. You may not believe this, considering our past history, but I'm pretty good at controlling those urges."

"No shipboard romances?"

"God, no."

A surge of relief told him he was already feeling slightly possessive. Not good. "I have to believe guys have tried. I mean, you're so...so..."

She watched him with a bemused expression. "Sensual. I'm a sensual woman. Is that what you're trying to say?"

"Yeah." Normally he had an excellent vocabulary, honed by hours behind a microphone, but Tyler had the ability to reduce his IQ by several points. "That's what I'm trying to say. So I don't understand, unless you hook up with somebody on the ship…"

"That's dangerous. The passengers are strictly off limits, obviously, and getting involved with a staff member can result in disaster if it blows up. I've seen it happen and it's not a risk I'm willing to take."

Alex gazed at her standing there in her flirty dress and come-hither shoes. "It's none of my business, but I don't understand how celibacy works for you."

Her cheeks grew rosy and her glance slid to somewhere over his left shoulder. "I haven't figured that out yet. It's the only negative factor in my career plan."

He wanted to laugh, but didn't dare. She'd constructed the perfect trajectory for herself, except that she'd left her sexual needs completely out of the equation. She hadn't successfully submerged them, either, despite what she'd said. Her choice of shoes told him that.

She straightened and looked him in the eye. "But FYI, I'm not a sex-starved woman who would be grateful if a virile cowboy came along to reduce her frustration level for a few days."

"I would never think of you like that." But he would think of her as a sensual, vibrant woman who needed to be loved. He sighed with regret. "It's probably better if we don't become involved while you're here. No point in starting something that could lead to problems."

"I agree."

"I wanted a chance to discuss that, which is the main reason I volunteered to bring your suitcase up and direct you to your room."

"I thought you were doing it to be a gentleman."

"No, to be gentleman*ly*. A true gentleman wouldn't have followed you up to the hayloft after the wedding reception. So don't ever mistake me for a gentleman."

"All right, I won't." Her eyes sparkled.

He wanted to kiss her, and he vividly remembered the feel of her lips on his. He resisted the impulse.

"So, Alex." She took a breath. "Let's forget about whatever chemistry we have and concentrate on your event."

He doubted he'd be able to forget about this attraction, but he moved into safer territory because that seemed to be what she wanted. "I will only admit this to you, but I'm feeling in over my head this first time. I have a marketing degree, but in Chicago they wanted me on air, so I—"

"Because you have such a great voice."

He shrugged off the compliment. He couldn't take credit for that because he'd never worked at trying to sound good. "It fit their criteria, I guess, but consequently I didn't get into the marketing end quite as much. I was part of the team that put on events for the station, mostly for charity, but this is my first solo effort."

She gazed up at him. "You'll be fine. You have a fabulous venue and people are more flexible than you think. If you keep your sense of humor, they'll keep theirs."

He understood why she was good at her job. "That's the best advice I've heard all day." He gestured toward the open bedroom door. "If you want to check out your room, I'll bring you some sheets and towels from the linen closet."

"Thanks. Just leave them by the door and I'll make up my bed later. Right now I need to change clothes if I'm going to be any good to you."

He could think of several ways she could be good to him, and none of them involved clothes. "Before I look for sheets, I need to see Gabe's bed. I can't remember what size it is." Picking up her suitcase, he carried it into the bedroom.

Oh, yeah. Now he remembered that Gabe's old room was furnished with an antique four-poster and dresser, which meant the mattress and box springs were a double rather than a queen or king. Alex had Jack's former room, which Jack had outfitted with a king-size bed set on a massive oak frame. The place was a man cave that was totally Jack. Jack would have taken the bed with him except he'd built it inside the room, and moving it would have been more trouble than building another one in his new house.

If Alex remembered right, the four-poster in Gabe's room had belonged to Archie and Nelsie Chance, the couple who'd settled on this ranch in the thirties and created the legacy that now belonged to their grandsons—Jack, Nick and Gabe. Like most guys in this century, Gabe thought a double bed was too small for two people, so he'd left the antique here to be used as a guest bed.

"What a gorgeous bed frame," Tyler said. "It looks old."

"I think it is. Don't quote me, but it might have been the marriage bed for Archie and Nelsie Chance."

"That's pretty cool." Tyler walked over and wrapped her hand around a carved post at the foot of the bed.

"Couples were willing to sleep closer to each other in those days, weren't they?"

"I guess so. Now a double bed is considered crowded with two people in it."

Tyler's grip on the bedpost tightened. "I suppose it depends on how much they like each other."

Alex remembered how her fingers had wrapped around his cock. He had to get out of there. He had to leave now, before he crossed the room and tested how crowded the conditions would be if he and Tyler rolled around awhile on that double mattress. Because they'd made do with a hayloft, he doubted that either of them would mind the size of the bed.

He set her suitcase on the hardwood floor with a soft click. "I'll get your sheets." Then he left the room and closed the door behind him.

The image of her manicured nails wrapped around the bedpost stayed with him. He wanted her hands on him, tangling in his hair, stroking his skin, caressing his penis. She was everything he'd ever wanted in a woman, and he was dizzy from craving her.

He needed to get over it. They'd set the parameters and he would abide by them. But he might not get much sleep for the next five nights while he lay across the hall from the woman who'd given him the most fantastic night of his life.

There. He'd admitted that making love with Tyler in the hayloft had topped anything he'd experienced with any other woman, including Crystal. The spectacular nature of that experience had been neatly contained in one night of craziness, but the situation wasn't so neat anymore.

Obviously he was still wildly attracted to her, and the

force of that attraction made him a little nervous. Ultimately, he'd be happier if he kept away from her. The more time he spent with her, the more right she'd feel and the more he'd want her to be his forever girl. And she couldn't be.

3

TYLER HUNG ON TO the bedpost to keep herself from walking right into Alex's arms. Her strong response to him scared her a little. No, it scared her a lot. She hadn't planned on this kind of complication.

Releasing her hold on the bedpost, she walked over to her suitcase, her legs trembling from the adrenaline rush of wanting Alex. Maybe she should leave, catch a flight out of Jackson and return to her little apartment in L.A. Then her longing for Alex Keller couldn't possibly create a detour on her carefully charted course.

She couldn't leave, though. Morgan would be crushed, and Morgan was the person Tyler had come here for. When Tyler had walked into baggage claim at the airport and caught sight of Morgan waiting for her, they'd both squealed and jumped up and down like teenagers. Their hug had been awkward because of Morgan's big belly, but that hug might have been the happiest, and the most tearful one, they'd ever shared.

No, Tyler couldn't pack up her marbles and go home just because Alex happened to be living here and he tempted her with the kind of bone-deep commitment that might make her forget all about her promotion opportunity. Unzipping her suitcase, she rummaged through it looking for jeans and a T-shirt, both of which she'd bought last week for this trip to the ranch.

She loved her job, loved the challenge of making a ship full of passengers happy while seeing the world she'd always dreamed of as a child. As a bonus, she could afford nice clothes and regular trips to the ship's beauty salon. She'd been raised to dismiss such things as unimportant, but her parents' disdain for material wealth had meant their kids never wore anything new and got haircuts at home.

Tyler agreed that character was more important than outward appearance, but she couldn't see anything wrong with being a worthwhile person who happened to be well dressed and well groomed. In the first place her job demanded it, and in the second place, looking good didn't mean she was shallow and materialistic.

Once she'd left home—or rather, the wildly painted van that had been a home on wheels for her entire childhood—she'd vowed to find a profession that allowed her to buy pretty clothes and patronize a good salon. And travel well. She adored seeing new places and having new experiences, but she never wanted to camp out again as long as she lived.

The cruise business was a perfect fit for her, with the tiny exception of having no room for a man in her packed schedule. Alex had quickly uncovered the one disadvantage to her chosen lifestyle. That might be another reason the night with him in the hayloft sparkled so brilliantly in her memory. She hadn't had many such experiences since taking a job with the cruise company.

She'd have to figure out how to fill that lack, but now

wasn't the time to worry about it. She was one world cruise away from nailing the job she'd coveted from the beginning—cruise director. Sure, it would be more responsibility, but she had tons of ideas and the job would give her the authority to act on them.

Tossing her dress on the bed and taking off her sandals, she put on the snug jeans and formfitting yellow T-shirt with the scoop neck. She hadn't brought anything baggy to wear because baggy wasn't her style. As a kid she'd been forced to wear clothes that didn't quite fit, so now she chose outfits that showed off her figure.

Alex might think she did that to attract a man, but that wasn't really her goal. She bought the outfits to please herself. She'd spent too much time as a child hating the shabby girl she saw every day in the mirror.

Once she'd put on socks and running shoes, she took a deep breath. Then she opened the bedroom door and stepped out into the hall. Alex leaned against the opposite wall, arms crossed as he waited for her, long legs stretched out, a tooled belt that drew attention to his narrow hips, and a chambray shirt that emphasized his broad chest and wide shoulders. Her heart rate kicked up. She couldn't help that automatic reaction, but she didn't have to give in to its power.

Male appreciation flickered in his gaze before he pushed himself away from the wall. His expression became a careful mask. "Ready?"

"Show me what you've got."

He laughed. "You might want to rephrase that."

"Is everything between us going to turn into a sexual joke? Because that won't work."

He started toward the stairs. "I'll try to do better if you'll try to avoid saying things like *show me what you've got.* You have to admit that line begged to be turned into something suggestive."

"I was referring to your…oh, never mind." She descended the winding staircase beside him, her palm sliding down a banister smoothed by countless other hands, and possibly a few fannies, too. The house and its history fascinated her. That kind of permanence and connection between generations was foreign, almost exotic, and she'd learned to appreciate exotic experiences during her travels.

She glanced down into the living room with its leather furniture grouped around the massive fireplace, and remembered that Alex was missing two of his three canopies for the open house. "Were you planning to make use of this space tomorrow?"

"I hadn't thought I would. This area seems more private. I've called the event an open house, but I wasn't really figuring on opening the actual house, just the grounds and the barn."

"If it rains, you might not have that luxury. How would Sarah feel about extending the event into the living room and possibly the dining room?"

"I don't know, but let's see if there are alternatives before we ask her. She might agree, but I doubt if the Chance brothers would like it. They're protective about this house."

Tyler paused at the foot of the stairs to glance around. "I can understand that. I—"

She was interrupted as the front door opened. A blast of cool air was followed by a broad-shouldered cowboy sporting a sandy-colored mustache. Until he took off his hat, Tyler didn't recognize that he was her brother-in-law, Gabe. She hadn't seen him since the wedding last August, and apparently he'd decided to grow a mustache over the winter months.

"Tyler!" He pulled her into a quick hug scented with horse and dust. "Thanks for coming. Morgan sounded so excited when I talked to her. I know it means the world to her that you made the effort."

"I'm glad it worked out." She stepped back and smiled at him. "I can tell you're treating her right. She's really happy."

"I hope so." Gabe turned and hooked his hat on a rack standing beside the front door. "We didn't plan for her to get pregnant this quick, but…" He shrugged.

"She doesn't seem to mind a bit."

Gabe scrubbed a hand through his hair, which bore the imprint of his hat. "No, she really doesn't, and I can't tell you how relieved I am about that. When we first got together she wasn't sure she ever wanted kids." He glanced over at Alex. "Looks like the two of you were headed outside."

"That was the plan," Alex said.

"Then you'd better get going. The clouds are moving in."

"We'll go fast," Tyler said. "I just want a quick overview."

Gabe looked puzzled. "Of what?"

"She's going to save my ass," Alex said. "Some of my plans for tomorrow have fallen through, but as luck would have it, an activities director from a major cruise line just showed up and offered to help me put on this shindig."

"That's the Chance luck working for you," Gabe said.

"But I'm not a Chance."

Gabe clapped him on the shoulder. "You're part of the

family, so that makes you an honorary Chance. As such, you might as well learn the family motto handed down from Grandpa Archie."

"Which is?"

"Chance men are lucky when it counts."

Alex sent the briefest glance toward Tyler. "Thanks. I'll keep that in mind."

Tyler waited until they were out the door and standing on the covered porch before she commented. "I saw that look."

"What look?" Alex had grabbed a gray-felt cowboy hat from the same rack Gabe had used. Holding it by the crown, he settled it on his head with practiced ease.

"The look you gave me when Gabe told you about the family motto. Just to be clear, the motto is 'Chance men are lucky,' not 'Chance men *get* lucky.'" But, oh, man, he'd increased his odds exponentially by adding the hat. She couldn't say what it was about a guy in a Stetson, but wearing one sure did multiply the sexy factor.

Alex laughed. "What made you think I had any such thoughts?"

"Are you saying you didn't?"

He gazed at her for a moment before answering with a brief smile. Then he turned to study the darkening sky. A tug on the brim of his hat brought it lower over his eyes. "We need to take that tour of the ranch ASAP before the storm hits."

Tyler's breath caught. The hat was a sexy addition, but when Alex took hold of the brim and pulled it down, she melted. One little innocent gesture created a soul-stirring image of courage and purpose, of protecting the weak, and shoot-outs in the middle of a dusty street at high noon.

That simple movement made Alex seem more focused and intense, even a little bit dangerous. No doubt about it, there was something compelling about a guy wearing a cowboy hat. For a gorgeous specimen like Alex, it was almost overkill.

She took a deep breath of air that already smelled of rain. "Lead on." She followed him down the porch steps. Once they moved away from the shelter of the two-story ranch house, the wind cut through the light cotton of her T-shirt.

"The hands set up bleachers over by the largest corral." Alex pointed to a spot where a small set of metal bleachers had been erected. "I'd planned to protect the guests with a canopy, but now I only have one, and the food and beverages should be under cover, either for shade or rain protection."

"Let's check out the barn." She started toward the large hip-roofed structure that was the biggest building on the property outside of the main house. "There should be places in there where people can get in out of the rain."

"At least it's clean as a whistle. The hands have been working on it all day. They'll go through again first thing in the morning, but they've put down fresh straw everywhere and set out some fresh hay bales which can be used for seating."

"I can smell the hay from here." And the scent turned her on. She still had a three-inch piece of it she'd plucked from the mounds scattered in the hayloft. It sat on a shelf along with her collection of souvenirs from her travels, and every once in a while she'd pick it up and sniff it. The aroma was fading, but her memories of Alex never had.

Last August as she and Alex had gathered up their clothes in preparation for leaving, Alex had explained that the ranch had outgrown the capacity of the hayloft and it was now strictly ornamental. A hay barn held the bales that supplied the ranch animals. But the old barn was the only structure left of the original ranch buildings, and so the Chance brothers threw some loose hay up in the loft every spring because their father had liked the picturesque way it looked.

The romance of that tradition had appealed to Tyler. She'd wondered if Jonathan Chance had enjoyed an episode or two in the hayloft himself. She'd asked Alex, but he hadn't known much about the family secrets at that point. Now that he was an honorary Chance, he might.

Two dogs were stretched out in front of the barn, one on either side of the open door. Tyler remembered them from her first visit last summer. At Alex and Tyler's approach, the dogs lifted their heads and thumped their tails in the dirt.

"Hey, Butch." Alex leaned toward the dog on the right side of the door. Butch was medium-size, with a short tan-and-white coat and a snub nose. Alex scratched behind Butch's ears and the dog's tail thumped faster.

"Right. This other one's Sundance." Tyler figured the dog on the left, all black with slightly curly hair, was her responsibility to pet. "Hi, Sundance." She stroked the dog's silky head. Dogs would have been a luxury when she was growing up, so she'd never had one, or a cat, either. She liked animals, but she wasn't used to them.

If an animal rooted a person to one spot, and Tyler thought maybe they did, then the Chance family must really be rooted with all the ones they had around here. Besides the horses, they had these dogs, a few barn cats and at least one goat, if she remembered correctly. Last summer she'd been a bridesmaid, so she'd been concentrating on the wedding instead of cataloguing the animals, so she could be wrong about the goat.

She certainly remembered the hayloft, though. The details of that area were permanently recorded in high def, probably even 3-D, and the movie flickered in her head every time she looked at Alex. Even if they never touched again, she would never forget those glorious hours in his arms.

Another gust of wind whipped up the dust at their feet and would have blown off Alex's hat if he hadn't grabbed it at the last minute. Thunder rolled overhead.

He straightened and glanced at the dark clouds hovering over the ranch. "We'd better finish up this tour and get back to the house." He walked through the large door and flicked a switch to his right, which turned on a row of ceiling lights that ran the length of the stalls.

As Tyler followed him into the barn, the scent of fresh hay swirling around her was an aphrodisiac more tempting than she could have imagined. Her body hummed with eagerness. They'd kissed here in the barn before climbing into the hayloft. The kiss had begun as gentle exploration and had ended with enough heat to melt all her inhibitions.

The open house, she reminded herself. She was here to evaluate the space for entertainment possibilities. The barn was quiet except for the sound of horses munching their evening meal. Somewhere a horse stomped a hoof, and another blew out a noisy breath. The scent of oiled leather mixed with the aroma of hay.

"I guess all the hands headed for the bunkhouse when they saw the storm coming," Alex said.

"Smart." She chose not to glance over at him as they stood in the center aisle of the barn only about two feet apart. Hearing his voice in this setting reminded her of how he'd murmured in her ear as he'd undressed her, and how he'd coaxed her to new heights of pleasure during that long, glorious night.

His voice had been a big part of the attraction early on. Hearing it coming through the sound system during the reception had begun the seduction, and by the time the festivities were over and she'd suggested moving the party to the hayloft, she'd been more than ready to hear that voice in a more intimate setting.

The open house, girl! You told him you'd help him plan his party! She cleared her throat. "If you lined the center aisle with tables for food and beverages, you could sweep out a few stalls and have potential seating in those. People could meander up and down this aisle and be close to the horses, which is what you want, right?"

He didn't answer.

"Right?" she prompted, turning to him.

"Yeah." His tone was husky, and he gazed at her with longing in his eyes.

Her heart began to pound. "Don't look at me like that."

"Can't help it." He took a step toward her.

She thought about moving back. She didn't. "We talked about this." But her words lacked all conviction.

"I don't want to talk." He reached for her.

"Me neither." With a groan she surrendered to the kiss she'd been craving for ten long months, the kiss she'd promised herself wouldn't happen, the kiss that was so...damn...good.

4

MISTAKES SHOULDN'T FEEL like this. Mistakes should torture a guy with regret and anxiety. But this one—and no question that it was a big mistake—filled Alex with incredible joy.

The moment he connected with Tyler's full mouth, his world made sense again. Kissing her was, he realized, his favorite thing to do. Cancel that. His second favorite.

She nestled against him and her body aligned with his as if they'd held each other only hours ago instead of months. His body remembered the fullness of her breasts, the curve of her spine, the press of her thighs. Predictably, within seconds of beginning this mistake of a kiss, he wanted to make more mistakes, bigger mistakes, juicier and more satisfying mistakes.

Judging from the way Tyler quivered and moaned softly when he thrust his tongue into her mouth, she had the same idea. She pushed her hips forward. He was already hard, already hotter than a branding iron. Somewhere in the middle of the kiss his Stetson toppled to the barn floor, and although he'd paid good money for that hat, he wasn't about to retrieve it now.

He was too busy to worry about a hat. He'd found his way under the back hem of her T-shirt to the clasp of her bra. Once that gave way, he slid one hand around and cupped her warm breast. Sweet heaven. How could a woman who felt so right be completely wrong for him?

She moaned again and arched into his caress. He knew in that moment that whatever they'd said while standing outside her bedroom meant nothing now. If he could figure out the logistics, she would surrender to this passion neither of them could control and she would worry about the fallout later.

Or maybe not. Gasping, she wriggled out of his arms and backed away from him. Her shirt was rumpled where her bra hung unfastened beneath it. Her breasts quivered with her rapid breathing and her eyes were heavy-lidded and dark with need. "This is crazy."

Heart hammering, he stared at her in helpless frustration as he gulped for air. His entire groin area ached from the restriction of his jeans. "I know."

She glanced around quickly, as if looking for something. "Did you...did you bring..."

"No." His sudden realization that she'd stopped him because she wanted to ask about condoms sent a new surge of desire through his system. "No, damn it."

"Then we can't..."

He wasn't going to let this moment pass. "You can." He started toward her.

She shook her head and backed up. "That's not fair."

"Let me decide that. I've missed touching you."

She took a shuddering breath. "But it's too one-sided. If we could just do it, then we could get it out of our systems."

If he hadn't been so jacked up on lust, he would have

laughed. She was seriously kidding herself if she believed one time would satisfy them. It hadn't the night in the hayloft and it wouldn't now.

He closed the distance between them. "You can't believe that."

"That's what I was telling myself while you were kissing me senseless." She stepped back and bumped against the latched door of an empty stall. "It seemed like a perfectly logical idea when you were unhooking my bra and I didn't have the self-control of a gnat."

He groaned. "You're torturing me."

"I know, and that's mean. We should just go back before this gets any—"

A loud crash and a flash of light was followed by a low rumble and the steady *ping* of rain on the barn's tin roof. The dogs came in and padded over to Alex, tails wagging slowly.

"Butch, Sundance, go lie down." He pointed to the tack room where they each had a bed.

With twin doggie sighs of resignation, they left for the tack room. When he turned back to Tyler, the rain had started to pound on the roof in earnest, and she had her hands behind her back and under her shirt as if she intended to fasten her bra. He was losing ground.

"I guess we'll have to make a run for it," she said.

"We could, but it'll probably let up in a few minutes. We could wait and see if it does."

She hesitated. "I suppose."

"So why not stop what you're doing and unlatch that stall door? There's a nice bed of hay in there."

Her lips parted and heat simmered in her gaze as it had earlier in the hallway outside her room. This time she didn't look away. "You don't give up, do you?"

"Not when there's something I want." His heartbeat hammered in his ears, almost drowning the rattle of rain on the tin roof. "I think you want the same thing."

Her breathing quickened. "Now you're the one torturing me."

"I can fix that." *Please let me love you.*

"Alex…"

"Tyler…" He waited, willing her to turn and unlatch that stall door, yet knowing that she might not. If she decided to run out into the rain, he'd have to run with her, because she couldn't arrive at the house dripping wet with him nowhere around. That would look bad.

She finished hooking her bra. "I'm going to see how hard it's coming down." Breaking eye contact, she walked to the front of the barn.

He scooped up his hat from the floor and followed her. If she insisted on making a run for it, he'd leave his hat on a shelf beside the door rather than ruin it in the rain. But he was still hoping she'd change her mind.

She peered out the door into the gray light. Rain slanted across the landscape, blurring the outlines of the ranch house and the twin spruces in front of it. "I think we should go."

He put his hat on the shelf by the door. "I'm warning you, you'll get wet."

She muttered something that sounded like *I already am.*

If that was an admission of how he'd affected her, he wanted to hear it again. "What was that?"

"Nothing. Let's go."

"Okay." He doused the lights, and once they were both out the door, he turned and shoved it closed.

She yelped, and he swung around in time to see her

land on her backside in the mud. He was beside her in three strides and leaned down to help her up. Except it didn't work out that way. She managed to upset his balance just enough on the mud-slick ground that he went down, too. By throwing himself sideways, he avoided landing on top of her, but he had mud splattered all over his clothes.

"I'm sorry!" She scrambled to her knees, rain dripping from her hair into her face. "Are you okay?"

"Yeah, other than the mud. Are you?"

"Yes, but…I don't want to track all this into that beautiful house."

There was a back way into the house for exactly this reason. It opened into the utility room adjoining the kitchen. There was even a narrow, seldom-used staircase that led from the kitchen to the second floor, an addition made when three growing, often dirty, boys had needed to get upstairs without making too big a mess.

But at the moment Tyler looked as if she'd entered a wet T-shirt contest. Surely any red-blooded male would forgive him for neglecting to tell her about the back entrance into the ranch's utility room and the staircase to the second floor.

"There's a cleanup sink in the barn," he said. "We can go back and get the worst of it off there."

"All right."

He felt a little bit guilty for leading her back into the barn, but not much. When he'd kissed her a few minutes ago, she'd kissed him back. Vigorously. Vows of chastity were all well and good for some people, but he and Tyler weren't those people. They needed each other too desperately.

Maybe they'd clean off the mud and go back to the

house without anything happening. It was possible. But he couldn't imagine four more days of nothing happening. To his way of thinking, they might as well get started now.

This time he didn't turn on the overhead lamps. Low lights mounted near the floor were on a dusk-to-dawn sensor, and they glowed softly, illuminating the floor so they wouldn't trip over anything and creating an ambience that suited the mood Alex hoped for. Rain hitting the tin roof added another romantic touch.

"Thanks for not turning on the lights," Tyler said. "I'm a mess."

"Not in my book." Even in low light, he had a good view of her yellow shirt plastered to her body. Her nipples made dents in the soaked material, and it was all he could do not to reach for her, mud and all. But the next move needed to be hers, not his.

She slicked her wet hair back and squeezed some water out of the ends as she glanced upward. "I like the sound of rain on a tin roof."

"Me, too."

She met his gaze briefly and looked away. "Where's the sink?"

"At the far end, beyond the last stall."

Her running shoes squished as she walked down the aisle between the rows of stalls. "Is there a goat in here, too? I seem to remember something about a goat."

"Yep, there's a goat." He followed her toward the back of the barn. "His name is Hornswaggled, and he shares a stall with a mare named Doozie. They're inseparable."

"Which stall?"

"Third from the end on the left."

Tyler detoured over to that stall and looked in. "Sure

enough. Hi, there, Doozie and Hornswaggled. How do you like this weather we're having?"

Doozie stuck her nose over the stall door and the goat's front hooves clacked against the wooden door as he propped himself against it to beg for his share of attention.

"They're so friendly." Tyler stroked Doozie's nose with one hand and scratched the top of the goat's head with the other.

Alex came to stand beside her. "The Last Chance prides itself on being a friendly place."

"I've noticed." She concentrated on the two animals instead of looking at him, but the color rose in her cheeks. "This horse isn't a paint like all the others."

"Nope. She was injured and needed a safe haven. Now she's fine, but nobody's willing to sell her, even if they can't breed her."

Dislodging Tyler's hand, Doozie moved closer to Alex, gazing at him expectantly.

He reached out and rubbed her silky neck. "Sorry, Dooz. I don't have any treats."

Hornswaggled bleated softly.

"Nothing for you, either, Horny."

Tyler groaned. "That nickname is so bad, Alex."

"Don't blame me. That's what all the hands call him. He came to the ranch with that name, and nobody's going to take the time to say all of it. Cowboys appreciate brevity."

Tyler glanced sideways at Alex as she continued to scratch the goat's head. "So how much of a cowboy are you these days? Do you ride the range and stuff?"

"I ride." He liked being able to say that. "Mostly I ride Dooz. Why?"

"Just wondered. Last summer you were still a city boy. You even told me you weren't the cowboy type, but you're…different now."

He wasn't sure if that was a good thing or a bad thing. Maybe she preferred city boys to cowboys. "How am I different?"

"Well, you dress differently, and your hair's a little longer. Your face seems a little more chiseled, but maybe that's because of your hair. Also, there's something else, something harder to define, an attitude…"

"Are you saying I have an attitude?"

"Not in a bad way. It's more like a quiet confidence."

He was flattered, but still he had to laugh. "I just admitted a while ago that I have all kinds of doubts about this event tomorrow. That doesn't seem like quiet confidence to me."

"This isn't about your job, it's about…your…" She took a deep breath. "It's about your sex appeal, okay? I have no business talking about it, because it will only make me want to do things I shouldn't do." She moved away from the stall door. "Where's that sink?" She started toward the end of the barn. "We need to get cleaned up and go back to the house. Dinner is probably ready, and I—"

He spun her around and pulled her into his arms, mud and all. "Let's do those things." Then he kissed her, knowing that she would kiss him back, knowing that this time he would take that kiss where he wanted it to go, and she would let him.

Her mouth tasted of rain and desire, and he knew the rest of her would, too. Heart pounding with anticipation, he began to strip her down, peeling her T-shirt over her head, unhooking her soaked bra, unbuttoning her

jeans. He encouraged her to help him in a voice hoarse
with need.

She did, nudging off her shoes, kicking away her wet
jeans, shimmying out of her panties. He warmed her
chilled skin with his mouth and his hands—stroking,
licking, kissing every fondly remembered inch of her.
She moaned and quivered in his grasp.

Her moan of delight was the music he'd yearned to
hear for ten long months. One night was all they'd had
together, and yet his feelings for her were so damn strong.
She seemed to be as caught up in the whirlwind as he
was. When he closed his mouth over her taut nipple, she
arched into him and held the back of his head, tunneling
her fingers through his wet hair as he sucked.

The tempo of the rain increased, urging him on. As
her body warmed, he moved lower. Finally he sank to
his knees and cupped her satiny bottom in both hands.
Ah, the scent of heaven—Tyler, fully aroused, wanting
him as much as he wanted her. He couldn't imagine anything better than that.

His tongue remembered her exotic taste and knew
the way to her sweet spot. There, waiting for him, needing him. He touched the tip of his tongue to her clit. She
gasped and clutched his head for balance. But she did
not pull back, did not tell him no. She was willing to
be vulnerable and let him love her, at least for this moment in time.

Filled with gratitude, he took her, claiming her with
an open mouth and a questing tongue. She was slick
with passion, and he savored the richness of her desire.
Her soft cries of delight spilled over him as he stroked
rhythmically with his tongue in time to the steady beat

of the rain overhead. He would give her this, even if they could share nothing else.

She began to tremble, and he used more pressure. With a groan that spoke of intense pleasure, she came, bathing his tongue in her juices. He drank joyfully, holding her, supporting her so she wouldn't fall.

At last her body grew quiet and she drew in a shaky breath. "Oh, Alex." She said his name on a sigh of happiness.

He couldn't ask for a better response than that. Slowly he stood, sliding his hands up her body as he rose to his feet. His legs were rubbery from the rush of adrenaline, and his cock was absolutely killing him. But a cowboy filled with quiet confidence would be stoic about such things.

Once they were face-to-face again, she looked into his eyes. "That was…" Her breath caught. "So good."

"Glad you liked it." He stroked her back as she nestled against him. He loved the transformation when a woman had a climax, and he especially loved watching Tyler lose every bit of the tension she'd held in her body. Having a work ethic like hers could take its toll. He should know.

"Mmm." She rested her cheek against his damp shirt. "I don't know what the heck I was thinking, letting you strip me naked and make me come."

"That you needed that?"

"I suppose. Anyway, I'm going to listen to the music of the rain and pretend it was fate."

"Good." He caressed her smooth skin, which was something he probably should stop doing, because the more he touched her, the harder he became.

"So what now?"

He frowned, wishing he had a better solution for the

next phase. "Unfortunately, we probably need to sponge the mud off our clothes and go back."

"I don't think you're ready to go back."

"It's not that I *want* to, but—"

She wiggled against him. "I'm not talking about whether you want to or not. I don't think you can do it physically."

"Excuse me?"

"I'm worried that in your condition, you'll have trouble walking." She reached down and rubbed the spot where the seam of his fly was threatening to give way under the pressure.

He drew in a sharp breath as her casual touch brought pleasure laced with pain. "I'll be fine." But his quick words sounded as strained as he felt.

"Yes, you will be fine. Very fine. I'll see to it." She stepped back and maintained eye contact as she used both hands to unbuckle his belt.

His heart thundered with anticipation, and yet she'd have to get to her knees on the barn floor. He grasped her wrists. "No."

"If you can do me, then I sure as heck can do you."

He held her fast, refusing to let her continue with her plan. "It's different. I had on jeans when I got down there."

"No worries." Glancing at the floor, she stretched out one shapely leg and used her elegantly polished toes to drag her crumpled jeans over to rest at her feet. "Voilà."

Then she met his gaze again. "Happy now?"

He groaned softly. "I think I'm about to be." He released her wrists with a sigh.

"You betcha, cowboy. Now hold still."

He tried, but watching her unbutton his fly and pull

down his briefs gave him the shakes. Her soft murmur of admiration nearly made him come, and when she put both hands on him—one circling his cock and the other cradling his balls—he had to close his eyes and lock his knees in order to remain standing.

Fabric rustled, and he knew she must have knelt on her jeans, but he didn't dare open his eyes. The sight of her there, poised for the next step, would be enough to send him over the edge. He'd made it this far, and he wanted… oh, yes…*that*…the flick of her tongue, the warmth of her mouth, the gentle suction…

He wouldn't last long. The sensation was erotic by itself, but knowing that Tyler was the one caressing him drove him slowly insane. He'd wanted her for so long, and now she was here, on her knees…

Even though he clenched his jaw, attempting to be the strong, silent type, a moan escaped. And another. He was breathing like a long-distance runner nearing the finish line.

And he was nearing the finish line. Her tongue danced along the underside of his cock, and then she did a swirling maneuver over the tip before taking him deep again. His penis touched the back of her throat.

And now he wanted to see. Opening his eyes, he took in the stirring sight of her drawing back, her cheeks hollowing to increase the pressure. Slowly she rolled his balls in the palm of her hand, creating a subtle yet powerful massage.

Dizzy with the need to come, yet desperate to prolong the ecstasy because this might never happen again, he combed shaking fingers through her luxurious hair, keeping his touch light even though she was winding him tight…and tighter yet. Once again she took him up to the hilt and slowly pulled back.

He was losing the fight. Control began slipping away as she used her tongue again before pulling his entire length deep inside. While holding him there and applying rhythmic suction, she pressed a ridge directly behind his balls…and he came in a rush. His surrender was total and vocal. He cried out and was very afraid his knees would buckle.

But, in truth, his center of gravity was buried in her mouth, which was the only logical reason he didn't fall down as a climax roared through him with the force of a tsunami. The movement of her throat as she swallowed sent a current of electricity from his cock straight up his spine to short-circuit his brain.

He had no idea how much time passed before she slowly released him and gently tucked him back into his briefs. When she got to her feet, he took a long, shuddering breath and tried to remember his name.

She cupped his face in both hands and stood on tiptoe to kiss him. "I think you liked that."

"That…" He paused to clear his throat. "That is the understatement of the year." Sliding his fingers through her still-wet hair, he cradled her head and gazed into her shining eyes. "I'm afraid our plan to avoid sex is a total failure."

"You could say that."

"So I guess we need a new plan."

"All right." Her gaze was steady. "How about great sex with no strings and no regrets?"

He nodded. "Might as well aim high."

"We can do it. We managed it last time." She said it with conviction, in the same tone she'd used when she'd assured him his event tomorrow would work out. He couldn't deny that her sunny approach to life appealed to him.

"Sure we can." He agreed with her because he had no choice. He'd craved her from the moment he'd laid eyes on her ten months ago. Now that she was within reach, he wanted to be with her day and night—especially night. If he felt any strings tugging at his heart as a result of spending time in her arms and in her bed, he'd just have to cut them.

Although she wasn't truly like Crystal, other than the fact that they both liked looking good, she still wanted a different life from the one he envisioned for himself. Good sex didn't mean he had to let himself fall for the woman, no matter how sunny her disposition was. *Right*.

5

TYLER CLEANED UP as best she could before they left the barn, but her wet clothes felt icky and no doubt she resembled a half-drowned cat. The rain continued to fall, soaking her hair and clothes even more, although Alex tried to shield her with his body. He wrapped his arm around her shoulders and she slid her arm around his waist as they started toward the house.

Normally she cared a lot about how she presented herself, but a world-shattering orgasm had mellowed her out tremendously. Even so, she still didn't like the idea of tracking the rain and mud onto the ranch's gorgeous hardwood floors.

"Are you sure there's no back entrance that leads to a mudroom?" she asked as they approached the front porch. "I'd think a ranch would have something like that."

"Um...well, it does."

"It *does?* Then why didn't you say so before?"

No answer.

She gave him a whack on the arm, but considering how solid his biceps were, she didn't think he felt much of anything.

He yelped in protest, anyway. "What was that for?"

"You know perfectly well! You lured me back into that barn on false pretenses!"

"Maybe." He didn't sound the least bit repentant. "Mad at me?"

"I should be. That was a very underhanded way to get me alone and naked." She heard the smile in her voice and was sure he could hear it, too.

"You're right. I'm thoroughly ashamed of myself."

"Yeah, I'll bet you are."

"I deserve to be sent straight to bed."

She laughed. "Stop it. We have things to do."

"We certainly do." He walked faster, urging her to keep up. "For one thing, I need to count the condoms stashed in my bedside-table drawer."

"You're getting carried away." And she was getting carried away right with him. Her wet panties had nothing to do with the rain and everything to do with the prospect of spending the night in bed with Alex.

Warnings whispered through her mind, threatening to erase her glow of satisfaction, and she pushed them away. Good sex was healthy and life affirming, like a trip to a spa. She'd soak up all the joy she could and not spoil it by anticipating the inevitable parting scene. It wouldn't rip her heart out. She wouldn't allow that.

"Getting carried away feels great," Alex said. "I haven't felt this good since..."

"Last August?" That would have been her answer. She hadn't felt this giddy since the night in the hayloft.

"'Fraid so. But that doesn't mean I'll get hung up on you. I can play by the rules."

"I know you can," she said with determined optimism. "It was naive of us to think we could keep our distance from each other while I'm here. I think facing the attraction and dealing with it is a realistic approach, don't you?"

"Absolutely. We both would have been on edge the entire time, which wouldn't have been fair to everyone around us."

"Right." She glanced at the ranch house as welcoming light shone through its many windows. "So where is this back entrance?"

"In the back."

"Very funny. Why are you still heading for the front door?"

"Because the utility room is right off the kitchen. Not only will we run into Mary Lou serving dinner, but the family dining room isn't far from the kitchen. Judging from the trucks parked in the driveway, everyone is gathered for the Friday night meal. Someone will hear us."

"But what about the mess we'll make in the main part of the house?"

"We'll take off our shoes—or in my case, my boots, on the porch. It's not that far to go through the hall and up the stairs. We can change clothes and come back down with nobody the wiser."

"I doubt that. I say somebody's going to pick up on the fact that we have more than friendship going on."

He pulled her to a halt. "And how do you feel about that?"

"It's not for me to say. I'll be leaving on Wednesday." She gazed up at him as rain dripped from her hair and eyelashes. Thank God for waterproof mascara. Although the rest of her might be a disaster, at least she wouldn't go into the house with raccoon eyes. "I guess we need to discuss this. Do you care if they figure out that we're involved?"

He hesitated briefly. "I guess it's none of their business unless it affects my work."

He was so adorably sincere that she chose not to mention how it had already affected his work. They still didn't have a plan for tomorrow. She'd make sure they did have one, but they'd become seriously sidetracked from working out the details of the open house.

"It may be nobody's business," she said, "but we each have a sister sitting at the dining table. I don't know about your family, but mine tends to think they have a right to an opinion about my behavior."

Alex combed his wet hair back from his forehead. "I'm sure Josie will say something to me. I made plenty of comments when she started seeing Jack, who had already broken her heart once. Okay, you're right. Let's get this out of the way. Josie will notice eventually, anyway."

"I'm not sure if Morgan will or not. She's so focused on this baby that she might be oblivious, but Sarah's nobody's fool. I get the impression she keeps pretty close track of what goes on around here."

"She does." He frowned. "In fact, I wonder if she already suspects something and that's why she put us in the same wing…"

"You think she's playing matchmaker?"

"No, probably not."

"I don't think so, either. She seemed really happy for me that I was up for this big promotion. Anyway, we won't confirm or deny that we have a connection and let people think whatever they want. But let's not sneak in as if we have something to hide."

He nodded. "The back door it is. There's a stairway

from the kitchen to the second floor, so we can go up that way to change. If anybody intercepts us, so be it." Wrapping his arm more securely around her, he started around the house.

"We have been out in the barn a fair amount of time, though."

"So?"

"So rather than let their imaginations run completely wild, let's tell them we've been cooking up alternate plans for the open house while we waited for the rain to stop. Finally we realized it wasn't going to stop and came ahead."

"All right." He navigated around a puddle. "By the way, do you have any alternate plans for the open house? Because I have zip."

She noticed that the rain had let up a little, but that didn't mean it couldn't start up again during the night. "The barn is definitely an option, but I still think we need to suggest using the living room and the big dining room."

"I thought you were worried about tracking up the floors just now? If you open up the main house and it's raining, that will—"

"Oh, geez." Talk about being distracted and missing the big picture. "Okay, scratch that. I'll figure out something else. Maybe it won't rain all that much."

"We can hope. But what about the entertainment? I'm not sure one lone guitar player is going to cut it, especially if he has to be talked into performing. I wanted something guests could have fun watching."

Now *that* she had worked out. "They can watch me."

"You? Doing what?"

Spinning away from him, she threw her hands in the air and belted out the opening lyrics to "Oklahoma."

He grinned at her. "I didn't know you could sing."

"There are lots of things you don't know about me, Mr. Keller. An activities director on a cruise ship has to wear many hats, and being able to sing and dance is a great thing to have on a résumé in my line of work." She executed a sloppy soft-shoe routine in the wet grass and finished with a little bow.

"You are so stinkin' cute."

"Yes, but do I get the job? Will you hire me as your entertainment for tomorrow's event? Me and Watkins, the reluctant guitarist?"

"Maybe. I know I can afford Watkins, but you're a professional. I don't know if I can afford you."

"Sure you can. I will work for…" She stepped closer and whispered a suggestion involving whipped cream and chocolate sauce.

He pulled her in tight, their wet clothes sticking together like Velcro. "To hell with making an entrance and having dinner with the family. Let's head back to the barn."

"Hey, you two," called a male voice. "Don't you have sense enough to come in out of the rain?"

Alex released her immediately. "Hey, Jack."

Tyler knew it had to be one of the Chance brothers who'd opened the screen door, but when she looked at the figure silhouetted against the light she wouldn't have been able to say which one it was. They sounded similar and all had the same broad-shouldered cowboy look. Apparently it was Jack, the oldest.

"We'll be right in," Alex said. "We were just—"

"I was practicing a number for tomorrow," Tyler said.

"Watkins and I will be filling in for the country band that canceled on Alex. We're going to give the entertainment a down-home feel." She remembered Jack as being dark haired and moody, but according to Morgan, his disposition had improved since marrying Josie.

"The band cancelled?"

"Afraid so," Alex said. "About two hours ago."

"I see. So are you also part of this number Tyler's practicing?"

Tyler realized Jack probably had witnessed the clinch. "We were discussing that," she said. "But I think not. He's not much of a dancer."

Jack chuckled. "I know he can't dance, but he tries."

"I'm not that bad of a dancer," Alex said. "It's just that all the Chance guys are like semiprofessional or something."

Tyler had noticed that family trait last summer and remarked on it. Sarah had told her they all took after their father, who was the best dancer she'd ever known. "Maybe I should let you help me with the entertainment for tomorrow, Jack."

"No can do. I'll have my hands full working with the horses. But you sounded great just now. I happened to hear you when I went to fetch myself a beer in the kitchen, and I was curious enough to stick my head out the door. Was that 'Oklahoma'?"

"Yes."

"Unfortunately the Last Chance is located in Wyoming. You know any songs about Wyoming?"

"No."

"Guess I'll have to teach you some, then. Alex, you might want to think about bringing your talent inside before she catches her death out there."

"We were heading in when Tyler decided she needed to audition for me," Alex said.

"Uh-huh. Well, Tyler, you've got a helluva voice."

"Thank you."

"Wrong tune, but helluva voice. Can we afford her, Alex?"

Alex's voice sounded choked. "I... Yeah, we should be able to meet her terms."

"Good to know. See you two inside."

The screen door banged shut and Alex lost it, doubling over and shaking with silent laughter. "Good God," he said, gasping. "If Jack only knew...what you named as your fee..." He gazed at her, still chuckling.

She smiled at him. "This way I won't have to claim it on my taxes."

"Yeah, I doubt there's a line item for being served up like an ice-cream sundae." He looked at her as if he'd like to start immediately. "Have you had sex with whipped cream before?"

"No, but I've always wanted to try it. Assuming you can smuggle stuff out of the kitchen."

"Don't worry about that. All you have to be concerned with is keeping the noise level down while I drive you crazy."

"Do you have whipped cream experience, then?"

"No." He winked at her. "But I've always wanted to try it. Shall we go in?"

"Okay. How do I look?"

"Beautiful."

"Liar."

"It's not a lie. You look like a woman who's been having fun, and that's always sexy to me."

"I have been having fun." She gave him a quick kiss.

"And I intend to have even more fun later on tonight." Then she started for the stairs leading to the back door.

"Damn, but you're hot, Tyler O'Connelli."

She glanced over her shoulder. "You're no icicle yourself, Alex Keller."

SPEAKING OF ICICLES, Alex could have used one to shove down his pants before he followed Tyler and her tight little tush into the house. The woman turned him inside out. She was right that they could never have managed four more days without falling into bed with each other.

Now that the dam had broken and they were committed to squeezing all the pleasure they could out of this time, he would ignore the ticking clock and make the most of every second he had with her. Of course, he wanted her all to himself 24/7, but that wouldn't be happening.

They were both committed to making the open house a success, and that would take up a chunk of time. Besides that, Tyler had come here to see Morgan, so whenever Morgan was around, Alex would back off.

And he could start now. Morgan met them at the door and ushered them into the room containing two large-capacity washers and a matching pair of dryers.

"Jack said you two got caught in the rain." Morgan's smile was merry, but her gaze was assessing. "I see he wasn't kidding."

"We're soaked and we're muddy," Tyler said. "We didn't want to track all through the house like this, so—"

"Stay right there, both of you," Morgan said. "I'll ask Sarah for a couple of bathrobes."

Alex pulled off his boots and his wet socks. "She has an idea something's going on," he said in an undertone.

"It's fine. I'll talk with her. She knows this cruise job doesn't give me much opportunity to date. She'll understand."

"Probably." But he noticed Tyler didn't sound quite as confident as she had out there in the rain. Neither was he. He wasn't looking forward to dealing with Josie's questions.

Last summer he'd tried to protect his sister from Jack, who had previously dumped her. Obviously Jack had learned the error of his ways and now spent all his time proving to Josie how much he loved her, but Alex hadn't known it would turn out that way.

Josie wouldn't approve of Alex having a temporary fling with Tyler any more than Alex had liked Josie hooking up with Jack. She'd see it as a heartache waiting to happen, and he couldn't promise her it wasn't. He couldn't very well claim to know what he was doing, either, considering that his marriage had failed miserably.

Maybe he'd steer clear of Josie for the next four days. That wouldn't be easy, but it wouldn't be impossible, either. He'd be involved in the open house tomorrow and the cleanup on Sunday. Josie liked to spend most of her weekend at the Spirits and Spurs because that's when the employees needed her the most.

But Friday nights were reserved for the Chance family to gather at the ranch house, and the hum of conversation and occasional bursts of laughter coming from the dining room told him the meal was in full swing. Josie would be sitting next to Jack and no doubt she'd already pumped her husband for information. She might try to corner Alex before the evening was over.

"Morgan said we need a couple of robes in here." Sarah walked into the utility room with two white terry bathrobes over her arm. Her eyes widened. "Good Lord, what happened to you two? Did you fall in the mud or what?"

"Something like that," Alex said.

"It was my fault." Tyler scrubbed her hair back from her face. "I made a run for it and slipped in the mud. Then Alex tried to help me up and I caused him to lose his balance. I'm sure we looked like Laurel and Hardy out there."

"Well, here's a robe for each of you." She handed one to Tyler before giving Alex his. "You should just leave your wet stuff here. Alex, turn your back while Tyler gets out of her clothes."

He couldn't very well say that he'd already seen Tyler naked quite recently, so he turned around and began unfastening the snaps down the front of his denim shirt. He could hear Tyler and Sarah murmuring behind him and the rustle of clothing.

"All clear," Sarah said in a louder voice. "You can turn around now, Alex."

He turned. Tyler's clothes were piled on the top of one of the washers and she stood there wrapped up tight in the terry robe.

The robe was bulky and too big, so it completely disguised her figure. Alex shouldn't have found a single thing to be turned on about, except that her feet were bare, and the polish on her sexy toes gleamed in the overhead light. His fevered brain kicked into fantasy mode again.

"There's a door in the kitchen to the right of the stove, Tyler." Sarah pointed in that direction. "Behind it is a stairway that will take you to the second floor. The boys used that route all the time when they'd come in from the corral. You have towels up there, right?"

Tyler nodded. "Alex brought me some."

"You don't have a private bath, I'm afraid. You'll have to share the hall bath with Alex, so you might as well take off and get a head start."

"I will, and thank you. Sorry to be so much trouble."

"It's no trouble, sweetie. Jack says you're going to pair up with Watkins to provide the entertainment for the open house tomorrow, which is a huge help. I feel guilty making you work on your vacation. I hope Alex is paying you well for that."

"Don't worry. He is."

Alex covered his reaction with a coughing fit as Tyler, cheeks pink, quickly left the room.

"Oh, dear." Sarah peered at him. "I hope you're not getting sick."

"I'm fine. Just swallowed wrong."

"Listen, it's not my place to interfere, but I think that girl is extremely focused on getting her promotion. And I don't blame her. That's impressive, being named a cruise director at her age."

Alex gazed into Sarah's blue eyes, so much like Gabe's. Although Sarah was a devoted mother to all three men, Gabe was her only biological child. Jack had been four when she'd married his father, and then baby Nick had appeared on the doorstep, the unexpected result of Jonathan's affair in the period between his divorce from Jack's mother and meeting Sarah. Sarah had accepted all three boys as hers to raise. In fact, she was fast becoming a second mother to him, as well.

"I know Tyler's dedicated to her career," Alex said. "And I think that's great."

"It is great. People should have jobs they love." Sarah laid a hand on his damp sleeve. "But it means she won't be sticking around here."

"No, she won't. I understand that, too."

Sarah squeezed his arm and let go. "I hope you do, because I've seen the way you look at each other."

"It'll be okay." He was touched by the gentle nature of her concern. No doubt Josie's warnings would come across like air-raid sirens.

"I probably shouldn't have put her right across the hall from you, but I didn't realize there was something going on between you two. Did it start last August?"

"Yeah."

"I wondered after I thought about your reaction when she showed up here today. She's a nice girl, and if I thought she'd consider staying, I'd be matchmaking like crazy. But she won't, so I want you to be careful."

"Thanks, Sarah." He leaned forward and kissed her cheek. "I will." Which was a damn lie, because it was too late to be careful. And he had a problem.

He could have dealt with the loss of great sex when Tyler left next week. He might not have been happy about it, but he could have managed.

Unfortunately for him, she'd chosen to sing "Oklahoma" in the middle of a rainstorm, and then she'd finished off her performance with a few dance steps. Watching her take that little bow, he'd felt his heart slip-sliding away. Halting that slide would be a real trick, but he'd have to try for both their sakes.

6

TYLER THOUGHT ABOUT waiting for Alex before going down to dinner and decided against it. They were liable to catch enough flak for their flimsy caught-in-the-rain story, so she'd demonstrate to the family that she and Alex weren't joined at the hip. She hoped they'd be joining different body parts later in the evening, but she'd like the next hour or so to be strictly PG-13.

She'd put on a clean pair of jeans and a black V-neck shirt. Then she added her turquoise necklace and earrings because…because she liked looking good. At times she wondered if she was too hung up on that.

Her job demanded that she be well groomed, and she'd always appreciated having a reason to dress well. But, to her surprise, she'd had fun getting all muddy and bedraggled. That would happen a lot on a ranch, where appearance wouldn't count as much as performance.

She contemplated that as an appealing change of pace and discovered she didn't recoil the way she might have a couple of years ago. She loved her job. She did. But sometimes the constant need to look great wore on her. She'd never admitted that to herself before.

As she descended the wide staircase to the first floor, she ran her hand along the banister again. Without Alex as a distraction, she could pause a moment and take in the welcoming sight of roomy leather chairs facing a gigantic rock fireplace. Framed family photographs lined the wooden mantel. A paperback lay on a small wooden table beside one of the chairs, as if someone had been quietly reading there and had left the book, planning to settle in for another relaxing moment later.

Home. The word hadn't meant much to Tyler over the years. Home had been a battered van until she moved out on her own. She couldn't call her tiny apartment home because she spent so little time there. Her collection of souvenirs was the only thing that marked it as hers. The cruise ship was luxurious, but it was where she worked. It wasn't home, either.

The Last Chance represented home to Morgan now. Tyler had thought her sister was crazy to tie herself to a man and then compound that by getting pregnant. Both Morgan and Tyler had witnessed how marriage and kids had absorbed nearly all their mother's time, giving her no chance to develop other interests or have a career.

But Morgan wouldn't be living the kind of life their mother had lived. Morgan would have a house and plenty of relatives around to help babysit. It wouldn't have to fall to the older siblings the way it had to Morgan and Tyler.

She'd taken Tyler on a quick tour before bringing her over here. Although Morgan's home wouldn't be quite this grand, it would be filled with light and space. It would be—no, it already *was*—a home.

Tyler pushed aside a prick of envy. She had the life she wanted, and it would only get better once she became a cruise director with the freedom to direct every aspect of the cruise experience. Someday in the far distant future she might want a home, but not yet, not when her dream was within reach.

Her route to the dining room took her down the same hallway she'd walked with Alex that afternoon. The left side was a wall of windows that provided a view of the Tetons during the day. Now the glass reflected the light from two wall sconces and the image of Tyler moving down the hall.

The right wall was covered with more framed family pictures, including some that looked as if they'd been taken fifty or sixty years ago. The O'Connelli family's vagabond lifestyle hadn't allowed for this kind of display. There had never been a wall available, and even a scrapbook would have been something to haul around and keep track of.

Tyler paused when she realized new pictures had been added, with people she knew well. She found a wedding shot of Morgan and Gabe, and another one of the entire wedding party, her included. Morgan hadn't offered her a copy, probably because she hadn't expected Tyler to want one. Keeping pictures around wasn't exactly an O'Connelli tradition.

It was obviously a Chance tradition, though. Next to that were the photographs of Jack and Nick's double wedding to Josie and Dominique. Tyler's heart warmed when she found Alex smiling happily in the group shot. He'd donned Western wear for the ceremony. Maybe that was when he'd started to transform into a cowboy.

Studying the picture, she identified two people who had to be Mr. and Mrs. Keller. They were both tall and had facial features that reminded Tyler of both Alex and his sister, Josie. Common wisdom said a father's appearance could indicate how his son would age. If so, Alex would still be a hunk in his fifties.

"I thought you'd already be tucking into your rib eye."

She glanced down the hall to find the man himself walking toward her. She must have been deep in thought to have missed hearing his booted feet on the hardwood floor. He'd put on a clean pair of jeans and a white Western shirt with pearl-covered snaps. The yoke of the shirt emphasized his shoulders, which she'd swear were wider than they had been last summer.

He'd obviously taken time for a shower, because his dark blond hair was still damp and he smelled like soap, the manly kind featured in commercials showing a guy lathering up his brawny chest. She wouldn't mind observing Alex doing that. In fact, she wouldn't mind being the person wielding the washcloth.

She looked into his gray eyes and wished they weren't expected at the dinner table. "I got caught up in the rogues' gallery. Are these two your folks?"

"Yeah." His expression softened. "They had such a good time. They might end up retiring in Jackson Hole, or at least spending their summers here and maybe winters somewhere a little warmer."

It all sounded so normal. Tyler decided not to mention that her parents didn't have a retirement plan. They just lived in the moment, taking life as it came. It drove her nuts. She'd already started an IRA.

Alex brushed his knuckle over her cheek. "You look nice."

"You, too."

He sighed. "We need to go. Mary Lou's probably keeping our food warm."

"So we'll go." She caught his hand and pressed it to her cheek before stepping away from him.

"Right. We'll go." But he didn't move, just continued to look at her.

With a shake of her head, she turned and started down the hallway. "Come on, Alex. They're expecting us."

"Yeah, they are." He fell into step beside her. "This is strange. I want to hold your hand, and yet I'd better not. I don't want to be all that obvious, like it's a done deal."

"I know." When they reached the large empty dining room where the midday meal was served, she could hear the buzz of conversation from the family dining area at the far end and through a set of open double doors. "I intended to get there ahead of you so we wouldn't look quite so much like a couple."

"So we won't sit together unless that's how it's set up and we have no choice. You should probably try to sit next to Morgan. That's who you're here to see, after all."

"And I plan to spend plenty of time with her. But she's the one who wants me to sleep at the ranch house."

He caught her arm, halting her progress. "And don't think I don't appreciate my good luck."

His touch was warm, seductive. She wanted to nestle into his arms and savor the feeling of belonging that she always felt there. "See?" She gazed up at him. "Gabe was right. You're an honorary Chance and that means you get some of the Chance luck."

He smiled and stroked her arm. "It seems to be working for me so far. I checked my condom supply and found an unopened box."

The question was out before she gave herself time to think. "And when was the last time you checked your condom supply?" Then she realized how jealous and possessive that sounded. "Don't answer that. It's none of my business."

His gaze was steady. "It's been a few months."

And she shouldn't be so damn happy about that, but she was. Whoever he'd been involved with hadn't turned into a serious girlfriend. She didn't want him to have a serious girlfriend, either, which was completely unfair, but the thought of him falling for someone made her miserable. How twisted was that?

He gave her arm a squeeze. "I'll be counting the minutes until we can open that box. Now, let's go face the family."

Tyler wasn't worried about that part. If she could handle a cruise ship full of passengers, she could deal with the Chances. In fact, she was looking forward to seeing them all together again and taking note of the changes that two more weddings had brought to the family dynamics.

As they walked into the dining room, all conversation stopped. Tyler glanced around quickly to make sure she recognized everybody. Sarah was at the far end of the linen-draped table, and on her right sat green-eyed Nick Chance and his bride, Dominique, a brunette with a pixie cut. The chair between Dominique and Alex's sister, Josie, was empty, probably waiting for Alex. Jack was next to Josie.

Gabe and Morgan sat on the far side of the table, and Morgan also had an empty chair beside her, no doubt reserved for Tyler. A pretty blonde woman who looked to be in her fifties occupied the next chair, and a ruggedly handsome man of about the same age sat next to her.

Tyler finally remembered who they were. The woman, Pam Mulholland, owned the Bunk and Grub B and B down the road and was somehow related to the Chance family. The man next to her was Emmett Sterling, the ranch foreman, and he was dating Pam. Coupling up seemed to be the norm around here.

"There you are!" Sarah was the first to speak. "You both clean up real good."

"Thanks." Tyler smiled. "It's great to see everybody again. And I sure hope you all have your thinking caps on, because Alex and I have been trying to figure out how to keep tomorrow's guests out of the rain. The barn is one option, but we need some more."

Nick glanced over at them. "I could have sworn you ordered some event canopies, Alex. I remember talking about it."

"I ordered three," Alex said. "But only one made it here. I've exhausted all the options for getting any more by tomorrow."

Jack set down his empty beer bottle. "The tractor barn. We'll move the equipment to a back pasture, temporarily cover it with tarps to protect it from the weather, do some cleanup, and use that space."

"That's a great idea," Alex said. "I didn't know that was possible, but—"

"Hold it." Mary Lou bustled in carrying a steaming plate in each hand. "No more talk of the open house until these two eat. Tyler, I want you over there between your sister and Pam. Alex, you can sit next to Josie." She deposited the plates at the designated places. "Who needs coffee?"

A chorus of requests went up.

"I'd love some, too," Tyler said as she walked around the table toward her chair. Before she made it there, Gabe came to his feet and pulled the chair out for her. She thanked him and glanced down the table, noting Sarah's pleased smile. "I'll bet you drilled manners into these guys when you raised them."

Nick rolled his eyes. "Tyler, you have no idea."

"Remember those Sunday dinners?" Gabe said.

Nick and Jack both groaned.

"Pure torture," Jack said. "She would use every blessed piece of silverware in the drawer and we couldn't eat until we'd correctly identified all of them. The forks were the worst. I was the only guy my age who could tell you what a seafood fork looked like."

"I was not about to raise a bunch of country bump-kins," Sarah said.

"Sounds like a great idea to me," Morgan said. "Be-tween Sarah covering manners and Jonathan show-ing them the finer points of country swing, I'd say the Chance boys got the perfect education." She patted her tummy. "I want the same for this little…kid."

"Ah, you almost slipped, Morgan!" Sarah's face was alight with anticipation. "You'll tell us the sex of that baby, yet."

Gabe looked fondly at his wife. "Nope. It's going to be our secret until July second."

"But I'm really serious about the manners and the dancing, Sarah," Morgan said. "I want this kid to be able to handle a fancy meal and navigate a two-step."

Tyler put her napkin in her lap. "It's not a bad idea to know those things. I had to learn on the job."

"You must have," Morgan said. "There wasn't a lot of formal training going on in the O'Connelli van."

"Lots of ideals, though." Tyler cut into her steak. Sud-denly she was starving. Making love to Alex had taken her mind off food, but now that he was across the table from her and completely out of reach, she breathed in the aroma of a meal carefully prepared, and she settled in to enjoy it.

"You're right about the ideals," Morgan said. "We were taught respect—of ourselves, other people and Mother Earth. That was a good thing."

"It is a good thing." Dominique looked across the table at Morgan. "That reminds me. Did you take your parents out to the sacred site while they were here for the wedding? It seems like something they'd like."

"There wasn't time. When they come back, I definitely will. They would love it."

Tyler swallowed a bite of the best steak she'd had in ages and cut herself another one. "What sacred site?"

Dominique gave Nick a warm glance before turning back to Tyler. "You should get Morgan to take you out there while you're here. It's a large, flat rock that's big enough for you to park a pickup on, although you wouldn't want to. The rock is granite laced with quartz. The veins of quartz sparkle in the sun...or in the moonlight."

Tyler figured Dominique and Nick had shared some moonlit time on that rock. She was intrigued. "And why is it sacred?"

"It's part of the Shoshone tribe's belief system." Emmett hooked an arm around Pam's chair and leaned forward to look down the table at Tyler. "When Archie and Nelsie Chance moved onto the ranch property, they discovered that the tribe conducted ceremonies out there, even though the land didn't officially belong to them. So Archie and Nelsie told them they were welcome to continue, but the tribe doesn't hold ceremonies much these days."

"Wow." Tyler glanced over at Morgan. "You have to take Mom and Dad out there next time they visit. They would eat that up with a spoon. I'm surprised you didn't make time while they were here last summer."

"I thought of it. I just…didn't want to encourage any weirdness during the wedding." She winked at Tyler. "If you know what I mean."

"Oh, totally. Good call. They could have decided you needed a shaman to bless your union, and no telling what else they would have dreamed up once they were inspired by an ancient Native American ceremonial site." Tyler turned back to Emmett. "So what's this sacred stone supposed to do for a person?"

"According to legend, it provides clarity. So if you're dealing with some issue and you're mixed up about it, the stone is supposed to help you figure it out."

"That could come in handy."

"Oh, it has," Nick said. Once again he and Dominique exchanged a fond glance.

Jack cleared his throat. "Then again, sometimes it's just a great place to share a few beers with your brother."

"That, too," Nick agreed.

"Well, now I have to see this sacred site," Tyler said. "I don't have any large issues I'm dealing with, but I still want to see it. After all, I was raised by flower children, so even though I've left that life behind, I haven't completely rooted out those woo-woo tendencies."

Gabe put down his coffee cup. "Neither has Morgan. We took a trip out there when we were deciding on names for the baby."

"Just don't call her Sunshine or Starlight," Tyler said.

"Or Moonbeam," Morgan said with a laugh. "Don't

worry. It'll be a gender-specific name that won't make a single person wince. I promise."

Sarah rolled her eyes and heaved a martyred sigh. "There you go again, tempting us with the fact that you both know whether the baby's a boy or a girl, and we don't. Why not just *tell* us?"

"Because we like the suspense," Gabe said with a laugh. "And we don't want any preconceived notions about this baby. This kid could decide to be a rancher or a foreign diplomat. We don't want anyone making plans for the kid's future based on gender."

"Other than teaching manners and the two-step," Morgan said. "I'm good with that."

Sarah tucked her napkin beside her plate. "Well, some of us are on pins and needles and can hardly wait until the official due date. Some of us are going quietly insane as we deal with this suspense you love so much."

"Then maybe this is the time to share our news," Josie said. "That might give you something else to think about, Sarah."

Sarah straightened and fixed a laserlike gaze on Josie. "Are you saying that you and Jack are…"

"Confirmed this morning." Jack's dark eyes glowed with pride. "Josie and I are going to have a baby."

The dining room exploded as chairs scraped back and everyone jumped up to give hugs, squeals and hearty congratulations. Tyler caught a glimpse of Alex enfolding Josie in a warm embrace, and for some unexplained reason that brought tears to her eyes. Maybe she was imagining how Alex would react when he received the news that he'd be a father rather than simply an uncle.

She couldn't really say why she was feeling so emotional. Babies were fine for Morgan and Josie, but Tyler wasn't into them, at least not at this point in her life. Babies equaled the loss of freedom to pursue work that she loved.

She understood there were trade-offs, but she wasn't interested in hearing about them right now. If she were totally honest with herself, she'd admit that listening to a woman rhapsodize about the joys of marriage and children might interfere with her enjoyment of the single life and her career success.

Maybe a part of her envied the spontaneous joy generated by Josie and Jack's announcement. The ship's crew celebrated things, too, but it was…different. The emotions around this table ran far deeper. She hadn't realized until now what she was missing, yet she wasn't willing to give up a dynamite career for that kind of connection. Or was she?

In the chaos surrounding Josie's announcement, Tyler was surprised to hear Alex's voice speaking her name. She turned to find him crouched beside her chair, his expression worried.

"Are you okay?" he asked. "You look a little pale."

She met his gaze. "Do you know where this Shoshone sacred site is located?"

"Yeah, I've been out there a couple of times."

She guessed that he'd gone because he needed to sort through his thoughts about Crystal. She decided not to ask. "Do you know if it's still raining?"

"No, but it was letting up about the time we came in. Why?"

"Because I'd like to go out there." She'd been so sure of what she wanted, and now doubts pelted her like hail. Her big promotion was within reach. She could always settle down later after she'd enjoyed that promotion for a few years. But it wouldn't be with Alex, and it wouldn't involve this family.

"Now?"

"Right now, if that's at all possible. Will that look too crazy?"

Alex stood. "I don't care if it looks crazy or not. If you want to go, we'll go. Let me get the keys to one of the ranch trucks."

She liked that he fell in with her gonzo plan so easily. Not all guys would. She liked many things about Alex, in fact. Too many things. The sacred site was supposed to give a person clarity. She desperately needed that.

7

TWENTY MINUTES LATER, Alex was at the wheel of one of the older ranch trucks, with Tyler belted into the passenger seat beside him as they bounced down a rutted road toward the sacred Shoshone site. Tyler had gone up to her room for a dark green hoodie, and he'd grabbed his denim jacket from the closet and an old blanket from the top shelf.

The night was cool, so he kept the windows rolled up on the truck. After the rain it wouldn't be particularly cozy on the granite, either, but he'd do what he could to compensate. He'd so hoped for an innerspring mattress tonight, but it didn't seem to be in the cards.

"By coming out here, I think we've tipped our hand," Tyler said. "Everybody must have guessed that we're… temporarily together."

"Oh, well."

"I just had to get out of there for a while."

Alex wasn't sure what was bothering her, but he had some ideas. "You looked a little freaked out after Josie made her announcement."

"I was, and I'm still trying to figure that out. You looked really happy, though."

"I was. This will be great for her and Jack, and Sarah's going to be in hog heaven with two grandchildren to run after. Plus, the kids will be close in age, so they can grow up together. It's nice for everyone concerned."

Tyler groaned. "Stop the truck."

He slammed on the brake. "Are you sick?"

"Not physically. I'm sick with guilt. Talk about self-centered! I dragged you out here when you should be back there celebrating with everyone. Please turn around and go back. I'm so, so sorry."

"Don't be." Alex took his foot off the brake and put it back on the gas. "I'd rather be out here with you."

"That's nice of you to say, but you're missing the festivities. I'll bet they moved the party into the living room and lit a fire. They're toasting those two babies, and you'll be the proud uncle of one and probably the adopted uncle of the other one. You should be there with Josie."

"She doesn't need me there. She has Jack."

"I should be there with Morgan."

Alex sighed. "That makes no real sense. You saw how Josie and Morgan instantly went into a huddle to discuss diet and exercise programs, and whether Josie can fit into some of Morgan's early maternity clothes."

"Yeah, I did. And that's great. They'll be a terrific support system for each other."

"Feeling like an outsider?"

She leaned her head against the back of the worn cloth seat. "Yeah, I guess I am. Maybe that's part of it. But to be an insider, I'd have to marry somebody and get pregnant right away. I won't do that, of course, but the power of suggestion is a scary thing."

Alex watched the road for critters. Back in Chicago he'd had to worry about other drivers. Out here he had to worry about hitting a raccoon or a skunk. "I suppose there is a lot of home-and-hearth sentiment swirling around the Last Chance right now."

"Which is so not me."

"I get that, Tyler."

"I know you do, which is one of the reasons I asked you to bring me out here. You may be the only person from that dinner-table crowd who truly understands that I'm not ready for a husband and kids. Morgan says she understands, but I can see in her eyes that she'd love to have me find a guy and settle down, maybe even in Jackson Hole."

"That's natural. I'm sure she misses you when you're gone for long stretches." He didn't want to imagine what his life would be like after she left, either. He was afraid the joy would leach right out of his days and nights.

"And I miss her, too, but that's the nature of the job. On the upside, I get to see amazing places all over the world, and the passengers are terrific, for the most part. Many of them have invited me to visit, and I'm sure their homes are gorgeous. You couldn't afford this type of luxury cruise if you didn't have plenty of money."

"Do you think you will visit them?"

"Probably not. The little time I have off I'll want to spend with family. Morgan's the first one to establish an actual home somewhere, but I'll bet the others will, too, eventually."

"And your parents? Will they finally stay put somewhere?"

Tyler chuckled. "I doubt it. I picture them waiting until we all have places of our own, and then they'll make the rounds. I've figured out that my dad is ADD. He can't stick with one job or one place for more than a month or two before he gets bored. I inherited the wanderlust, but I've been able to keep this job for almost six years. And I love it. It's perfect for me."

"I'm sure it is." And yet…now he wasn't so sure. She kept saying how much she loved her lifestyle, almost as if she needed to keep repeating her dedication to the job to ward off any change to the plan. Or maybe that was wishful thinking on his part.

Tyler peered out the window. "It's very dark out here, isn't it?"

"Especially tonight, with all the clouds. I'm afraid you won't see the moon glittering on the quartz unless I use a flashlight."

"You have one, though, right?"

"There should be one in the glove compartment."

As she reached to open it, he remembered what else was in there. She'd waited on the porch while he'd brought the truck around, and he'd used that opportunity to shove a handful of condoms into the glove compartment. A handful was excessive, but he hadn't had time to figure out how many he might need, so he'd just grabbed some.

Sure enough, the minute she opened the compartment, several condom packages tumbled out and fell to the floor of the truck. She began to laugh. "Are the ranch trucks normally stocked with these?"

"No. That was me doing the stocking." And the sight of them had jump-started his libido.

"I see. That's quite a supply."

"I didn't want to run out." But as eager as he felt to have her, even those might not be enough.

"Is that so? I don't remember needing that many in August. Have you shortened your recovery time?"

He wouldn't doubt it. She seemed to be affecting him more strongly than she had last summer. "I guess we'll find out, won't we?" And soon, very soon.

"That depends on whether there's a flashlight in here. It wasn't snake season when I lived here as a kid, but last summer I distinctly remember being warned about walking around in the dark without a flashlight because of snakes."

"It was warmer then. August." He didn't want her to get distracted thinking about wildlife. He wanted her mind to be firmly where his was—on sex. "It's too cold out for varmints to be out moseying around."

She glanced over at him. "Listen to you, sounding like Yosemite Sam! I'm beginning to think you have turned into a real cowboy, after all."

He lapsed into a slow drawl. "In that case, ma'am, could I interest you in going for a little…ride?" He wanted her so much he could taste it.

She reached over and stroked his thigh. "Sounds like fun."

"I guaran-damn-tee it." Ah, that single touch was all it took for his cock to strain against his fly.

Moving her hand, she rubbed his crotch.

He drew in a quick breath. "You might want to be careful, ma'am. That gun is loaded."

"I can tell." She continued to fondle him. "Are we there yet?"

"We're close, and I'm not talking about the sacred site, either." Clenching his jaw, he brought the truck to a stop and switched off the engine.

"Why are we stopping?"

"Honey, we're just getting started." He opened his door and the overhead light flashed on. He turned to her and raked her with his gaze. "By the time I come around to your side, I want your jeans and your panties off."

"Are all cowboys as bossy as you?" Her eyes darkened and excitement trembled in her voice.

"Don't know. Don't care. Just do it." He couldn't remember ever being this desperate to have a woman. He'd hoped to hold out until they reached their destination, but he couldn't see himself driving another ten feet, let alone another mile, without some relief.

When he opened the passenger door and the dome light came on again, he was greeted by the welcome sight of Tyler shoving her jeans and panties over her ankles. She'd already taken off her shoes and socks, which left her dressed only in her shirt and green hoodie. He didn't need those off right now.

She glanced at him, her cheeks rosy with excitement. "I did it, but I think you're crazy."

"Most likely." He scooped up a condom packet from the floor at her feet and unbuttoned his fly.

"I don't know how you plan to manage sex under these conditions."

"I'll figure out the logistics as we go." The situation was fast approaching the critical point. He got the condom on in record time. "Turn toward me."

But as she did that, he could see it wouldn't work to take her that way. With the first thrust, he'd knock himself out cold on the roof of the cab. He leaned in and cradled the back of her head with one hand so he could kiss her, although a kiss would only make things worse for him. But he needed to kiss her, needed to feel that plump mouth moving against his.

He could go on kissing her forever, if only he weren't ready to explode. He used his free hand to explore the wonders between her silky thighs, and she wrapped her arms around his neck and started moaning softly.

He lifted his mouth a fraction away from hers. "Wrap your legs around my waist. I'm going to pick you up and reverse our positions so I'm sitting on the seat."

"Where will I sit?"

"On me, little lady."

"Okay."

As fast as she was breathing and as wet as she was, she probably would have said okay to any suggestion he made, including doing it on the hard ground. But he wasn't that frantic...yet.

Putting one arm around her shoulders, he slid the other one under her bottom and lifted her out of the truck. Fortunately he remembered to bend his knees, which gave him better leverage and kept him from throwing his back out or banging her head on the same truck roof he was trying to avoid. He thought longingly of the king-size mattress in Jack's bedroom, but he'd make do with the conditions he'd been given.

He only staggered once as he turned around, but she gave a little cry of alarm and tightened her grip.

"Everything's fine. Keep your head down."

"If you drop me, Alex Keller..."

"I won't." He made contact with the seat and slowly sank back, propping his butt against it. They were almost in a doable position, except she was still mostly out of the truck.

She nibbled on his lower lip. "So what's your next move, Houdini?"

"I'm thinking."

Keeping one arm around his neck, she reached down and took hold of his dick, condom and all. "I know where this belongs."

His voice was hoarse. "Me, too. I'm just not sure how to…"

"This is turning into a number from Cirque du Soleil."

"I know."

"Let me maneuver a bit."

Unwrapping one leg from around his waist, she held on to his cock as if needing it for balance while she propped her knee on the seat next to his hip.

Her grip threatened to send him over the edge, so he started counting backward from a hundred to distract himself.

"Are you doing a countdown?"

"If you don't hurry, that's exactly what it will turn into."

"Scoot back a little."

He obeyed and kept counting.

She managed to get the other knee in position so she was straddling him. "Move back a little more."

He followed her directions and then, miracle of miracles, they were there. His cock was poised at the entrance to all things special. Her mouth found his, and she suckled his tongue as she slowly lowered her hips, taking his throbbing penis bit by torturous bit.

He resisted the urge to thrust upward. She'd engineered this feat, and she had the right to tease him. He took satisfaction in knowing she was teasing herself, too. After that night in the hayloft, he knew exactly how much she liked having him deep inside her. She'd told him all about that…in detail.

When at last he was in up to the hilt, she drew back to

look into his eyes. In the glow from the dome light, her eyes flashed with dark fire. "There," she said, her voice husky. "Mission accomplished."

He swallowed, so overwhelmed by the sensation of being inside her again that he wasn't sure he could form an actual word. "Nice," he murmured at last.

"Yeah." Her gaze held his as she began to move.

Bracketing her hips with both hands, he closed his eyes, the better to savor this moment. He'd made love with several women in his life, and not one had welcomed him the way Tyler did. He wasn't sure how she did it, but somehow she opened to him in a way no other woman ever had. And, at the same time, she gathered him in close, as if wanting him, and only him, to learn the secrets of her body.

Leaning forward, she brushed her lips over his. "You okay?"

"I'm so okay it's frightening."

"I wasn't sure. You closed your eyes..."

"I wanted to... I needed to concentrate on..." He pushed up, not much, but enough to tighten the connection, lock it in. "On this."

"You're not imagining I'm someone else?"

He opened his eyes at once. "God, no. Is that what you thought?"

"For all I know, some woman broke your heart again and I'm handy."

"Come here." He guided her closer and kissed her, putting all the gratitude, tenderness and passion he felt into that kiss. Then he drew back. "You're not a substitute, Tyler. There's no one like you. No one."

She framed his face in both hands as she glided up and down, up and down. "Last summer, I think you wanted to forget." She moved a little faster, her breath coming in quick gasps.

"Maybe." He lost himself in the depths of her eyes. "Now I want to remember. I want to remember how it feels to be loving you."

"That sounds serious." It wasn't an accusation, just a statement.

"Not that serious," he lied. His climax stalked him, ready to pounce. "Don't worry. I'll let you go."

"I know." Her hips pumped faster. "Don't think about that now."

He laughed. "Who's thinking?" His grip tightened and the blood roared in his ears.

Her voice was low and intense. "Not me. I'm coming. Oh, Alex, this is so…"

"Yeah…" The sound of their ragged breathing drowned out everything but the slap of her thighs against the denim of his jeans as she hurtled toward her orgasm.

She took him with her. As the spasms rocked her body, he erupted, driving upward in an instinctive impulse to plant his seed deep in her womb. He understood that she wasn't asking for anything but this, sex for the sake of mutual pleasure. But his body, responding to signals hundreds of years old, had other ideas.

His body would just have to get over it. Any thoughts that Tyler had been affected the way he had were dashed once she'd recovered enough to talk.

"Well, that was fun." She laughed but didn't meet his gaze. "However, getting unwound from each other will be more of a challenge than untangling a strand of Christmas lights."

So, they were supposed to keep their comments superficial. He could do that. "How are you at untangling Christmas lights?"

"Pretty good. Let me move first."

"I think that's a given. If I move first, you're going out the door and into the dirt."

"Hold on to me."

He cleared his throat. "You bet."

"I meant that literally, not figuratively."

"I know." He wished she hadn't felt the need to remind him, though. And once she lifted her body free of his, he battled a sense of loss that didn't bode well for his future peace of mind.

"If I swing around and put both feet on the floor, then I think you can slide out, and I can sit back down in the seat."

"You must be a whiz at Twister." There. That was the right tone to set. Fun and games. He hoped he could maintain that attitude.

"I am good at Twister. And cruise ships are also a marvel of spatial economy, so I've learned a lot there, too." She put her right foot on the floor mat. Then, bracing both hands on the back of the seat, she put her other foot on the floor, giving Alex room to duck underneath her and climb out of the cab.

He murmured his thanks, and once she was sitting on the seat, he closed the door, which turned off the dome light. That gave him the necessary privacy to deal with the condom and button up. By the time he came to the driver's side of the truck and opened the door, she was once again dressed in her jeans and was putting on her shoes.

She'd braced one foot on the edge of the seat so she could tie her laces, and her hair fell forward, obscuring her face so he couldn't read her expression. He would have thought she was totally cool and in command of herself except for one thing. Her fingers trembled and she was having some trouble tying her shoe.

Apparently she was as shook up by their lovemaking as he was. The breezy way she'd talked to him afterward had been her way of trying to maintain some distance. He'd promised not to cause problems for her, but it seemed he had, anyway.

"Maybe we should just go back," he said softly as he climbed behind the wheel.

"We can't." She finally tied her shoe and switched feet to work on the other one.

"Why not?" He left the door open so she could see what she was doing.

She yanked at the laces, as if that would stop her fingers from quivering. "Because we told everyone we were coming out here to take a look at the sacred site, so we need to look at it. I don't want to have to make something up if anybody asks what I thought."

"I can describe it for you, if that's all you—"

"No, I want to go out there." She finished tying her shoe and turned to him. "Maybe it will help."

"I think what might help is me keeping my hands off you for the next four days."

She gazed at him, her dark eyes troubled. "That's just it. I don't want you to. Making love with you seems like the only worthwhile thing in the world right now. Maybe if I stand on that rock, I'll get my sense of purpose back."

"All right." He closed the door and started the engine. "But no matter how that rock affects you, I'm backing off. I'm not about to derail your dreams."

8

THEY RODE IN SILENCE the rest of the way, which turned out not to be very far. Tyler's body still hummed with awareness of Alex. She was tuned in to his breathing and the subtle sound of denim against the fabric of the seats. Even in the dim light from the dash, she could make out the movement of his thighs as he worked the pedals on the truck.

And she knew, even without looking, that he was aroused again, despite his vow to keep his hands off her from now on. She drew in his musky, masculine scent and imagined she could read his heated thoughts and his desperate attempt to tamp down his desire.

She'd fed that desire with her behavior, and she took full responsibility for the turmoil she'd created for both of them. She'd been the one who'd suggested they work together on tomorrow's event. Yes, he'd initiated the kiss in the barn, but she'd wanted it as much as he had.

So they'd talked themselves into the idea that they could have a lighthearted affair and then go their separate ways. But now her future plans seemed like pale, lifeless things compared to the warmth of the Chance family unit and the heat she and Alex had created in the past few hours. She was terrified by that. She'd worked too long and too hard to abandon those plans on a whim, just because the image of a different future had appeared tonight.

"It's up ahead," Alex said. "I don't know if you can see the rock yet. It doesn't stick very far out of the ground."

Tyler peered into the darkness. "I think I see it."

"I'll swing around so the headlights will help you catch some of the sparkle." Alex veered to the left and then turned the truck so it was parked across the road. The headlights illuminated the surface of a flat rock about the size of a cruise ship's lifeboat once it was lowered into the sea.

"Huh." Tyler gazed at the subtle white stripes of varying widths, some only a few inches, some more than a foot. They did indeed sparkle. "It's quartz."

"Yep."

"My folks would love this rock. Quartz is supposed to be good for meditation, and it's also a healing stone."

"Which fits with the local lore about this place," Alex said. "Emmett told me that years ago he tried digging down to find the bottom of the rock, and after about seven feet he gave up. I'm sure somebody with special equipment could measure the depth, but nobody's ever done that."

"So it's like an iceberg," Tyler said. "We're only seeing the smallest part of it."

"True." He gazed out the windshield at the rock.

"I guess now would be a good time to test its powers. Rain's supposed to have a purifying effect on the quartz."

"I read that."

She glanced over at him. "You read up on crystals?"

"I thought I might as well, once I'd made up my mind to take a trip out here. I resisted the idea for weeks, thinking it was too mystical for me. Plus, Crystal is my ex's name."

"I hadn't thought of that."

"Josie's the one who finally convinced me to come out here. She said I was still angry, which wasn't doing me any good, and maybe it was perfectly appropriate to use a crystal to stop being angry with Crystal."

"Was this after I was here?"

He nodded. "Maybe a month or so after."

"I can sure believe you were still angry in August. There was an edge to you, something a little fierce about the way you made love."

He looked stricken. "I didn't hurt you, did I? I know we got kind of wild in the hayloft, but—"

"No, nothing like that. It was more a mental thing. I could sense that anger Josie was talking about."

"Do you sense it now?"

"No." She hesitated. "But I think…I think you're still wary."

"You're calling *me* wary? You, the person who's scared to death that marriage is contagious?"

"Yes. You're wary. If I suddenly reversed course and said I was giving up my career and wanted to settle down here at the Last Chance with you, I'll bet you'd run in the other direction."

He held her gaze for several long seconds. Then he looked out at the rock sparkling in the headlights. "We haven't known each other long. I'd hate like hell to make another mistake."

"You think it was your fault that the marriage didn't work out?"

"No, but we shouldn't have married in the first place. If I'd thought about it beforehand, I might have realized that Crystal would get bored. She needed more excitement, more action, so she finally went out and found it."

Tyler frowned. "I'm sorry." She'd suspected that Crystal had cheated on him, but hadn't been sure until now.

"It was just a bad combination."

"You mean a loyal person hooking up with a disloyal person?"

He smiled. "Thanks for that. I meant that I was focused on work, and she hadn't expected that from me because I was a party animal when we met in college. So was she, and she never changed. I did."

"I think that's called growing up."

"Or is it just different needs? You're not really like her, but the job you love is full of parties and exotic destinations. My ideal life would be putting in a hard day's work and relaxing quietly at home with…somebody special."

That sounded way too appealing, and she found herself longing to be that *somebody special* in his cozy scenario. Dangerous, dangerous thinking if she expected to stay on course. With that kind of temptation, she could get sucked into the marriage-and-baby whirlpool before she knew what was happening.

"You're right," she said. "We do have different visions of how we want to live our lives."

"That's all I'm saying."

"I'm going to see what the rock has to say." She opened her door. "Would you mind leaving the engine running and the lights on while I get out?"

"Nope." He put the truck in Neutral and set the emergency brake. "I'll come with you."

She thought about snakes as she hopped down from

the truck, but she also didn't think Alex would have let her get out if he'd been worried about her safety. She trusted him to do the right thing. She just didn't totally trust herself.

He, on the other hand, didn't totally trust her, but she didn't take that personally. He wasn't ready to trust any woman yet, unless maybe she was the cookie-baking, curtain-sewing, nesting type. And that was fine. A lack of trust on his part was a good thing if it kept her from falling for him.

He met her at the front of the truck and offered a steadying hand as she stepped up onto the damp rock. She decided not to mention that he'd vowed not to lay a hand on her ever again. Being a gentleman didn't really qualify, anyway.

Besides, he released her hand right away. "You're now standing on the sacred site revered by the Shoshone Indians for…"

"Centuries?" She looked down at her feet.

"Who the hell knows? Let's just say it's been a long, long time."

She took a deep breath of the cool air scented with pine, and focused on her dilemma. Did she plow forward and grab her career opportunity, or should she open her heart to the possibility of a home and family, maybe even with this man?

But no answer came to her. "Are we supposed to say anything?"

"Like what?"

"Like an incantation, a special chant, a Native American prayer." A breeze sighed through the tops of the evergreens nearby, but it was only the wind, not some magical message.

He shrugged. "I never did, but if that appeals to you, go for it."

"Alex! I'm looking for a mystical experience, here. I want clarity of purpose."

"Hmm." He glanced at her before gazing off into the blackness surrounding them.

"I could use a little help. I mean, you've been here before, and obviously had a positive experience, so if you'd be willing to make a suggestion instead of staring off into space, I'd appreciate it."

"When I was here last fall, I was alone." He continued to look into the inky night as if mesmerized by the darkness.

"I realize that. Maybe alone is better, but I'd rather not have you leave me here in the cold and dark with potential wild animals around, if you don't mind."

"I wouldn't do that, Tyler."

"Good. So when you were here, how did you maintain your focus?"

He cleared his throat. "Like I said, I was out here by myself, so naturally it didn't strike me as a particularly sexual place."

"Well, it's not. It's a very hard rock which looks wet and extremely uncomfortable."

"Does it?" He turned, allowing her to see the glow of desire in his eyes.

Despite the unsexy conditions, she responded with a rush of heat. "Yes, it does. This is not a good place for sex, if that's what you're thinking."

"Are you sure? Because to me, it looks like the perfect place to pull you down, strip off your clothes and pump into you until neither one of us can see straight."

Her breath caught. As she imagined him doing that,

her panties grew damp and her nipples became tight buds of anticipation. She swallowed. "I suppose that's another way of looking at this place."

"I was hoping for clarity about us when I stepped onto this rock."

"So was I. Sort of, anyway. I mean, clarity about my job, and what I—"

"Turns out I have clarity." He closed the gap between them but didn't reach for her. "I can see clearly that although I want to be noble and leave you alone, when I have a chance to touch you, kiss you and slide my cock deep inside you, I'm going to take it. What sort of message do you get from this rock?"

She ached with longing. She had no answer to what the future held for her, but she knew what she needed in the present. "It's...becoming remarkably similar to yours."

"I guess the rock has spoken."

"Are we really going to do it right here?"

"Yes, I believe we are." Pulling her into his arms, he began working her out of her clothes.

She decided not to let that become a one-sided situation and started working him out of his clothes, too. It was complicated by his boots and her shoes, but eventually they accomplished what they both had in mind.

He pulled her close and feathered a kiss over her lips. "I have a blanket in the truck."

She was hot, achy and desperate. "I don't want to wait for no stinkin' blanket. We'll use our clothes."

"The rock's wet," he said. "They'll get messed up again."

"I don't care." She pushed the discarded clothes together into a makeshift bed and stretched out. "Perfect."

"You know, it is. Except you're lying on something important."

She started to get up.

"Stay there." He knelt beside her. "I'll have fun finding it." Leaning over to kiss her, he fondled her breasts with one hand while he reached underneath her.

The maneuver, which stimulated her both in front and in back, was driving her insane with wanting. Clutching his head in both hands, she forced his mouth away from hers. "Stop fooling around."

He chuckled. "I thought that's what we were here for."

"No, we're here so that you can get down to business, so either you find that little raincoat toute de suite, or I'm getting up and finding it for you."

"Yes, ma'am." He produced the foil packet and tore it open.

"And don't litter."

"Wouldn't dream of it." He shoved the foil packet under the pile of clothes before kneeling between her thighs. "Is the rock too hard?"

"No." And even if it had been, she wouldn't have told him at this point in her frenzied state. Some things were worth suffering for.

"I'm glad, because I really, really need to do this."

"And I really, really need you to. Forget the foreplay."

"Nice to know." With a quick movement of his hips, he thrust deep and joined them together. Then he groaned softly. "Damn, that's good."

"Uh-huh." When she felt him there, the tip of his cock touching her womb, her world shifted and settled into place. She wasn't supposed to feel this sense of completion, wasn't supposed to want this more than anything else in her life. But she did.

He stayed still for a moment, his arms braced and his chest heaving. "I'm glad I left the headlights on."

"So you can see the sparkle?"

"Yeah. In your eyes." He drew back and eased forward again. "I never realized how they light up when I do this."

She ran her hands up his muscled arms and clutched his powerful shoulders. "So do yours. I couldn't see your face very well in the hayloft." And because of that, he'd remained a shadowy memory, one more easily relegated to her fantasy life.

But the man gazing down at her while he loved her with slow, steady strokes was not the least bit shadowy. His gray eyes focused intently on her face and the tiny lines at the corners crinkled as he subtly increased the pace. Faint stubble roughened the strong outline of his jaw, and his beautifully sculpted, highly kissable lips parted as his breathing became more ragged.

She would never forget the way he looked, poised above her like this, his eyes filled with the need to drive into her over and over. His neck and jaw muscles were tight. Instinctively she knew he was holding back his own orgasm until he'd given one to her.

"I love the way you move with me." His eyes darkened as he changed to an even faster rhythm. "I love the way you lift your hips and meet me halfway. Like that, and, ah…like *that*."

"Because when you push in deep it's…so good. So very…" She gasped as she rose to meet him again. The pressure and friction set off little explosions of delight building to what she knew would be a mind-blowing orgasm.

Around them, the night was still, forming a silent backdrop for their labored breathing, the soft rumble of the truck's engine and the intimate, liquid sound of his rhythmic strokes. Each time he made the connection that sent shock waves vibrating through her system, she whimpered in anticipation. He coaxed her closer...and closer yet. She moaned softly and dug her fingers into his shoulders.

"No need to be quiet." He shifted his angle to bring more pressure on her clit. "This isn't the hayloft. No one can hear you yell."

"Guess...not." A sense of freedom washed over her. She arched upward with a groan of intense pleasure.

"Open that beautiful mouth for me. Let it out." He pumped faster.

Feeling reckless, she welcomed the next thrust with a joyful cry.

"That's good. Again."

The more she cried out, the more excited she became. Giving voice to her pleasure intensified it, hurling her toward her climax at warp speed.

"Now I want to hear you coming." He bore down, his movements rapid and focused. "Go for it, Tyler. Be loud. I know you're close. I can see it in your eyes."

She gulped for air. "Be loud...with me."

"I'm right behind you. That's it..."

She yelled as the first wave hit.

"Louder!"

"Oh, God! Alex! *Alex!*"

"Louder!"

Her climax lifted her right off the rock and she emptied her lungs in a wild cry of triumph that echoed through the trees.

True to his word, he followed with a deafening bellow as he plunged deep and shuddered against her, his cock pulsing. With a groan he pushed forward, as if to go even deeper.

She wrapped her legs around his, locking him in tight. Slowly he lowered himself until his weight was on his forearms and his body rested lightly against hers. His breath was hot as he nuzzled her throat and behind her ear.

He raked his teeth along the curve of her shoulder. "I could eat you up."

She drifted in a dreamy haze, satisfied in a way she'd never been in her life. "Bet you didn't bring the whipped cream."

"No." He licked the hollow of her throat. "Too bad, because you won't be able to yell like that when you're in my bed."

"Being quiet can be fun, too."

"With you, everything can be fun." Leaning down, he flicked his tongue over her nipple. "I can hardly wait to squirt whipped cream all over your hot body and lick it off."

"That's if we ever leave this rock." She couldn't imagine moving. Apparently endorphins had made her oblivious to the rocky surface, because she could swear they were lying on a cloud.

"Oh, we'll leave it." He lifted his head and feathered a kiss over her lips. "Much as I like lying naked here with you, I'd rather not let the truck run out of gas and strand us on this rock."

"How much gas is in it?"

"Don't know. Didn't check it when we left." He nibbled on her lower lip. "Should have, I guess."

"Maybe we should get up."

"Mmm." He settled in for another kiss.

Tyler realized that kissing Alex was an activity that was excellent all by itself. Even when she'd just had amazing sex with him, she still enjoyed every second of having his lips moving on hers because he was so good at it, so sensuous, so…

He lifted his mouth away a fraction. "Listen."

Her heart raced as her imagination ran wild. "What do you hear? Footsteps? A bear? A moose? What?"

"I don't hear anything, anything at all." He lifted his head. "And that could be a problem."

"Because?"

"I'm afraid the truck's stopped running."

"Are you saying—"

"We're out of gas." He paused. "Did you bring your cell phone?"

"No. Did you?"

"No."

"So what are we going to do?"

He sighed. "Walk."

9

"BUT WAIT." Alex untangled himself from Tyler, and as cool air hit his overheated body, his brain started to work again. "This isn't your fault, so it's not fair to make you walk back. I'll go to the house, get a can of gas and bring it here in a second truck. I'll be fast. You can stay here."

"Not happening."

"No, seriously, it'll be fine." He turned away from her so he could deal with the condom. Before they left, he'd toss it in a bucket in the back of the truck where he'd put the other one.

"You think you're going to leave me out here by myself?"

"You'd be perfectly safe. You can lock yourself in the truck if you're worried about wild animals." He felt like a total idiot for getting them into this fix. Running out of gas, for Chrissake. Teenagers did that kind of thing, not a grown man, and certainly not a self-confident cowboy.

But he'd do whatever it took to correct the situation. Too bad the whipped-cream fantasy would have to be sacrificed, but there was always tomorrow night, or the night after that. They had time…some, anyway.

"Alex, I'm not staying out here with the truck while you walk back. I'm going with you."

He turned around to find her sorting through their damp clothes. "I won't be gone long. We're probably only about five or six miles from the house, so I can walk that in about an hour, maybe less if I jog part of it. I'll be back to get you in an hour and a half, tops."

"If you're worried about me keeping up, I'm in good shape. The *Sea Goddess* has a weight room and a jogging track." She stepped into her panties and pulled them over her hips.

He knew she was in good shape. He'd had his hands all over her tonight, and there wasn't a bit of flab on her. She was all sleek, toned, sexy woman. "I'm sure you can make it fine." He walked over to the pile of clothes to search for his briefs.

"Damn straight I can."

"That's not the issue. The issue is…look, I screwed up by not checking the gauge and noticing the tank was almost empty. I don't want you hiking back to the house because of my stupidity. Stay here and relax."

"No." She pulled on her jeans next instead of searching for her bra.

As she buttoned and zipped her jeans, Alex took a moment to appreciate the sight of her standing topless in the headlights, her dark hair cascading down her back. Her breasts were truly a work of art. One lock of her hair had fallen forward over her shoulder and curled lovingly around her nipple. Alex wanted to step closer and tease her nipple with that tendril. And then he would…*stop thinking about that,* is what he would do. Right now.

He was the doofus who'd managed to strand them out here, so he needed to forget about sex and concentrate on fixing the mess he'd made. He located his jeans and shook them out. "Please stay here," he said. "Let me take care of this." He pulled on the jeans and his belt buckle clanked.

"No way." Her gaze flicked over his belt and his open fly.

For one crazy moment he wanted to say the hell with going back to the ranch house. They had privacy and a generous supply of condoms. They could spend the night making noisy love and walk back in the morning.

But he had obligations in the morning. The open house began at ten. The ranch hands would be up before dawn, but they needed him there to supervise. The tractor barn had to be prepared, the setup for the music arranged and final touches made to the barn. Besides, he'd prefer this rendezvous with Tyler be kept on the down-low, so that meant returning under cover of darkness.

"Listen, Alex." She propped her hands on her hips, which made her look even more like a centerfold. "I'm the reason we're out here in the boonies, remember? If it weren't for me, you'd be at the house enjoying your third glass of celebratory champagne in front of a warm fire."

He deserved a medal for not going over and hauling her back into his arms. "And thank God you suggested coming to the sacred site. You have to know I'm happy about that. My dick is *really* happy about that."

"Okay." She smiled. "Point taken. But if I hadn't insisted on leaving the engine running and the lights on, I'll bet we would have had enough gas to get back, or almost back, so I'm accepting part of the blame for this, like it or not." She picked through the clothes again and came up with her bra.

"Accept all the blame you want. Just stay here while

I get the gas and another truck. Then we'll drive tandem back to the ranch and all will be well."

"No." She fastened her bra in place.

He shoved his arms into the sleeves of his no-longer-white shirt. "Yes."

"No, Alex!" She picked up her black shirt and started pulling it over her head. Her next comment was delivered while she still had the shirt covering her face. "It would be way too scary out here alone." Then she pulled the shirt down, her cheeks red with embarrassment.

He stopped fastening the snaps on his shirt. "You'd really be afraid?"

She shrugged. "I know I shouldn't be, but I grew up in a family with seven kids, so somebody was always around. Nowadays I spend most of my life on a cruise ship full of passengers. When I'm in L.A., I live in an apartment building with three hundred tenants, give or take. Don't make me stay all by myself out in the middle of nowhere. Please."

His protective instincts roared to life. He closed the distance between them and gathered her into his arms. "I didn't mean for you to be scared. I'm sorry."

She clung to him and pressed her cheek to his chest. "It's not something I like admitting. After all, I travel the world. I'm the most independent woman in my family. Everybody thinks I'm invincible."

"I won't tell anyone. And I certainly won't make you stay here. We'll walk back together, and we'll sing camp songs on the way, if that will help."

She groaned. "Not camp songs. My parents *love* camp songs, and I've heard enough to last me a lifetime. If I never hear 'Kumbaya' again, that's fine with me."

"Then we can sing drinking songs."

"We don't have to sing at all." She gazed up at him. "Just don't leave me."

His heart twisted. She was begging him not to leave her tonight, and yet she would be the one doing the leaving next week. The irony wasn't lost on him.

Now that they had a plan, they both moved quickly. After pulling the flashlight out of the glove compartment, Alex turned off the headlights and climbed out of the truck.

Tyler wanted to be in charge of the flashlight, so he gave it to her. But after seeing that she intended to keep it switched on all the time and fan it lighthouse style over the muddy road and the grassy meadows on either side, he had to say something. "Maybe we should conserve the batteries."

"Conserve the batteries? That sounds like something out of *Survivor*. Are we in more trouble than I thought?"

"We're not in any trouble, but the flashlight would be nice to have if we need to see something specific."

"Like what? A snake?"

"Not a snake. Like I said before, it's too cold." He was thinking more of a bear, but decided not to mention that critter. He chose something that sounded more cuddly. "You know, like a raccoon."

"Raccoons are kind of cute. I wouldn't mind seeing a raccoon."

"Anyway, you should probably use the flashlight sparingly. I don't know how old those batteries might be."

She didn't look happy about that. "You're saying that I can't leave the flashlight turned on because the batteries could go dead any minute?"

"Yeah, pretty much."

She muttered something to herself and turned off the flashlight.

"What was that?"

"Nothing."

"It was too something. Spit it out, O'Connelli."

"I just wonder what sort of outfit this ranch is, that's all, with trucks almost out of gas and dead batteries in the flashlights."

He cleared his throat so he wouldn't laugh. Nerves could make people say funny things. "It's the person driving the truck who's supposed to keep it gassed up, and I didn't do that, so my bad. The flashlight batteries may last for hours, but I don't know that, so I thought we should use the flashlight only when we have to."

She took a deep breath. "Fine." She started off again, but she was walking noticeably faster, which wasn't such a good idea on a muddy, rutted road.

He lengthened his stride to keep up with her. "You might want to watch out for—"

"What?" She glanced around wildly and stumbled over a rut. Although he caught her before she fell, she still managed to splash the legs of their jeans with mud. "What was I supposed to watch out for?"

"Ruts."

"Well, damn." She flashed him a quick grin. "Thanks for catching me. Falling down in the mud once is an accident. Twice begins to look like a habit."

"Well, we didn't." He massaged her shoulders. "I would kiss you, but I know what that could lead to, and we need to get back."

"I wouldn't let you kiss me, cowboy."

"Is that a challenge?"

"No." She backed away from his touch. "Not a challenge, so get that note of anticipation out of your voice. You have a way of making me forget where I am, and where I am is in the woods in the dark, and that's *not* where I want to have sex."

"Actually, me neither." He stepped forward and placed a quick kiss on her nose. "Let's go. We'll hold hands."

"Okay." She laced her left hand through his and held up the flashlight with her right. "At least I didn't drop this."

"Good." He squeezed her hand, enjoying the way her fingers fit through his as they started walking again. "See, this isn't so bad, taking a walk along a country road after a rain, breathing in the fresh scent of pine, listening to the wind in the—"

Noise exploded to their left in a wild series of yips and barks before several dark shapes hurtled across the road about twenty feet in front of them.

Tyler gasped and squeezed his hand so hard he winced. Then she switched on the flashlight and swept the area, but nothing was there. "Dear God, were those *wolves?*"

"No, coyotes. Most likely going after a late dinner. Maybe a rabbit."

Gradually her grip on his hand loosened. "Okay, I vaguely remember about coyotes from when I lived here as a kid."

"They won't hurt you."

"I know. But let's leave the flashlight on. If it gives out, it gives out, but having that beam pointing the way makes me feel comfier."

"Sure, why not. The batteries will probably last."

They walked along in silence while Tyler made periodic sweeps of the muddy road with the flashlight beam.

After they'd gone about a mile, she squeezed Alex's hand. "Hey. What does this remind you of?" She stuck the flashlight under her chin in *Blair Witch Project* mode.

He laughed. "Looks like you're feeling better about being out here in the wilds of Wyoming."

"You must think I'm such a wimp."

"Not at all. In fact, it's nice to know you're not perfect."

"Oh, I'm far from perfect, Alex."

"If you ask me, you're pretty damn close."

"Ha! I have a million little irritating habits."

"You do?" He glanced over at her in surprise. "Like what?"

"I take really long showers and I like to hog the bathroom. So be forewarned, because we're sharing."

He'd forgotten that. "Then if you're taking too long and I need to shower, I'll just climb in with you." If he hadn't been holding her hand, he would have missed the fine tremor that ran through her.

"Um, yeah." She cleared her throat. "Thanks for planting *that* idea in my head."

"You don't like it?"

"Oh, I like it a lot. Too much, in fact. And we've already established that in the middle of the dark woods is a bad place to have sex, so now I get to be frustrated."

He stroked her palm with his thumb. "Think of it as building the anticipation."

"Stop it, Alex." She pulled her hand away. "It's not fair how you can do that."

"What?" His masculine ego felt very good right now.

"Make me want to drag you off into the dark woods even though it's filled with lions and tigers and bears, oh, my." She swallowed. "I just remembered something. There actually are bears in these woods, aren't there?"

"There can be."

"Shitfire."

He swallowed his laughter, knowing she wouldn't appreciate it. "I doubt we'll come across one tonight."

"Have you seen any since you've been here?"

"A couple of times."

She gave a little wail of distress and grabbed his hand. "Now, *that's* scary. Okay, let's talk about something else, like…like what songs I should perform tomorrow. Obviously not 'Oklahoma.' Any ideas after being a DJ in Jackson for a few months?"

"Country is the obvious choice. How are you with country tunes?"

"I know some Faith Hill, Tim McGraw, Taylor Swift, Martina McBride. Will that work?"

He nodded. "Perfect. Watkins will know all that."

"I'll get with him in the morning. What about a sound system?"

He got a kick out of how her tone became more brisk and efficient when she switched into business mode. "We'll use mine. That was one of the things I had my folks ship out from Chicago last summer. People around here like having a DJ they can hire for parties, so I do gigs on the side. Speaking of that, people still request plenty of John Denver's stuff."

"I know a few of his. 'Annie's Song,' 'Country Roads,' 'Rocky Mountain High.'"

"Those are good. He also has one called 'Song of Wyoming' and Watkins knows it. If you could learn that, you'd make Jack very happy."

She laughed. "I promise to learn it if you promise to

make sure Jack's around to hear it. Just my luck he'd be off riding some horse in a demonstration and miss the whole thing."

"We'll coordinate. But be sure and sing 'Annie's Song' at some point. Everybody likes that one." And he shouldn't have requested that she sing it, he realized after the fact. He didn't just like that song. He loved it. Now that song would be forever linked to her, and that could be bad.

"I hope I remember all the words," she said. "I hate having to look at lyrics while I sing."

"If you don't know them, I do." He was into it now, so he might as well help her. If he didn't give her the correct lyrics, somebody on the ranch would.

"Then I should practice it while you're here to coach me." She started singing in her clear, lilting soprano.

The song went right to his heart, as he'd been afraid it would. He doubted she was giving the lyrics any personal meaning, but he couldn't seem to help doing exactly that. The words fit the way he felt about her. For the first time in his life, a woman filled up his senses exactly as Denver had described in the song.

Now every time he heard it he'd remember walking down the road with her while she sang to him. Great. His favorite tune, ruined. But it would be a crowd-pleaser tomorrow. He might have to find reasons to avoid listening.

He couldn't avoid listening to it now, though. She stumbled over the line about rain, which seemed sort of telling when he stopped to think about it. He recited the lyric and she sang it, this time without hesitation. Maybe her first screwup had nothing to do with her imagining how the song applied to them. That was probably just his sappy interpretation of her thought process.

"So how was that?" she asked after she finished. "Okay?"

"Wonderful." His voice sounded rusty and he had to clear his throat. "Terrific. You have a great voice."

"It's a nice song," she said softly. "I've always liked it. It speaks of an elemental connection."

"Yeah." He felt his heart slide another notch toward the danger zone. "I know."

"How far do you think we've walked?"

"A little over two miles or so. I'd say we're close to the halfway point. How are you holding up?"

"Great. No worries. And the flashlight is working just fine." She flicked it over the road and then moved the beam out over the meadow to their right. "What's that out there? It looks like a big rock."

A chill went down his spine. "It's not a rock. Don't shine the light over there again. And just keep walking."

"Alex…" The flashlight beam wiggled, indicating she was shaking.

"Don't panic. Let me have the flashlight." He took it from her quivering fingers.

"It's…it's…"

"Yes." He squeezed her hand. "It's a bear."

10

TYLER HAD NEVER hyperventilated before. She'd always wondered what that would be like when she heard other people talk about it. Now she knew. She literally couldn't breathe.

"Come on." Alex tugged on her hand. "Just keep walking along the road. Let the bear know we're just moving through."

She edged down the road but kept her eyes trained on the indistinct blob that Alex had identified as a bear. Little by little she sucked air into her tortured lungs. "Are you sure it's not a rock?"

"I saw eyes and fur. It's not a rock."

"What if it charges?"

"It looks like a black bear to me, so I doubt it will if we don't act threatening. It seems to be simply watching us. Walk on the other side of me if that will make you feel better."

She accepted that invitation, even though it felt cowardly to put him between her and the bear. "B-but what if it ch-charges?" she repeated, needing an answer, wanting to be ready with a strategy.

"Then we'll both raise our arms and yell at it. The idea is to look as big and menacing as possible to scare it off."

Despair tightened her chest. She couldn't imagine facing down a charging bear and she didn't seem to have enough air in her lungs to create a decent yell. "Is there a plan B?"

"In the first place, I don't think it will charge. In the second place, yelling should scare it off."

"But if it doesn't?" Although she craned her neck to look back over her shoulder, she'd lost track of the blob that was supposed to be the bear. The shadows blended together, and she pictured it moving closer, stalking them.

"Some people say you should lie down, curl up and pretend to be dead."

"If I did that, I'd probably just go ahead and die of fright."

"Well, you don't have to worry about that, because the bear isn't coming after us."

"How do you know that for sure? How do you know it isn't sneaking up on us?"

"I just…think it would have made a move by now."

She didn't want a tentative answer at the moment. "You don't know a whole lot about bear behavior, do you?"

"Some. Not a lot."

She could see the internet headline: Couple Mauled by Rampaging Bear. Everyone would click on that. She had the prospect of either dying from her wounds or being hospitalized, but either way, she'd miss the world cruise and her window of opportunity for the promotion.

But then she had another thought. If she didn't die of her wounds, she'd be hospitalized along with Alex, and if he didn't die of his wounds, they could recover together. She wouldn't have to make any decisions about her career because fate would have made them for her. And she could find out whether she and Alex were meant to be.

"I think you can stop worrying now," Alex said. "We've passed a bend in the road, and no bear is lumbering along behind us. I'm sure the one we saw is either still sitting in the meadow or has gone off to forage for grubs under a fallen log."

"That sounds so Disneyesque. I've always loved cartoons about bears, but I have to tell you, when face-to-snout with the real thing, it's different."

"I agree." He let out a breath.

"There, see? You were worried, too."

"I wasn't worried for myself, but I didn't want anything to happen to you."

"That's very sweet." She wouldn't have wanted to be mauled by a bear, but now that the possibility was receding in the distance, she also had to give up the fantasy that she and Alex would nurture each other back to health and they'd discover in the process if they were suited to each other.

Instead it looked as if she had to carry on with her world cruise and earn that promotion. That was her first choice, of course, but the recovering-in-the-hospital scenario didn't sound all that bad, either. Staying in Wyoming didn't feel quite like the prison sentence she would have expected it to feel like, which meant she was still conflicted.

"Want the flashlight back?" he asked.

"You can keep it." Now that she understood what she might accidentally see while sweeping the flashlight beam over the landscape, she wasn't so eager to do that. "Are you sure it was a black bear and not a grizz?"

"A grizzly bear? No. A grizzly would have been more aggressive."

She shuddered to think what that would have been like. "Well, anyway, when you tell this story to your grandchildren, you should suggest that it might have been a grizz. That will keep their attention better than if you just call it a bear and they're thinking teddy bear. But everyone knows a grizz is a fearsome creature to watch out for. You'll look like a hero for calmly strolling past it."

"In order to have grandchildren, I have to have children. I don't even have a wife, let alone kids."

"But you will, Alex. I saw how you looked when Josie announced she was pregnant. You want kids." And that was part of her dilemma. She hadn't thought she cared much about starting a family, but when she looked at Alex…her priorities shifted. He'd make a great dad. She wasn't ready for those thoughts, though, if she intended to be a cruise director by next year.

"When Crystal and I were married I wasn't thinking in terms of kids, maybe because she was so into partying. But now, I admit I think about it. Josie's already said that I'm considered part of the family, which means I could build on the ranch if I wanted."

"Would you do that?" Tyler was intrigued with the idea that the Last Chance could become a community of extended-family members. A few times during her childhood her parents had become part of communes, but her restless father had never been able to stay for long.

"I don't know. I'd have to…" He paused and tugged on her hand. "Do you hear a truck coming?"

"Yes, I do! I've been so busy talking that I missed

the sound. Who would be driving down the road at this hour?"

"Somebody looking for us."

"Oh." She thought about being discovered in a bedraggled condition yet again. At least this time her green hoodie and his denim jacket disguised most of the damage to their clothes. "I feel like a teenager caught out after curfew."

"Yeah, well, I'm the dummy who didn't check the gas gauge, so I'll handle the explanation."

"What are you going to tell them?"

"Depends on who it is."

The sound of the engine grew louder as headlights appeared around a curve in the road. The beams bobbed up and down as the truck drove slowly over the deep ruts.

Tyler peered into the darkness, but all she could see were the headlights coming closer.

Alex shaded his eyes. "That's Gabe's truck. I recognize the front grille. And he's driving like an old lady, which tells me Morgan's in the truck and he's worried about jostling her too much. We might as well walk to meet them."

"Listen, before we see them, I have a thought. How about we agree to tell them everything?"

"*Everything?* Don't you think that's TMI?"

"Not everything, as in *everything*. But I want them to know that we spent the night in the hayloft last August and we're renewing that…acquaintance."

"But won't that give them the wrong idea? Like we might be getting serious?"

"Not if we explain it as a…"

"As a what, Tyler?"

The truck drew closer. "I'll figure it out." In the light

from the approaching truck she could see the doubt in his expression. "I just want to make sure you're okay with me giving them a little bit of background. I don't want Morgan to think I'm...well, that we're..."

"Wild? Promiscuous?"

"Something like that, yeah. I mean, she is my big sister, and I've always looked up to her."

Alex chuckled. "I'll have to find out if Josie's always looked up to me. Dollars to doughnuts she'd deny doing that."

"She might deny it, but I'll bet she does. I idolized Morgan when we were younger, but I also wanted to make sure I did my own thing, which is why I got into the cruise business. She would never have considered the lifestyle I've chosen."

"You went into that field just to be different from her?"

"Well, not *just* that." Tyler realized how her statement must have sounded, but she hadn't taken up the cruise business as a reaction to Morgan's dream of becoming a real estate agent in Shoshone. She'd had plenty of other reasons.

"It's also a great life," she said. "I love ships, and water, and the travel opportunities." Though she had to admit that she was so busy during a cruise that she didn't have much chance to actually see the ports where the ship docked. She had enough time to grab a quick souvenir from a nearby shop and that was about it.

"They're almost here," Alex said. "I'll leave the explanation to you, then."

"Thanks."

The truck stopped and the dome light came on as Gabe

opened the driver's-side door. Sure enough, Morgan was sitting in the passenger seat. She gave a little wave.

Gabe left the truck running and the headlights on as he jumped down and came toward them. "Since you're hoofing it, I'm guessing you ran out of gas."

Alex walked toward him and shook his hand. "Good guess."

"We brought a can. After Jack realized which truck you two had taken out here, he mentioned that it was low on gas, so Morgan and I volunteered to ride to the rescue."

"That was really sweet," Tyler said. "Thanks."

"It was Morgan's idea," Gabe said. "You know Morgan, like a mother hen, especially these days. Where's the truck?"

"Back at the site," Alex said. "It's late, so you can just give me the can and take Tyler back home, if you wouldn't mind."

"That's ridiculous," Gabe said. "We can drive you both there. We can squeeze Tyler up front with us and you can ride in the back. Even if I'm going slow because of Morgan's condition, it'll still be a lot faster than you walking."

"We accept." Tyler glanced over at Alex. "We both have a big day ahead of us tomorrow. We need our sleep."

"That's what I'm thinking," Gabe said. "So hop on in the back, Alex. Tyler, let me get the door for you."

"I'll help her in." Alex moved quickly around to the passenger side.

Tyler almost laughed at the possessive note in Alex's voice. If Gabe hadn't known the situation before, he could certainly guess it from Alex's overly gallant behavior. Well, it didn't matter what Gabe suspected.

She'd fill in her sister and brother-in-law on the short drive back to the sacred site.

"Hey, there, little sis," Morgan said as Alex handed her up into the cab.

"Hi, Morgan." Tyler gave Alex's hand a squeeze before releasing it. "Thanks, Alex."

"Make sure your foot's out of the way before I close the door," he said.

Tyler tucked in next to her very pregnant sister, and it was a tight fit. "Morgan, if I'm crowding you too much, I can ride in back with Alex."

"Nope, this is just ducky," Morgan said. Then she lowered her voice. "And I want to talk to you, so don't ride in back."

"All righty, then! I'm in, Alex, so go ahead and close the door."

Once all three of them were in the front seat, Gabe rolled down his window. "Holler when you're aboard, Keller!"

"I'm in!" Alex called back.

Gabe glanced over at Morgan and Tyler. "You two okay?"

"We're perfect," Morgan said. "You have no idea how many times we had to ride squished together when we were kids. The folks would load up on groceries and maybe buy more camping equipment, which meant we had to pack in like sardines. This is nothing."

Gabe released the emergency brake. "I just want to make sure all's well with my two ladies and the little... one."

Morgan blew out a breath. "You're going to let it slip yet, Gabriel."

"Even if you did," Tyler said, "I can keep a secret. And besides, I'm leaving."

"Uh-huh." Morgan held on to the dash as the truck bounced over a rut. "That's exactly what I wanted to talk to you about. Please tell me you're not going to break that poor boy's heart."

"Hearts aren't involved," Tyler said. "It's a physical attraction, plain and simple."

"I've never known a physical attraction to be simple. Have you, Gabe?"

"I need to concentrate on my driving."

Morgan sighed. "It's a country road, not a twelve-lane freeway. Give us the male perspective. Do you think there's any such thing as a purely physical relationship between a man and a woman?"

"I suppose there can be," Gabe said cautiously.

"Really?" Morgan turned to him. "Have you experienced that yourself, then?"

"Uh…well, I…wow, this road is really tricky. I need to be on my toes. Sorry. Can't let myself get distracted or we might end up in a ditch."

Morgan sighed again. "I can see that you don't want to talk about it, and I'm not sure I'd believe you, anyway. People, especially guys, like to say they've had relationships that were only about the sex, but I wonder if that's ever true, unless you're paying for it."

"And we're definitely not talking about *that*," Gabe said. "In fact, I don't think we should talk about any of this. Let Tyler and Alex work this out however they want. They don't need us to be interfering in their private business."

"Thank you, Gabe," Tyler said. "I appreciate that sentiment."

"It's easy for him to say." Morgan clutched the dash again. "He's not your sister."

Gabe laughed. "Hell, I hope not. That would make me a transvestite and you a lesbian and both of us incestuous. We could get on any talk show in the country."

Tyler couldn't help giggling. She'd forgotten how funny her brother-in-law could be.

"Look, you two can yuk it up all you want, but I'm worried about Alex, and I'm worried about you, too, Tyler. I know you, and I don't think you're any more capable of having a no-strings-attached affair than Alex is. At least one person's going to get hurt, and maybe both of you will."

"So what are we supposed to do about it?" Tyler had thought all those things and would love some answers. "Sarah put us across the hall from each other, and even if she hadn't, after what happened last August we probably would have found some way to be together."

"Last August?" Gabe and Morgan said in unison.

Tyler had meant to lead up to the subject, but the discussion hadn't gone quite the way she'd anticipated. "After the reception, Alex and I took a bottle of champagne and had a private party up in the hayloft."

"No kidding?" Gabe sounded intrigued. "How was that? Because I've always sort of—ouch!" He rubbed his arm where Morgan had pinched him.

"This isn't about exploring your hayloft fantasies," Morgan said, all business. "It's about Tyler and Alex and what happens now. So have you two been keeping in touch since then?"

"No. He was getting over a divorce and I was leaving the next day. I knew I might see him when I came back this time, but I thought he was at the radio station and lived in Jackson. I expected that he might show up for a meal or something, but we'd both agreed what happened in August was a onetime thing."

"Hmm." Morgan put a protective hand over her belly as the truck jolted over another rut. "But judging from the way you two came back together like two refrigerator magnets, I—"

"Refrigerator magnets." Gabe chuckled. "I like that."

"Unfortunately, it fits," Tyler said. "We can't seem to keep away from each other, but it can't turn into anything permanent. I'm not ready to find my soul mate."

"Neither was I," Morgan said. "He showed up, anyway."

Gabe smiled at her. "Thanks. That sounded sort of like a compliment."

"It was a compliment. I'm very grateful that you wouldn't take no for an answer."

"Yeah," Tyler said, "but at least you weren't planning to travel the world for the next several years."

"No, but I had no intention of popping out babies, which was the main sticking point between us." She waved a hand over her belly. "And here I am, fifteen months pregnant and counting."

"But you still have your real-estate career. In order to be with Alex, assuming he'd even want that, I—"

"He wants that," Gabe said. "I recognize that goofy expression whenever he looks at you. I'm sure he has issues, what with Crystal cheating on him and everything, but I think that boy is working up to a second try at matrimony."

Tyler groaned. "I don't want him to work up to a second try if it involves me! I'd have to give up everything!"

Morgan gazed at her. "Then if that's the way you feel, you should probably stay away from him."

"You can sleep at our place," Gabe said. "I'll take the couch and you can share the bed with Morgan."

"That's really sweet, Gabe, but I'm not putting you out of your bed when there's a perfectly good one at the ranch house. It's my problem, and I'll solve it. If you're convinced Alex is headed toward a serious commitment, then I need to exercise some self-restraint."

"It's really no problem for me to take the couch," Gabe said. "Morgan's tossing and turning most of the night, so it's not like I'm getting all that much sleep, anyway."

Tyler laughed. "So you're offering me the bouncy bed?"

"It's not that bad," Morgan said. "He exaggerates."

"In any case, I'm not coming home with you. Alex and I are adults, and you shouldn't have to separate us like a couple of teenagers. I'll handle it."

Morgan sighed. "I hope so. Because if you don't, the next person you'll have to deal with will be Josie. From what I hear, Alex was torn up after his divorce, and she doesn't want a repeat of that."

"I wouldn't, either." Tyler's stomach began to hurt.

"Plus, if Josie's upset, then Jack will be, too, and before long you're liable to have the whole fam-damnly involved in the drama."

"Shit." Tyler squeezed her eyes shut. Then she opened them again and looked over at Morgan. "I didn't mean to come here and cause problems. Maybe it would be better if I left."

"Please don't." Morgan hooked an arm around her shoulders and hugged her. "I love having you here. Just stay out of Alex's bed."

"Yeah, you shouldn't leave because of this," Gabe said. "Besides, maybe I'm wrong about Alex and he's not looking for anything permanent. I shouldn't have said anything."

Tyler glanced over at him. "Yes, you should have. Besides, my main purpose in coming here had nothing to do with Alex. I came here to see my big sis—my *very* big sis."

"Watch yourself, toots." Morgan gave her a nudge. "One day this could be you."

"But not anytime soon." She saw the truck parked up ahead. "And we've arrived at our destination."

"One last chance," Morgan said. "You can still come home with us instead of going back to the ranch. We can pick up your things early in the morning."

"Thanks, but no thanks." Tyler took a deep breath. "I'm going to take care of this."

11

With the noise of the engine and the windows rolled up, Alex hadn't been able to make out any of the conversation taking place in the truck's cab. He heard some laughter, but also a fair amount of murmuring that sounded like a serious discussion. Although he might be getting paranoid, he suspected they'd been talking about him.

Once the truck stopped, he vaulted down and grabbed the gas can out of the truck bed. He wondered whether Tyler would elect to stay with him or ride back with her sister and Gabe. She'd said that spending time with Morgan was important to her, so he couldn't get upset if she decided to ride with them. In fact, he would suggest it.

Gabe left the engine running and the headlights on so that Alex could see to put in the gas. Then he and Tyler both climbed out.

Alex unscrewed the truck's gas cap. "Hey, Tyler, I was thinking you might want to ride back with your sister and Gabe. I'll have this under control in a sec, and then you guys can take off."

"That's okay," Tyler said. "I'll ride back with you."

The happiness spreading through him because of that

remark wasn't a good sign that he was keeping a handle on his emotions. He'd wanted her to ride back with him, and climb the stairs to the second floor with him, and maybe even take a long, hot shower with him before they tumbled into his bed.

From all appearances, she wanted those things, too. "If you're sure." He tipped the gas can and shoved the nozzle into the tank. There was something sexual about it, not that his mind was tending in that direction or anything.

"I'm sure."

Once the gas can was empty, Alex handed it back to Gabe. "I appreciate you and Morgan coming out here."

"No problem."

"See you tomorrow." Alex shook Gabe's hand. He'd never had brothers, and suddenly he had three. He was enjoying the hell out of that.

"I'll be there early," Gabe said. "I want to run through a couple of the cutting-horse demonstrations before the crowd arrives."

"I trust there will be a crowd. The RSVPs show there will be, but—"

"They'll show up." Gabe smiled. "You advertised free wine and food. Folks will come just for that."

"Yeah, but I don't want them to eat us out of house and home without buying a bunch of horses."

Gabe shrugged. "It's worth a shot. We haven't done something like this before. We always depended on Dad's charisma to charm people into buying. It's time to try a different approach. I'm looking forward to it."

"Me, too. Thanks again for coming all the way out here."

Tyler stepped forward. "Yes, thanks, Gabe." She gave him a hug. "Good luck with your sleeping arrangements."

He grinned at her. "No worries. She's uncomfortable and wants this to be over, and I sure can't blame her for that. She's been a trouper, considering that not so long ago she wasn't even interested in having kids."

"She sure is now," Tyler said. "You should have heard her talking about decorating the baby's room, and hanging a tire swing in back of your house, and building a sandbox. That kid will have the childhood she didn't, and she's loving that idea."

"That's good to hear. I—"

"Hey, Gabe," Morgan called from the truck. "Tell the lovely folks good-night. The mother of your child needs to go home now."

"You got it!" Gabe winked at them. "I'll give her a nice backrub and she'll mellow out." Touching two fingers to the brim of his hat, he walked back to his truck. As he climbed in, he called out to Alex. "I'll wait until you start 'er up before I leave."

"Okay." Alex quickly screwed on the gas cap. "I'll do that now." He hopped in the cab, inserted the key in the ignition, and the engine turned over immediately. That, too, seemed like a sexual thing. Apparently everything reminded him of sex.

He leaned out of the truck. "We're good to go! Thanks!" Leaving the truck running, he climbed down and walked around to open the door for Tyler, but she was already in the process of stepping in. He thought that was a good sign, too, that she was eager to get back to the ranch house so they could be alone in a more comfortable setting.

"Thanks for keeping me company on the ride back," he said, taking hold of the door handle.

"I wanted to."

He smiled at her. "I'm glad, because—"

"We need to talk."

His smile faded. In his experience, those were not the four words a guy wanted to hear when he was anticipating some hot sex. That kind of talk usually meant that the hot sex he'd been looking forward to was not going to be happening, after all.

"Okay." He closed her door with a sense of foreboding. As he walked back around to the driver's side, he speculated about the conversation she'd had with Morgan and Gabe.

Something they'd said had altered her viewpoint. He could feel it. She was more reserved, definitely not in the same mood as when she'd suggested whipped cream and chocolate sauce. She wasn't even in the same mood as when they'd hiked down the road and he'd coaxed her quietly past the bear sitting in the meadow. *Damn.*

Climbing into the cab, he closed his door and put the truck in Reverse so he could back around and head down the road again. "What did Morgan and Gabe have to say?" He maneuvered the truck so that it was facing in the right direction and put it in first.

"Basically, they think we're playing with fire."

"How so?" He stepped on the gas and looked at the gauge as the truck moved forward. Too bad he hadn't checked that gauge hours ago. Then Tyler wouldn't have had that unfortunate powwow with her sister.

"Morgan doesn't believe there's any such thing as a purely physical relationship, and Gabe thinks you're looking for Ms. Right."

"No, I'm not." Well, maybe he had a little bit in the past, but right now he was living for the moment. When Tyler left, he might start looking again.

"Well, they're both convinced that you're going to fall for me, at which point I'll break your heart, and the entire Chance clan will be out for blood, especially your sister, Josie."

Alex blew out a breath. "I'm not surprised by that evaluation, but it's a load of bull."

"I'm not so sure."

He gave her a quick glance, but it had to be quick considering the condition of the road. "Look, I know the score. How can you break my heart when I'm completely aware that you're leaving and you don't want a permanent relationship with anyone?"

"You might think you could change my mind."

"What kind of guy would try to change your mind? You've worked hard to get where you are and you've told me several times how much you love your job. A man would have to be pretty self-serving to try to keep you here under those circumstances. I hope you already know this about me, but I'll say it anyway. I'm not that kind of man."

"I know you're not, but—"

"But what? Do they imagine that after you leave on your cruise I'll go into a decline? That I won't be able to function, do my job, be happy?"

"Maybe something along those lines."

Alex swore softly under his breath.

"Look, I'm sorry, but I don't want to be the cause of major friction in the family."

"That would only happen if I reacted the way they're predicting I will." He tried to get a grip on his temper.

"It's not really their fault that they anticipate the worst. When I first came to Jackson Hole, I was pretty beat up. I spent a lot of time hiking and trying to figure out what went wrong between Crystal and me. I'm sure Josie hated that I was so unhappy."

"I'm sure she did. I have brothers. A twin brother, in fact. If some woman worked him over, I'd want to take her apart. That's why I understand where Josie's coming from."

"But this is totally different, Tyler. You've been straight with me from the beginning. You have your career, which you love. You're not ready to give it up, not even for the kind of incredible sex that you and I have. You've never once suggested that you might stick around."

"No, I haven't."

"My point, exactly!" He slapped a hand against the steering wheel. "Crystal promised to love me forever and then discovered that didn't work for her, so she made other arrangements behind my back. I was blindsided. With you, I can see in all directions. If I get hurt, it's because I wasn't watching where I was going."

"*Are* you watching where you're going?"

"You bet." Unfortunately, he hit a rut he hadn't noticed and they both bounced at least an inch off their seats. "Sorry."

"I hope that wasn't symbolic."

"No, it was just a damn rut. And I hope that you haven't let Morgan and Gabe's dire predictions bother you, because I'm just not that fragile."

She gazed out the window and didn't respond.

"Looking for the bear?" He hoped she was, because maybe that would remind her of the good times they'd had and the good times they could continue to have. He was prepared to give her up on Wednesday morning. He wasn't prepared to give her up tonight.

"Is this where we saw it?"

"The meadow is coming up on your right. Want me to slow down?"

"Yes, but if I yell, speed up."

He downshifted and eased along the road next to the meadow. "See anything?"

"No." She had her face plastered to the window like a little kid. "Oh, wait… I see it, Alex! Can you stop?"

"Sure." He put the truck in Neutral and put on the emergency brake.

"See it? Over to the left, close to the trees."

She'd given him the perfect opportunity to lean over and rest his arm along the back of her seat. She smelled like heaven. "Yeah, I see it." A dark shadow moved through the grass.

"It's walking away from us."

"You sound almost sad about that." He resisted the urge to comb her hair aside and kiss her neck.

"I'm a lot braver in the truck than on foot. And it really is kind of thrilling, isn't it?"

"Yeah." Seeing the bear didn't rank as high on his thrill-o-meter as some other experiences he'd had tonight, but he was glad to know that she was more enthusiastic than afraid. He wouldn't build that into anything, though. He wouldn't start thinking that she might someday make her home in Wyoming just because she was excited about seeing a bear in the wild.

"I almost can't see it anymore. I'll bet it's a grizz."

"It's not, but you're welcome to tell your grandchildren it was."

She laughed. "Okay."

Her affectionate laughter stirred him and he couldn't help himself. Brushing her hair from her shoulder, he placed a gentle kiss on the side of her neck. With nothing more than the press of his lips against her silky skin, arousal began teasing him again. He'd already had more sex in a few short hours than in the past several months, and yet he still wanted her. Amazing.

She sighed. "Please don't, Alex."

"Don't?" He nuzzled behind her ear. "Is there something you'd rather have me do?" He slid his other hand over her warm thigh. But when he started to reach between her legs, she squeezed her thighs together, closing him out.

"No," she said. "Don't do that, either. That's what I've been trying to explain. We can't have sex anymore."

He drew back to stare at her. In the lights from the dash, he couldn't see her expression very well. "Are you serious?"

"Like a heart attack."

"So you believe what Morgan and Gabe said to you?"

"I believe that I've already caused problems between you and your sister. Trust me, I understand how protective a sister can be, and now that she knows about you and me, you won't be able to so much as frown without her thinking it's because of us."

"So I'll set her straight."

Tyler shook her head. "She won't buy it."

"Damn it, this isn't any of Josie's—"

"Sure it is." Tyler's voice softened. "You've admitted she was the person you came to when you were hurting. That makes it her business if she thinks you're about to put yourself in harm's way."

He hated to admit she had a point, so he said nothing.

"Morgan's been there for me plenty of times, too." She shifted on the seat to face him more squarely. "If she wants to give me advice, I can't tell her to shove a sock in it. That's not fair. Besides, it was good advice. We are playing with fire."

"Speak for yourself."

"Okay, I will. I could get burned, too, Alex."

"I don't see how that could happen. You'll be the one leaving."

"Do you think I'll forget you the minute I step on that plane?"

He shrugged. "Maybe. Isn't that what you did last summer?"

She looked away and fiddled with the strings dangling from her sweatshirt hood. "Not exactly."

That sucker punched him. He'd suspected earlier tonight, when she'd had trouble tying her shoes, that their lovemaking had affected her more than she wanted to let on, and that had worried him. But he'd pushed that worry away by remembering how easily she'd left him last summer.

He took a deep breath. "But you didn't contact me."

"You didn't contact me, either." The shadowy light revealed that her mouth was set in a grim line. "I figured you forgot about me the minute I left."

"I didn't."

"Well, I didn't forget about you, either. So from the moment I saw you standing in the ranch house kitchen, I've had an internal debate with myself because I know having sex with you could lead to an emotional mess when I have to leave on Wednesday. But then you kiss me and the debate's over."

Alex squeezed his eyes shut. "God, I'm sorry, Tyler."

"It's not all your fault. I've been a willing participant."

"Yeah, but—" He opened his eyes and faced her, knowing he had plenty of blame to shoulder. "I made the first move in the barn. And then on the rock, you were hoping for clarity and I gave you an orgasm."

Finally, a smile. "Don't apologize for that."

"Just don't ever do it again, right?" He ached all over, which made him realize that from the beginning, despite his claims to the contrary, he *had* hoped she'd change her mind about leaving. That made him a self-serving guy, after all.

"We need to demonstrate to your sister, and everybody else, for that matter, that we've dialed it back, that we're just friends now. I think if we can prove that to them in the next four days, they'll all relax."

"How about you?" He really wanted to hold her, but that wouldn't help either of them and she probably wouldn't let him, anyway. "Will you relax?"

"I don't know, but it's a better plan than carrying on an intense affair right up to the minute I leave the ranch. Until Morgan started questioning me, I was thinking we'd try to squeeze every drop of pleasure out of our stolen moments together."

"That was my plan." And to illustrate that he was indeed a self-serving jerk, he still wanted to follow that plan. He wouldn't, but he wanted to.

"There's a good chance we'd both go into withdrawal if we did that."

Sighing, he leaned his head back against the window. "I was willing to risk it for myself. I didn't want to admit that I might be risking it for you."

"I'm a big girl. I should be able to watch out for myself. And I will, starting now."

"Will you be okay?"

"Maybe not immediately, but eventually."

He groaned. "I don't want you to hurt, Tyler. I never wanted that."

"I'll get over it."

"I know it's not an excuse, but Crystal didn't seem to suffer much when she left, and I...I made the mistake of thinking you had the same ability to cut a guy out of your life without agonizing over it."

"Because I'm a party girl?"

"You're not a party girl. I know that. But you're used to having lots of people around, and I thought...never mind what I thought."

"That having all those people around, I wouldn't miss you?"

"Yeah, I'm afraid that's exactly what I thought. I hope someday you can forgive me."

"Oh, Alex, I already have."

He suspected she might be on the verge of tears, which made him *really* want to hold her. But he no longer trusted his own motives.

"We should get going," she said. "It would be very bad if we ran out of gas again."

"That's for damn sure." Squaring up in the seat, he released the emergency and put the truck in gear. They drove the rest of the way in silence, and he used the time to plan how he'd get through the next few days without being able to touch her.

He'd known that once she left, he'd miss her like crazy, and he hadn't been looking forward to that. But somehow this prospect seemed worse. He could see the logic of it, but in practice it would be sheer torture.

One thing he knew without a shadow of a doubt. If he heard the intro to 'Annie's Song' tomorrow, he would get the hell out of there.

12

TYLER WOKE EARLY to the sound of rain on the cedar roof. Climbing out of the four-poster, she tugged at the hem of her short nightgown and padded over to the pair of double-hung windows. Blue bandanna-print curtains that hung on either side of the windows were obviously for decorative purposes only.

How freeing to have so much property that privacy wasn't an issue. Tyler peered out through the raindrops sliding down the glass. She assumed the Tetons were visible from the front bedrooms, but the back ones like hers looked out on pastureland that sloped gently down to a line of trees that appeared ghostly in the mist. She wondered if Archie Chance had cleared that pasture for his cattle back in the forties.

A few head grazed there this morning, but they were only rented cattle for the cutting-horse demonstrations Gabe and Jack had planned for the open house. She glanced at the small alarm clock sitting on an antique bedside table. She'd set the alarm for six-thirty, but it was only a little past six. She walked over, shut off the alarm and crawled back under sheets that had been hand-embroidered and a quilt that also looked handmade.

She thought about Alex across the hall and wondered if he'd slept. Probably. Men seemed to be able to sleep no matter what anxieties plagued them. She'd slept, too, but not straight through.

She'd woken up several times, and each time she'd fought the urge to go across the hall and climb into bed with Alex. Keeping her hands off him would be a challenge, but she'd do it.

Part of her restlessness had to do with Alex, but part of it had to do with a bed that didn't rock. Most of her nights were spent on the move as the *Sea Goddess* sailed from port to port. She'd always told herself that she liked that gentle movement and that it lulled her to sleep at night.

And she did like it, but…there was something really nice about a big log home set firmly on a foundation. The view out her window wasn't the vast ocean, but from the second story she had a wide vista, and in some ways it was more interesting than the unbroken horizon of the open sea.

Lying snuggled under covers that carried the scent of lavender and cedar, she allowed herself to admit things that would have been unthinkable a few weeks ago, maybe even a few days ago. She was beginning to question how much longer she wanted to be in the cruise business, how much longer she was willing to live in a tiny efficiency apartment in the middle of L.A.

Thanks to Morgan, she was seeing what a real home might feel like. Even sleeping in this bed, which quite possibly belonged to the couple who'd built this ranch, had contributed to her sense of a solid, enduring legacy. Of ownership. She didn't own anything but a few sticks of basic furniture and her clothes. Suddenly that seemed uncomfortably rootless.

Thoughts of Alex were tied in there somewhere, too, but she'd be a fool to imagine settling down with him. In the first place, he hadn't asked her to. In the second place, she'd need a way to earn a living, and the Last Chance didn't require the services of a cruise director.

Although she had savings that would carry her a little while if she left the cruise company, she'd have to find a new job. She'd made up her mind at an early age that she'd always have a job and never be dependent on someone else the way her mother was. Her father had earned whatever money they had and her mother had spent all her time economizing and taking care of children, which weren't highly marketable skills.

Tyler had marketable skills, but she wasn't sure if or how they'd translate from sea to land. Maybe they would and maybe they wouldn't. She'd definitely have to start over with whatever career she dreamed up for herself. In the meantime, she had a good chance at a wonderful promotion that would give her a nice salary increase. She couldn't afford to turn her back on that. Could she?

The aroma of coffee brewing and bacon frying brought her back to the present. A quick glance at the clock told her she needed to leave this cozy bed and start her day. She'd promised to help put on this party, and she was a person who delivered on her promises. She had arrangements to supervise and a quick practice session to schedule with Watkins, the guitar-playing ranch hand.

Pulling on the same terry robe Sarah had loaned her the night before, she gathered up her toiletries and opened her bedroom door. Whoops. She had either bad timing or good timing, depending on how she wanted to look at it.

Or how she wanted to look at *him*. Alex stood in the bathroom doorway, his hair damp, his jaw freshly shaven, and his gaze resting firmly on her. He wore only a towel.

He'd wrapped it casually around his hips, and it was all she could do not to step forward, slip a finger between towel and damp male skin, and pull. From the way his gray eyes smoldered and the towel twitched, she had a good idea what would happen after that.

His broad chest, lightly covered with dark blond hair, lifted as he took a deep breath. "Good morning." His sexy DJ's voice reached out to her, tempting her to move closer.

With great effort, she stayed where she was. But even from here she could smell soap, shaving cream and his citrusy aftershave. The longer they stood there staring at each other, the more those man-made scents mingled with the heady fragrance of good old-fashioned desire, both his and hers. Just like in "Annie's Song," he filled up her senses.

She swallowed. "Good morning to you, too."

"Sleep well?"

"Fine. You?"

"Fine." His hot glance traveled slowly down her body to her toes, before making a leisurely journey back up to her face again.

Her body warmed and moistened as if he'd caressed every inch of her and paid special attention to all the secret places that longed for his touch. Her breathing grew shallow. "That wasn't fair."

"Why? You just did it to me."

"I did not!" But she flushed, knowing that she probably had done exactly that, starting with his shaven jaw, moving to his bare chest, and sliding down his taut stomach to the knotted towel. She'd imagined that he was aroused beneath it. Her once-over had been as sexual as his.

"Okay, maybe I did," she admitted. "But you caught me by surprise."

"You forgot we were sharing a bathroom?"

"No, not really. I just didn't expect to come out of my room and find you standing there…practically naked."

"Do you want to establish rules for hallway attire?"

"No."

"I'm glad to hear it, because I put on the towel in deference to you. When I'm up here by myself I don't even bother."

"I see." She wanted him so much she was starting to shake. She clenched her hands around the toiletries bag.

"In fact, if we'd continued the way we'd planned yesterday, I wouldn't be wearing a towel even if you were here. But then, you wouldn't be wearing a bathrobe, plus whatever nightgown you have on."

"How do you know I'm wearing a nightgown?"

"I looked you over very carefully a moment ago, and there's a piece of lace sticking out where your robe isn't closed all the way."

"Oh." She clutched the lapels of her robe in one hand, not sure whether she wanted to hold it together or rip it open. Actually, she did know what she wanted, but she'd made a decision and she would abide by it.

"I wondered if you slept naked. We've never actually been in the same bed together, so I was curious about that."

She was curious about how he slept, too, but she wasn't going to ask. Besides, she already suspected what the answer would be. The thought of him lying naked in a king-size bed fanned the flames that licked at her body, tightened her nipples and dampened the bikini panties that went with her short nightgown.

"The bathroom's all yours." He stepped out of the doorway and started down the hall.

She'd taken two steps forward when he turned, and she froze in place, not sure what he might do, not sure what her response would be. She wanted to be strong, but if he came back and pulled her into his arms...

"I'll share a tip with you," he said, "because I have to say, you look as if you're feeling as horny as I am."

"You're wrong. I'm—"

"Be that as it may, the shower's a great place to work off some of your frustration. You might even want to detach the showerhead. It has several settings."

She longed for a snappy comeback, but her brain had been pickled by a flood of hormones. She managed a choked "Thanks."

"You're welcome. Enjoy." He continued to his room and walked inside. He didn't bother closing the door.

And why should he? They'd agreed not to have sex anymore, so closed doors shouldn't be necessary any more than she should have to bunk down with her sister, Morgan, to avoid climbing into bed with Alex again. They were adults who should be able to control themselves.

And she was hanging on by a thread. Once she was in the bathroom with the door closed, she thought about his suggestion. If he hadn't been standing in the hall wearing only a towel, she might not be in this condition. Even then, if he hadn't given her that look, she might still have been okay. All the talk about what she wore or didn't wear to bed had been the final straw.

Stripping down, she turned on the shower, stepped inside and unhooked the showerhead. Sometimes a girl had to do what a girl had to do.

ALEX WONDERED why he tortured himself, and decided he did it because she was torturing herself, too. He'd been doing his best to maintain control. He'd thought of her all through the long night, but he'd stayed in his room. This morning, while passing her door, he'd resisted the strong compulsion to go climb in bed with her.

But, oh, how he'd wanted to. Instead he'd taken a right turn into the bathroom where he'd sought release under the shower spray. Sometime later, shaved, showered and mellow, he'd exited the bathroom feeling proud for staying away from her. Then she'd come out of her bedroom and looked at him as if she wanted to eat him up.

She'd even had the nerve to protest when he returned the favor. Irritated by how quickly she got under his skin, he'd delivered that stupid parting shot about the showerhead. But the last laugh was on him. The image of her taking his suggestion was burned into his brain, and his cock was so hard he couldn't fasten the fly of his jeans.

Damn it, he was not having solo sex again. He was stronger than that. He would distract himself…somehow. Pulling off his boots and stripping off his jeans, he paced the length of his bedroom while counting backward from a hundred. When that didn't work, he did it by threes.

He heard the shower go on and began to hum to drown out the sound, because he knew, he just *knew* what she was doing in there. He'd had to open his big mouth. Only a wall separated him from Tyler, who was most certainly standing in that shower using pulsing water as a substitute for him. A soft moan that barely penetrated the wall confirmed it.

His imagination painted a vivid picture of Tyler braced against the shower wall as she moved the spray over her breasts, her stomach, and at last centered it where it would do the most good. He couldn't hear her breathing quicken, couldn't hear her gasp, but he knew how she'd sound, because he'd been there enough times when she was climaxing.

Teeth clenched, he stalked over to the double-hung windows set side by side and focused on the Tetons, hoping the mountain range would give him some perspective. No such luck. Gray clouds hung low over the peaks, and no doubt at that altitude it was snowing. He thought about the French meaning of *teton*—tits—which took him right back to Tyler, naked in the shower.

Leaning his forehead against the cool glass, he took a deep breath, and another, and another. The shower had stopped running. Thank God. Of course now he pictured her toweling off. She'd rub the soft terry over her wet body and her breasts would shift gently with the movement of the towel. Would she imagine his hands there? His mouth?

He was a mess.

After what seemed like an eternity, the bathroom door opened and the sound of her bare feet moving over the hardwood floor made him suck in another deep breath to keep from going after her. Then her bedroom door closed.

He grabbed his towel and hotfooted it back to the bathroom. The delicious scents left behind by the woman he couldn't have assaulted him, but that couldn't be helped.

He shoved back the shower curtain and discovered she'd neatly replaced the showerhead after her little orgy.

Turning on the cold tap, he stripped off his briefs, stepped under the icy spray and closed the curtain. He figured she'd be able to hear him taking a second shower. Oh, well. He'd promised to keep away from her. He hadn't promised to make it look easy. Managing this new regime was liable to take a lot of running water.

TYLER DIDN'T HAVE to think very hard about why Alex was taking another shower. After she'd allowed the showerhead to do its job, she'd expected to be less needy, but instead she'd kicked her libido up a notch. So she'd shut off the hot water and finished her shower with cold.

If Alex was having as much trouble as she was dealing with their sexual attraction, he might have needed a session with cold water, too. If so, their predicament was bordering on ridiculous. They were indeed behaving like a couple of refrigerator magnets, just as Morgan had said.

She dressed quickly, choosing a pair of tight black jeans with rhinestones decorating the back pockets. She'd bought those on a whim, thinking the bling might be too sparkly for a working ranch, but if she was supposed to be the entertainment, they'd be perfect. High-heeled boots, a black silk blouse and chandelier rhinestone earrings added more glamour to her look. She dried her hair quickly, piled it on top of her head and fastened it with tiny combs and hairpins, several of which were decorated with rhinestones.

Yes, she looked sexy as hell, and Alex wouldn't appreciate that. But she couldn't worry about the effect on Alex. She'd spent enough time looking like a bedraggled waif.

Now she intended to show off her other side, the woman who directed activities aboard a luxury cruise ship, the woman capable of dazzling the Last Chance's open-house guests. If she put them in a buying mood, that would benefit everyone and would ultimately help Morgan and Gabe. Alex would just have to deal with seeing her like this.

As she put the finishing touches on her makeup, she heard him coming down the hall, his booted feet striking the wooden floor with swift precision. He didn't pause beside her door on his way toward the stairs. Good. They'd made it through their first morning of waking up within twenty feet of each other.

She would have to talk with him, though. They had to work together this morning, unless he'd decided against using her help. She hoped he hadn't. He needed her, and not only in a sexual way.

On her way down the curved wooden staircase, she spotted Sarah coming from the west side of the house.

Sarah glanced up and gave a low whistle. "You look stunning."

"Thank you."

Sarah waited for her at the bottom of the steps. "I love my sons to pieces, but I wouldn't have minded having a girl, too. Girl clothes are so much more fun than boy clothes."

"So, are you hoping Morgan has a girl?" Tyler walked with Sarah through the living room where the scent of wood smoke lingered from the night before.

"A little bit, maybe, although I'll be thrilled no matter what she has. Now that Josie's pregnant, I have another shot at a girl. I'm hoping for several grandchildren, so statistically at least one has to be female, right?"

"You'd think so." They headed down the hallway. "In any case, those grandchildren will be lucky to grow up in such a beautiful place."

"Yes, they will. I only wish Jonathan had lived long enough to be able to teach them to ride and take them on fishing trips. He was so looking forward to that someday."

"I'll bet you miss him." Tyler had a sudden realization of what it would be like to be married to someone for all those years, and it seemed…nice. Sure, their time together had been cut short, but they'd had each other for more than thirty years, and they'd obviously enjoyed that time to the fullest.

"I miss him every day," Sarah said. "But—and I hate to admit this—now that he's gone, the boys are coming into their own in a way they might not have if he'd lived. Even Alex is part of the new order. Jonathan would never have hired someone to handle marketing. He thought he could do a better job of selling horses than anyone."

"Did he?"

"He was good, but that made us dependent on his personality to turn a profit. He was the brand, not the Last Chance. Alex wants to make the Last Chance a brand that will endure regardless of the people involved. It's a better way to move forward, and we wouldn't be there if Jonathan had lived."

"That's such a positive way to look at it." Tyler already respected the heck out of Sarah Chance, but this discussion added a new layer of high regard. As they walked into the empty dining room, sounds of frantic activity, including Alex's laughter, came from the kitchen.

Sarah smiled. "Now, *that's* the sound of progress."

"You're really good about accepting change, aren't

you?" Tyler thought she could take a lesson from Sarah on that subject.

"It's a survival mechanism, sweetie." Sarah glanced at her. "Change comes whether we embrace it or not. I've decided to embrace it."

"That makes you a very wise lady."

"I don't know about the wise part, but I sure as hell am flexible. Come on. This will be a big day, and I need coffee."

13

ALEX KNEW HE had to talk to Tyler, but at least here in the kitchen, with Mary Lou bustling around getting ready for the caterers to arrive, he wouldn't be tempted to haul Tyler off into a dark corner and kiss her until they were both breathless.

"Hey there, cowboy." Mary Lou gave him a smile. "Emmett and Jack just left. Get yourself some coffee and I'll be back in a sec to fix you something." She ducked into the walk-in cooler.

He got a kick out of her calling him cowboy. He wasn't sure he deserved the label yet, but he was working on it. He poured himself some coffee and took a sip. Ah, that helped unscramble his brain. Mary Lou made terrific coffee.

She emerged from the cooler carrying a wheel of cheese. "How about some bacon and eggs?"

"I don't want to put you out." If he'd arrived earlier instead of angsting over Tyler, he could have eaten with Emmett and Jack and saved her the extra trouble. "I'm late getting down, so I'll just grab something."

"Oh, no, you don't. People can't just 'grab something'

in my kitchen. Not while I'm still alive and kicking. You need a proper meal." She set the wheel of cheese on the counter. "And breakfast is the most important meal of the day."

Alex smiled. "My mom used to tell me that all the time."

"So sit yourself down and make both me and your mom happy."

"Thanks. That would be great." Alex pulled out one of the kitchen chairs and sat, although he wasn't sure how much he could eat, as keyed up as he was over Tyler.

"What do you hear from your folks?" Mary Lou turned on the large griddle, tossed several bacon strips on it and cracked eggs into a bowl. "Are they coming back out this summer?"

"They already have reservations with Pam at the Bunk and Grub for August."

"They should stay here." As the bacon began to sizzle, Mary Lou nudged it with a spatula and grabbed a wire whisk for the eggs. "We have the room, and we'll get the plumbing fixed on that other wing before August."

"Yeah, but Sarah won't take any money from them, and they want to stay a couple of weeks. Pam's willing to let them pay for their lodging, although I'm sure she's giving them a cut rate."

"But they're *family*," Mary Lou said. "They shouldn't have to be paying for anything."

"I know." Alex was distracted by the sound of Tyler's and Sarah's voices as they made their way toward the kitchen. When he raised his mug to take another sip, his hand shook. Damn it, Tyler was driving him batshit crazy. "Maybe I'll get them to buy a place out here and that will solve the whole problem."

"Good idea." Mary Lou turned toward the doorway as Tyler and Sarah walked in. "Just in time for some bacon and eggs. I made extra just in case."

Alex had prepared himself for the sight of Tyler walking into the kitchen. Or rather, he thought he had. But he wasn't nearly ready to see her looking like this.

He'd wisely put his coffee mug on the table once he realized his hand was shaking. If he hadn't, the mug would have dropped from his nerveless fingers when he caught his first glimpse of her.

Lord almighty. He'd seen her in an old-fashioned bridesmaid outfit last summer, in a sexy turquoise dress yesterday, and in jeans and knit shirts after that. In between he'd been treated to the sight of her in a terry robe, and not least of all, gloriously naked. But he hadn't seen her dressed to dazzle.

"Good morning." He managed a smile that encompassed both Sarah and Tyler, although he couldn't have said what Sarah had chosen to wear if his life depended on it. Tyler was the only person in the room as far as he was concerned.

"Same to you, Alex." Tyler glanced his way briefly before sauntering over to the coffee urn in her high-heeled boots.

Her jeans fit with amazing precision, and the rhinestones on the back pockets winked at him when she shifted her weight. Dodging that cock-stirring sight, he lifted his gaze to her upswept-hair arrangement that exposed her tender nape. The updo seemed sexier than when she wore her hair down, maybe because he imagined pressing his eager lips to the back of her neck, burying his fingers in that glossy hair and coaxing it loose as he breathed in the scent of shampoo and desire.

Her earrings sparkled and swayed as she poured herself a mug of coffee and turned, heading for the table. The view from this angle was just as dangerous as the flip side.

She'd left the top three buttons undone on her black silk shirt, and the shadowy hint of cleavage revealed by the open neck of the shirt would make any man who wasn't dead want to unfasten that fourth button. Alex supposed her outfit would be a hit today when she performed, but for him personally, it was cruel and unusual punishment.

She sat across from him and cradled her mug in both hands. "Have you talked to Watkins?"

He was so busy remembering how her hands had cradled his balls that he almost missed the question. His response came a little late, like a tape delay. "Not yet."

"Can you call him on his cell?"

"Uh, no. Watkins thinks a real cowboy shouldn't carry one. But I can call Jeb. Jeb's young enough not to give a damn what real cowboys do, so he packs a cell. He'll be able to get Watkins and tell him we need him up here." Alex pulled his phone out of his jeans pocket.

"He should bring his guitar," Tyler said.

"Right." Alex wondered if he would have remembered to say that. He needed to get his head in the game, and fast. He quickly made the call to Jeb, who promised to send Watkins up to the main house pronto.

"This is exciting." Sarah joined them with her own mug of coffee. "What a great idea—Watkins and Tyler."

"Well, he hasn't agreed yet." Alex had a sudden image of Watkins developing stage fright and refusing.

"He will." Sarah smiled at Alex over her mug. "You

know he loves to perform, but he'd be shy about doing it alone for an event like this."

Tyler put down her coffee. "I'd planned on three one-hour sets. Is he up to that?"

"He should be." After answering the question, Alex turned back to Sarah. "I'm counting on his inner rock star to show up." Focusing on Sarah was a better idea than looking across the table at Tyler with her cleavage and her flashy earrings. He'd been right to make sure other people were around when he had to deal with her. If he couldn't block out the memories of her silken skin and tempting kisses, he could mute them slightly in a crowd.

"Watkins will come through for us," Sarah said. "By the way, Jack called while I was getting dressed. He's already down at the tractor barn moving the equipment out. We'll serve the food and drinks in there. I think that's where Tyler and Watkins should perform, too, don't you?"

"Probably," Alex agreed. "We can move the stage I'd planned to use for the country band in there. I'll warn you that the stage is rustic, but I think it'll work."

Tyler looked over at him, her manner totally professional. "I'm sure it'll be fine. How are the acoustics in the tractor barn?" It was as if she'd pulled on a protective shell along with the flashy outfit.

He'd been in the barn a few times. "I doubt they're very good, but at least you won't get wet."

She sipped her coffee. "That would be a nice change."

She *would* have to reference the times they'd been wet together. He wanted to chew the furniture. How was he supposed to function today when he so desperately wanted a woman who was now off limits? He needed her help, no question, but he hadn't counted on her wearing a fantasy costume that was now burned into his retinas.

"I'm sure the acoustics are terrible in that barn." Mary Lou started passing out plates of bacon and eggs.

"I hope you made a plate for yourself, Mary Lou," Sarah said.

"I did, as a matter of fact. Let me get my coffee." Mary Lou joined them at the round oak table. "As I was saying, if we intend to make a habit of this, we should figure out a covered venue that would be semipermanent. There's no time to do it today, but it should be finished by the time Alex has another event."

"That would be terrific." Alex grabbed the new topic with relief. "Good thought, Mary Lou." He cherished many things about the Last Chance, but he especially loved the democratic spirit that invited everyone who worked there to voice an opinion about how things should be run.

"Jonathan would have loved the idea of live entertainment as part of this." Sarah looked around the table. "He also would have loved the way everyone's pitching in to boost sales." She winked at Tyler. "Even if we draft someone into service who's supposed to be on vacation."

"It's not a problem," Tyler said. "This is my cause, too, you know. If the ranch does well, then so much the better for my sister, Morgan, and the mystery kid."

Sarah put down her fork. "So you still haven't found out if she's having a girl or a boy?"

"Nope. That has to be the most closely guarded secret in the universe."

"I suppose I'll just have to wait." With a sigh of resignation, Sarah picked up her fork. "But I would really love to know, because…" She paused as her cell phone chimed. "Excuse me. That's Gabe." She left the table and walked out into the large dining room to take the call.

Mary Lou glanced over at Tyler. "You look mighty pretty this morning, like you belong on a country-music video or something."

"Why, thank you." Tyler's expression warmed. "What a nice thing to say."

Alex felt like a complete jerk. He'd been so busy controlling his reaction to her that he hadn't paid her a single compliment. No wonder she'd been so prickly toward him. She'd probably expected him to say *something*.

Better late than never. "You do look great, Tyler. Fantastic."

"Thanks." Her protective barrier seemed to crack a little. "I asked Sarah if it was too over the top, but she seemed to think it wasn't."

"It's not. It's great." He could kick himself for not saying anything when she'd first walked into the room.

Sarah returned, tucking her phone in her pocket as she came over to the table. Instead of sitting down, she picked up her plate and mug. "I'm going to drive out to Gabe's."

"Nothing's wrong, I hope," Mary Lou said.

"I'm sure everything's fine. Morgan's had a few mild contractions, which she's convinced are Braxton Hicks, but Gabe wants me to stay with her so he can do the cutting-horse demonstration without worrying."

"Probably it is Braxton Hicks." Tyler shoved back her chair and stood. "But I—"

"Who's Braxton Hicks?" Alex left his chair, too. He didn't like the sound of this, for many reasons. "Have I met the guy? What's he doing out at Morgan and Gabe's house, anyway?"

Tyler glanced at him. "Braxton Hicks contractions

are named after the doctor who identified them. Basically it's false labor. I remember my mother having it with my little brother."

"Oh. Well, then." What he knew about childbirth could be written on the head of a pushpin.

"Anyway, I'd like to ride out with you, Sarah," Tyler said. "If everything's fine, Gabe can bring me back when he drives here."

Sarah shook her head. "She specifically said you weren't to come. She agreed I could sit with her, but she wants you to stay here and get ready for your gig."

"But I can still get ready after I come back."

Sarah came over and wrapped an arm around Tyler's shoulders. "Look, I know she's your sister and you want to make sure everything's okay, but I promise to call if I need reinforcements. Morgan made it very clear she expects you to stay and sing your little heart out."

Tyler hesitated. "I left my cell phone upstairs. Will you please wait to leave until after I've called her?"

"Sure, I can do that."

"Thanks." Tyler hurried from the room.

Alex didn't realize he'd watched her go until Sarah spoke.

"She's a beautiful girl, Alex. I can see why you're smitten."

He swung back to Sarah and opened his mouth to issue a denial, but her knowing smile stopped him. "I'll get over it," he said.

Mary Lou left the table and came over to join them. "You're going to have to, I'm afraid. One look at that outfit of hers and I can see why she's perfect for her job on the cruise ship." She gazed up at Alex. "Have you ever been on one?"

"No." Crystal had pestered him to go on a cruise, but he'd resisted because the ones she'd suggested looked like one big party to him.

"I have, about ten years ago, for the hell of it. The staff was a fun bunch, and I'm sure Tyler's personality fits right in. She's found her niche."

"I'm sure you're right. I have no intention of trying to change her mind about that, either. I—"

"Okay, I'm staying here," Tyler announced as she came back into the kitchen. "You're right that she's adamant about that, and I don't want to argue with a hormonal pregnant lady. I'm afraid if I go out there she'll be so upset with me that she might go into real labor."

"Wise decision." Sarah patted her arm. "I promise to keep you informed, but I'm guessing it will be a quiet day out at Gabe's. Maybe I'll trick Morgan into telling me what she's having." She glanced over at Alex. "But promise that you or one of the boys will call and give me updates on how the sales are going."

"You bet. Let's hope your cell phone rings off the hook."

"That would be wonderful. By the way, I rounded up some umbrellas and left them by the front door. Tyler, you should use one for sure when you go outside. I'd hate to see you ruin your outfit and your hair walking through the rain."

"Thanks. I'll grab one on the way out."

"Okay, I'm off." As Sarah left the kitchen, she narrowly missed bumping into Watkins, who came barreling in toting his guitar in a case.

His face was ruddy with excitement, but he took one look at Tyler and his smile sagged. He set down his guitar case with a thud. "Dang, Alex. I don't have the clothes for this."

Tyler looked crestfallen. "It's too much, isn't it? I was afraid of that, but I—"

"No, no," Watkins said. "You're beautiful in that outfit. Folks will love it. You look like a star. Whereas I'm just going to look like an old cowboy."

"Which is exactly how you're supposed to look, Watkins," Mary Lou said. "Have you ever heard that expression 'fade into the background'?"

Watkins smoothed his mustache with nervous fingers. "'Course I have."

"That's your job. Play a little guitar and fade into the background. You don't want rhinestones flickering all over your buns, calling attention to yourself. Tyler's the one they're supposed to look at."

Watkins nodded. "I suppose that's right." He gazed at Mary Lou. "I remember a time when you used to wear rhinestones, Lou-Lou."

"Watkins, for heaven's sake! Don't start with that Lou-Lou nonsense." And Mary Lou blushed.

Alex stared at her in shocked surprise. He didn't think he'd ever seen her blush. Could it be that once upon a time, Mary Lou and Watkins…nah, probably not. He had sex on the brain.

And an event to get into gear. "All right, then. I was thinking the two of you could use the living room as a practice space, if that sounds okay."

Tyler glanced at Watkins. "I'm fine with that, if Watkins is. By the way, is Watkins your first name or your last name?"

"That's his last name," Mary Lou said. "He doesn't

like people using his first name. I happen to know it, because we...well, never mind. I just happen to know it."

"And I'd appreciate you keeping that information to yourself, Lou-Lou."

"You keep calling me Lou-Lou, and I'll make a general announcement of your first name. I'm sure there are a lot of people working here who have no idea what it is."

"I'm happy to call you Watkins, then." Tyler exchanged a glance with Alex that said plainly she was thinking the same thing he was. Mary Lou and Watkins had a past.

Alex consulted his watch. "I'll start setting up the sound system in the tractor barn. I'll call you when I have it ready for you to test."

"In case it slipped your mind," Watkins said, "I don't carry one of those cell-phone contraptions."

"I know. I'll just call the house."

"Better yet," Tyler said, "call my cell. That's simpler."

He looked over at her. "Okay. What's your number?" As she gave it to him, he added it to his list of contacts. It was a dangerous thing to do because now he'd have something he'd never allowed himself before—a way to connect with her once she'd left.

"You should give me yours." She held her phone poised, ready to record the numbers.

As he recited the information, he wondered if she realized the significance of putting these numbers into their respective phones. She could always erase it after she left, of course. So could he. But he knew he wouldn't erase it and he'd bet money she wouldn't, either.

She saved the number and glanced up. "All set. Watkins, let's go into the living room and make some music."

Watkins picked up his guitar case. "I'm right behind you."

After they were gone, Alex couldn't resist turning to Mary Lou. "What was that all about?"

"Nothing." She looked at least ten years younger than she had a few minutes ago.

"Oh, yes, it was. It was something."

"Oh, we had a little flirtation years back."

"Uh-huh." Alex was fascinated. The longer he lived at the Last Chance, the more layers he uncovered. "And?"

"And he wanted to marry me. I have no intention of marrying anyone. Fun and games are fine, but I don't intend to sign some legal document. So he got all bent out of shape, and that was the end of that."

Alex took note of the new sparkle in Mary Lou's eyes. "I'm not so sure it is the end."

"It is. He had to just forget about me." She met his gaze. "The same way you'll have to forget about Tyler."

"Hmm." Guitar chords drifted through the house, followed by Tyler singing the opening lines of "Annie's Song."

"I love that tune," Mary Lou said.

"Yeah, me, too."

"Watkins used to sing it to me." Mary Lou cleared her throat. "Well, I have stuff to do."

"So do I. I think maybe I'll go out the back way so I don't disturb them."

"I think I'll close the kitchen door so they don't disturb *me*."

Alex nodded. "Good idea." As he left the house, he heard the pocket door between the kitchen and the main dining room close with a decisive thump. Mary Lou wasn't about to let that song get to her. And neither was he.

14

TYLER HAD THOUGHT maybe Alex would stick around to hear a number or two. If for no other reason, he should want to know whether she and Watkins sounded okay together. So maybe she'd also wanted him to watch her perform when she had musical backup and wasn't walking down a muddy road in wet, wrinkled clothes. Maybe she'd wanted to show off a little.

But Alex had left the building. She wasn't even sure if he liked her outfit. He hadn't made a comment until after Mary Lou had sort of shamed him into it. Then she had an unpleasant thought. Maybe Crystal used to dress in flashy clothes. Tyler wouldn't doubt it.

So maybe Alex wouldn't want to know that she was rethinking her entire future. He might not care that Mary Lou's suggestion of building a permanent stage on the property had given Tyler the germ of an idea that might change everything.

She pushed the idea to the back of her mind while she concentrated on rehearsing with Watkins, who turned out to be a very talented guitar player and a decent backup singer. They discovered several country tunes they both knew, and then Watkins taught her "Song of Wyoming."

"That should satisfy Jack," she said after making it through without flubbing any of the lyrics. "He wanted me to sing a Wyoming song."

"That's a good one." Watkins strummed his guitar. "You do a nice job with it, too. Ever recorded anything?"

"Oh, some of us who perform on board made a CD we sell to the passengers, but otherwise, no."

"I wouldn't mind trying it sometime, but then, I don't know who would buy it."

"If Alex keeps holding these events and you keep playing, you might build a fan base."

Watkins shrugged. "I was thinking more of you and me recording something, but then, I guess you'll be leaving."

"Yeah." Tyler thought about the brainstorm she'd had earlier. If it became a reality, it could lead to her doing many future gigs with Watkins. "Let me ask you something."

"Shoot."

"Other than the Fourth of July celebration, does Shoshone host any other community events?"

"Not especially. Everybody decorates for Christmas, but that's about it. Why?"

"Because I think there's a missed opportunity here. It's a great little town, with the Spirits and Spurs, and the Shoshone Diner, and the Bunk and Grub, and the Last Chance, of course. I could see a country music festival doing well."

Watkins's eyebrows lifted. "You think?"

"I do. And maybe another time, an antique-car show.

And entertainment would be a part of that, too, of course."

"I like looking at those old cars all polished up." Watkins idly picked out a few notes on his guitar. "Hey, what about one of those historical-reenactment groups? And the townspeople could get into it, and dress up like in days of the Old West."

"Exactly!" Tyler's excitement grew as she saw Watkins warm to the idea. "And maybe a winter festival with an ice-sculpting contest."

"And a snowshoe race, and sleigh rides. I think there's an old sleigh around here someplace. A few other folks might have a sleigh tucked away in a barn."

"I love the idea of sleigh rides. So romantic." She shouldn't be picturing riding in a sleigh with Alex, but she couldn't help it.

"But I don't know who would organize all that." Watkins frowned. "It's hard enough to get the Fourth of July stuff together. Most folks don't have the time."

"But it would be so worth it. It would bring more visitors to the town, which would be good for business, including the Last Chance."

Watkins nodded. "I can see that. But like I said, nobody has the time to organize it."

"Well, the merchants would have to get together and hire someone."

His gaze sharpened. "You wouldn't have someone in mind, would you?"

"Uh, I'm not sure. I'm just thinking out loud."

"That's a lot of thinking for someone who's planning to vamoose the middle of next week."

She gazed at him and hoped he was the strong, silent type with an emphasis on the silent part. "I'm thinking of making a change, but I don't want people to know that yet."

"By people, do you mean Alex?"

"Well, him, but everybody, really. I just got this idea, and I don't… I'm just not sure if it's the right move. I especially wouldn't want my sister to get wind of it and start hoping I'll move here."

"I can keep quiet. But let me say this. If you end up sticking around, then you and me, we need to record something. I know a guy in Jackson who has a little studio. I haven't felt quite ready to go there, but I like the way we sound together. I'd be ready if you went with me."

His expression was so hopeful that she almost promised him that she'd stick around, but she controlled the urge. She had to think about this some more. The idea of putting down roots, of creating an actual home, was sounding better the more she considered it. But Alex was a huge part of the equation, and there was no point in pretending that he wasn't. He was a key element, and she wasn't sure how he'd react to all this.

Her phone chimed and his number came up. If she kept his number in her phone, she'd assign it a ringtone. Ha. There was no *if* about it. No matter what happened in the next few days, she would keep his number saved on her phone.

She did her best to project breeziness when she answered. "Hey, there. How's everything shaping up?"

"I'm ready for you."

She gulped. Surely he hadn't said that. Spoken in his seductive radio voice, the words were guaranteed to fire up her libido.

He cleared his throat. "Let me rephrase that."

"Please do."

"The equipment is set up. You can come anytime."

"You might want to rephrase that, too."

A gusty sigh came over the line. "Damn it, Tyler."

"Easy there, big boy. Don't lose your sense of humor. We'll be there in a few." She disconnected the phone and smiled brightly at Watkins. "Let's go."

"All righty." He opened his guitar case and settled his instrument inside. "I have to admit that I was a little worried about how this would turn out, but now I'm really looking forward to it."

"So am I." Like a fool, she still hoped Alex would catch her act and discover that he…what? Tyler took a deep breath. She might as well admit that she was falling for the guy. Shoot, she'd started falling for him last August, and this trip only confirmed that he had a hold on her. She'd like him to be in the same condition.

"You might want to take one of those umbrellas," Watkins said as they walked toward the front door.

In her preoccupation with Alex, she'd been ready to walk out the door without one, but she quickly remedied that. "How about you?"

"I'll be fine. It's not raining much anymore."

They stepped out on the porch and she could see that was true. Still, she'd spent time on her hair, so she'd use the umbrella.

On the way to the tractor barn Watkins talked about country artists he admired. She listened with half an ear while she continued to think about Alex. She couldn't blame him for being on edge. He was incredibly attracted to a woman he thought would leave him.

Up until recently, she'd thought she would, too. But the idea of settling down in Shoshone was growing on her. She was beginning to feel as if she belonged here, and these people, unlike the crew and passengers of the ship, wouldn't be leaving after a few months.

Alex could tip the scales if she knew for certain that he wanted her to stay. But he obviously saw things in her that reminded him of Crystal, and he'd already said he didn't want to make another mistake. Unfortunately, she was running out of time. If she truly intended to leave her job with the cruise line, she should tell her boss immediately and offer to train a replacement.

"What do you think of Martina McBride?" Watkins asked.

Tyler dragged herself back to the present and Watkins, her new BFF. "I like her style."

"I think you sound a little bit like her."

"That's a nice compliment, Watkins. Thanks." She hoped talking to Watkins about her new plan hadn't been a terrible mistake. He wouldn't blab it to anyone, but he might be crushed if she changed her mind.

But maybe she wouldn't have to change her mind. Maybe everything would work out and there would be a fairy-tale ending. Telling herself that, she walked through the large double doors of the tractor barn.

She spotted Alex standing on a wooden stage at the far end of the building talking to Jack, Emmett and a cowboy she didn't recognize. There was no doubt he was a cowboy, though. He had the long-legged, broad-shouldered build of the breed and the requisite jeans, boots, yoked shirt and hat.

But then, so did Alex. He'd obviously retrieved his gray Stetson from where he'd left it in the horse barn the night before. He fit right in with the other three cowboys standing up on the stage.

Watching Alex deep in conversation with the other

men, Tyler felt a glow of pride. He'd been knocked around emotionally by a cheating wife, but he'd come out here and rebuilt his life. She admired him for that, but there was more going on in her heart than simple admiration. She'd fallen in love with the guy.

That would be great if she knew for sure that he loved her back, but she didn't. He wanted her, but that wasn't the same thing. She was excited about her idea for making a living here in Shoshone, but if Alex didn't return her love, she'd be better off cruising the world until she got over him.

"I wonder who that guy is," Watkins said. "He looks vaguely familiar, but I can't quite place him."

"Maybe he's an early arrival for the open house."

"Maybe."

"Let's go find out." Tyler glanced around the barn. "And after we get introduced and do a sound check, I want to see if I can brighten up this place."

"We don't have much time left. Only about an hour."

"A lot can happen in an hour." A lot could happen in two minutes. Two minutes ago she hadn't admitted to herself that she was head over heels in love with the tall cowboy in the gray Stetson. Now she had, and that changed everything.

ALEX KNEW THE MINUTE Tyler walked into the barn, although he continued to talk to the others as if he hadn't noticed her. She belonged on a stage gleaming with footlights and draped in velvet curtains, not here in a tractor barn on a rough plywood platform. As much as he might selfishly want her to stay, she didn't belong in Shoshone, Wyoming. Her outfit underscored that with agonizing finality.

As she approached the stage, he excused himself and walked over to make sure she could navigate the crude steps in her high-heeled boots without tripping. He held out a supporting hand and she took it with a smile that burrowed deep into his heart. God, how he was going to miss the warmth of her touch, the lilt of her voice and that incredible smile.

"Thank you." She released his hand as she took the last step up to the rustic stage. "This looks great, doesn't it, Watkins?" She turned back toward the ranch hand as he trudged up the steps carrying his guitar case.

"It'll work." Watkins paused to gaze at Alex. "Let me tell you, this woman can sing."

"I know."

"I mean, she can *sing*."

"I believe you." Apparently Tyler had made a conquest, which didn't surprise Alex one bit. In a couple of hours she'd make several more when the guests started to arrive. Any guy with eyes and a brain could tell she was exceptional.

Watkins glanced past Alex to the far side of the stage. "Is that Clay Whitaker over there talking to Jack and Emmett?"

"Yep. I guess he used to work here."

"He did, indeed. Somebody said he came to Jonathan's funeral, but I must've missed him."

Alex looked over at the group. "He just graduated with a degree in animal science and he thinks Jack should hire him to run a stud program."

"Well, hallelujah." Watkins brightened. "I always thought that might be a good idea, but Jack's dad liked to breed paints the old-fashioned way."

"So what's the modern way?" Tyler asked.

She had to ask. "Artificial insemination," Alex said, hoping that would end the discussion.

"So why would Jack's father object to that?"

"I'm not sure, but it doesn't really matter, I guess." There. Now maybe they were done with the topic.

"I can tell you exactly why," Watkins said.

Alex groaned inwardly.

"See, if you're providing the semen, you have to collect it before you freeze it and ship it out. The collection method was the sticking point for Jonathan Chance. He thought it was degrading for a stallion to be tricked into mounting a dummy instead of the real thing."

Alex chose not to look at Tyler.

"Oh. I had no idea how it was done," Tyler said. "I suppose you can't send the stallion into a little room with copies of *Playmare* magazine, can you?"

Watkins laughed. "No, ma'am. And it is tricky, because it's best if you have an actual mare who's in season, and then—"

"You know what, Watkins?" Alex said. "You might want to weigh in if you're in favor of the program. Emmett's all for it, but Jack's still a little hung up on doing things the way his dad wanted them done."

"Odds are, Jack will be outvoted," Watkins said. "I've heard Nick and Gabe discussing this as an option. Clay left here headed for college, so I'll bet he's studied up on how best to do this. Plus, we know him. I always liked Clay." Watkins set down his guitar case. "But you're right. I should at least go over and say hello."

As he walked away, Tyler glanced at Alex, her gaze mischievous. "If this becomes a reality, you'll have to come up with a marketing angle for it."

"Probably."

"Maybe something along the lines of 'When you think of semen, think of the Last Chance first.' How's that?"

"Oh, Tyler." Alex shoved his hands in his back pockets and stared up at the dusty rafters until he lost the urge to kiss that beautiful laughing mouth of hers.

"Don't forget what I said. The secret to getting through today is keeping your sense of humor."

He looked into her bright, beautiful eyes. "I promise to work on that."

"Good. Now let's test the mic and find out if we have a hellacious echo in this barn."

"I already did and you do."

"Hmm." Tyler surveyed the empty space. "Tables and chairs will help, especially if the tables are covered. But we need more. How about bringing in some hay bales and stacking them around in random places?"

"We can do that."

"Then maybe dress them up with any spare saddle blankets and a few coils of rope."

Alex adjusted the fit of his hat to give his hands something to do besides reach for her. "You're talking about an artistic arrangement, right?"

"Yeah. And I'm thinking if we can round up enough vases, we should see if we can put wildflowers on all the tables."

"I'm afraid artistic arrangements and flower vases are out of my area of expertise."

"Which is why you hired me."

"For no pay." The minute the words were out, he wanted to bite his tongue. She *had* specified how she wanted to be paid, and it had involved whipped cream and chocolate sauce. They wouldn't be enjoying that treat together after all.

"Right," she said. "For no pay." She laughed softly. "That must mean I'm doing it for love."

The word sucker punched him and he had to look away. Hearing that word coming out of her mouth so easily, so lightly, as if it meant nothing, was more than he was ready to take. But hearing her say it reminded him of why he would encourage her to go back to the life she wanted, why he would make no attempt to stop her. He was doing it for love.

15

BODY LANGUAGE DIDN'T LIE. Only a blind person could have missed the way Alex flinched when Tyler mentioned the word *love*. And it was her fault. She shouldn't have put that out on the table in such a casual way. How else was he supposed to react?

After all, she'd been emphasizing all along that she would leave at the end of this visit. Logically, he'd try to protect himself from getting hurt. No, she shouldn't have introduced that loaded word, and certainly not as a joke.

She wasn't surprised when he left the barn while she and Watkins ran through a few numbers to test the sound system and get comfortable on the stage. True, she'd asked for hay bales to absorb the echo. That gave him a legitimate excuse to duck out, but he could have stayed for one song, or even part of a song.

But he didn't, so if she'd imagined his gaze finding hers while she performed "Annie's Song," if she'd imagined being able to read something more in his expression than pure lust, if only for a second or two, that wouldn't be happening. She would have to risk telling him straight out that she was considering a change and hope his reaction was positive. But not now, when they had a job to do and precious little time to do it.

They raced the clock to get everything ready before the first guests arrived. Fortunately Josie showed up to help with the table-and-chair arrangement, which saved some time. Then she left to check on how things were going with Mary Lou and the caterer.

Tyler directed the action like a general commanding her troops as seasoned ranch hands hurried into the tractor barn carrying a vase of wildflowers in one hand and a rope or saddle blanket in the other. Then Dominique arrived with several large framed action shots of Gabe, Jack and Nick riding Last Chance horses. She propped the pictures in the midst of the hay bales and then helped arrange lariats and saddle blankets.

By ten the drizzle had let up, but the skies remained cloudy and threatening. Gabe muttered about putting on demonstrations in the mud after all the time spent grooming the horses. But inside the tractor barn, old-fashioned lanterns, flowers and Western paraphernalia had transformed the space into a warm and welcoming venue.

Emmett Sterling came to stand beside Tyler as she surveyed the finished product. "Not bad," he said. "Pam asked me to tell you she wanted to come over and help, but the Bunk and Grub is packed with folks who either flew in or drove in for the open house, so she's tied down to her kitchen this morning."

"That's good, right?"

"Oh, you bet. Pam's thrilled with the extra business this event brought in. This helps the diner, and I'm sure Josie will have a crowd at the Spirits and Spurs tonight. It's all good."

And Tyler could keep the ball rolling for Shoshone

merchants. With her help, business could be even better. But all that depended on Alex's reaction to her plan. If he didn't care for her the way she cared for him, she'd only be letting herself in for major heartbreak. No matter how much she might like to establish a home here, she couldn't imagine doing it if Alex rejected her.

"Well, I see a few folks coming in, so I'd better start socializing," Emmett said. "Thanks for all your help, Tyler."

"My pleasure."

As the crowd continued to grow, Watkins approached, his grin flashing beneath his mustache. "It's showtime, Miss O'Connelli."

Her spirits lifted at his enthusiasm. She wasn't sure how she'd manage it, but she was determined to come back between cruises and help Watkins record that CD he so desperately wanted. At least she could do that much.

She linked arms with him. "Then let's make us some music, Mr. Watkins."

THE OPEN HOUSE was in full swing, and Alex already counted it a success. So far Jack had reported several sales to Sarah, and Alex had overheard enough comments to know that many other guests were seriously considering buying a Last Chance paint. Even some who weren't prepared to commit today were good prospects for the future.

Alex had tried his damnedest to block out Tyler's music and had done a decent job of it. She and Watkins had taken a break and he'd used that time to check on the buffet table to make sure it was well stocked. But now they were headed back on stage, so he turned to leave the tractor barn.

Before he could make his escape, Jack stopped him. "I've run the idea of a stud program past a few people here, and there's definite interest. It looks like we're going to hire Clay, but we'll need you on the marketing end."

Alex nodded. *When you think of semen, think of the Last Chance first.*

"Maybe you could get with him before he leaves today and set up a time next week to talk about that. He's staying in Jackson right now, but we'll probably bring him out here soon so it's more convenient for everybody. We have space in the bunkhouse."

"Sounds good." Of course, *of course,* Tyler had chosen this very moment to launch into "Annie's Song."

Jack paused to listen. "She's good."

"Yeah." He pictured himself erecting shields around his heart, but it wasn't working.

"I was impressed that she learned 'Song of Wyoming.' I was sort of kidding about that, but she took it to heart. I really—" Jack stopped talking to peer at him. "Hey, are you okay? You look a little green around the gills, buddy."

"I'm fine. Listen, I'll make a point to hook up with Clay next week. But right now I need to check with Mary Lou and make sure we got all the food we paid for."

"Yeah, right. We don't want to be shortchanged." Jack seemed satisfied with the explanation and went back to watching Tyler. "Tyler and Watkins sound great together, don't they?"

"Yep, they do. See ya, Jack." He headed toward the main house, although he had no reason to talk with Mary Lou. Still, it might not be a bad idea to see if she was happy with what the caterers had brought.

He went in the back way so he could wipe his boots off and avoid tracking mud into Mary Lou's spotless kitchen.

She paced the gleaming tile floor, her cell phone pressed to her ear. "Yes, I think you should call the midwife. Oh, here's Alex." She glanced up and motioned him forward.

"I'll send him to get Gabe, in case Gabe's in the middle of a demonstration. No, you're not being an alarmist, and this needs to be handled, regardless of the open house. Don't worry about that. Right. Gabe will be there soon. And probably Tyler, if I know that girl. Keep in touch." She disconnected the phone.

"The baby?"

Mary Lou looked at him. "The kid's decided to make an early appearance. Sarah said things are progressing quickly, especially considering it's a first baby. I want you to send Gabe out there, and come to think of it, send Nick, too, in case the midwife doesn't show up fast enough."

"Nick? Why Nick?"

"He's delivered plenty of foals. He should be able to deliver a baby if necessary."

"All right." Alex caught her sense of urgency and turned back toward the laundry room.

"Go out the front. It's faster. And take keys to one of the trucks in case you need to drive somebody. I'm thinking that could be Tyler, once she finds out her sister's about to deliver this baby."

"Got it." He started out of the kitchen and turned back. "The open house is still—"

"I know. I'll deal with that. We have Jack and Emmett, plus Dominique and Josie. Watkins can play a little solo guitar. It won't kill him. Go, go!"

Alex went, grabbing a set of truck keys from a hook as he dashed out the front door. He spotted Nick over by the corral where Gabe was demonstrating the skills of his champion cutting horse, Top Drawer. Mud flew as Top Drawer wheeled left, then right to keep the cow from returning to the small group of cattle on the far side of the corral.

Several people sat in the bleachers and leaned forward intently. No wonder so many people had expressed interest in buying a Last Chance paint. Gabe and Top Drawer put on one hell of a show. But the show was over, at least for today.

Alex lengthened his stride as he headed toward the corral. "Nick!"

Nick turned immediately, took one look at Alex and hurried over. "What's up?"

"Sarah just called Mary Lou. Morgan's gone into labor."

"Shit."

"Apparently she's not fooling around about it, either. Gabe needs to go out there, and so do you, just in case the midwife isn't available."

Nick's expression shifted from shock to determination. "You got it. She'll be fine. The baby will be fine."

"Absolutely. Listen, I'll find Jack and tell him, and then I'm driving Tyler to Gabe's house. She'll want to go."

"Yeah, Morgan will want her there." Nick reached over and squeezed Alex's shoulder. "See you at Gabe's, buddy." Then he turned and loped back to the corral.

Alex changed direction and made his way quickly across the space between the corral and the tractor barn. Tyler was singing Faith Hill's "This Kiss," but Alex didn't allow himself to imagine she was thinking about him as she sang. He couldn't afford to get emotional right now.

Fortunately, Jack was standing right inside the door where Alex had left him a few minutes ago. Alex quickly filled him in on the situation. "I'm taking Tyler to Gabe's house," he said.

Jack nodded. "Don't worry about anything here. I'll handle it. But I want to know what's going on out there. Everybody else will be too involved in the process to think of it, so I'm counting on you to keep me informed."

"I will." Alex started toward the stage. He could tell the second Tyler knew something was wrong, because she flubbed a lyric. But she covered it well and finished the song while he stood to the left of the stage and waited.

As applause and cheers echoed around her, she murmured her thanks into the microphone. "Excuse me a moment, folks. Someone needs to talk to me." She tucked the mic back in its stand and walked to the edge of the stage. Her dark eyes were wide with alarm and her poise seemed to have deserted her. "What is it?"

"Morgan's in labor."

"Oh, God." She gulped for air. "It's too soon, isn't it?"

"Don't worry. It'll be fine."

"I've been around for home births. I have to go."

"I know. I'll take you. Do you want to announce that you're leaving or let me do it?"

She closed her eyes, and when she opened them again, the seasoned professional was back in charge. "I'll do it. I'll tell Watkins to take over."

He waited while she talked to Watkins, who nodded and patted her arm. Then she went back to the mic. "Well, folks, you're in for a treat. Something's come up and I'll have to skedaddle out of here, but that means you'll get to hear even more from my talented partner in crime! Please welcome an amazing musical talent, the masterful Mr. Watkins!"

The crowd responded with cheers, especially after Tyler handed Watkins the mic and leaned down to kiss his ruddy cheek. Then she skipped off the stage as if she didn't have a care in the world.

Alex moved over to the steps, though, and extended a hand as she started down.

She took it and held on tight. Her hands were clammy and she wobbled a little coming down the steps. Obviously she was frantic with worry over Morgan, but she'd put on a good face for the crowd gathered in the tractor barn.

Alex longed to take her in his arms and comfort her, but she wouldn't want to waste time with silly hugs when they could be on their way to Gabe's house. He continued to hold her hand, though, and she made no effort to pull away.

"I assume Gabe knows," she said as they left the tractor barn and took a shortcut to the back of the house where the trucks had been parked for the day.

"Gabe's on his way out there, along with Nick."

"Nick?" She glanced up at him. "Why is he going?"

"To help." Alex wished he hadn't mentioned Nick, because it made the situation seem even more dicey, but he couldn't take back the information. Besides, she'd find out when she got there, because Alex would bet that Gabe and Nick were already racing down the road.

"Why would Nick need to…oh. In case the midwife doesn't make it in time."

"Yes." They reached the truck, the same one they'd

driven out to the sacred site, and he opened the passenger door for her.

"I can get myself in. Just hurry up and get this buggy in gear."

Giving her hand a squeeze, he jogged around to the driver's side, hopped in and closed the door.

"Do we have gas?"

Alex turned the key in the ignition. "We have gas."

"Then move it, cowboy."

He pulled around the house and onto the circular driveway. "I will, once I get past all the parked vehicles." Fortunately he knew the way, although he'd only been out to Gabe's place a couple of times. Gabe's road branched off the main one leading to the ranch house, so Alex had to navigate past the visitors' cars and trucks parked on the shoulder until he reached the turnoff.

Like the other roads on the ranch, the one to Gabe's was graded but not paved, which meant it would be slick with mud. Plus, it had several wicked curves. Alex shifted into four-wheel drive. "You buckled in?"

"Yes."

"Good. This could get slippery."

"I don't care. I just want to get there as fast as we can."

"All right." Alex was still learning his way around horses, but when it came to driving, especially under difficult road conditions, he knew his stuff. For someone who'd navigated Chicago's Outer Drive in an ice storm, this was child's play. He gripped the wheel and stepped on the gas.

Tyler sucked in a breath, but she didn't say a word as the truck fishtailed through curves and plowed through puddles without slowing. Mud sprayed the windows. Alex flicked on the wipers so he could see, but he didn't touch the brake. Even so, the trip seemed to be taking forever.

"You okay?" He kept his eyes on the road.

"Yep."

"I'm going as fast as I can."

"Good."

"She's going to be okay, Tyler."

"I know." But her voice shook.

Finally he rounded the last curve and pulled in right behind Nick's truck, which was also covered in mud. Sarah's SUV, having been driven at a reasonable speed, was cleaner.

Tyler quickly unlatched her seat belt. "Thanks. I didn't know you could drive like that." Then she opened the door, hopped down and ran toward the house.

It took him a second to realize that sometime during the wild ride she'd shucked her high-heeled boots so she could make that run more easily. Alex followed at a slower pace. This wasn't his family, and he didn't want to intrude on whatever was happening inside the house.

Plus, if he wanted to be honest with himself, he wasn't sure how he'd react to seeing a woman give birth. If he fainted or got sick to his stomach, that would be bad.

So he paused and looked around at the stacks of lumber covered in tarps. The log exterior of the two-story house was complete, but the interior was still a work in progress. Morgan and Gabe joked about living in a construction zone, but Alex could tell they loved every minute of being out here together.

They were building a life together, and Alex envied them that. He didn't know squat about building a house, but the Chance brothers did. They would help him. Living at the ranch house was nice, but this—creating a home from scratch, almost like the pioneers, really appealed to him.

But he couldn't imagine doing that just for himself. He'd want to share it with someone, and he didn't need to think very long about who he'd choose if he could. Then he remembered how she'd looked up on stage and squashed that thought. She didn't belong here.

Holding that thought, he approached the house. He was almost at the door when Morgan's scream shattered the silence. He hurried forward. God knows he'd be of no practical use. But whatever was happening, Tyler was part of it. He wanted to be there for her.

Morgan's next scream came as he followed muddy footprints through the living room toward the master bedroom. Heart racing, he said a little prayer that she wasn't dying, and that the baby wasn't dying, either.

But when he heard a loud cheer coming from the bedroom, he let out a sigh, dizzy with relief. It was okay. He stood in the doorway, still feeling a little like an outsider.

From here he couldn't see much of Morgan, who was surrounded by Tyler and Sarah on one side and Gabe on the other. Nick stood at the foot of the bed holding a bloody, slimy baby who scrunched up its little face and let out a wail of protest.

"She's *beautiful*," Morgan said, gasping. "Isn't she beautiful, Gabe?"

Gabe cleared his throat and leaned down to kiss his wife. "You're beautiful," he said, his voice raspy.

"A girl." Sarah seemed to be lit from within. "I have a granddaughter."

"And I have a niece," Tyler said as tears ran down her cheeks. "A beautiful little niece."

"Hey, she's my niece, too." Nick was busily wiping

the gunk off the little kid. "Okay, you guys. Now we know the first grandbaby is a girl. But we don't know her name."

"You tell." Morgan tugged on her husband's hand.

Gabe snuffled. "No, you." His voice was still thick with emotion.

"All right," Morgan said softly as she kissed Gabe's hand. "Her name is Sarah Bianca, after her two grandmothers."

"Oh, my goodness." Sarah lost it and began weeping openly.

A lump in his throat and envy in his heart, Alex backed away from the doorway. Everything was fine and nobody needed him. To stand there during this emotional family moment seemed wrong, so he retreated to the living room, moved aside a newspaper, and sat on the couch.

God, he wanted to be part of something that wonderful, though. He ached with longing to have a woman love him the way Morgan loved Gabe. Crystal never had, and he could see that now. He hadn't lost her so much as that he'd never truly had her.

"I wondered where you were."

He glanced up to find Tyler standing in front of him, a smile on her tear-streaked face.

She sniffed and swiped at her eyes. "Isn't it wonderful?"

"Yes." He discovered his throat was still tight with emotion. "I'm really glad everything's okay."

She nodded. "I couldn't figure out where you were, so I came looking for you."

"I… It didn't seem as if I should…"

"You could have come in. But I know what you mean.

I stepped out for a while so that they could all bond. I'll have my chance later."

"Yeah. At least you still have a few days before you have to leave."

"About that." She gestured toward the couch. "Could I sit down?"

"Oh! Sure!" He tossed the newspaper on the coffee table. "Sorry."

"That's okay. It's been a confusing kind of day." She settled herself on the couch next to him. "And I'm about to add to the confusion, but I have something to discuss with you. I have an idea."

He angled his body so he could look at her. She was so incredibly beautiful and he wanted to remember her like this, her face glowing with happiness. "What kind of idea?"

Her gaze was soft and her smile warm. "What would you say to me giving up the cruise business and setting up shop as an event planner for the town of Shoshone?"

For one shining moment he allowed himself to embrace the thought that she would settle down here. He let himself imagine that she was falling in love with him and they could have the kind of life that he longed for, full of trust and joy and…okay, plenty of sex.

But then reality smacked him in the face. Of course she'd come up with this idea now. She'd just been put through an emotional wringer, first thinking her sister's life was in danger, and then witnessing the birth of her niece. She was awash in family sentimentality. She wasn't thinking straight.

He took a deep breath. "I'd say you'd be making a huge mistake."

Her smile faded. "Why?"

"Tyler, you've worked for this promotion for years. You've told me before how much you love your job, and now you're going to throw that all away?"

"Maybe I want something else instead."

"You just think you do because of all that just happened. Your sister's had a baby, so naturally you're trying to figure out how to spend more time here. But you don't have to take a drastic step like dumping the job you love."

"Or maybe you don't want me to dump the job because that would put more pressure on us than you're ready for."

"I didn't say that!"

"You didn't have to. It's written all over your face. I scared you to death with that suggestion, didn't I?"

"This isn't about me. It's about you, and your future."

"Right. My future." She stood. "I see it very clearly now."

"Good. That's excellent. Because you don't want to let the emotions of the moment carry you away and make you do something you'll regret."

"That's for damn sure. Listen, you probably need to get back, so don't worry about me. I can ride with Nick. You can go on."

He could tell she was furious with him for telling her the truth, but he'd done it for her own good. "Tyler, I—"

"No, really. I'll get back just fine. See you." Then she walked down the hall toward the bedroom.

Well, hell. He supposed that's what he got for trying to be a good guy. Blowing out a breath, he got up and walked outside. It was raining again. Perfect. Just perfect.

16

TYLER OFFERED TO spend the rest of her vacation time out at Morgan and Gabe's house so she could help with baby Sarah. That had the added benefit of avoiding Alex almost entirely. She should have known better than to think he'd welcome her idea.

She really had thought he might react with excitement once he understood what she had in mind. Watching a new life come into being had made her decide to lay everything on the line and find out if Alex wanted her to stay.

But he didn't want that, obviously. He'd looked horrified at the thought of her moving permanently to Shoshone. Well, he wouldn't have to worry about that now.

Gabe drove her to the airport in Jackson on Wednesday. "I can't tell you what this has meant to Morgan and me, having you here when Sarah was born," he said as he pulled her suitcase out of the back of the truck. "Sometimes I worry that Morgan is a little overwhelmed by my family, and so to have you here sort of balanced the scales."

"I'm glad." She gave him a hug. "I'll come back as often as I can, but you know the schedule."

"I know."

"And you'll have my mom and dad visiting next month. I'm sure they'll bring more of the tribe with them, so Morgan won't get too lonely for her family."

"Guess not." Gabe smiled at her. "But I can tell she's closest to you. So come back when you can."

"I will." She damn sure wasn't going to let the threat of dealing with Alex keep her away. "Expect to get some baby stuff from Greece."

"I'm sure Sarah will have all sorts of exotic clothes and toys. Travel safe." With a wave, he hopped back in his truck.

Travel safe. The operative word in that was *travel.* She was going to be on the move, and if she kept herself constantly in motion, maybe she wouldn't notice that her heart was truly and completely broken.

ALEX THREW HIMSELF into his job. The first part of the week he did it to pretend she wasn't still at the ranch. After she left Wednesday morning he put in even more hours as he pretended she wasn't gone. Sometimes it worked. Mostly it didn't, but he had obligations and he was determined to honor them and prove that he wouldn't go into a blue funk because of Tyler.

Early in the week, he talked with Clay Whitaker about marketing plans for the stud service, which would be operational within the next month. Another open house had already been scheduled for July, as well. Despite the interruption caused by the early arrival of baby Sarah Bianca, who had been dubbed SB by the hands, the open house had been a rousing success with multiple sales.

Interest in the Last Chance paints had increased exponentially, and the Chance brothers wanted a repeat of the event. That was impossible now that Tyler was gone, but everybody agreed that Watkins had been a hit. Instead of hiring outside entertainment, the family had voted to hire Watkins and pay him over and above his normal wages as a ranch hand. They'd settled on a fee and had authorized Alex to make the deal.

Alex put off talking to Watkins because he had the distinct feeling Watkins wasn't happy with him. He figured it had something to do with Tyler leaving. Watkins might have thought Alex would ask her to stay and then Watkins would have someone to jam with. Too bad about that.

Early Friday morning, Alex decided to get it over with and talk to Watkins. He found the stocky ranch hand in the barn caring for the horses. Watkins was grooming Gold Rush, a butterscotch-and-white paint previously ridden only by Jonathan Chance Sr.

Nick had opted to ride the flashy gelding in last year's Fourth of July parade, and now the hands thought of Gold Rush as Nick's horse. But Watkins had a fondness for the animal and usually made time to take a currycomb to him a few times a week.

He glanced up when Alex walked over and leaned against the door to Gold Rush's stall. "Morning, Alex." His greeting was curt and he went right back to brushing the horse.

"Morning, Watkins." Still pissed, obviously.

"We'll be doing another open house the middle of next month," he said as an opener.

"That's nice." Watkins kept grooming Gold Rush.

"Everybody really enjoyed your guitar playing, and we'd like you to be the entertainment again. We're prepared to pay you this time."

"Not interested."

"What?" Alex had expected a short conversation, but not a refusal.

Watkins didn't look up. "Sorry. I'm not interested."

"Why not?"

Watkins turned to face him, the currycomb still in his hand. "If it was just the Chance boys asking, I might do it. But since you're involved in the whole thing, I'm going to say no."

Alex stared at him. "Okay, what's this about? You've been crossways with me for days now. I want to know why."

"Because you don't have the good sense to appreciate Tyler, that's why."

"Are you kidding? I appreciate the hell out of her! She's an amazing woman who's doing the job she loves. I realize it would have suited your purposes to have her stay, but that's just plain selfishness on your part."

Watkins gazed at him. "I guess I can say this because technically you're not my boss."

"No, I'm not. Get it off your chest, Watkins."

"Pardon my saying so, but you are one stupid son of a gun."

Alex hung on to his temper with difficulty. "I don't doubt that, but you seem to have some specific stupidity in mind."

"I do." Watkins tossed the currycomb into a plastic bucket that held several grooming tools. "Tyler had this great plan she was all excited about. Considering the fact she left, I'll bet she didn't even mention it."

Alex had an uneasy feeling. "I don't know. She might have."

"If she did, you're even dumber than I thought. She and I talked about it before the open house, and she had big plans for this town. She wanted to be the organizer, get the merchants to hire her to put on communitywide events. Is any of this sounding familiar?"

"Maybe." Good God. Had he been so wrong about her state of mind? "So you're saying she had this idea before the open house even started?"

"That's right. But she asked me not to say anything. I think she was trying to figure out how you felt about her before she committed to it. She knew it would suck to be seeing you all the time if you didn't return her feelings."

Alex felt as if Watkins had punched him. "Did she… did she say she had…feelings for me?"

"Hell, no. She wouldn't have spilled her guts like that. She has her pride. But I've been around a few more years than you, and she had all the signs. Every number she sang, she was looking for you. When she left for L.A., after all, I figured she decided not to tell you anything."

"She mentioned it to me after SB was born. And I thought…I thought she was just reacting to all the drama with her sister. I didn't know she'd dreamed it up before that."

Watkins blew out a breath. "Well, I'm glad she's gone, then. Like I said, you don't have the good sense to appreciate her. I hate that you hurt her, but she's well rid of you."

"Hurt her? I was trying to *help* her!"

"By rejecting her?"

"Yes, damn it! She needs more than this!"

Watkins looked him up and down. "She needs more than you, that's for sure, if you can't see that she's crazy about you. You should have been thanking your lucky stars instead of letting her get away." He pushed open the stall door. "Excuse me. I have work to do."

After he left, Alex sagged against the stall with a groan of despair. She wanted him. And not just because they clicked sexually. She wanted what he wanted, to build a life together here in Shoshone, and she'd figured out a way to use her skills to earn a living, which was so very important to her. Clever, clever girl. Stupid, stupid man.

And now she was on her way to…no, wait! Today was Friday. The ship sailed out of L.A. tonight! Pulling his phone out of his pocket, he scrolled through his contacts until he found her. He'd considered erasing that number. Thank God he hadn't.

His fingers trembled, but he managed to type out a brief text message which he deliberately put in caps. C U 2NITE LOVE ALEX. As he pushed the button to send it on its way, he prayed he wasn't too late.

THE *Sea Goddess's* ENGINES rumbled, churning the water beneath the ship. Tyler's stomach mimicked the motion of the propellers. In six years of cruising she'd never been seasick, but she might break that record this afternoon before the ship ever left port. The *Sea Goddess* would sail in exactly one hour, and she hadn't heard a word from Alex.

Despite the frantic pace of the day as she checked last-minute details in the morning and began greeting passengers boarding in the afternoon, she'd pulled out her phone to look at Alex's text message dozens of times. She'd memorized the short message, but still she had to look at it.

There was no mistaking the meaning. He intended to see her before she left. If so, that cowboy had better be riding a really fast horse.

But it was the other part of the message that glowed like a field of diamonds in her mind. LOVE ALEX. He wouldn't have typed that in casually, like the kind of stupid throwaway line she'd given him the day of the open house. She had to believe he wouldn't have typed it at all unless…but she dared not speculate too wildly.

And he wasn't here.

She'd positioned herself by the embarkation doorway to greet passengers as they came on board. Some were returning passengers eager to chat. In the middle of one of those conversations with a darling couple in their eighties, Tyler's phone vibrated.

Her heart raced and blood surged through her, roaring in her ears in a deafening rush. She excused herself from the couple and stepped away from the door. She was shaking so much she could barely hold the phone to her ear.

"Alex?"

"I'm outside the ship. They won't let me in. Can you come out?"

She gulped. "I shouldn't, but…five minutes. I can give you five minutes."

"Give me ten."

"Five, cowboy." Her throat was so tight she could barely speak. "You'll have to talk fast."

"Then don't hang up. I'll start now. I'll talk to you while you're coming down."

"Okay." Phone to her ear, she hurried over to the staff at the security-check station. "Don't let them leave without me. I'll be *right back*."

Both guys lifted their eyebrows but didn't say anything.

"I promise." Then she started down the ramp to the dock. Nearly all the passengers were aboard, so she only had to work her way around a couple of latecomers.

"Can you hear me?" Alex said in that seductive radio voice.

"Yes. I'm walking down the gangplank now."

"Thank God. Thank *you*." His voice caressed her. "I've been such an idiot, Tyler."

"Have you?" She searched the dock area below her as she descended, but didn't see him yet. California sunshine bathed the dock and the blindingly white ship as carts buzzed around bringing in last-minute supplies.

"Dumb as a box of rocks. But I'm a hell of a lot smarter now."

"How so?"

"I should have trusted you to know what you wanted instead of thinking I knew best what you needed."

She took a shaky breath. "True. I'm not Crystal."

"Not even close. And…I finally understand that loving each other is the only thing that really matters."

Tyler grabbed the railing for support as her knees began to quiver. "Loving?" Her voice squeaked on the word.

"Loving." His voice didn't squeak. It fell into that incredible register that turned her insides to warm goo. "I intend to love you like you've never been loved, for the rest of our lives. We'll build a life together in Shoshone, but we'll travel, too, because I know how much that means to you."

"But...but...I can't...Alex, the ship is ready to sail."

"I know. It's okay. I can wait."

Joy spread through her brighter than sun on the ocean waves. "Give me a couple of weeks so I can train someone to take over."

"It'll seem like forever, but I'll wait for you."

"Where are you?" She stepped onto the dock and looked around.

"I'm over here, behind the gate."

She saw him then, a tall, broad-shouldered cowboy in a snow-white shirt, snug jeans, leather boots and his favorite gray Stetson. "I hope you're not going to wait right there for two weeks."

His soft laughter sang along her nerve endings. "I will if I have to. But I'd rather fly to meet you wherever it is you get off the ship after you're released from your contract. Make it someplace romantic like Casablanca."

"You got it."

"Could you hurry a little bit? My five minutes is almost up."

"Right." Phone still to her ear, she began to run.

"God, you're beautiful," he murmured.

"I've missed you...so much." She was out of breath by

the time she reached the gate, but it didn't matter. Nothing mattered but seeing him, touching him. Her gaze locked with his as she flashed her pass and the security guard opened the gate.

"I love you, Tyler." Slowly he lowered his phone.

She stepped through the gate and into his arms. "I love you, Alex." As he wrapped those warm, strong arms around her, as his lips found hers, she knew five minutes wasn't long enough. A lifetime wouldn't be long enough to spend loving Alex. But she would give it one hell of a shot.

* * * * *

COWBOY UP

To Rhonda Nelson, friend, top-notch painter of walls, and valued source of story ideas. Thanks for my freshly painted walls and your excellent suggestion for Clay's job description.

Prologue

CARRYING HIS COFFEE MUG, Archie Chance joined his wife, Nelsie, for their evening ritual of rocking on the front porch, gazing at the mountains and discussing…whatever came up.

Archie settled in his chair and took a sip of his coffee before broaching the subject on his mind. "What do you think about frozen semen?"

Although some women might have been taken aback by such a question, Nelsie didn't bat an eye. "Are you fixing to freeze yours?"

That made him laugh. How he loved this woman. "Nope. Don't think there would be much call for my semen considering that I've only been able to produce one son in all these years."

"That's because you go for quality and not quantity."

Archie gave her a smile. Their son, Jonathan, now fifteen, had turned out pretty damned well, if Archie did say so. The boy lived and breathed ranching just as Archie had hoped he would. There was no question that Jonathan would take over the Last Chance when the time came.

"So whose frozen semen are you interested in, then?" Nelsie asked.

"Goliath's. I've been reading about folks shipping frozen bull semen all over God's creation and making money doing it. Seeing as how the Last Chance is still a cattle operation and Goliath fetches a hefty stud fee, I wondered if I should look into it."

Nelsie's rocker creaked softly as she appeared to ponder that idea. "Goliath might not take to having his semen collected."

"I know."

"I would imagine he prefers to impregnate cows the old-fashioned way."

"Too bad. It's the sixties. Times are changing. Goliath needs to change with them."

Nelsie turned to gaze at him. "And you need more money to get this horse venture off the ground."

"Yeah." He cradled his mug in both hands and watched the fading light play across the flanks of the Grand Tetons. "It's a hell of a lot more expensive than I thought it would be, Nelsie, and it may take years, but someday the Last Chance is going to be known for raising the finest paints in Wyoming."

1

July, present day

THE STALLION'S SCREAM of sexual frustration ricocheted off the walls of a shed that smelled like fresh lumber and honest sweat, both human and horse. The Last Chance Ranch baked under a sun that shone with uncharacteristic ferocity. Clay Whitaker, who'd recently been put in charge of the ranch's stud program, wiped his face on his sleeve.

The new shed could use an air-conditioning unit—humans would appreciate it, at least. The horses probably wouldn't care, judging from the ardor of Bandit, the black-and-white paint that claimed a higher stud fee than any other stallion in the Last Chance Ranch.

Despite the heat, Bandit seemed desperate to mount the mare contained in a small pen only a few feet away. He would never get the chance. The pretty little chocolate-and-white paint named Cookie Dough was a decoy.

Instead of mating the old-fashioned way, Bandit would have to make do with a padded dummy so that Clay could collect the semen, freeze it and ship it to a customer in

Texas. Shipping frozen horse semen promised to add an increased revenue stream to the ranch operation, or so Clay projected it would.

Nick Chance, middle son of the family that operated the ranch, was on hand to help. A large-animal vet, Nick, co-owned the Last Chance along with his older brother, Jack, his younger brother, Gabe, and their mother, Sarah. Clay had known all of them for ten years.

Theoretically, sperm collection was a simple task. Nick would keep a firm grip on Bandit's lead rope as the stallion mounted the dummy, and Clay would move in with a collection tube. Instead, Bandit seemed determined to get to the mare, and both men's yoked Western shirts were stained dark with sweat.

Nick glanced around the small shed. "We need to get us some air-conditioning in here."

"That's exactly what I—" The rest of Clay's response was drowned out by another scream from Bandit, right before he did exactly as he was supposed to and mounted the dummy. Grasping the tube, a twenty-five-pound piece of equipment designed to keep the semen at an even temperature, Clay moved in for the crucial part of the operation.

When Bandit was finished, both men stood back to let the stallion rest on the dummy for a moment.

Nick glanced over at Clay. "Shall I offer him a cigarette?"

"Very funny."

"I invited Jack to watch, but he declined."

"I'm not surprised." In fact, Clay would have been amazed if Jack had shown up for Bandit's session. Jack didn't much like the idea of collecting and shipping frozen semen, but he recognized times had changed and had agreed to let Clay put his animal science degree to good use.

Still, Bandit was Jack's horse, and Jack thought the collection process was completely undignified. Maybe so, but Jack couldn't argue with the income it would generate. Being in charge of this new operation meant Clay had an important job at the ranch he loved so dearly, but it also allowed him to give something back to the only real family he'd ever had.

Orphaned at three, he'd been shuffled through a series of foster homes until turning eighteen. Then he'd come to work at the Last Chance, where Sarah and her husband, Jonathan, had treated him more like one of their sons than a hired hand. But he'd formed the strongest bond with Emmett Sterling, ranch foreman and the closest thing to a father Clay had ever had. Emmett had recognized that Clay had a brain, and encouraged him to save for college.

Working while he attended school had meant taking six years to complete a four-year program, but now he was back. Jonathan Chance's death from a truck roll-over almost two years ago had shocked Clay and made him even more determined to use his education to benefit the family.

Bandit slowly lifted his head as if he'd recovered enough to dismount from the dummy.

"Guess we're about done here," Nick said. "I'll take him back to his stall and then get Cookie Dough."

"Thanks." Clay hoisted the canister to his shoulder and left the shed. On his way to the tractor barn and the incubator he'd set up there, he had to pass by the horse barn, and he glanced around uneasily.

Emmett's daughter, Emily, had arrived late last night

so she could help celebrate her dad's sixtieth birthday tomorrow. Her white BMW convertible—sporting a California vanity plate that read SURFS UP—sat in the circular drive, top down and tan leather upholstery exposed to the sun. Well, that fit the impression Clay had of her—spoiled and irresponsible.

He'd met her at her father's fiftieth birthday, soon after he'd come to work at the ranch; but Clay hadn't seen her since. She might have visited while he was away at college, though she'd made it obvious ranch life didn't suit her.

Emmett had sent her large chunks of his paycheck every month when she was a minor, so the guy was always broke. After she came of age, everyone expected Emmett to have more money. He didn't, and eventually it had come out that he was still writing sizable checks to his daughter.

Although Clay would never say so to Emmett, he—along with most everyone at the ranch—resented the hell out of the ungrateful little leech. When he'd first met Emily, he'd done what any normal eighteen-year-old guy would do when confronted with a gorgeous blonde. He'd flirted with her.

She'd said in no uncertain terms that cowboys weren't her style. The rejection had stung, but her disdain for cowboys in general had to be even more hurtful to her father. Clay had vowed to forget her hot little body and continue about his business.

Unfortunately the image of her Daisy Dukes and low-cut blouses had stuck with him, no matter how often he'd tried to erase the memory. He could still close his eyes and see her prancing around like she was in some beauty pageant. With any luck she'd packed on some pounds in the past ten years and wouldn't look like that anymore. With any luck, he wouldn't have direct contact with her at all.

So much for luck. Here she came, long blond hair swinging as she walked out of the horse barn with Emmett.

Clay swallowed. Sure enough, she'd put on a few pounds—in all the right places. Her black scoop-necked T-shirt had some designer name across the front and, to Clay's way of thinking, the designer should've paid Emily for the display space.

Her Daisy Dukes had been replaced by cuffed white shorts that showed off a spectacular tan. She'd propped oversize sunglasses on her head and now she pulled them down over her eyes as she glanced in his direction.

Clay had no trouble picturing her wearing a bikini and sipping an umbrella drink while she lounged by the pool in her hometown of Santa Barbara. He imagined her smoothing coconut-scented suntan oil over every inch of that gorgeous...

Whoa. He'd better shut down that video right quick. No way was he lusting after Emily Sterling. That was a mistake on so many levels. For one thing, he didn't even *like* her, and he prided himself on only getting involved with likable women.

Emmett looked at him and nodded in approval. "Looks like you got 'er done."

"We did." Clay dredged up a polite smile as he drew closer. "I'm glad your daughter arrived okay." He made out the letters on the front of her shirt. BEBE, with an accent mark over the last *E*. Probably French for *babe*. Appropriate.

"She showed up about eleven last night," Emmett said.

"I never thought I'd be grateful for cell phones, but I sure am when she's on the road. Emily, do you remember Clay Whitaker?"

"She probably doesn't." Clay adjusted the collection tube, that was getting heavier by the second. "That was a long time ago. Anyway, nice to see you again, Emily. If you'll excuse me, I need to—"

"Do what?" She motioned to the metal tube balanced on his shoulder and grinned. "That thing looks like a rocket launcher."

"Um, it's not. Listen, I really have to—"

"At least tell me what it is, then."

"Semen collector," Emmett said helpfully.

"Really?" Emily took off her sunglasses and peered at the tube. "So did you collect some semen just now?"

"Yes, and I need to get it into the incubator."

"And then what?"

"Oh, it's a whole process," Emmett said. "Clay studied how to do it when he was in college, and now the Last Chance can ship frozen semen all over the country. All over the world, if we want."

"Flying semen." A ripple in her voice and a glitter in her green eyes suggested she was trying not to laugh. "What a concept. That canister is pretty big. Is there that much of it?"

Dear God. Clay couldn't have come up with a worse topic of conversation if he'd tried all day. "Not really. There's insulation material, and...and..."

"The AV," Emmett said.

"What's an AV?"

Of course she'd ask.

"It's an artificial va—" Emmett stopped and coughed, as if he'd finally realized this really wasn't a fit subject to be discussing with his daughter, who hadn't been raised on a ranch and wouldn't be used to a matter-of-fact discussion of female anatomy.

Clay stepped into the breach. "Artificial vacuum," he said. "It's an artificial vacuum."

"Huh." Emily's brow furrowed. "I'm not sure I understand. Something's either a vacuum or it's not."

Emmett put his arm around her shoulders. "It's complicated. And very technical. Anyway, we need to let Clay get on with his job."

"Right." Emily flashed her even, white teeth and winked at him before replacing her sunglasses. "I don't want spoiled semen on my conscience. See you later, Clay."

"You bet, Emily." He headed off, cursing under his breath and trying to ignore his gut response to that smile. If he didn't know better, he'd classify that wink as flirting; but that couldn't be right. She'd told him once that she was a city girl who had no intention of getting mixed up with a shit-kicking cowboy, and he wasn't about to make the same mistake twice. The perception that she'd flirted with him just now was only wishful thinking on his part.

Stupid thinking, too. How could he have sexual feelings for a woman who continued to bleed her hardworking father for money while sneering at that good man's lifestyle? A woman like that shouldn't interest Clay in the least and definitely shouldn't stir his animal instincts. Ah, but she did. Damn it, she did.

Maybe she presented a challenge to his male ego and all he really wanted to do was take her down a peg. He was far more confident around women now than he had been ten years ago, and he realized that they found him attractive. Could be he'd like to prove to Miss Emily that a shit-kicking cowboy could ring her chimes better than any city boy.

He wouldn't follow up on that urge, though. Emmett had been like family. The guy was his idol. That meant Clay wasn't going to mess with Emily. End of story.

"CLAY WHITAKER SEEMS to have turned out okay." Emily congratulated herself on sounding vaguely interested, when inside a wild woman shouted *Take me, you bad boy! Take me, now!*

She watched Clay walk across the open area between the horse barn and the tractor barn. A girl could get used to that view—tight buns in faded jeans and shoulders broad enough to easily support a large canister of horse semen. Horse semen, of all things!

She was dying to know how that process worked. Biology had been her favorite subject in high school, but her mother, a buyer for Chico's, had steered her into fashion design. Unfortunately, she had no talent for it.

Collecting horse semen—now that would be interesting. Apparently it was a sweaty job. The back of Clay's shirt clung to his sexy torso and the dark hair curling from under his hat made him look as if he'd stuck his head beneath a faucet. The guy was hot in more ways than one, and pheromones had been coming off him in waves.

He must have had those same deep brown eyes when he was eighteen; but, if so, they hadn't registered with her. Today was a different story. Looking into his gorgeous eyes had produced an effect on her libido that was off the Richter scale. Either Clay had acquired a boatload of sexual chemistry over the years, or she'd been a stupid seventeen-year-old who hadn't recognized his potential.

She wondered if she'd been rude to him back then. At the time she'd been full of herself and full of her mother's prejudices against cowboys. If she had been rude, she hoped he'd forgotten it by now. He probably had, after not seeing her for so long.

"Clay's developed into a top hand." Emmett studied her as if trying to guess what was going on in her head.

"That's good to hear." She didn't want him to figure out what she was thinking, either. "I know you're fond of him." In fact, she'd been a little jealous over the years when he'd bragged about Clay, although she'd never admit that to her dad. On the other hand, knowing Emmett had Clay had eased her conscience about not visiting more often.

"He's a good guy," Emmett said. "So, do you still want that coffee?"

"What? Oh, right! Yes. Absolutely." At home she'd developed a midmorning Starbucks habit, something she'd confessed to Emmett during their tour of the barn when she realized she was running low on energy. But the encounter with Clay had boosted her spirits without the benefit of caffeine. Still, coffee was always welcome. She fell into step beside her father as they continued on to the house.

"I don't know if I told you that Clay got his degree in animal science this spring."

"I don't think you mentioned that." She knew he wasn't comparing Clay to her, but still, she'd dropped out of college because she couldn't see wasting the money when she didn't know what she wanted to study.

Her mother kept pushing retail, preferably involving

fashion. Emily's heart wasn't in it, and finally she'd told her mother so. She'd briefly considered marine biology and had volunteered in the field, but that hadn't felt quite right.

Her current receptionist job couldn't be called a career decision, either. She sighed. "When I see somebody like Clay, who has his act together, I feel like a slacker."

Emmett shook his head. "Don't be too hard on yourself. Some people take longer than others to figure out what they want to do."

"Maybe so, but Clay's had so many obstacles to overcome…"

"We all have obstacles."

"I suppose, but you told me he spent his childhood going from one foster home to the next. That's major trauma."

"You haven't had a bed of roses, either, what with no father around."

"That wasn't your fault, Dad." She hated that he still felt guilty about the divorce, nearly twenty-five years after the fact. Before she'd been old enough to think for herself, she'd accepted her mother's assessment that Emmett was to blame for the divorce. Gradually she'd come to see that it had been a bad match that was doomed from the start.

"It was partly my fault," Emmett said. "First off I let your mother take you to California, and then I only came over to visit two or three times."

"Yes, but Santa Barbara isn't your kind of place." They'd reached the steps going up to the porch and her dad's boots hit the wood with a solid sound she'd missed hearing. She'd missed other things, too, like the way his gray hair curled a little at the nape of his neck, and how his face creased in a smile and his blue eyes grew warm and crinkly with love when he looked at her.

She hadn't always appreciated how handsome he was because she'd been so influenced by her mother's assessment of cowboys as unsophisticated hicks who went around with a piece of straw clenched in their teeth. Her dad did that sometimes, but he also moved with fluid grace, and he was as lean and muscled as a man half his age.

He blew out a breath, which made his mustache flutter a bit. "Doesn't matter if it's my kind of place or not. I should've visited more often." He paused with one hand on the brass doorknob. "I'm sorry for that, Emily. More sorry than I can say."

"It's okay." Bracing her hands on his warm shoulder, she rose on tiptoe and leaned in under the brim of his hat to give him a kiss on the cheek. "I've always known you love me."

"More than anything." His voice was rough with emotion. "Which is why we both need to get some coffee in us before we turn into blubbering fools and embarrass ourselves."

"And a Sterling never turns into a blubbering fool."

"That's exactly right." Clearing his throat, Emmett opened the door and ushered her inside.

Although the main house didn't have air conditioning, the thick log walls kept the rooms cool even in the heat of summer. The second story helped, too. Emily adored the winding staircase that, according to her dad, had been expertly crafted more than thirty years ago by the Chance boys' grandpa Archie.

Emmett had told her that Archie had been a master carpenter who'd designed every aspect of this massive home for both beauty and practicality. Even Emily's mother, who pretty much despised anything to do with ranching, had once confessed that she found the house to be spectacular.

A huge rock fireplace dominated the living room, and although no fire burned there, the scent of cedar smoke had worked its way into the brown leather armchairs and sofa gathered in front of the hearth. No doubt the large Navajo rugs hanging on the walls had absorbed the smell of the fire, too. Its woodsy fragrance combined with that of lemon-oil furniture polish would always be connected in Emily's mind to the Last Chance.

She'd assumed salt air and ocean waves were her favorite backdrop; but walking into this living room late last night had felt a bit like coming home. Because her dad's little cabin was small, Emily stayed upstairs in the main house when she visited. She hadn't thought she was particularly attached to the place, but last night she'd realized that wasn't true. She loved it here.

Her dad caught her looking around the living room. "Maybe if I'd provided your mother with a house like this," he began, "then she—"

"She still wouldn't have been happy. Face it, Dad. She isn't content unless she's living by the ocean near some really good shopping."

"I discovered that too late."

"So did she." And Jeri had never remarried, which told Emily that her mother had loved her dad and probably still did. Although Emma might be the feminine version of the name Emmett, Emily was darned close. "She married you without stopping to think that she finds horses and dogs exceedingly smelly."

Emmett laughed. "And she's right, they are. But I happen to love that about them."

"Believe it or not, I kind of do, too."

He thumbed back his hat to look at her. "I had a feeling you did."

"All along I've pretended that taking barn tours and riding was a drag, but the truth is, I've always looked forward to being around the animals."

"You'd better not let your mother hear you say that."

"I know. I suppose I thought it would be disloyal to her if I said I liked them." She gazed at him for several seconds. All her life she'd been told that ranching was nothing but dust, horse poop and endless drudgery. Because of that she'd told herself her visits were only an obligation to maintain a connection with her father.

She'd let three years go by since the last time, and she might not have made the trip this summer except that her father was turning sixty. To her surprise, she was really glad to be here. And she'd finally admitted to her dad that barns and horses appealed to her.

In fact, she had the urge to spend more time hanging out at the barn and getting to know the horses. Of course, that could have something to do with Clay Whitaker. Clearly if she wanted to see more of Clay she'd need to become involved with the animals he tended.

She turned toward her father. "Do you think we could take a ride this afternoon?"

"I might be able to work that out. I need to pick up some supplies today, and maybe we could stretch that into a little shopping trip in Jackson." He brightened. "I could ask Pam to come along so you could meet her. You two could shop while I warm a bench outside."

"That sounds great, Dad." Actually, it didn't. He'd told

her last night about Pam Mulholland, who owned the Bunk & Grub, a bed-and-breakfast inn down the road. It seemed her father had a girlfriend, and Emily wasn't sure how she felt about that. "But I meant a horseback ride."

"Oh. I'm afraid that's not in the cards for today, sweetheart. I really do have to run several errands and I'm not sure how long they'll take. Sure you don't want to come along?"

She couldn't blame him for thinking she'd love to go shopping. Three years ago she'd been all about buying stuff, partly because she'd known it would please her mother if she came back with clothes. "It's funny, but now that I'm here, I feel like staying put," she said. "Maybe I'll just take a walk around the ranch this afternoon." *And see what Clay's up to.*

"A walk?"

She smiled at his puzzled expression. "I know. Cowboys don't walk, but I do."

Emmett looked down at her feet. "Then you'll need to put something on besides those sandals."

"I packed the boots and jeans I bought when we went shopping in Jackson last time I visited."

"You still have those?"

"They're like new. I felt like a fake wearing them in Santa Barbara. I'll probably feel like a fake wearing them here, but I want to give it a shot."

"Okay." He gave her a look that was pure protective dad. "Promise me you won't try to go riding by yourself."

"I promise." Years ago she would have resented the implication that she couldn't handle riding alone. But she hadn't been on a horse in three years, and she was old enough now to appreciate his warning as a gesture of love. "I know my limits. I can ride a surfboard like nobody's business, but I don't have much practice on a horse." She paused. "Maybe one of the hands could go with me."

"That's an idea. I could send Watkins."

She remembered Watkins as a shortish, older guy with a handlebar mustache. Nice enough, but not the person she had in mind.

"No, not Watkins," her dad said. "He has a toothache and would spend the whole ride talking about it."

"Then how about—"

"I could send Jeb, but...I don't know. That boy gets distracted by a pretty face. I'd ask one of the Chances, but Nick's scheduled to worm our little herd of cattle, Gabe's off at a cutting-horse event, and Jack's taking Josie to the obstetrician today." He glanced at Emily. "I did tell you that Josie's pregnant?"

"Yes. You gave me the rundown last night, and I think I have it all straight. Josie and Jack are expecting their first. Gabe and Morgan have little Sarah Bianca, who's one month old. Nick and Dominique are waiting a bit before having kids."

"Right. Okay, let me think. There must be somebody I would trust to take you."

She did her level best to sound indifferent. "I don't suppose Clay could go."

"Hey, that's a great idea! I don't know why I didn't think of it. I'll ask him."

Bingo.

2

FOR THE FIRST time since he'd come to live at the Last Chance, Clay dreaded lunch hour. Years ago, before Clay had come to the ranch, Archie had begun a tradition of gathering everyone in the main house at midday so that news could be exchanged and plans made. In fact, when the east wing had been added, Sarah had suggested creating a large lunchroom because the family dining room had become too crowded.

The new space held four round tables that each sat eight, and windows on the north and east provided light and spectacular mountain views. Hands ate in the bunkhouse for breakfast and dinner, rotating the cooking chores among themselves, but they considered lunch a treat, both for the setting and the food. Sarah insisted on tablecloths and cloth napkins because she believed in adding a little class. The guys tolerated that because Mary Lou Simms, the family's cook, always put on a mouthwatering spread.

Mary Lou's cooking was one of the many things Clay had missed while he was in Cheyenne going to school. Today's menu featured fried chicken, potato salad, corn on the cob and biscuits, all served family style. The heaping platters and bowls coming out of the kitchen smelled as good as they looked, and normally Clay would have been licking his chops.

Instead, he was on Emily Alert. She'd be here, sure as the world, and he wanted to stay as far away from her as possible. He hesitated just inside the doorway and scanned the room, which was already filling up.

"Just the man I want to talk to."

He recognized Emmett's deep voice as the foreman gripped his shoulder from behind. Clay turned, knowing that Emmett wouldn't be walking into the lunchroom alone. As expected, Emily stood beside him, and to Clay's surprise, she seemed unsure of herself.

Even more surprising was her outfit. She still wore the scoop-necked T-shirt with BEBÉ splashed across the front, but she'd traded the shorts for a pair of jeans that looked as if they'd never seen the light of day, and tooled boots with nary a scuff mark on them. Clay found it hard to believe that she'd decided to dress like the locals so she could fit in better, but that's exactly what her change of clothes appeared to suggest.

"Let's find us a place to sit," Emmett said.

Clay stifled a groan. Trapped. He'd considered skipping lunch completely, but he was starving and he hadn't come up with a decent excuse for staying away. Traditions had taken on new significance since Jonathan's death, and the hands made every effort to be there at noon each weekday.

Nick and his wife, Dominique, a tall woman with her glossy brown hair cut short, sat at a table with Sarah. Emmett ushered Emily in that direction, and Clay had no choice but to follow.

Nick stood as Emily approached. The Chance boys, thanks to a firm hand from Sarah, had the manners of diplomats. Sarah's mother, Lucy, had been an NYC runway model, and Sarah had inherited her mother's classic beauty and carriage. Although she was in her mid-sixties and her sleek bob was silver, she could pass for a woman fifteen years younger.

Sarah had taken over Clay's education in the social graces, too, and he was grateful. She gave a slight nod of approval as Clay helped Emily into a chair and introduced her to Dominique, who hadn't been part of the ranch the last time Emily visited.

Finally he sat down, and there was Emily, right beside him, giving off a fragrance that reminded him of sun and salty air. He'd only seen the ocean once, during a brief vacation taken by one of his foster families. On that trip he'd noticed lots of girls who looked like Emily, blond and wearing skimpy clothes to show off their tans. She was exotic, and he was, unfortunately, drawn to that.

He'd hoped to escape sitting at the same table with her, and now here they were knee-to-knee and thigh-to-thigh. If Clay had thought he could get away with it, he would have scooted his chair closer to Sarah, on his other side. But that would look too obvious, so he worked on not making body contact.

No one else sat at their table for eight. Once the food had been passed and everyone had started to eat, Sarah glanced over at Emily with a friendly smile. "You look like you're getting serious about this ranch visit. I don't think I've ever seen you in jeans and boots."

"Nope, you haven't." Emily put down her drumstick. "I bought these a while ago, but this is their first outing. I'm hoping I'll be able to go riding this afternoon."

"The problem is, I have errands to run," Emmett said, "so I thought maybe Clay could take Emily out for an hour or so." He bit into a fried chicken breast.

Yikes. This was getting worse by the minute. Fortunately, Clay had an excuse. He quickly chewed and swallowed a forkful of potato salad. "I'd be glad to, but I have plans for this afternoon."

"Collecting more semen?" As Emily picked up her drumstick again and looked at him, she had a definite gleam in her eye. "I find that fascinating. I'd love to watch."

Damn it, she *was* flirting. Well, it wouldn't get her anywhere. "Sorry, but that's not on the schedule. I have another job I need to do." He buttered his ear of corn and sent a pointed glance in Sarah's direction. She'd deliberately created some errands for Emmett to run today because they needed him gone for a few hours so they could start setting up for tomorrow night's party.

Emmett expected a party, of course. But Sarah had decided to surprise him by switching the venue from the Spirits and Spurs—Josie's bar in the nearby small town of Shoshone—to an old-fashioned cowboy cookout where they'd all ride in on horseback. Clay thought Emmett would love that, so he'd volunteered to truck the tables, benches and firewood out there and build a fire pit.

"That's true, you do have chores this afternoon," Sarah said. "But you might be able to work in a ride after they're done."

"Maybe I could help with the chores," Emily said.

No. That's all he needed, to be stuck alone with her on party detail.

"That's a great idea," Sarah said. "Then he'll be done

that much faster. I would take you out riding myself, Emily, but I've got a list a mile long."

Emmett split open a steaming biscuit and piled butter on it. "And it's all to do with my sixtieth, I'll bet. I keep telling you folks not to make a fuss over this."

"We're not making a fuss," Nick said. "We'll all head to the Spirits and Spurs tomorrow night like we usually do for special occasions. We'll have some drinks and a meal. Somebody's liable to drag out a birthday cake, but that's about the extent of the fuss."

"It better be. And no presents. Is that understood?"

"Too late, Dad," Emily said. "I hauled presents all the way from Santa Barbara, and you're gonna open them or else."

His expression softened. "Sure, sweetheart. I'll make an exception for you, but nobody else had better be showing up with packages."

"I can't guarantee that won't happen." Nick put down a corn cob and reached for another. "But I can guarantee that some of them will be gag gifts, so you might as well resign yourself to the process, Emmett. The hands deserve to have their fun at your expense."

The foreman sighed and raised his eyes to the ceiling. "Good thing these decade birthdays don't come more often." Then he turned his attention to Dominique. "And I suppose you'll be taking pictures."

She paused, her fork in midair, to give him a sweet smile. "Don't I always?"

"Yes, and they're fine pictures, mostly because I'm not in them. So take pictures of everybody else if you want, but the world doesn't need a record of me opening up a box with a whoopee cushion inside or blowing out a bunch of candles. And I sure as heck don't want to see my mug hanging with your other work in that gallery in Jackson."

Emily laid a hand on his arm. "The world might not need a record of you holding a whoopee cushion and blowing out candles, but I do." She glanced over at Dominique. "Please take a gazillion pictures of my dad during his party, okay?"

Dominique gave Emily a thumbs-up. "You've got it."

Clay listened with interest. Emily didn't sound like a spoiled brat who was only interested in the money she could squeeze out of her dad. Instead she sounded like a daughter who dearly loved her father and looked forward to celebrating his birthday.

She might be putting on an act for the benefit of those sitting at the table, though. As far as he knew, she was still accepting monthly checks from this man even though she was certainly old enough to earn her own living. Still, Emmett obviously basked in Emily's affection. Clay hadn't realized until now how much the guy adored his only child.

That kind of parental devotion used to set off a wave of longing in Clay, but these days he was more philosophical about being an orphan. After all, he'd been taken in by the Chance family. He might have started off life at a disadvantage, but he'd wound up pretty good.

And although Emmett wasn't technically his father, the guy filled that role in everything that mattered. He'd latched on to Clay from the get-go and always had his back. Emmett seemed to recognize that Clay needed an advocate. But maybe Emmett had needed Clay, too, as a stand-in for his absent daughter.

So now Emmett was asking Clay to take Emily riding. That was a gesture of trust, no doubt about it. Sarah's suggestion that Emily help him with party chores was a decent idea, too.

He could be gracious and take her with him out to the meadow. She could carry the benches and find rocks for the fire pit. It wasn't so much to ask that he include her after all the support Emmett had given him over the years.

He turned to Emily. "I'd appreciate it if you'd help me with the chores I have, and then we should be able to take a short ride later this afternoon."

Her answering smile dazzled him more than it should. "I would love that. Thank you, Clay."

"You're welcome." He looked away before she could see the effect she had on him. Heat shot through his body and settled in his groin. The rush of sexual awareness left him so shaky that he dared not pick up his fork or his water glass in case somebody noticed how he was trembling.

Good God, he wasn't some inexperienced teenager anymore. In the time since he and Emily had first met he'd had two serious girlfriends and several who would've liked to become serious. These days he knew his way around a bedroom and understood a thing or two about pleasing a woman once he got her in there.

And yet, one brilliant smile from this California girl had reduced him to the hormonal kid he'd been ten years ago. She hadn't wanted him then, but he had a strong suspicion she wanted him now. He wasn't sure why, because she sure as hell wasn't interested in sticking around Jackson Hole, and he was here for the duration.

Curiosity, maybe. She'd never indulged herself with somebody like him and had decided now was as good a time as any.

But none of that mattered, because no matter what she had in mind, nothing would happen between them. Emmett's trust guaranteed that. Clay would sooner cut off his right arm than betray the man who'd encouraged him to be the person he was today.

EMILY WASN'T SURE how she managed to eat anything at all as the meal progressed, and several times she almost dumped food on herself. Sitting next to Clay was like surfing in a storm—exhilarating but dangerous. He'd showered and changed before coming to lunch, and she almost wished he hadn't. His pine-scented cologne was nice, but she preferred the raw energy of his sweat-soaked body.

She wasn't sure who was generating the most sexual heat as they sat side by side eating lunch, but she sensed that he was as turned on by her as she was by him. He was nervous about that, though, and she didn't blame him. He clearly idolized her father, and anyone with half a brain would be able to tell that Clay was a principled guy. He wouldn't want to do anything that would upset Emmett.

She didn't want to upset Emmett, either, so her fascination with Clay was a tricky business. As much as her dad wouldn't want Clay seducing her, conversely he wouldn't want her seducing Clay, especially if she didn't have any intention of sticking around. And she didn't.

Maybe on this visit she liked the ranch better than she had before, but that only meant she considered it a good vacation spot. There was really nothing for her to do here. She didn't possess the particular skill set that would make her a...what had her dad called Clay? A top hand.

No, she was a far cry from being a top hand. She still

hadn't figured out what she was good at. She loved to surf, but not enough to make a pro career out of it. Fashion design was out, and retail sales bored her to tears.

But she wouldn't solve her career dilemma hanging around the Last Chance. Once her visit was over, she'd return to her receptionist position at a medical complex in Santa Barbara. Maybe she'd go out with the cute doctor who kept asking her for a date. She hadn't been seriously involved with anyone since last year, when a surfing buddy had proposed.

She'd realized he was far more emotionally invested than she was and had gently turned him down. Besides, she had no business marrying someone when she didn't know where her life was headed. She wished she could be more focused, like Clay. Spending time with him this afternoon might give her some insights. At the very least, she'd be able to enjoy the sexual buzz they had going on.

As the meal ended and everybody stood to leave, Clay helped her from her chair—a gallant gesture she wasn't used to from the men she knew. "Thanks." She turned to him. "Do you have a cell phone?"

"Yes. Why?"

"I thought you could call me when you're ready for me to help you."

He grinned. "How about if I just come up to the house and get you?"

Oooh. Great smile. She curled her toes into the leather soles of her boots. "That works."

Emmett put an arm around her shoulders and kissed her on the forehead. "If you go riding later on, see if somebody will loan you a hat."

She glanced up at him. "Why do I need one?"

"For the most part, to keep you from being sunburned."

"Dad, I surf every weekend, and nobody wears a hat while they're on a surfboard. I have a good base tan and I have sunglasses. That's enough."

Her father looked over at Clay. "Would you see that she puts on a hat before she goes out? I know we have extras lying around somewhere."

"Excuse me." Emily inserted herself between the two men. "I will not be treated like an obstinate female who needs to be managed by the men who know more than she does."

Clay laughed. "Then don't be obstinate. Wear a hat."

"Why should I?" She was intrigued by the fact that he was joking with her instead of getting irritated. She liked that kind of easygoing attitude.

"Because you're at a higher altitude here than you're used to, so the ozone layer's thinner and you could still burn. Besides that, if you're going to help me this afternoon, you're going to sweat, and the hat will keep the sweat from running in your eyes. I suppose you could wear a do-rag, instead, but personally I think the hat would look better on you."

Well, then. She hadn't thought about the value of a hat as an accessory. She should have, after being conditioned in that direction for most of her twenty-seven years by her fashion-conscious mother. If Clay thought she'd look better in a hat, no further argument was needed.

She turned to Sarah, who had been standing to one side watching the action with obvious amusement. "Got a hat I might be able to borrow?"

Sarah nodded. "Come with me."

3

EMMETT GLANCED AT CLAY. "Look, I hope she won't be in your way this afternoon. I didn't ask what you had on your agenda."

And Clay wasn't at liberty to discuss that. "It'll be fine." He would make it so, regardless of his strong attraction to the golden California girl.

"I invited her to come with me so she could do some shopping—my treat, of course. To my surprise, she wanted to stay here, instead."

"Huh." That surprised Clay, too.

"I know. I thought she loved to shop. Three years ago when she came to the ranch, we made a couple of trips into Shoshone, but the stores there aren't what she's used to. So when I took her back to the airport, we built in extra time for her to browse through those fancy places in Jackson."

"She was here three years ago, then. I wondered how often she'd made it over."

Emmett looked sad. "Not often enough, but I can't blame her for that. It works both ways. Like I told her this morning, I could have made more trips to Santa Barbara."

"Yeah, but..." Clay thought of the freeways and the traffic snarls and grimaced.

"I don't relish that area, either. But until this time, I didn't think she relished staying on the ranch—yet she comes to see me, even so."

"What do you mean *until this time?*"

Emmett rubbed the back of his neck. "I took her on a tour of the barn, like always. In the past, she acted like that was no big deal. I could tell she liked the horses, but she wouldn't let herself really get into it. I figured her mother had brainwashed her pretty damned well. But this morning was different. Apparently she's starting to think for herself."

"That's great." Clay hoped the foreman wasn't making too much of a passing fancy on Emily's part. He didn't want the guy to get his hopes up that Emily would suddenly turn into a cowgirl.

"I know what you're thinking, son."

Clay's chest tightened with emotion. He loved having Emmett call him *son*, even though he knew that cowboys used that word loosely and Emmett probably didn't mean it in a literal sense. "I'm not thinking anything, Emmett," he said.

"Sure you are. You're thinking that I'm an old fool who imagines his daughter is going to magically fall in love with ranching."

Clay sighed. "You're not an old fool, but it would be only natural if you—"

"Don't worry. I made that mistake with her mother. I knew California was where Jeri wanted to be, but I thought I could convince her otherwise."

Something in Emmett's expression told Clay that those wounds had never healed. That might be another reason

Emmett hadn't taken many trips to see Emily. He would have had to see his ex, too, which would have been painful if he was still in love with her.

Clay thought he might be and wondered if Pam Mulholland had any inkling of that. The two had been dating for more than a year without making a commitment. Emmett said that was because Pam had way more money than he did, but that might not be the whole story.

By now the dining room was empty except for Clay, Emmett and Watson, who had recently started helping Mary Lou clear the dishes in exchange for extra dessert.

Mary Lou bustled over, her gray hair in disarray as usual and her cheeks pink from working in a warm kitchen. "Did you two get enough to eat? I'm about to serve Watson an extra piece of cherry pie, and you're welcome to have a second serving if you want one."

Emmett patted his flat stomach. "Thanks, Mary Lou, but I couldn't fit in another bite. You outdid yourself again."

"Thanks, Emmett." She beamed at the praise. "I do love my job. How about you, Clay? More pie?"

"It's tempting, but no thanks."

"All right, then." She began stacking the dessert plates from each place setting at their table.

Watkins came out of the kitchen and headed toward them. "Hey, quit doing my job, Lou-Lou."

Her cheeks turned a shade pinker. "Then speed it up there, Watkins. We need to get this place clean."

"We will, we will. Leave those for me and go cut me a nice big piece of your delicious pie. And put some ice cream on top." The stocky cowboy winked at her as he reached for the dishes in her hand.

"Oh, for heaven's sake. If you insist." She handed over the dishes and walked back toward the kitchen.

Instead of stacking plates, Watkins gazed after her. "What a woman."

Clay watched in fascination. He'd thought something might be going on between Watkins and Mary Lou, but he hadn't been sure until now. "Are you sweet on her, Watkins?"

Watkins nodded, which made his handlebar mustache twitch. "Have been for years. Once I tried to get her to marry me, but she claims she's never marrying anybody. So I backed off, but lately…let's just say I might be making progress."

Emmett clapped him on the shoulder. "Clearing dishes and complimenting her on her cooking just might get the job done. Not that I'm an expert on women. What's your opinion, Clay?"

Clay held up both hands. "Don't ask me about women. They're a mystery."

"Ain't that the truth." Watkins glanced toward the kitchen. "Well, my pie should be about ready. Catch you later, boys."

After he left, Clay looked at Emmett and raised his eyebrows.

Emmett shrugged. "He's been carrying a torch for a long time," he said in a low voice. "You may not believe it, but she used to be a real babe."

"You know, I can believe it. And I've always loved her spunky attitude. I—" He stopped talking when Emily walked into the room. Talk about a babe. The snug T-shirt and form-fitting jeans would make any guy take a second look, but Clay had a thing about women in cowboy hats.

This one was tan straw, a warm-weather alternative to felt. The brim curved downward in both the front and back so it partly shielded her eyes in a sexy, flirty way. The more Emily adopted a Western style, the more Clay liked what he saw.

"How's this?" she asked as she came toward them.

Clay dialed back his response several notches. "It'll do."

"Good choice." Emmett's weathered face glowed with pride. "Fits nice."

Sarah appeared and crossed to where they were standing. "Looks good, huh? Fortunately we wear the same size."

"Sarah said I could keep this," Emily said. "But that seems silly if I'm only going to wear it while I'm here."

Some of the glow faded from Emmett's expression, and Clay ached for him.

No matter what Emmett had said about not expecting too much, it was obvious he'd allowed himself to hope that Emily wouldn't abandon her newfound interest in the ranch once she left. He nodded. "Guess so. Wouldn't want to let a good hat end up in the back of a closet. Well, I'd better get going if I intend to finish up those errands in town."

"Oh, that reminds me." Sarah pulled a slip of paper from the pocket of her jeans. "Here are a few more things I need while you're there. Also, Pam called and asked if you'd stop by the Bunk & Grub, and I'd really appreciate it if you'd look in on my mother and make sure she remembers about the party tomorrow night."

Emmett looked over the list. Then he trained that piercing blue gaze on Sarah in a manner Clay knew well. It meant that Emmett suspected something was going on and he intended to find out what. "You wouldn't be stacking up the errands to keep me away from the ranch all afternoon because of some scheme or other, would you now, Sarah?"

"Goodness, no! Why would I do a thing like that?"

"Because I've known you for thirty-some years, and you look like you're up to something. I'm warning you, if I come back from town and a passel of folks jump out of the bushes yelling 'surprise,' I will be one unhappy cowhand."

Sarah patted his arm. "I promise that won't be happening. Besides, your birthday's tomorrow."

"Which means the only way you could surprise me is to stage the party tonight. I wouldn't put it past you, either."

"You are so suspicious." Sarah gave him a big smile. "You will love your birthday party, Emmett, and it will take place on your birthday, not the night before."

"Time will tell if you're putting me on or not. Anyway, I'll see you folks later, and there had better not be any shenanigans taking place while I'm gone." Settling his hat on his head, he left the dining room.

Sarah studied the beamed ceiling of the dining room and twiddled her thumbs as his footsteps receded down the hall leading to the living room. Only after the front door had opened and closed did she drop her gaze to Clay's and burst out laughing. "He's *such* a baby when it comes to birthdays."

"He knows something's going on," Clay said.

"What is it?" Emily looked eagerly from one to the other. "*Are* you going to surprise him tonight?"

"No." Sarah glanced over at the door to the dining

room as if worried that Emmett might have crept back down the hall. "Emily, go make sure he's left."

"Be right back." Emily hurried out of the dining room.

Sarah moved closer to Clay. "He really will love this cookout. But if he knew about it in advance, he'd pitch a fit because we're going to extra trouble on his behalf."

"You're right, he would."

"But it's going to be so perfect. I realized this morning that you'll need to dig two fire pits, one for the bonfire and one we can let burn down to coals for grilling the steaks."

"I can do that."

Emily came back in, her face pink with excitement. "He's really gone. So what are you planning?"

"Clay can explain it all. I need to go check with Watkins, if he's still in the kitchen. His guitar was missing a string and I need to make sure he's fixed it."

"He's still there," Clay said, "but you might want to knock before you go in."

"I *see*." Sarah grinned. "Thanks for the warning. Catch you two later. Call if you run into any glitches." Then she walked toward the kitchen. "Sarah Chance is on the move!" she called out. "If there's anything going on you don't want me to see, you'd better cease and desist immediately!"

Emily looked at Clay. "What the heck is that all about?"

"Just a little romance between Watkins and Mary Lou. Come on. We have tables and benches to load into the back of a pickup."

"Okay." She fell into step beside him as they headed down the hall lined with windows on the right and family pictures on the left. "This visit is turning out to be way more interesting than I expected."

That patronizing remark set his teeth on edge. Added to her comment about not needing the hat once she went home to California, he decided to broach the subject of her attitude. "You know, this ranch may not be your favorite place in the world, but could you pretend it is, for your dad's sake?"

She stopped in her tracks. "Wow. You are definitely hostile."

He spun to face her. "I suppose I am. I love that man like a father, and you—"

"I love him like a father, too. *My* father, in fact."

He wondered for the first time if she resented all the attention Emmett had devoted to him. "Point taken."

She gave him a brief nod, as if at least that much was settled. "Anyway, I don't want to give any impression that I might like to live in Wyoming. To me, that would be crueler than being honest about my feelings. My mother gave him that kind of false hope, and I think he's still hurting because of it."

Clay hated to admit it, but she made sense. He wished she loved ranching the way Emmett did, but if she didn't, pretending could possibly do more damage. He took a deep breath. "You're probably right. I apologize. I have no business sticking my nose in, anyway."

"Sure you do. You love him. And from the way he raves about you and your accomplishments, I think he loves you, too."

"He raves?"

"Oh, yes. He brags about the way you carefully saved your money for tuition and then worked odd jobs while you took classes in Cheyenne. He was so proud of your grade point average. And when you got that scholarship, he mentioned it to me several times."

Clay gazed at her as his understanding grew. "It's a wonder you don't hate my guts."

"At times I did, although I don't like admitting that. Besides, he was born to be a dad, and I haven't given him much chance at that. Knowing you were here relieved my feelings of guilt."

"Still, I'll bet you got tired of hearing about my accomplishments."

She shrugged. "It's hardly your fault that I'm not focused like you and can't for the life of me figure out a career. My dad's not likely to brag about my surfing ability, so that leaves him with nothing to boast about when it comes to his only child."

"Do you have a job?"

"Of course I have a job. How do you think I support myself?"

He decided not to mention that he'd been convinced she didn't support herself, that she was living off the money Emmett sent her every month. She might not appreciate knowing that most everyone at the Last Chance knew he sent checks and wondered why when he was no longer financially obligated. They all assumed Emily was living on that money, or at the very least, only working part-time to supplement his generosity.

But her finances and her job situation were absolutely none of his business. "I'm sorry," he said. "I was out of line starting this conversation in the first place, and we have a lot of work to do before your dad comes home. We should get going." He started back down the hall.

"Going where?" She lengthened her strides to keep up with him. "You still haven't told me the plan."

Briefly he outlined the details. He wondered if she'd find it hokey, but she responded with enthusiasm.

"That sounds like so much fun! Sometimes we have bonfires on the beach and cookouts, too. Usually some-body brings a docking station for their iPod instead of having live music, but a guitar player sounds terrific. Will there be dancing?"

"That's an excellent question. Knowing the Chance family, there should be dancing."

"Yay! I love to dance. I…just realized that I have no idea if my dad dances or not. I should know that, shouldn't I?"

"Not if you've never been around when dancing was part of the program." He reached the front door and opened it for her.

"Thanks." She tossed her hair back over her shoul-der and smiled at him. "I'm enjoying all the gallantry around here."

"Sarah insists on it, and besides, it's the cowboy way to show respect toward a woman." He stepped onto the porch and closed the door behind him. That's when he looked out at the circular drive and noticed her convert-ible, top still down, leather upholstery exposed to the sun.

He couldn't stand it. "Do you have your car keys with you?"

"No, but I can get them. Is my car in the way?"

"You can leave it there, but you need to put the top up. You'll ruin the leather seats."

"It's stuck."

He glanced over at her. "Permanently?"

"I don't know. I pulled over at a rest stop around eight last night and decided to put the top down for the rest of the way, so I'd be sure and stay awake. When I got here, it wouldn't go back up. I meant to say something to my dad this morning, but he was so excited about the barn tour and then I got interested, too. My convertible wasn't a top priority."

Once again, Clay had been guilty of assumptions. He needed to stop making them when it came to Emily. "We don't have time to fix it now, but if you'll get your keys, you can put it in the tractor barn so at least it's out of the sun. The tables and benches are stored down there, so drive on down and I'll meet you."

"Good idea." She glanced at the BMW. "It's eight years old, and things go wrong with it. My mom found it in the paper and thought I should have a classy car, but sometimes I think I'd be better off with something more practical."

Clay couldn't agree more, but he could tell the purchase had been more about pleasing her mother than pleasing herself. Emily Sterling didn't fit into the box he'd created for her, and that might put him on dangerous ground.

Ignoring her sexy body was one thing. Resisting a cry for help from someone who wasn't sure of her place in the world would be much more difficult. He'd been there, and no one should have to face that kind of insecurity alone.

4

EMILY FETCHED HER KEYS from her room and roasted her
fanny driving the convertible down to the tractor barn.
Maybe that was just as well. Searing her backside might
serve as a reminder that little girls who moved too close
to the fire could get burned.

No matter which way she looked at it, giving in to her
instincts with Clay wouldn't be a good thing. Oh, except
for the obvious, which involved glorious sex with a guy
who had *hero* written all over him. The catch was just
as obvious.

If her dad found out, no doubt he'd be disappointed
in her. She couldn't imagine that he'd condone a superficial fling with Clay, and that's all it would amount to.
She didn't want to disappoint her father any more than
she already had.

Even worse, he might be disappointed with the apple
of his eye, Clay Whitaker. The two men had a special
relationship, and she had the power to ruin it. No doubt
her dad had told Clay that a Wyoming man should steer
clear of a California girl. Emmett certainly wouldn't want
to see history repeating itself with his own daughter.

So she was faced with an afternoon in the company of a man she found wildly sexy, yet she couldn't do anything about it. To make matters even more complicated, he showed definite signs of a mutual attraction. She could tell by his heated looks, the tone of his voice and the occasional bulge in his jeans.

Knowing he didn't quite approve of her wasn't the turnoff for her that it should have been, either. No doubt about it, Clay would have preferred a cowgirl who fulfilled all of Emmett's unspoken dreams. Instead she was a city girl who spent her free time riding a surfboard instead of a horse.

Despite that, Clay wanted her, and Emily had the uncharitable urge to show him how a California surfer girl could destroy his control. Let him disapprove of her all he wanted—she'd bet that, given the opportunity, she could make him crazy with lust. It would be satisfying, indeed, if she could reduce him to begging for the chance to sink into her hot body.

She approached the large metal tractor barn. Clay had driven a dark blue pickup to the entrance and was letting down the tailgate as she drove past him. It was a simple task, so how come he looked so sexy doing it? She'd never made out in the bed of a pickup, but she wouldn't mind giving it a try with Clay.

By the time she pulled into the shadowed interior of the tractor barn, her hormones were dancing to a hip-hop beat and her noble intentions had taken a hike up the trail into the Grand Tetons. To hell with an uncomfortable truck bed. Her BMW was a four-passenger with a backseat, and she was ready to invite Clay to join her there. But that was *such* a bad idea.

Gripping the leather-wrapped steering wheel, she

closed her eyes and willed herself back to sanity. She'd driven here to celebrate her dad's sixtieth birthday, a major milestone. She would not muck it up by having sex with his protégé, no matter how yummy the guy was.

"Are you okay?"

She opened her eyes to find Mr. Yummy himself standing next to the driver's side of the car, his hat pushed back and his dark eyes filed with concern. For a split second she pictured telling him exactly what was on her mind, which involved getting naked and then squirming around on the warm leather upholstery of her car.

The tractor barn seemed empty of people other than the two of them, and if she'd judged their chemistry correctly, the event would be over in minutes with very little chance they'd be discovered *in flagrante delicto*. Of course, she wasn't figuring in birth control as part of this fantasy, and she didn't think Clay was the sort to be packing.

With a deep sigh, she gave up the whole concept. "I'm fine. The transition from the heat to the shade made me a little dizzy, is all."

He opened the car door for her and stood back. "You don't have to help me load the tables and benches. In fact, you don't have to help do any of this. I'll be back in a couple of hours and we can go riding then, if you still feel up to it."

"I want to help." She climbed out of the car and moved a safe distance away from him. As she'd suspected, they were very much alone in the cool and cavernous tractor barn.

"After all, this party is for my dad." She decided not to look directly at him and risk more eye contact. She was already on edge, and sexual tension wound tighter with every second they stood together inside the deserted barn. "Let's get started."

"Okay." His voice was suspiciously gruff. "You'll need these."

She had to look at him to find out what he meant by *these*. He was frowning as he held out a pair of leather work gloves.

That's when it occurred to her that he might not want to take her with him. She'd invited herself along, and with Sarah and Emmett jumping in to second the idea, he hadn't had much choice.

She didn't take the gloves. "Maybe I shouldn't go with you, after all. I don't know the routine and I might get in your way."

"But you said you wanted to."

"I know, but this isn't all about me. If my going will complicate things, then—"

"Take the gloves." His tone gentled. "I could use the help."

She hesitated a moment longer, and then decided that she really did want to be a part of setting up the party for her father. "All right. Thanks." She took the gloves and pulled them on. They were huge on her. Laughing, she held up both hands. "Look, Minnie Mouse."

He smiled. "Sorry. That's all I could find."

Instantly she was contrite. "I'm not complaining. I think it's sweet that you thought to give me gloves in the first place. They'll work fine." That's when she made the mistake of looking into his eyes, and the air went out of her lungs.

Oh…dear…God. She hadn't seen heat like that in… maybe she'd never seen heat like that. It was a wonder she didn't go up in flames. Parts of her felt as if they might combust at any moment.

Muttering a swear word under his breath, he dropped his gaze. "This is no good," he said, his voice husky.

"You're right. I won't go." She took off the gloves and held them out.

He lifted his head and looked at her. "That's not right, either."

"Sure it is." She shook the gloves. "Take these back, and I'll just go on up to the house."

He stared at the gloves. Then, with another muttered oath, he took them and tossed them into the front seat of her car.

"What on earth are you doing?"

"Making a mistake." He grasped both her wrists and drew her toward him.

She should have resisted. She didn't. Her heart beating furiously, she gulped as the distance between them grew smaller. "You don't want to do this."

"Oh, yes, I do." Releasing his hold on her wrist, he took off his hat. That went into the front seat, too, followed by her hat.

"But you said it's no good." She began to tremble.

"It isn't." Sliding his hand around her waist, he pulled her into his arms. "Tell me to stop and I'll stop."

She couldn't believe any woman on the planet had that kind of willpower, especially when said woman had fantasized about the body she was now plastered against. Gazing into dark eyes that promised a thousand delights, she wanted every single one. She spread her hands over his muscled chest and felt his quick intake of breath and the staccato beat of his heart.

"One kiss." She struggled to breathe normally. "Surely we can handle that without causing a major problem."

"Right." His head dipped lower. "Maybe we won't like it."

Fat chance. "Maybe not." Her eyes fluttered closed.

"At least we should find out." His warm breath caressed her lips.

"We should." Anticipation shot fire through her veins. "But what if we like it?"

"We'll worry about that later." His lips settled over hers.

Nice, she thought. *We fit.* He tasted of cherry pie and coffee. She sighed with pleasure, wrapped her arms around his neck and leaned into him. This would be a good kiss. This would be—whoa! He changed the angle and delved deeper. The kiss intensified until the word *nice* no longer applied. *Wicked,* maybe or *wild,* or…

No words. She had no words for what he was doing to her now. She opened wider, craving him as she'd never craved a man, demanding he give her more, and yet more…her nipples tightened and moisture gathered between her thighs. Digging her fingers into his shoulders, she arched against the bulge straining the fly of his jeans, and whimpered.

And then he stopped kissing her. Gasping, he held her tight and leaned his forehead against hers. "I was afraid of that."

"Kiss me again." She heard the plea in her voice and yet she couldn't help it. Sometime during the kiss she'd lost a sense of separateness, and now she could no longer tell whether the vibration she felt was her heart beating or his. She wanted to be caught up in the whirlwind once more, just once more.

He drew in a ragged breath. "If I kiss you again, we're going to end up naked on the nearest flat surface."

Her body hummed with excitement at the thought.

"And we both know that can't happen."

Slowly but inevitably, his words doused the fire raging inside her. Of course he was right. Loosening her grip on his broad shoulders, she eased out of his arms and took a couple of steps back.

She combed her fingers through her hair and flipped it over her shoulder as she gazed at him. "What now?"

Hands on his lean hips, he sent her an unhappy glance. "This is such a loaded situation that I don't even know where to start. Your dad trusts me. If I ended up seducing you, then—"

"Hold it right there, cowboy. I'm a big girl. That means no man is going to seduce me unless I want him to. The whole seduction issue cuts both ways. Let's say that *I* seduced *you*. That would be betraying my dad's trust, too, you know."

"I don't know how you figure that."

"Think about it. A beach-loving California girl gets involved with a dyed-in-the-wool Wyoming ranch hand. We know how that story turns out and so does my dad. He'd accuse me of being careless with the feelings of someone he loves like a son, someone who—" She stopped herself before she said "someone who was raised in a series of foster homes and probably has abandonment issues." He wouldn't appreciate her pop psychology evaluation.

Clay's smile was grim. "I'm a big boy. No woman seduces me unless I want her to."

She could almost see the shields going up around his heart. "That may be true, but my dad is not going to be

happy no matter who is the seducer and who is the se-
ducee. Both you and I know the story of his failed relationship, and he certainly expects us to be smarter than
that."

"I thought I was, but…" He made a sweeping gesture
with his hand. "You sorely tempt me, Emily Sterling."

"Ditto, Clay Whitaker." But if she hadn't fully considered it before, she now realized that a casual fling was
the last thing a man like Clay needed. He'd had enough
temporary relationships over the years. She didn't need
to add her name to the list.

"Emmett wouldn't be happy to know about this attraction," Clay said.

"No, he would not." Emily met his gaze. "I guess we
have to make sure he doesn't find out, which means no
more…no more…"

"Just no more," Clay said quietly. "No more, Emily.
Like you said, we know the story wouldn't turn out well."

No, it wouldn't, but she wanted to lighten the mood.
"That kiss was a humdinger, though."

"It was." He seemed to realize she wanted to end this
on a teasing note. "I was hoping you were a slobbery
kisser or that you would suck too hard on my tongue."

"You kissed me hoping I'd be bad at it? That's twisted."

He shrugged. "It would have solved my problem if
you'd been a lousy kisser."

"I see." She gave him a long look. "For the record, I
suck on tongues exactly the same way I suck on…other
things."

He let out a low groan. "Now *that* was a low blow."

"You're the one who calculatingly kissed me hoping I
would slobber on you or dislocate your tongue."

"I had to do something! You were driving me crazy

with that traffic-stopping figure of yours and your cute little Minnie Mouse impersonation. A guy can take only so much, you know."

Satisfied she'd established an appropriately light and breezy mood, she let it drop. "All right. Let's call a truce and get those tables and benches loaded."

"You still want to come out there with me?"

"Yes, I do. Now that we've had this experience, and we've talked everything out, we both understand how we need to behave toward each other."

He raised his eyebrows. "Oh? And how is that, exactly?"

"Friendly, but not too friendly, if you know what I mean."

"I might."

"Accomplishing this job together will prove that we can interact without any hanky-panky."

"Fine. But you're not allowed to talk about how good you are at sucking…things."

"I promise not to discuss my sucking expertise."

"Good. The tables and benches are right over here." He started off, his long strides putting distance between them as he headed for a corner of the barn.

She picked up their hats and her gloves from the front seat of her car and followed him. She hoped they'd averted a disaster. He'd swept her away with that kiss, and if he hadn't called a halt, no telling what would have happened.

Yes, he'd made the first move, but he was a guy. Guys were conditioned to make the first move. She hadn't stopped him, and she could have. She should have. Clay had the body of a Greek god, but he could also have a heart of glass. She'd do well to remember that.

EMILY TURNED OUT to be a good and efficient worker. She did her share of the loading and made a couple of good suggestions for how to fit everything in. Once again, she'd surprised him by pitching in so eagerly. If he didn't know about the monthly checks she took from Emmett, he'd think she was a great person, someone he'd like having for a friend.

Maybe he'd have an opportunity to ask about those checks because that was the piece of the puzzle he didn't understand. He couldn't blame her for preferring the beach to the ranch. She'd been raised to think that way. But taking money from her father when he obviously wasn't a wealthy man—that made no sense at all.

Thinking about her accepting financial aid helped a little bit as he tried to ignore the enticing little droplets of sweat that rolled down her throat and into her cleavage. He reminded himself about those checks when she leaned over the tailgate and stretched the denim covering her delicious backside. She didn't have to do anything special to turn him on. Just looking at her got him hot.

He shouldn't have kissed her. Then again, the kiss might have worked to his advantage if he hadn't enjoyed it. Just because a woman was beautiful didn't mean she could kiss worth a damn. At least that's how he'd justified what had probably been a stupid move on his part.

Now he knew that she could kiss. She'd also informed him she could do other things with her mouth, things that he didn't need to be thinking about. Of course he couldn't seem to think about anything else, especially when she stopped to drink water from the canteen he handed her and fit her mouth around the opening. Damn.

He'd focused on the task at hand as best he could, and at last the truck was loaded. While Emily filled up the canteens, he tucked a couple of shovels in the back. He didn't know if she'd want to help dig the fire pits, but he'd offer her the chance. She seemed to enjoy physical labor.

Too bad for Emmett's sake that she didn't like ranching, because she had the kind of attitude that made for a good hand. She cheerfully accepted hard work and adapted to whatever conditions she found herself in. She didn't seem to mind getting dirty, either, which totally surprised him.

As she walked back to the truck with both canteens slung over her shoulder, he moved around to the passenger side and opened the door for her.

She turned that wonderful smile on him. "That's just so nice, Clay," she said as she climbed in. "I didn't realize how much I like having a man hold my chair and open my door for me."

"Like I said, Sarah deserves the credit. She won't tolerate sloppy manners from the men on her ranch." He felt guilty being praised for gentlemanly behavior when he'd taken full advantage of his position by the door to enjoy the snug fit of her jeans as she climbed in.

Under the circumstances he should be treating her like a kid sister and avoiding any sexual thoughts whatsoever. Yeah, right. She'd turned him on the first time he'd met her, and nothing had changed. If anything, his attention had become more intense.

God, he should never have kissed her. What had he been thinking? He hadn't been thinking—that was the answer. He'd walked over to her car and seen her sitting in it with her eyes closed and her hands clenched around the steering wheel.

Instantly he'd worried that she was sick, and with Emmett gone, he was responsible for her well-being. But then she'd opened her eyes and he'd known right away that she wasn't sick. No, she was sexually aroused. And it didn't take a genius to know he was the lucky guy who'd created that situation.

They'd managed to feed each other's fires until he couldn't stand it another second. He shouldn't have reacted that way, and he should probably regret that he'd shoved aside his misgivings and kissed her. But he didn't regret it. That kiss was the way kisses should always be—a trip to the sun and back.

He made sure she was tucked inside before he closed the door of the truck. Then he walked around to the driver's side. He'd left the keys in the ignition, a common habit around the ranch. Sliding in behind the wheel, he began to understand the mess he was in.

Just sitting next to her in the cab was going to be torture. The air-conditioning didn't work in this truck, and the heat from her body amplified the impact of her perfume. A whiff of sea and sand mingled with the scent of a healthy, sexy woman to create an aromatic cocktail that could get him drunk in no time.

Maybe with the windows down, he'd manage to survive the trip without pulling over and reaching for her. He started the truck.

"How far away is the spot where we'll have the cookout?"

"Not far." But with her sitting right next to him, it might turn out to be the longest damn drive of his life.

5

"I DON'T THINK I've ever been on this road." Emily focused on the scenery, which somewhat distracted her from the virile cowboy in the driver's seat, the one she longed to kiss again, but would not.

So instead she admired the wildflowers that created a carpet of purple, yellow and white in the meadows they passed. She watched flocks of birds fly away at their approach and rabbits hop into the underbrush by the side of the road. She'd been on trail rides with her dad, but she'd been so determined not to like Wyoming that she'd missed its beauty.

Ahead of them, the snow that still remained on the summit of the Grand Tetons glittered in the sun. She'd never been here in the winter and had never tried skiing, although she had friends who loved it. She'd avoided finding anything positive about Jackson Hole, and that was a shame.

"Emmett never took you out to the sacred site?" Clay had to talk over the noise of the engine and the tables and benches rattling in the back.

"No, I would have remembered that." She felt sad

that her father hadn't mentioned the landmark, but she didn't blame him. She hadn't been particularly enthusiastic about any of the local attractions, so why should he? Maybe she was finally old enough to realize that she didn't have to keep harping on her love of all things California. By now, Emmett got it.

"This road leads to the site." Clay avoided a particularly deep rut. "We'll have the cookout in the meadow east of there."

"What's sacred about the place?"

"There's a big flat rock about the size of a parking space there. The stone is gray granite with white streaks of quartz through it."

"Sounds pretty."

"It is, especially when the sun or the moon shines on it. Then the quartz sparkles."

Emily laughed. "That works for me. I like shiny, sparkly things."

"We'll stop on the way back so you can take a look. Back when Archie and Nelsie were alive, the Shoshone Indians used to worship on that spot, so they've always been allowed on the property. But I don't think the Shoshone have been there for years."

"It's for religious services?"

"Well, not exactly."

"What, then?"

He glanced over at her. "According to the Shoshone legend, if you have an issue to resolve or uncertainties in your life, being on that rock will give you clarity. Morgan's parents—have you met Morgan?"

"Not yet. Tomorrow night I'm supposed to meet everyone."

"Anyway, her parents are into all the New Age stuff,

so Morgan knows about it, too. She says that quartz is supposed to be a powerful crystal."

"I've heard that. One of my surfer friends is into crystals." Emily could think of at least two issues she wouldn't mind having clarity on. Her purpose in life would be one. The other one was sitting next to her. "Have you ever tried it?"

He didn't answer right away, which told her that he probably had tried it and didn't want to admit that he had.

"It's okay," she said. "I'm from California, remember? The land of woo-woo. I just want to know if this rock works or not. I could use some clarity in my life."

"I came out here a few months after I'd landed the job working for the Chances. I wanted to know if it would last."

"The job?"

"I suppose, but I wanted to know more than that. A job was one thing. But I was starting to become attached to the people—Sarah, Jonathan, Emmett. I wanted to know if I'd finally…"

She sensed this had been an important moment for him and he didn't share it with many people. She felt honored he'd even considered sharing it with her. "Finally what?" she prompted gently.

He blew out a breath. "If I'd finally found a home."

Her heart ached for him. Of course he'd longed for some permanent place that would always welcome him. That was the thing he'd been denied his whole life. "Did…did the sacred site give you an answer?"

"Sort of. Something that had been knotted up in me seemed to relax, and I took that to be a good sign. Then a raven flew over and pooped on my shirt." He laughed. "I'm not sure what that was supposed to mean."

"That's easy. Shit happens."

"Maybe that was the message. Anyway, the Chance family, along with Emmett, have given me a home base, so whether the rock was telling me that or not, my life has worked out so far."

"I'm glad. You know, if my dad had been willing to move to Santa Barbara like my mother wanted him to, he wouldn't have been here when you came to the ranch."

He looked over at her. "You mean like that saying, that things happen for a reason?"

"Sort of, yeah."

"That hardly seems fair." He frowned. "I don't like the idea that you had to give him up so that I could have him."

She was tempted to say that Clay might have needed her dad more than she had, but she decided against it. No man liked to appear weaker than a woman, even psychologically. "In any case, if he couldn't be with me, then I'm glad he was here for you."

Clay drove along silently for several minutes. Finally he spoke again. "Do you believe that saying?"

"Which one?"

"That things happen for a reason."

She thought about it. "I guess I do. For the most part, anyway. Why?"

"Then please tell me why you and I have run into each other again this summer. If there's a reason besides torturing me with things I can't have, I'd love to know what it is."

He spoke with such feeling that she was taken aback. "Am I really torturing you?"

"Not on purpose, I'm sure. Wait, I take that back. Your comment about your sucking ability was absolutely on purpose, and I've been tortured by that ever since."

"I shouldn't have said that."

"So *now* you realize it, when it's too late to do anything about it."

She leaned back against the headrest and controlled the urge to smile as a very naughty idea came to her. "Maybe it's not really too late."

"Oh, yes, it is." His tone was heated and tinged with desperation. "In case you've forgotten, we've already had this discussion. From now on we're going to be friendly, but not *too* friendly. In other words, it's too late."

She couldn't stop herself from grinning. This could be a real adventure, something she'd never offered a man in quite this way before. And it wouldn't count as an actual fling. "Come on now, Clay. What's a little oral sex between friends?"

He swerved to the side of the road and hit the brakes so hard the load in back rumbled in protest. *"What?"*

She turned her head to look at him. "Think of it as a friendly gesture to keep you from going off the deep end. You just admitted that I'm torturing you."

"Yeah, but—"

"Since it's my fault for putting that thought in your mind and now you're struggling with sexual frustration, then it seems only fair that I relieve your condition so that you can continue on about your business."

He stared at her, his eagerness evident in the strained fabric of his jeans, but his gaze wary. "What…what about our plan not to get involved with each other?"

"I'm not proposing marriage, or even an affair." The more she thought about this, the more she liked the idea. "I'm simply offering an answer to your problem. Nobody ever has to know."

"I can't believe you're saying this."

"Can you believe I would do it?"

His breathing quickened. "Yes, I sure as hell can, and that's what's driving me insane. I've had an X-rated movie going in my head ever since you broached the subject in the barn."

Taking off her hat, she set it on the dash. Then she unbuckled her seat belt and turned toward him. "I should never have teased you with that remark. Let me make it up to you."

"I'm not sure this is a good idea."

She glanced at his crotch. "You're being outvoted."

"No surprise there." His chest heaved as he dragged in a breath.

"It's a reasonable solution." She rested her hand on his thigh and felt the muscles bunch. Excitement churned through her at the thought of what she wanted to do. "And it won't take long."

He closed his eyes and leaned his head back. "That's a given."

Slowly, as if approaching a wild animal, she reached for his zipper. "You need this, Clay."

"Yes," he murmured. As the zipper rasped in the stillness, he groaned. *"Yes."*

HE COULDN'T BELIEVE he was allowing her to do this, but the way she'd explained it made some crazy kind of sense. She *was* responsible for his inflamed state, and she'd suggested helping him out by performing exactly what she'd hinted was her specialty. If he didn't take that pleasure now, he'd never have another chance.

She was right that no one ever had to know. He'd suffer through slivers under his fingernails before he'd tell anybody about *this*. He squeezed his eyes shut and groaned as she fumbled her way through the unveiling, and then…oh, man.

This was frickin' *incredible*. Her warm fingers wrapped around what felt like the most intense hard-on he'd ever had in his life. She'd volunteered to ease his pain, and only an idiot would pass up the opportunity.

Grateful didn't even begin to describe his state of mind. But when her breath whispered across the head of his cock, he had no state of mind. He had no mind, period.

He braced himself for contact, tightening his hands into fists and clenching his jaw. He'd always prided himself on his control, and he'd need every bit of it when she…ahhh…heaven. Her tongue. Licking. Stroking. Teasing. So good, so very, very…*good*. She deserved those bragging rights.

Someone moaned. Could've been him. He wanted to open his eyes. Didn't dare. And yet, he wanted to see, wanted the visual. To keep forever.

Had to risk it. Had to look. Holding his breath, he watched the golden top of her head as she lowered her mouth down over his cock. Her hair curtained her face, tickling him as she lifted up again, curling into her mouth, getting in her way.

She pushed the damp strands away. Then she tried to pull her hair back with her free hand, but it wouldn't stay. She made an impatient sound low in her throat.

The vibration from that sound nearly made him come, but he conquered the urge, because he knew what needed to be done. Unclenching both fists, he scooped her silky hair back and held it at the nape of her neck.

And now…now he could watch. Her cheeks hollowed and her eyelashes fluttered as she moved rhythmically up and down, up and down, up…his control slipped a notch…and down…up…she did something with her tongue and he gasped…down…once more…and up… blood rushed in his ears…*now.*

With a ragged cry, he came, his cock pulsing inside her warm mouth. She sucked more vigorously as she swallowed, and swallowed again. Pleasure rolled over him in waves so strong he was afraid he might pass out.

But he didn't, and gradually the world came into focus and he slumped against the seat. A raven perched on the hood of the truck and stared at him. Good thing a bird hadn't flown in the open windows of the cab, although he might not have noticed. A bear could have tried to climb in and he might not have noticed.

Emily released him gently with lingering kisses, and then she tucked his johnson carefully back into his jeans. He realized he was still gripping her hair, caveman style. He let go and she sat up.

"Emily, that—" He sounded like a rusty hinge, so he cleared his throat and tried again. "That was unbelievable."

She smiled and combed her hair back from her face. Her green eyes sparkled and her lipstick was gone, but her mouth was rosy from all that activity. "Better, now?"

"You have no idea."

"See how easy that was? Problem solved, and nobody has to be the wiser."

"You can damned well count on me not to say anything." Now that he was recovering from his state of bliss, he noticed that although his breathing had returned to normal, hers hadn't. The rapid rise and fall of her breasts brought his attention to another fact—under her T-shirt and bra, her nipples were standing at attention.

"My lips are sealed," she said. "It's our little secret."

Intrigued with his new thought, he studied her. Her cheeks were flushed and when his glance traveled over her, she shivered slightly. "Emily, I'm thinking that by solving my problem, you've created one for yourself."

"What do you mean?"

"Maybe now you're the one jacked up on sexual frustration."

She waved a hand dismissively. "Maybe just a little. No problemo."

"That's not fair. Do you want me to—"

"No!" She drew back against the door. "I mean, no, thank you, although it's kind of you to offer."

"It's not kindness that prompted me. I want to." Now that he understood what had happened, his fingers itched to slide inside her panties and return the favor.

"It's a bad idea. One little episode like we just had can be pushed under the rug. Making out all afternoon—not so much. We could slide right into a full-blown affair if we're not careful, and the more we get involved, the more likely we'll be found out. Besides, we have work to do."

"That's a fact. But if we skip the horseback ride, then we'd have time for me to even the score." And he'd love to do that. Giving her a climax now seemed like a most excellent concept, and no one would ever have to know about that, either.

She shook her head. "We're already even. I created a problem for you and now I've taken care of it. We need to move on."

"What's the matter? Are you afraid to let me see you lose control the way I just did?"

"Of course not! I'm trying to minimize our involvement. Anyway, giving a guy an orgasm just involves unzipping his pants. With a woman it's more complicated."

"Not really." He was growing impatient with her stubborn refusal.

"It is, too, more complicated. Your…equipment is all external. Mine's internal."

"Insignificant details."

"Anatomically speaking, it's not insignificant at all."

"Practically speaking, it is. I might have to unfasten your belt and unbutton your jeans, but that takes no time. I'm a cowboy. I know my way around a pair of women's britches."

"I'm sure you do."

"All I need is room to maneuver." He gave her a lazy smile. "If you'd said yes five minutes ago instead of arguing with me, you'd be having an orgasm right now." He watched the pupils in her eyes dilate as desire gripped her. "What do you say?"

"No." She swallowed. "Please start the truck."

"I think you'd really like it."

"That's not the point. We need to draw the line somewhere. What's done is done, and we can put it behind us and forget about it."

He stared at her in disbelief. "You expect me to forget about it?"

"Why not? It was one quick climax to lower your stress level, not much different from a sneeze or a cough. No big deal."

"*A sneeze or a cough?* You're kidding, right?"

"Studies have shown that a good sneeze is very similar to—"

"You're seriously telling me that you'd just as soon sneeze as come?"

She looked away, her color high. "Well, that may be a slight exaggeration. My only point is that a climax isn't that big a deal."

"If you say so." He straightened and reached for the ignition. "But then, I'm willing to bet you've never had one courtesy of a cowboy."

6

EMILY HAD PLENTY of time to think about cowboys and climaxes during the next two hours. After she and Clay unloaded the tables and benches, they collected piles of rocks to line the fire pits. Then she threw herself into the job of digging the smaller one in hopes the sweaty labor would eliminate her desire for sex with the gorgeous guy working a few yards away.

No dice. While shoveling, she tried to distract herself by concentrating on her natural environment. But the scent of warm grass and the distant gurgle of a creek only reminded her that she was alone in this glorious place with a man who'd offered to give her pleasure. Even though she wouldn't allow herself to look directly at him, she was aware of every move he made.

Finally, when the pit seemed deep enough, she laid down her shovel and rewarded herself with a quick glance in Clay's direction. Oh, dear God. He'd taken off his shirt.

Considering his parting shot, he'd probably done it on purpose. She couldn't be sure of that, because it was hot work. If she could have taken off her shirt she would have. Women weren't given the same leeway to strip down, though, and that left her overheated both inside and out.

A smart woman would save herself some grief by turning away from the rhythmic flex of biceps, pecs and delts every time Clay drove his shovel into the ground. Emily wasn't very smart since she couldn't stop staring. Obviously he'd worked shirtless at other times over the summer, because his skin had been kissed to a golden hue by the Wyoming sun.

Tossing his shovel aside, he began lining the pit with rocks, which meant he had to lean down. A lot. Each time, the soft denim of his jeans pulled tight across his picture-perfect ass.

Emily tingled all over. *Oh, baby.*

As if sensing her ogling, he looked at her, his face shadowed by his hat brim, his expression unreadable. "Tired?"

Tired of being noble. "A little bit, I guess."

"Then take a break. You've done plenty, and I can finish up with the rocks. Go on over to the truck and relax."

"Maybe I will." But if she stopped working she'd have nothing to do but watch him, and that wouldn't help her condition at all. She pointed to a faint set of tire tracks leading toward the line of trees. "Does this go to the creek?"

"Yep. If you can hang on for a few more minutes, I'll drive us over there and you can splash some cool water on your face."

Her face wasn't the main area that needed cool water, but she wasn't about to tell him. "If you don't mind, I'll walk on over now."

He shrugged. "Suit yourself. Just follow the tracks and they'll take you straight to the bank of the creek.

I'll pick you up when I'm done. And thanks for all your help, Emily. You're a hard worker."

"You sound surprised."

"To be honest, I am a little bit surprised."

That irritated her. He might be yummilicious with his bronzed shoulders gleaming in the sun, but she couldn't let him get away with insulting her. "Look, I may not have a college degree and a career plan, but that doesn't mean I don't know how to work."

"It's not about school or jobs. It's…" He paused, braced his hands on his hips and blew out a breath.

"Spit it out, cowboy. You've come this far, so you might as well get it off your chest." *Your incredibly muscled chest.*

"Hell, this is none of my damned business, but I like you, and I can't figure out why, when you're perfectly capable of supporting yourself, you still take money from your dad every month."

She stared at him. "What in hell are you talking about?"

"I'm talking about the checks he sends you. That money might seem like nothing to you, but it's a good portion of his paycheck."

She folded her arms, so ready to take this cowboy down several notches. "You have no idea what you're talking about. That money doesn't come out of his paycheck. It's part of my inheritance from my grandparents."

He hesitated for a moment, but then he shook his head. "That can't be right. The ranch is a small place. Somebody would know about an inheritance."

"He's a private man. Which brings up my first question. How do you know he sends me money? Are you two so close that he confides all his financial secrets?"

She didn't like the idea that Clay was privy to things even she didn't know.

"It's not just me. We all know. Even though he gets a decent salary, he never has spare cash, and it didn't take a genius to figure out he was still mailing checks to California."

She went from angry to horrified. "Are you saying that everyone at the Last Chance thinks I'm sponging off my father?"

"Well, yeah, but—"

"That's *awful!* I'm surprised anyone's nice to me."

His voice gentled. "They're nice to you because of Emmett."

She closed her eyes in dismay. Then slowly she opened them again. "And I suppose no one has thought to tell my dad that they think his daughter is a spoiled brat who's soaking him."

"Of course not. Why would we? That's why I asked you about it. You don't seem like the kind of person who would do that."

"I'm not that kind of person! It's an inheritance!"

"How do you know that?"

"Because he told me. Are you now claiming my father's a liar?"

"No, I'm not. But it doesn't add up, Emily. The guy never has extra money, and it seems like his parents would have left him something, too, especially if they trusted him enough to manage your inheritance."

She wished his logic didn't make so much sense. "He's not the type to spend on himself, that's all. Maybe he's tucked his portion away in a bank."

"I don't think so."

"And I don't think you're qualified to have that opinion, unless you've been peeking at his bank statements."

Clay sighed. "I haven't, and neither has anyone else. But we all know that he refuses to marry Pam Mulholland because she has more money than he does, so if he has some inheritance stashed away, then—"

"They're that serious?" Emily's stomach tightened. Sure, her parents had the right to find somebody else, especially after all these years, but again, that was logic talking.

"I think they might be in love, if that's what you mean. But your dad's old-fashioned, and doesn't like the idea of marrying somebody who's better off financially."

"This is crazy. None of it makes sense."

He stepped closer. "I can see you're upset, and I'm sorry. But I couldn't keep quiet after the way you've been working this afternoon. Your actions don't fit the reputation you have around here."

"Thank you." The concern in his dark eyes comforted her, but the nearness of his sweaty, virile body threatened to obliterate her good sense. She had a sudden vivid image of sex on a picnic table. That was a bad idea on so many levels, with the most obvious one being a lack of birth control.

He gave her a wry smile. "You know, in some ways it would have been easier on me if you'd been a brat."

"Sorry to disappoint you." She'd better get out of here before the chemistry between them took complete control of the situation. "Listen, I'm going to walk to the creek and think about this. I obviously need to have a discussion with my dad, but—"

"Tomorrow's his birthday."

"Right. I mean, maybe there really is an inheritance,

but I tend to think you're right that he made it up, for whatever reason. Confronting him with this won't be easy for either him or me."

"No, probably not." His voice was rich with compassion.

Hearing that compassion was a turn-on. Or maybe hearing him recite the alphabet would be a turn-on. Still, he was the only sounding board she had right now, and listening to his reaction might help her figure out what to do.

"There's something else," she said. "I've banked all the money instead of spending it."

"All of it?"

"Yes." She peered up at him. "Is that so hard to believe?"

"It shouldn't be, now that I know you better, but I would have expected you to spend at least part of it."

"So will he, and he may be upset that I haven't. But at eighteen I had no clue what I wanted to do with my life. At twenty-seven, I still don't know. I wanted to save the money until I had a better chance of spending it wisely, whether it's for a college degree or to start my own business."

"You must have a fair amount tucked away by now."

This part of her life she could be proud of. "I seem to have a knack for investing, so I've done well with what he's sent me over the years." She paused. "But I'm not sure how he'll take any of this, so can we…can we keep this conversation just between us for now?"

He nodded. "That's a given. But don't you want to set the record straight with everyone at the ranch?"

"I'd love to, but my dad comes ahead of worrying

about what everyone else thinks of me, so I want to proceed with care."

"Understood."

"All right, then." She resisted the urge to touch him. Even a small gesture like putting her hand on his arm could ignite the passion smoldering just beneath the surface of their seemingly calm discussion. "Are you sure you don't need me to stay and help finish up with the rocks?"

"I'm sure. Take some time alone to think this through."

"Okay. See you soon." She turned and began walking down the widest of the two tire tracks through the meadow.

"I'll drive over shortly," he called after her.

"Thanks!" She hoped that by the time he did, she'd have some plan for dealing with her father. But she also needed a plan to deal with Clay.

Now she realized why he'd had that prickly edge to him. He hadn't liked being attracted to someone he didn't approve of. Now that he knew she wasn't taking advantage of Emmett, he had no reason to dislike her. As he'd said, she'd made it tougher for him.

Tougher for herself, too. Still, they might make it through without giving in to their feelings for each other. As he'd said before, he didn't want to risk damaging his relationship with Emmett. Besides, she was no psychologist, but she had to believe that, as a former foster kid, Clay would want to avoid anyone who was guaranteed to leave him.

Those two issues loomed larger the more distance she put between her and the dark-eyed cowboy. Their problems arose when they spent too much time near each other, and the concerns that should keep them apart…

didn't. She couldn't do much to prevent their close proximity for the next hour or so, but once they'd returned to
the ranch, she'd keep out of the danger zone.

She reached the trees about the time she had that
thought, and stepped gratefully into the shade. She
caught the flash of a sunlit patch of water through
the maze of trunks and headed for the liquid sound the
creek made as it slid over rocks and fallen branches.
Somewhere she'd read that cascading water gave people
a more positive outlook.

Maybe the creek would help her mood as she considered how to broach the money subject with her dad.
She'd wait until the day after his birthday, though. He'd
probably be embarrassed that he'd been caught in a lie
he'd been telling her for nine years.

She wasn't sure what had motivated him to disguise
the checks as an inheritance, but she could guess. He
wanted to guarantee that she'd take the money without guilt. Her dad knew all about guilt. Apparently he'd
blamed himself for being an absentee father, and sending
her money every month soothed his conscience.

But when he found out that she'd touched none of it,
how would that affect him? She didn't know for sure,
but she was afraid he'd take it as a rejection of his loving gesture. And all the guilt he'd sloughed off as a result of sending those checks would come roaring back.

No, she couldn't bring up the subject until after his
birthday. Sarah had gone to a great deal of trouble to
make the celebration special, and Emily would be a
most ungrateful houseguest to ride in and spoil it all.
That would show her to be easily as selfish as everyone
thought she was.

She reached the creek and sat down on a fallen log to

take off her boots. Until today she hadn't worn them for more than five minutes, and they weren't broken in. Dangling her feet in the water seemed like an excellent idea.

Leaving her boots and her borrowed hat by the log, she looked for a place on the bank that would allow her to sit, but no log or branch had fallen into a convenient position and the rocks were wet. If she wanted to put her feet in the water, she'd have to wade in. So be it. She rolled up her jeans and edged down the embankment.

She gasped as her toes made contact with the icy creek, but as a surfer, she could take the cold. She also had excellent balance, so standing on smooth stones while the water rippled around her was child's play.

As she congratulated herself on solving her problem of achy, sore feet, she glanced across the creek—which was only about as wide as an average hotel room—and came eyeball-to-eyeball with an SUV-sized bull moose. At least, she assumed it was a bull moose. He looked a little bit like Bullwinkle, and his antlers could have served as a coatrack for a family of six, which probably meant this was a male.

She stood very still, and so did the moose. He seemed as surprised to meet her as she was to meet him, but Emily thought the moose had the advantage in this encounter. She vaguely remembered news stories of people being trampled by a large moose, but hadn't that been in Alaska?

This was a Wyoming moose, and she could hope that they were friendlier. Maybe the only thing this guy wanted was a cold drink. So far as she was concerned, he could drain the creek dry. She would just stand there, not moving.

The moose, however, didn't seem willing to stay on

his side of the stream. When he stepped into the water with what Emily now viewed as killer hooves, she panicked and tried to move backward on the slippery rocks. She went down in a very ungraceful sideways move that tossed her into deeper water.

That could be a good thing. A moose might not be able to trample her to death in three feet of water. Still, she could certainly drown in that depth if she didn't get her head out soon.

Flailing to the surface might not be wise with Bullwinkle around, but she had this little issue of breathing. Grabbing at mossy rocks, she managed to get her head up far enough to gulp for air and take a quick moose survey. No Bullwinkle.

Getting out of the creek while wearing soggy jeans and a T-shirt was tricky, but she managed it right as Clay appeared. Of course he'd show up while she was in the middle of making a fool of herself. He'd put his shirt on but hadn't fastened the snaps, so his glorious chest was still fully visible when he hurried forward and the breeze caught and parted the material.

"What happened?" He offered his hand to help her up the embankment.

"Would you believe I was pushed by a moose?"

"I thought I heard something crashing through the trees when I got out of the truck. You must have scared the hell out of him."

"Oh, yeah." Emily found solid footing and paused to shove her dripping hair out of her eyes. "I had him on the run, no question."

Clay released her hand and stepped back to survey the damage. "I have a blanket in the truck."

"That would be nice." A blanket sounded good right

now, but it could lead to…several things. She decided not to think about the various options, for fear she'd become invested in one of those outcomes.

Now that she was out of the water, her clammy clothes felt icky and cold. If Clay hadn't been right there, she would have peeled them off, but she wasn't supposed to be doing anything that could be construed as sexual. Removing clothes could easily be interpreted as an invitation.

In truth, she wouldn't mind making such an invitation, if only her conscience would check out for a while. She was shivery and he looked warm and cozy. More than that, she could tell by the gleam in his eyes that he still wanted her, and that was reassuring, considering that she must look like a bedraggled mess.

He gazed at her a moment longer, and then glanced around. "Where are your boots and hat?"

"Over by that log." She pointed to the spot, but her wet jeans were so heavy she felt cemented to the ground.

As if he understood that completely, he walked over and grabbed her stuff. "Hold these."

She took everything, and before she realized what he had in mind, he'd swept her dripping self up in his arms and moved off through the trees as if he carried women all the time. She felt silly being thrilled by such a macho gesture, but her romantic, little heart loved it.

Still, she was a modern woman with modern sensibilities. "You don't have to do this," she said as he tromped through the underbrush, crushing leaves and twigs under his boots. "I can walk."

"No, you can't. Going barefoot in the forest is a really bad idea, and your jeans are so wet you'd probably stain the leather of those top-of-the-line Ropers. I can't stand to see a good pair of boots suffer."

She laughed. "So this has nothing to do with me and everything to do with my boots."

"Oh, I wouldn't say that."

"Meaning?"

"Meaning that once I get you to the truck, you'll want to take off those wet clothes and wrap up in the blanket. I have a strong suspicion that somewhere in that process, we're going to get very friendly."

Desire slammed into her with the force of a medicine ball in the gut. She glanced up at him, but all she could see was his very determined profile. "That's not a good idea."

"Probably not, but there's an air of inevitability about it. Besides, no one should go through life believing that an orgasm is no different than a sneeze. That's just pitiful."

7

CLAY HAD APPROACHED the creek with the best of intentions. Emily was absolutely right that any sexual move on his part would raise the stakes. In the afterglow of the amazing climax she'd given him, he hadn't cared. But digging a fire pit and hauling rocks tended to steady a guy and help him face reality.

In his case, facing reality meant staying away from Emily Sterling. Now that he had his degree and a great job, he was ripe for commitment, but his dream girl would love ranching and specifically love the Last Chance. Sarah Chance had already told Clay that he could have a little plot of ranch land whenever the domestic urge hit.

He could see that day coming soon, although he hadn't dated anyone since moving back to Jackson Hole. He might want to remedy that so that he wouldn't be susceptible to a beautiful woman like Emily—the wrong woman who'd shown up at the right time.

His mind had been clear and focused until he'd arrived to discover that she'd fallen into the damn creek. His mind was still clear, but it was focused on an entirely different goal. As he carried her back to where he'd parked the truck, he tried to imagine getting through the next thirty minutes without touching her naked body. Sadly, he wasn't that strong.

If only she didn't want him as much as he wanted her, then maybe he could have ignored this opportunity. But she did want him. He could tell by the way she wrapped her free arm around his shoulders and pressed her body close. Her heat penetrated her wet clothes so thoroughly that he wouldn't be surprised to see steam rising as he strode through the woods.

"I'm turning into a lot of trouble, huh?" She shifted her weight and snuggled against him.

He stifled a groan as his cock responded. "Yeah, you sure are."

"Would you believe I drove over here to spread sunshine and love?"

"Yep." The navy blue pickup came into view. "You spread quite a bit of it when you unzipped my jeans this afternoon."

"You're really not going to forget that, are you?"

"Never."

"Never? Oh, come on. Aren't you being a little too dramatic?"

He walked around to the back of the truck. "Emily, a guy might forget a woman's birthday or the loaf of bread he was supposed to bring home from the store, but he'll never forget a spectacular blow job."

"Oh."

"That's my Guide to Guys tip for the day." He paused at the rear of the truck. "Now just sit tight on the bumper while I get the blanket." He eased her down to the chrome-plated surface. "Is it too hot?"

"No, actually, it feels good."

He imagined warmth working itself through her wet jeans to the part of her body he was personally focused on. The warm bumper might give her a jump start on pleasure. "I'll take your boots and hat."

She handed them over and glanced up at him, her green eyes mischievous. "So it was spectacular, huh?"

He met her gaze. "You've set the bar pretty high, but that's okay. I'm up to the challenge." As he walked around to the cab and deposited her hat and boots inside, he wondered if she'd been able to tell that he was just plain *up*, period. The prospect of caressing her until she came apart in his arms was causing his johnson some discomfort, but without condoms, he'd have to ignore that side effect.

"I've never agreed to a thing, you know," she called out from her perch. "I can ride home in the truck bed so I won't get the seat wet. No blanket required."

He took that for token resistance and grabbed the old wool blanket from behind the seat. "Emmett would never forgive me." He carried the blanket to the back of the truck. "But it's up to you. Is that what you want?"

She'd finger-combed her wet hair and she looked like the winning contestant in a wet T-shirt contest. For all the good her bra and shirt were doing her, she might as well be naked. That idea sounded good to him.

"I don't want to get you in trouble with my dad," she said. "Or get me in trouble, either, for that matter. Let's face it, I'm here for the short term. With your...background, that makes me a liability to...to your mental health."

Clay sighed. "So you're worried about me because I was a poor foster kid, is that it?"

"Well...yeah."

"Do me a favor and forget that, okay? I'm not an emo-tional cripple, and I can handle this situation just fine."

She gazed at him. "All right."

"So now we're back to you. What do *you* want?"

"What I want is to get out of these miserable clothes ASAP. But even if I take them off now, they won't magi-cally get dry in time, so what have I gained?"

He smiled. "Something I can guarantee you'll never forget, either."

"You're incorrigible." Her reprimand didn't have much punch to it, especially considering the glow of excitement in her green eyes. "You and I both know I can't go back to the ranch wearing nothing but a blanket." She swung her bare feet back and forth.

He noticed purple toenail polish and realized he liked that she was playful when it came to such things. "Sure you can, especially if you have on underwear. And in this heat, your bra and panties will dry in no time."

"You mean while I'm wearing them?"

He didn't mean that and she damn well knew it, but he'd play the game. "They'll dry a hell of a lot faster draped over the tailgate." He held her gaze so that she wouldn't mistake his meaning. While her underwear dried, he'd be doing his level best to make her very, very wet.

"You're seriously suggesting I walk back into the house wrapped in a blanket?"

"Why not? You fell in the creek and then used the blanket to protect your modesty while you took off your shirt and jeans so you wouldn't get the upholstery all wet."

"And you think everyone will buy that?"

"In the first place, you might be lucky enough to

make it upstairs without being seen. Even if you are seen, it won't matter as long as you treat it like an accident you had to handle in the best way you could. But I can guarantee that if I haul you home in the back of the pickup, I'll hear about it from your dad. That's not how a cowboy treats a lady."

She studied him for several seconds. At last she seemed to come to a decision. "How does a cowboy treat a lady?"

He let out a long, slow breath. "Let me show you."

"But what if somebody comes?"

He just grinned. No need to say a single thing.

"I didn't mean it like *that*. What if somebody shows up here while we're…involved?"

His heart hammered in anticipation. She was considering it. "Highly unlikely."

"Then…yes."

Glory, hallelujah, he'd won. He might regret this later, but at the moment he was filled with jubilation. She would go along with the plan, and his insides did a victory dance. He started forward, but she held up her hand like a traffic cop.

"I'll take care of the beginning stages." She reached for the hem of her T-shirt and, to his delight, peeled it off over her head. Because the shirt was so wet, he'd known in advance that her bra was a white lacy affair that offered a tantalizing glimpse of her nipples, tight as wild raspberries under the confining lace.

Even so, his heart hammered at the prospect of touching her there, of drawing a taut nipple into his mouth and rolling it with his tongue… He was so mesmerized by the prospect that he almost missed the T-shirt when she tossed it at him. But he'd played basketball at a community youth center when he was a kid, and his reflexes were still decent. He caught the wadded-up shirt in one hand.

"It feels so great to have that gone!" She stretched her arms over her head. "Now for the jeans. If I stand on the bumper, will you help me get them off?"

He laughed. "Oh, yeah." He realized that somehow she'd managed to turn the tables on him. He'd intended to seduce her, but it seemed to be going the other way. "But stand on the same spot where you've been sitting, so the chrome won't be so hot."

"Good idea." Swinging her legs up onto the bumper, she took hold of the tailgate and pulled herself to a standing position with her back to him. "I'm steadier turned this way. If I hold on, can you just—"

"You bet. Glad to help." Laying the folded blanket on the end of the bumper and his hat on top of that, he reached around and worked at the metal button, that didn't want to go through the wet buttonhole.

"If you'll hold on to me, I can try," she said.

"Nope. I've about got it. There it goes." He took hold of the zipper, which wasn't easy to deal with, either, but at last he was able to slide the jeans over her hips.

Only thing was, her panties wanted to come along for the ride. What the hell. She'd planned to take them off anyway.

As he exposed her smooth skin, she sucked in a breath.

"Can't help it," he muttered. "Everything's stuck together."

"Mmm."

His pulse quickened. She had such a curvy, tempting backside. Before he'd quite realized what he intended to do, he'd leaned over and pressed his mouth against her cool skin.

"Clay…"

He couldn't tell whether she'd said his name as a protest or a plea. But when he flicked his tongue over the same spot, she whimpered in a way that removed all doubt. Green light. He nibbled and kissed his way across the small of her back as he moved to her other silken cheek.

The scent of arousal called to him, and he slipped his hand between her thighs. She was still trapped in her jeans, so he didn't have much room to maneuver, but he couldn't resist. There. He found her moist entrance and her hot trigger point.

Her ragged breathing told him that he could make her come in seconds. But that wasn't his plan. He didn't want her to climax while tangled in wet denim. So he teased her lightly, all the while placing kisses on her delicious bottom. Then he withdrew his hand and savored the impatient noise she made in the back of her throat.

"Not yet," he murmured as he peeled her jeans and panties down to her ankles. "Step out."

She did, and he shoved them aside. They fell on the ground, but he was past caring about that. "Turn around. I'll help you."

He steadied her by holding on to her waist as she pivoted on one bare foot and found purchase with the other. He would never forget the sight of her purple toenails as she braced her feet on the chrome bumper.

Slowly his gaze traveled upward, past her tanned, shapely legs to a spot that had never seen the sun, the golden triangle that marked his ultimate destination.

She swallowed. "Clay, I'm feeling a little shy. Maybe we should—"

"Shh. Let me look. You're so beautiful, Emily." Her decision to stand on the bumper had accidental benefits he hadn't realized until now. By reaching back to grasp the tailgate, she'd angled her lace-covered breasts forward, and they were at the perfect level.

Heart racing with excitement, he glanced up at her. "Now this is what I call a tailgate party."

Her shallow breathing and flushed cheeks revealed her excitement, even though she frowned at him. "So help me, Clay, if someone shows up I'll kill you."

Holding her gaze, he unfastened the front clasp of her bra. "Want to move into the cab?"

"Yes…" She moaned as he smoothed back the lace and cradled her breasts in both hands. "No…I don't know."

He began a slow massage as he leaned in to kiss her full lips. "When you do, tell me."

Her eager welcome was his answer. She kissed him with enough enthusiasm to make him dizzy. Desire pulsed through him with such urgency that he fantasized spreading the blanket on the ground, unfastening his jeans and taking her.

Gasping and fighting for control, he drew back and looked into green eyes wild with passion. "Damn, Emily."

She gulped for air. "We should stop."

"I know." He brushed her rock-hard nipples with his thumbs. "I can't." He kissed her again, thrusting his tongue deep as his cock strained against the fly of his jeans.

She groaned and pushed her breasts against his palms, reminding him that she had other delights he'd promised himself. He never expected to have this chance again, and he didn't want to miss anything. Reluctantly leaving the pleasure of her hot mouth, he kissed his way down to her breasts.

"I want you," she said, her voice breathless. "I want you so much."

He circled her nipple with his tongue. "I know."

"Are you sure…" She panted as he tugged on her nipple with his teeth. "You really don't have any…"

"No." He licked a path over to her other breast.

She groaned again. "I need you."

"I'm here." Still teasing her quivering breasts with his mouth, he reached between her damp thighs. She couldn't have his cock, but she could have this. As he pushed his fingers in deep, she tightened around him in response.

Aching with needs he couldn't satisfy, he stroked her steadily. The liquid sound mimicked the rhythmic beat of mating, and yet it wasn't. She was so wet, so responsive, so perfect. And he'd never know the joy of sliding into that pulsing channel. He'd never join with her in the way a man was meant to unite with a woman.

Her soft cries grew faster and more desperate, and he increased the pace. As she came, her contractions squeezed his fingers and her warmth bathed them in the sweet nectar of release. He stifled a groan of frustration.

He'd spent a good part of his life wanting what he couldn't have. Now it seemed he'd have to add Emily Sterling to the list.

THE MOST INTENSE orgasm of Emily's life was followed by boneless languor, and she gratefully accepted the help of Clay's strong arms as he eased her down from her precarious perch and carried her around to the passenger side of the truck. She felt like a rag doll as he leaned into the cab and deposited her carefully on the seat.

Moments later he was back with the blanket, but she couldn't imagine wrapping herself in it while she was still glowing like an ember. She tucked the blanket beside her tilted head and against the seat, and looked out the windshield at the trees that surrounded the front part of the truck. Clay had pulled it partway into the forest, probably to shade the cab.

The back, however, had been open to the meadow, and that's where she'd chosen to let Clay give her an orgasm. Now that she'd done it, she wondered if that explained why the experience had been so intense. She'd never allowed herself that kind of sexual adventure in the great outdoors.

Clay opened the driver's side door and climbed in. He had her panties in one hand, and he draped them over the steering wheel before turning toward her. "You okay?"

She surveyed his extremely handsome and remarkably pulled-together look. He'd put on his hat, fastened the snaps of his Western shirt and tucked his shirttail into his jeans. She, on the other hand, was sitting here with the hairstyle from hell and wearing absolutely nothing, not even a hat.

Oh, wait. Her bra still dangled loosely from her shoulders. "I'm fine," she said, "but I must look like something the cat dragged in."

"No cat I've ever known has dragged in anything so beautiful."

His compliment warmed her. In fact, everything about this man, from his deep voice to his thrilling touch, made her feel treasured. "Thanks, Clay. That means a lot coming from you."

"Why?"

"I don't think there's an insincere bone in your body. You say what you mean and mean what you say."

"I sure try to."

"And for the record, you delivered on your promise." She looked into his dark eyes. "I will never, ever forget what just happened."

He turned sideways in the seat and reached over to cup her cheek. "Me neither." Tipping his hat back, he leaned across the console and gave her a gentle kiss. Passion hovered in the background of that kiss, lending a rich undercurrent to the sweetness of the gesture.

She sensed that if she held his head and demanded more, he'd give it. Then they'd land right back where they'd been moments ago, mindless with the force of their need for each other. They'd already created problems for themselves. No point in making things tougher.

Gradually he released her and settled back in his seat. "I hope you're not disappointed, but we'll have to skip visiting the sacred site today."

She almost laughed. As if she gave a flip about that after what they'd shared instead. "I'm not disappointed."

He glanced at her and smiled. "Good."

"In any sense of the word."

"Even better." He held her gaze. "We can stay here as long as you like, but eventually we have to go back to the ranch house."

"I know." Sitting up, she pulled her bra together and fastened the clasp. Then she reached for her panties hanging on the steering wheel.

His hand closed over hers. "I didn't mean you should rush. These aren't even close to dry."

Just that much contact was enough to send shivers up

her spine. "I should put them on anyway. People might already wonder why we're not back yet." She pulled her hand out from under his and took the panties. They were still damp and she didn't relish putting them on; nevertheless she slipped them over her feet and up to her knees.

"There's a simple explanation for the delay. You wanted to explore the creek and then you fell in. I doubt anybody's paying that much attention to how long we've been out here."

"Maybe not, but I was supposed to be helping you so that you'd be finished in time to take me for a horseback ride." Holding on to the dashboard with one hand, she lifted her hips so she could drag on the clammy underwear.

"Here, let me." He leaned over, grasped the panties and pulled them up with quick efficiency.

Just as quickly, she was aroused and ready for action. She froze in place as she fought the urge to ask him to reverse the process. Those talented hands of his could give her another mind-blowing orgasm in no time.

"You can sit down now," he said gently.

She swallowed. "I should probably sit on the blanket instead of the seat, if you wouldn't mind unfolding it for me."

"Sure."

Positioning the blanket brought him back in close proximity. As she felt his warm breath on her bare arm and caught his musky scent, she gritted her teeth to keep from begging him to love her some more. He acted so nonchalant about helping her. He must not be feeling the same tension.

"*Now* you can sit down."

"Thanks." She lowered herself onto the blanket and

stared out the window as she tried to get her heartbeat back to normal.

"I probably shouldn't tell you this, but I want you so much right now I can't see straight."

She groaned and buried her face in her hands. "No, you shouldn't have told me." Lifting her head, she looked at him, knowing he'd be looking right back. "What are we going to do about this?"

"I have no idea. Spending the next few days being around you and not able to touch you is liable to drive me crazy."

"Ditto."

"I should never have let you give me that blow job."

"I should never have let you touch my hoo-ha."

He stared at her in obvious frustration. Then slowly he began to grin, then to chuckle. Finally he was full-out laughing.

"What's so funny?"

"Us! We're ridiculous! We're consenting adults, and we should be able to have sex with each other if we want to."

"Yes, but as we've said several times, my father would have a fit if he found out. I don't know if he'd be more upset with me or with you, but he would definitely be upset."

"So we'll make sure he doesn't find out. We'll make sure nobody knows."

She shook her head. "Even if that's possible, it's not just about him, it's about you. What if I break your heart?"

His smile never wavered. "Trust me, Emily, if there's

one thing I've learned, it's how to guard my heart. This isn't about my heart. It's about a totally different part of my anatomy."

8

EMILY PULLED THE blanket around her. "Let me think about it."

That wasn't the answer Clay had hoped for. "Don't think too long." He started the truck and slowly backed it in an arc so he was facing the meadow again. "When are you leaving?"

"Probably Saturday. I made the trip in one day on the way here, but it's close to seventeen hours. I might break it up going back. I'm supposed to be at work Monday, and I don't want to be wiped out."

He put the truck in gear and started back to the graded road. He hadn't given much thought to her decision to drive, but it was a hell of a long way. "Why didn't you fly?"

"I wanted to save a few bucks."

And here he'd thought she was a spendthrift. Instead she might be a beautiful cheapskate. "Yet you have all this money stashed away."

"I do, and you know what? I feel like giving it back to him."

Clay winced. "I wouldn't, if I were you. I don't think his pride could handle that."

"Maybe I could tell him I won the lottery and wanted to share."

"I—"

"No, that's a really bad idea," she said. "Assuming he's already lied to me about where the money's coming from, I don't want to compound that by creating a second lie in order to give it back."

Clay sighed with relief. "Good. Besides, he wouldn't take it, no matter what story you cooked up. I'm sure in his mind he's the parent who's supposed to give to the kid, not the other way around." From the corner of his eye he saw her nod.

"You're right," she said. "But I promise you, if he needs anything as he gets older and doesn't have savings to cover it, I'll find a way to help him."

"So will I. I know how it feels to depend on the kindness, or sometimes the unkindness, of strangers."

She was quiet for several moments. "You don't have to answer this, but I really want to know what it was like."

He thought about taking the fifth because he didn't enjoy talking about those days. But he had just told her that he knew how to guard his heart, so maybe she needed to understand. "You feel like somebody lost in the desert with no water and no shade. You see this oasis, but when you get there, it's a mirage. Eventually you stop believing in the oasis and you learn to survive without water and shade."

"But what about the Last Chance? Isn't that a real oasis?"

"I want to believe it is, and it's the closest thing to a

home I've ever had, but I'm still a hired hand. I sleep in the bunkhouse, and I don't own any part of the ranch."

"Emmett thinks of you like a son."

"I know he does." Guilt pricked him. "Which is why he trusts me with you."

"As he should! You would never let any harm come to me."

"No, I wouldn't." He cut the wheels to the left and the truck bounced over a small ditch as he drove onto the dirt road leading back to the ranch. "But I doubt he'd want me fooling around with you, either."

"More for your sake than mine. He doesn't want you falling for a California girl the way he did."

Clay looked over at her. "That might be part of it, but you're still his little girl, and any man with intentions like mine would probably face a loaded shotgun."

"But I'm twenty-seven years old!"

He couldn't help laughing, because her exclamation made her sound no more than five. Without makeup and wrapped in a blanket, she didn't look twenty-seven, either. More like seventeen. But she probably wouldn't appreciate hearing that.

"I don't think it matters what age you are," Clay said. "I hope I'll be a dad someday—I've watched how they behave with their kids, so I can learn something. They may try to treat their sons and daughters the same, but they don't. They're way more protective of those girls."

"I wouldn't know about that." She sounded sad. "My dad wasn't ever around long enough for me to find out if he'd be protective or not."

Instantly he regretted ever bringing up the subject. "I'm sorry. I have a bad habit of thinking nobody's had childhood problems but me."

"If we're comparing, I certainly had it better than you, though. At least I had a mom and a home."

"There was a time I would have given anything for that, but who knows? I might not have ended up on a ranch, and I love that life. It suits me to a T."

"It does."

He felt her gaze on him and turned to see her smiling in a way that made his groin tighten. "You probably shouldn't look at me like that while I'm driving."

"Why not?"

"Because it makes me want to pull over and ravish you."

"Ravish me?" She laughed. "That sounds like fun."

"I guarantee it would be, but you said you had to think about whether you and I should have any more sexual adventures together."

"I do have to think about it. And not because of my dad's disapproval, either. Still, we might want to hold off until after his birthday."

"Which gives us one whole day?"

"And night."

He groaned. "I can't convince you to sneak out of the house tonight and meet me in the barn?"

"No. My dad will only turn sixty once, and I don't want to risk upsetting him on his big day. Either with a discussion about this supposed inheritance, or by carrying on a secret affair with you."

"You're right." He blew out a breath. "You are so damned right. I'm being selfish to even think of it."

"No, you're not. I've thought of it. I've imagined all kinds of scenarios."

"Yeah?" That gave him hope. "Like what?"

"You don't want to hear them while you're driving."

"You are a hard woman." He avoided a rut partly to save the shocks but mostly because bouncing around with an erection was extremely unpleasant. "And you're turning me into a hard man."

"Now that's funny."

"No," he said with feeling. "Believe me, it's not."

LUCK WAS WITH EMILY, and she made it upstairs without anybody seeing her. She'd been given Nick's old room, although according to Sarah none of the furnishings were the same. Apparently Nick had cherished the bed he'd had in there and had taken it to his house.

Sarah had put a secondhand bed and dresser in the room temporarily while she searched for something more distinctive. Emily hadn't thought much about the room, but as she walked around after a quick shower in the bathroom across the hall, she pictured it with a king-size bed and dresser.

The headboard and footboard of the bed would be made of some kind of rugged wood with old-fashioned brands burned into the surface. The dresser would be constructed the same way, and a red leather armchair in the corner would give the room a splash of color. She liked her vision so much she thought about telling Sarah.

If Sarah had an idea of what she wanted, she might be able to find someone to make it. Emily thought about coming back when everything was done, and how much she'd enjoy sleeping in a room she'd helped design, in a house that she loved. Then she brought herself up short.

What was she doing, turning into some sort of Western girl? One day of hot sex with a cowboy and she'd gone native? How her mother would wrinkle her nose at that.

As if to prove that she was from California and proud

of it, she dressed for dinner in a short white skirt and a black tank top. Then she piled on the gold jewelry with big hoop earrings, a three-strand gold necklace and gold bangles on her arm. For good measure she added a gold ankle bracelet and wedge-heeled sandals.

When she walked down the curved staircase to the living room, she found Sarah sitting there drinking wine with a blond woman who looked to be in her late fifties.

"Emily!" Sarah called out. "I wondered if you'd turn up. I have someone I want you to meet."

As Emily walked toward the two women seated in leather armchairs she wondered if, like it or not, she was about to meet her father's girlfriend.

"Hello, Emily." The woman stayed seated but held out her hand. "I'm Pam Mulholland." She had a warm, firm handshake and kind gray eyes.

Emily wanted to instantly dislike her, but she wasn't the sort of woman to inspire instant dislike. Her dimpled smile of welcome invited Emily to smile back. "I'm glad to meet you. My dad has mentioned you." She didn't add *several times* because that would give more importance to the relationship. At this point, Emily didn't want it to be important.

"And he's certainly mentioned you to me! He's very proud of you."

"That's nice to hear." It was the polite response, but Emily couldn't imagine what her father had to be proud of. She hadn't done much of anything.

She was so focused on Pam that she didn't notice Sarah had left to get another glass from the liquor cabinet until Sarah held it out to her already filled with wine. "Oh! Thank you, Sarah."

"I took a chance that you like red, but please, watch out for that skirt."

"I do like red. Thanks." Obviously she was meant to join them for a little chat. She'd rather not, but she'd taken the wine and now she was caught. She chose a seat next to Sarah. "Is...uh...my dad home yet?"

"Any minute, now," Sarah said. "We're waiting dinner for him, since we sent him off on all those errands to make sure he was gone for the afternoon, we can't very well start dinner without him."

"I should have gone with him," Pam said. "I could have made sure he didn't get sidetracked, but I had so much to do. I'm training the girl who'll take over for me tomorrow night when I come to the party, and she has lots to learn."

"A bed-and-breakfast must be a big responsibility." Emily studied Pam and noted some similarities to her mother—both Pam and Jeri had fair complexions and a nice smile. But Emily's mother had an edge to her, a sharpness that was missing from this woman. Pam definitely seemed softer. She also dressed like a westerner in a yoked shirt and jeans.

"It doesn't seem like a big responsibility to me," Pam said. "But I've been doing it for a while. I suppose it's overwhelming to someone who's just being introduced to the job."

Sarah beamed at her friend. "I'm excited because you're finally getting a whole night off. I don't think you've taken the night off since you bought the place."

"No, I haven't, but Emmett's sixtieth warrants my full attention."

"Indeed." Sarah raised a glass in Pam's direction.

"Which reminds me, Emily. How did you and Clay make out at the picnic site?"

Emily was grateful that she hadn't just taken a mouthful of wine, because if she had, it would have spurted all over her white skirt. "Just fine," she said in a voice that sounded almost calm. "The tables and benches are all set up and the fire pits are ready."

"That's great. So here's my plan. We have a yearling named Calamity Sam who's recently developed a phobia about the noise of plastic bags. Gabe keeps meaning to work with him, but he's gone so much with his cutting-horse competitions that he hasn't had time. I've asked Emmett to work with Sam tomorrow morning. Desensitizing a horse with a phobia is a tedious job, and it should keep Emmett occupied so we can sneak our nonperishables out to the picnic site."

"And tomorrow afternoon I'm going to develop a plumbing problem at the Bunk and Grub," Pam said. "While he's fixing that, you can haul the perishables out there."

"Can I help in any way?" Emily didn't want her dad's girlfriend to contribute more to the plan than his only daughter.

"Absolutely," Sarah said. "You can be part of the Calamity Sam plan. Two people are usually more effective. While Emmett calms the horse, you can rustle a plastic bag. This may take more than tomorrow's session, but we need to cure that colt of his phobia. I think Emmett will be happy to show off his horse-training skills for you."

"I can do that. After all, I came here to spend time with my dad." She gave that last sentence extra emphasis.

"And he's absolutely thrilled to have you here," Pam said. "So am I, for that matter. I've been eager to meet you after all the wonderful things Emmett has told me about you."

"He has?" Emily had a hard time imagining her dad bragging about her and fought the impulse to ask what those wonderful things had been.

"Of course. He thinks you're so smart, and he envisions great things for you once you settle on a career."

Emily grimaced. A smart dilettante wasn't particularly admirable. "Finding a career has taken far too long, I'm afraid. You'd think by twenty-seven I'd have more direction in my life, but instead I'm working at something that pays the bills but doesn't really interest me all that much."

"My, my." Pam exchanged an amused glance with Sarah. "Twenty-seven already and you don't know what you want to be when you grow up. Sweetie, I was past fifty before I figured that out."

"As for me," Sarah said, "I married Jonathan and that made the decision for me. I was a rancher's wife. But I chose the man, not the vocation. I didn't realize until after the wedding that I'd made a career choice at the same time. Turns out I love it, but I didn't know I would. Jonathan's first wife wasn't so lucky. She hated ranching and left."

"She did?" Emily had never heard that story. "Like my mother?"

"Not exactly like your mother." Sarah took a sip of her wine. "Diana left her son, Jack, behind. He was only four."

Emily gasped. "She *left* him? How could she do that?"

"I don't know, but Jack had some major problems dealing with his mother's abandonment. Thank God for Josie. She's helped him come to terms with it. I think having a baby is the best thing that could happen to them because Jack can give that kid the security he didn't have."

Emily shook her head in amazement. "And all this time I thought he was your son."

"Well, he is. Just not biologically."

Emily wondered what other important facts she'd missed over the years because she'd visited the ranch under protest and had kept a protective shell around herself the entire time. "I can't imagine what it must have been like for Jack. At least I've known all along that both my parents love me."

"And that's a gift," Pam said. "I can vouch for the fact Emmett loves you dearly. You should see his face light up when he talks about you."

Emily discovered that she couldn't dredge up a single ounce of resentment toward this woman. Pam obviously loved Emmett, and that had to be a good thing. If he couldn't have his daughter around all the time, he should have someone like Pam to brighten his days.

His objection to marrying a wealthy woman seemed silly and old-fashioned. Emily hadn't planned to champion Pam's cause, but now she was inclined to do exactly that. Life could be rough sometimes, and it made no sense to reject love when it was offered.

The front door opened and Emmett came in.

"Speak of the devil." Pam set down her wineglass and stood. "Hey, stranger! Did you get lost in the feed store?" She started toward him.

"I did not. But Ronald's jacked up the price on that watering trough you wanted, Sarah."

"I hope you got it anyway."

"I did, but it took forever. I looked for one with a small

dent in it, but then I had to haggle with him for thirty minutes before he knocked a few dollars off."

Pam chuckled and gave him a kiss on the cheek. "You're a good bargain hunter, Em."

"Thanks." He smiled down at her. "I try."

Emily had thought she might be uncomfortable seeing a woman being affectionate with her dad. But from the way he was looking at Pam, he obviously returned her love—whether he was ready to admit it or not. Emily was happy for him.

Sarah stood. "Now that you're here, we can have dinner. Let's go tell Mary Lou to start serving."

Picking up her wineglass, Emily stood, too. "So who will be here for dinner?" She vaguely remembered the evening meal as a boisterous affair with all the Chance boys in attendance. But so much had changed since her last visit.

"Just us," Sarah said. "Now that the boys are all married with homes of their own, we've designated Friday as family dinner night. The other nights, sometimes it's just me and Mary Lou." Carrying her wineglass, she headed for the hallway that led to both dining rooms—the large one used at lunchtime and the intimate one for gatherings of family and close friends.

Pam fell into step beside Sarah, leaving Emily to walk with her dad. Emily was impressed with that small gesture, that showed more than words could that Pam wasn't the possessive type.

"And we've also had Alex the past few months," Pam said. "He's been a regular up until recently."

"You're right. Can't forget Alex." Sarah glanced over her shoulder at Emily. "I don't think you've met Alex, but he's Josie's brother and our marketing director. He flew to Casablanca last week to meet his girlfriend, Tyler."

"Casablanca! How exotic."

"Tyler works on a cruise ship," Sarah said.

"But maybe not for much longer," Pam said as they all continued down the hall. "Have you heard anything from him?"

"Not yet, although he might have called Josie. In any case, I predict we'll be planning another wedding soon. I should probably hang out my wedding planner shingle, at the rate we're going."

Pam laughed. "You know you wouldn't want to do it for strangers."

"No, I wouldn't. But for family and extended family, it's fun. I love having young people around."

"So is Clay coming to dinner?" The minute Emily asked the question, she wished she could take it back. Clay had told her himself that he was just a ranch hand. He might fall into Sarah's category of *young people*, but so would many of the hands, and they all ate in the bunkhouse.

Sarah paused and turned back toward Emily. "I hadn't planned on it, but I could call down to the bunkhouse and see if he'd like to come up. I hadn't thought about the fact you might appreciate having someone your own age at the table."

Pam had also turned to face Emily. "Good point. Poor Emily will probably be bored stiff listening to the old folks all evening."

"No, no, that's not true!" Emily hoped she wasn't blushing and was afraid she was. "I'm perfectly happy with present company. I forgot that Clay would naturally eat down there and not up here. Obviously I'm not used to ranch routine. Forget I brought it up."

Sarah gave her a long look. "You're sure? Because he's welcome at the table and it would only take a phone call. We have a direct line to the bunkhouse."

"I'm absolutely sure." Emily linked her arm through her father's. "I'm here to hang out with my dad. It's been a long time since we've had dinner together."

"Too long," Emmett said.

Emily decided to start her campaign right now. "Even better, I'll have a chance to hang out with Pam, too. And just so you know, Dad, I think she's terrific."

Pam smiled at her. "What a nice thing to say. The feeling's mutual."

"Then let's get this mutual admiration society into the dining room." Sarah started down the hall again. "I'm starving."

"Me, too." Pam fell into step beside her.

Emmett didn't move immediately, and because Emily had linked her arm through his, she either had to wait until he did or urge him to get going. She waited, but she had a feeling she knew why he'd hung back.

Sure enough, he fixed her with a father-knows-best look. "I hope you're not getting interested in Clay."

"Of course not, Dad." Good thing noses didn't really grow when a person told a fib.

"He's really attached to this ranch, and we both know you're not into ranch life."

She was beginning to question the truth of that, and whether she really disliked ranches or she'd been conditioned to dislike them by her mother. But she nodded, because now wasn't the time to discuss it. He might think she was only saying it to justify her interest in Clay.

"Exactly. I'm a California girl," she said.

"And a beautiful one, at that. You looked cute in your jeans and boots, but this is the real you, Emily."

"I suppose." She'd have to find a way to wash out those jeans so she could wear them again tomorrow.

"I don't have to tell you why I feel so strongly on the subject."

"No, you don't. I get it."

"It's not just my own history, but Clay's. He may pretend to be tough emotionally, but his first eighteen years were rootless. That had to take its toll."

"I'm sure it did. Don't worry, Dad. I understand."

"Good. Now let's go eat."

Her heart was pounding by the time they set off down the hall again. She hadn't come here to cause problems, but she was causing them, all the same. She'd slipped up just now by asking about Clay. He seemed to think they could carry on right under everyone's nose without getting caught, but so far she wasn't demonstrating any talent for subterfuge.

There were a bunch of reasons why she had no business even trying to conduct an affair with Clay. She needed to tell him that staying away from each other was the best option. But that didn't mean she had to like it.

9

CLAY WAITED UNTIL the bunkhouse was dark and the hands were all snoring before he slipped outside. Hard work and fresh air guaranteed that the guys always slept like the dead. Usually Clay did, too. But tonight there would be no sleep for him until he'd seen Emily.

He figured if they could avoid getting caught, then it didn't matter whether they waited until after Emmett's birthday or not. And they for sure wouldn't get caught tonight. Clay had been sitting around outside talking with the guys before everyone turned in. Emmett had walked past on the way to his cabin and given them a wave.

So Emmett was in for the night, and the ranch house, near as Clay could tell from here, was also dark. He knew which room Emily was in. Somebody, maybe even Emmett, had mentioned that Sarah was giving Emily Nick's old room while she was here.

Clay knew the inside of the house like the back of his hand. Whether the Chances had taken pity on him or whether Nick and Gabe had plain liked him, he'd felt more like a friend to those guys than an employee, and he'd had the run of the place. He knew exactly where Nick's window was on the second story of the west wing.

All the windows had screens on them this time of year, so tossing a pebble at the window wouldn't have the same effect as it would have with glass. Still, he figured enough pebbles tossed would eventually get her attention. Then it would be time to see if she'd go for the next stage; that would take her cooperation and removal of the screen.

Every bedroom on the second floor was equipped with a rope ladder in case of fire. The ladders had been Sarah's idea, according to Nick, and the boys had all embraced the concept with enthusiasm. They'd never needed them to escape a fire, but those ladders had seen plenty of use before the Chance brothers were of legal drinking age.

After that, the boys had used the ladders once in a while for old times' sake, just to keep their comings and goings secret from their folks. Clay was willing to bet a rope ladder was still stored in Nick's closet.

He was planning on it, in fact. All Emily had to do was let down the ladder the way Rapunzel let down her hair in the fairy tale, and...

Well, and nothing, if she'd decided against having sex with him. But he hoped to hell she wanted to, and in case she did, he'd tucked a couple of condoms in his pocket. The scheme was virtually foolproof because nobody else was staying on the second floor in either wing at the moment.

So he was on his way, showered, shaved and dressed in clean clothes. He'd considered whether to wear his hat. Obviously he didn't need one at night, but he sensed the cowboy mystique intrigued her.

He'd worn the hat, and he'd keep it on long enough for her to see him standing below her window looking...

cowboylike. Actually, he'd need to keep it on when he climbed the ladder because he didn't relish leaving his precious hat on the ground where anything could happen to it. The hat would be in the way later, but it might serve a seductive purpose in the beginning.

He had a half moon to see by, and his eyes had adjusted to the light enough that he could find his way around to the back of the ranch house without a lot of trouble. He tripped a couple of times on protruding rocks, but only because nerves were making him clumsy. Thank God the Last Chance hadn't installed motion detectors.

Jonathan Chance had hated the things, that he claimed lit up every time a raccoon sauntered by and probably would malfunction if an actual intruder came around. Jonathan had counted on the unpaved road into the ranch to discourage would-be burglars. That and always having at least one dog on the place, although dogs had to be locked in the barn at night because of wolves and coyotes.

Clay heard a pack of coyotes yipping off in the distance as he rounded the end of the house and walked toward Emily's window. No light showed there, either. He wondered if she was asleep.

He stood in the shadows debating whether to wake her up. She had been up late the night before after driving almost seventeen hours to get here. She deserved a good night's sleep.

But he couldn't assume she was actually sleeping. If today's sexual adventures had left her as hot and bothered as they'd left him, she'd be lying up there drifting on a cloud of ultimate frustration. She might decide to do something about that, even though she was alone.

Clay had considered that option to solve his own problem and had discarded it. He couldn't see going that route unless he struck out completely with Emily. But she might not be thinking that he was standing down here ready to climb a rope ladder to get to her. She might be pleasuring herself right this very minute.

That was enough motivation for him to pick up a small pebble and toss it at her window. It didn't make much noise, so he picked up a slightly larger stone and threw that. When the second stone only rustled lightly against the screen, he went for the next size up. Once again, nerves made him clumsy and he missed the window.

The rock, for that's what it truly was rather than a pebble, hit the side of the house, hard. The loud crack sounded like a well-placed blow from a hammer. Instantly a light flashed on in her room. She appeared at the window and gazed into the darkness.

But as he knew—and she might have to find out—the light made it harder to see into the darkness. It gave him a perfect view of her, however at least from the waist up. In his fantasies about this moment, she'd been wearing a black lace negligee. In reality, she had on a white tank top. With her long blond hair down around her shoulders and her golden tan, she looked very much like a California surfer girl.

But she wasn't in California now, and he didn't really care what she had on. If all went according to plan, she wouldn't be wearing it much longer. As it was, he could tell she wasn't wearing a bra, and that was a good start.

She shrugged and started to turn away from the window. He'd been thinking so intently about the next step that he was neglecting the critical part, getting her to let him in.

The window was open, so she ought to be able to hear him. "Emily," he said in a stage whisper. "Down here."

She whirled back and crouched down to peer through the open bottom half of the double-hung window. "Clay?"

He stepped closer so he could talk more normally. As he gazed upward, he had to smile. Her nose was making a dent in the screen as she pressed forward, trying to see him. "Turn off the light and you can see me better."

She moved away from the window and the light went out. When she came back, she was just a shadowy figure behind the screen. "It is you."

"Yeah." He thought it was a good sign that she didn't ask him why he was there. "Listen, there should be a rope ladder in Nick's closet."

"A *ladder?* What in heaven's name…oh."

"We need to talk." It was the opening line he'd decided on, but he had much more than talking in mind.

She laughed softly. "That's the biggest con in the world and you know it. You don't want to talk."

"Yes, I do."

"Not much, though."

"All right, how's this? I can't sleep knowing you're so close by, so I decided to come over here and check on you. Were you asleep?"

"No."

"Why not?"

"None of your beeswax."

Now it was his turn to laugh. "I have my answer."

"Look, if you were picturing me lying in bed pining for you, then—"

"Actually I was picturing you lying in bed giving yourself a climax and wishing I could be there to do it for you."

Her breath hissed out. "Stop that."

"Will you go look for the ladder?"

"Then what? There's a screen on here."

"You can take that out and pull it inside for now."

"You seem to know all about this process."

"I used to watch Nick do it all the time. Will you go get it?"

"I thought we decided to wait until after my dad's birthday."

"That seems like a waste of a perfectly good night. FYI, your dad is fast asleep in his little cabin. Everyone else on the ranch is also fast asleep. Nobody will ever know that I've been up there."

"Unless they heard you heave that boulder against the side of the house."

"I accidentally missed the window."

"Good thing. You probably would have broken it. That would have been difficult to explain, don't you think?"

He blew out a breath. "Please get the ladder."

"If I do, it doesn't mean anything."

Oh, yes, it does. "All right. I understand."

The light flicked on again and he heard her rummaging around in Nick's closet. After the light went out, she came back to the window. "I found the ladder."

His heart rate picked up considerably. He checked to make sure the condoms were still safely tucked in his pocket. "Just take out the screen. Once you do that, the ladder will hook right over the window sill."

"You know, maybe I should just come downstairs and unlock the front door for you."

"It's not a good idea. The stairs creak quite a bit, and there's always the chance Sarah will hear that, or hear the front door open. She's a parent, and according to her, parents' ears are tuned for that kind of thing. Plus I'd have to leave the same way, and all that running up and down creaky stairs will get us caught for sure."

Emily sighed and started working on the latches holding the screen. "If you say so, but this doesn't seem like the brightest idea in the world, either. This screen is kind of awkward, and I...whoops! Watch out!"

Clay dodged out of the way as the screen came down. Fortunately for anyone below, the frame was made of lightweight aluminum and couldn't do much damage. Unfortunately for the screen, that same aluminum crumpled like paper on impact.

Emily leaned out the window. "You okay?"

"Yep." He picked up the screen. "This thing's a little bent, though." He was thinking more like totaled, but he didn't tell her that.

"Oh, great. You'd better leave while you can. That screen coming down is sure to alert somebody."

"Maybe not. I'll step into the shadows."

"What about the screen?"

"I'll take it with me. We'll figure out some way to explain this if we have to." He was too close to victory to worry about how he'd replace the screen without anybody knowing about it. He stashed the screen behind a bush growing close to the house. Then he counted to one hundred while he waited to see if either Sarah or Mary Lou would sound the alarm.

All quiet. Well, except for the intense pounding of his heart. He moved back to the window. "Let down the ladder."

A few thumping sounds indicated she was hooking it to the windowsill. Then the rope ladder tumbled down in a beautiful cascade. He looked upon it as his personal stairway to heaven.

She leaned out of the window again. "You'd better go slow and test this thing. It looks as if it's been sitting in that closet for years."

"I'm sure. It almost qualifies as an antique. I'm surprised Nick hasn't had it bronzed." He took her advice and balanced on the bottom rung to make sure nothing would give way. The ladder held. "I'm coming up."

"There's something medieval about this, like you should have a sword."

He glanced up. "Sorry. Left my sword at home."

"But I noticed you wore your hat." She sounded amused.

"I feel naked without it."

"Really?"

"Not exactly, but I am used to it. I...damn." As if talking about the hat had been a jinx, a sudden breeze lifted it right off his head. It dropped to the ground, the very ground where he hadn't wanted to leave it.

"Oh, dear." She sighed dramatically. "Now you're naked."

He had a difficult choice. He could go back for the hat and look like a dork who was more concerned about his hat than a rendezvous with a hot woman, or he could leave it and hope a raccoon didn't carry it off. He left the hat.

Another few seconds of climbing, and he pulled himself through the window. It wasn't a graceful entrance, but at least he was now in her bedroom where there was, conveniently, a bed.

She'd backed away from the window to give him room to climb in and stand upright. Once he did that, he felt more in control of the situation. He pulled the ladder back inside and closed the window.

"That means no breeze," she said.

"And no bats."

"Bats?" She put a hand to her chest. "We could have bats in here?"

"You go around leaving windows open with no screens, and you sure could. They're harmless, but there's no point in having one accidentally fly in and scare itself to death."

"Not to mention freaking me out."

"I'd protect you. Besides, like I said, they're not a threat to you."

"Sorry. I grew up in suburbia. Between a bull moose charging me and potential bats in my bedroom, I'm experiencing a little too much *Wild Kingdom* for comfort."

"And that's not even counting the human animal who climbed in your window."

"Exactly." She stood in the shadowed room, her arms crossed over her chest. Besides the tank top, she was wearing boxers in what looked like a plaid design. The combination was somehow sexier to him than a black negligee would have been. Or maybe it was just because Emily was wearing them.

"Actually, I was more worried about the noise than the bats," he said, hoping to calm her fears a little.

"You're assuming there will be noise. I made it clear that allowing you to climb the ladder doesn't mean I've agreed to have sex with you."

"Why not?"

"Because I'm not good at this cloak-and-dagger stuff. When I was walking down the hall to dinner with my dad, Sarah and Pam, I opened my big mouth and asked if you'd be coming to dinner, too."

He could see how that might have attracted some attention, but maybe it wasn't so bad. "That's natural enough. You're not expected to remember who eats where."

"No, but I could have asked if any of the hands were joining us for dinner. Instead I specifically asked about you, and my dad picked up on it."

A whisper of uneasiness distracted him slightly from his single-minded need to take her to bed. "What did he say?"

"That he hoped I wasn't becoming interested in you because we're from two different worlds, and besides, you had a rough time as a kid. I told him I was not interested in you. Which is, of course, a lie. I think he knew it was a lie, too."

Clay ignored the warning bells in his head. "So tomorrow we'll behave like polite strangers."

"Wouldn't it be a lot easier if we behave that way now, and you go back down the ladder?"

He propped his hands on his hips and gazed at her in the semidarkness. He couldn't see her all that well, but he could hear her breathing, and she wasn't as calm as she'd like him to think. "Is that seriously what you want me to do? Leave?"

"It would make our lives a lot simpler tomorrow."

"Would it, really? I've given this a lot of thought."

She chuckled. "I'm sure you have."

"Oh, and you haven't?"

"Yeah, I have, too. I haven't come up with any answers, either. It's a touchy situation, but I keep thinking if we can keep a lid on it for another twenty-four hours, then—"

"I don't know about you, but I see this like a pressure cooker. If I go back down that ladder right now, the steam builds up and by tomorrow night we might both be ready to blow."

"That's one way to look at it."

If he judged only from her tone of voice, he might believe she was looking at the problem rationally. But there was a breathless undercurrent to her words that told him she might be nearing the breaking point, too.

He decided to press his advantage. "On the other hand, if we let off some of that steam tonight, then we might be able to hang around each other without the same level of tension."

"That's another way to look at it." Her voice quivered ever so slightly.

"Which way do you want to look at it, Emily?"

She cleared her throat. "Did you by chance bring condoms?"

"Two."

"Then maybe we should use them."

It took him only a split second to close the distance between them and sweep her up in his arms.

10

FROM THE MOMENT she'd looked out the window to discover Clay standing there, Emily had known it would end up this way, with both of them naked in her bed. Clay had been the image of a determined male, with his legs braced and his shoulders back—a man on a mission. He wanted her and even though she knew they shouldn't, her own hunger was too strong to deny.

She wasn't convinced that his theory of a pressure-cooker made sense, but it meant that she was flat on her back, writhing against the sheets while he kissed every available inch of her. That couldn't be all bad, could it?

"I want to turn on the light, but the curtains aren't heavy enough," he murmured as he brushed his mouth over the very top of her nipple. "Can't attract attention."

"Why do you need the light?" She was proud of herself for managing a complete sentence while he was driving her slowly insane.

"To see your face."

"My face?" She gulped for air as he used his lips and tongue to devastating effect. "What about my naked body?"

"That, too." He traced a path down the valley between her ribs. "But I love how your eyes widen and your pupils get huge when you're excited."

She didn't want to make this *too* easy. "What makes you think I'm excited?"

"Do you usually wiggle around like this?" He dipped his tongue into her navel.

She arched up off the mattress. "All the time. I have an itch."

"Then let me scratch it." And in one swooping motion, he tucked his head between her thighs, slid both hands under her bottom and zeroed in.

She nearly lost what was left of her mind. She wasn't a stranger to this maneuver, but she had to admit Clay's technique topped every experience she'd ever had. For the next several minutes, he owned that territory. If he hadn't thrown her a pillow to muffle her cries, she would have brought the house down as he made her come in a spectacular fashion, and then repeated the fireworks display moments later.

Limp and covered in a sheen of sweat, she was vaguely aware of a condom packet being ripped open, and then he slid into her, smooth and easy, his way paved with two delicious orgasms. He felt so good there that she summoned the energy to rise and meet his second thrust.

An electric impulse rocketed through her at that firm contact, and she knew she wasn't finished yet. Her pelvic muscles tightened without her consciously willing it, and he groaned in response.

She'd recovered enough to remember they had to be quiet. "Shh," she whispered. "Shh."

He pumped again. "But it's so good, Emily. So damned good."

"I know, but we can't make noise." Wrapping her legs around him, she held on and gloried in the way he filled her to the brim. "Kiss me. That will absorb most of the sound."

He covered her mouth with his and began to thrust, long and slow at first, and then faster. She muffled his low, urgent moans and held him close, but not so close that he couldn't move. She needed the urgent rhythm as much as he did, wanted to come...once more...just once...*more*.

With one mighty push, he buried himself deep, his muted cries joining hers as she lifted her hips and shivered in a glorious explosion of pleasure. He shuddered in her arms as the rapid pulsing of his cock teased her womb. She'd never been this susceptible to a man's virility and power. Must be the cowboy in him.

At last he eased his mouth from hers. "Perfect," he murmured. He rocked his hips forward, bringing them even closer together. "Perfect."

"Yes." In the darkness she held him tight and wished this moment never had to end.

CLAY WASN'T SURE how much time passed before he roused himself to go across the hall to the bathroom and dispose of the first condom. Yes, he'd brought two, but that didn't mean he had to use both of them. In consideration of his beautiful bedmate, he should probably leave the way he'd arrived and let her rest for whatever hours remained of the night.

Feeling extremely chivalrous, he returned to the room and wondered what the hell he'd done with his clothes. Once she'd agreed to take him into her bed, he'd thrown them every which way, although he'd kept track of the jeans pocket with the all-important condoms. Now, however, he was having a little trouble locating a few key items, such as his briefs and his shirt.

"You're not leaving, are you?"

He glanced toward the bed and could dimly see her propped up on her elbow, gazing at him. "I thought maybe you'd want to sleep," he said.

"You climbed a rope ladder and risked your reputation to make this all happen. Why worry about a silly thing like sleep?"

He abandoned the search for his briefs and walked toward the bed. "I'm not worried about me, but you must be exhausted."

"I'm feeling very, very mellow." She held out a hand to him. "But that's different from being exhausted. Besides, I've never had the pleasure of a totally naked Clay Whitaker. I can't see you without turning on a light, but I can use the Braille method. Come down here so I can explore."

Only a stupid man would refuse an invitation like that. He stretched out on his side next to her. "I'm just your standard-issue male," he said.

"I can testify *that's* not true." She reached down and took hold of his very happy johnson. "Exhibit A. This particular item is way above average."

He didn't care to know how she was able to judge that. Funny how quickly possessiveness could set in, even when he knew she wouldn't ever commit to him.

"And when you consider the whole package, then you're a bargain at any price." Sliding her hand under his balls, she balanced each one in her palm. "There's nothing standard about you, Whitaker. Everything is supersized."

He loved having her hands on him, but he pretended to take her fondling in stride. "I don't know that it matters all that much."

"It matters." She traced a line up the underside of his penis, that was beginning to show interest in resuming the program. "The added value here increases the friction for me, which is all kinds of good. And these—" She caressed his balls again. "I could feel them brush my skin with each thrust. That's the kind of experience a girl remembers."

"Good to know." Yes, he was definitely going to use that second condom. "Now it's my turn." He ran his knuckles across her breasts. "Kissing you here and having you arch up because you want my mouth all over you is almost enough to make me come."

"That's nice." Her low, sexy voice egged him on.

"And you taste good, too."

"Spearmint toothpaste."

"I meant here." He slid his hand between her thighs and stroked up and in, his fingers creating the sweet music of sex as he moved them slowly back and forth.

She moaned. "That feels…"

"Nice?" He rotated his thumb lightly over her clit.

"More than nice." Her breath caught. "I've never been so…"

"Neither have I." So soon, and he was hard again, throbbing with the need to have her.

"Should we…" She whimpered softly.

He found her G-spot with his middle finger and smiled as she began to pant. "Should we what, Emily?"

"Worry."

"Not now. Right now I'm going to kiss you so you can yell if you want." He angled his mouth over hers and concentrated on that G-spot until she came so lustily that he wondered if she'd bite his tongue in her frenzy. But she didn't. He eased his hand free and caressed her slick thighs. "That was fun."

"Uh-huh." Gasping, she flopped back on the bed. "I mean it, Clay." She gulped for air. "I'm not usually like this."

"I'm not, either."

"From the moment I saw you today with that canister of semen on your shoulder, I wanted to jump you."

He started to laugh and turned his head into the pillow to mute it.

"I suppose that does sound funny, but honest-to-God, you looked so manly."

He cleared his throat. "I never thought of semen collection as a way to get girls."

"I'm sure it's not that. Well, maybe it added to the mystique since you'd just been involved in something sexual and you had the evidence to prove it."

"If all that's true, what's my excuse? Why have I been in a constant state of semiarousal ever since I saw you this morning?" He was in a state of full arousal now, but he could wait.

Once he used the second condom he'd have no reason to stay and risk being discovered here in the morning. And lying in the dark talking was nice. Although sex was never far from his mind when he was with Emily, he just liked being here, sharing the same space.

"You tell me," she said. "I've had boyfriends before, obviously, but I can't imagine any of them climbing a rope ladder in the middle of the night just to have sex with me."

"This is going to sound dorky as hell, but I think it's the long buildup."

"What buildup? We just saw each other this morning."

"Yeah, but apparently I've wanted you for ten years."

"Wow. No wonder you've been talking about pressure cookers. That's a long time to have a boner."

Once again he had to turn his face into the pillow to keep from hooting out loud. "Okay," he said once he could speak again. "It wasn't that bad. It's not like I've thought of you constantly for ten years. That would be pathetic."

"And crazy. I wasn't that memorable."

"Oh, you were damned memorable in your short shorts and low-cut blouses. You may not remember me, but I sure as hell remember you. I flirted with you like crazy."

She was quiet for several seconds. "I sort of remember, and I'll bet I wasn't very nice to you, either. I'd hoped you'd forgotten."

"Nope. But all this sex has taken the sting completely out of it."

"I apologize for being such a jerk back then, Clay. It only shows how stupid I was at that age. What horrible things did I say, if you don't mind me asking?"

"You told me in no uncertain terms that cowboys weren't your type."

She rolled to her side, facing him. "Those were my mother's words and I was dumb enough to parrot them without thinking whether it was true for me. I'm so, so sorry for being mean and rude."

"But cowboys really aren't your type," he said softly. He'd do well to remember that simple fact.

"I don't know." She reached for him, brushing her

fingers over his chest. "You're my type, and you're a cowboy."

"Yes, ma'am."

She chuckled. "I like it when you sound like that. Maybe cowboys are my type, after all." She toyed with his nipples.

He drew in a deep breath. If she kept that up, they'd be searching for the second condom very soon. "But the thing about cowboys is that they tend to hang out at ranches. That could be a problem for a surfer girl." He said it lightly, but he hoped she'd heard what he was trying to tell her.

"I guess so." She moved her hand lower and encountered his rock-hard penis. "Oh my goodness." She wrapped her fingers around it. "What are we doing talking when we could be engaged in something far more stimulating?"

"Beats me." He didn't want to admit he'd been holding off using the last condom because then he'd have to leave. Technically the relationship was supposed to be about sex, but for him it had already gone beyond that. When he'd woken up this morning he'd thought he didn't much care for Emily Whitaker. What a difference a day made.

"It's party time." She rubbed her hand up and down, her touch firm enough to make her intentions clear. "Do you know where your condom is?"

"Yes. Don't stop what you're doing."

"Wouldn't dream of it."

Leaning back, he reached blindly over the side of the bed, located his jeans and pulled them onto the mattress. Once he'd taken out the condom packet, he shoved the jeans to the floor and tore open the wrapper.

"Wait. I want to put it on."

"In the dark?"

"You did."

"I've had lots of practice."

"Let me try. I've always wanted to and never felt I could ask before. It seemed too personal, somehow, and I was worried I'd mess up."

"So you're turning the guy you barely know into a guinea pig?" He was secretly flattered. It meant she felt more comfortable with him than she had with other guys.

"Funny, but it feels like I know you really well."

"You will if you fumble the condom application. All that contact is liable to have an undesired effect, like early liftoff, if you know what I mean." He handed the condom to her and hoped for the best.

"So you can give me instructions."

He groaned. "Just let me do it."

"No. Lie down. It's probably good for you to have somebody else in charge once in a while."

"Fine. You can be in charge of pulling up the ladder after I leave. How's that?"

"Boring. I'm in charge of this. Go on, now. Lie down."

He stretched out on his back and wondered what he could think about that would keep his climax at bay. Not his work, that was for sure. That was all about stallions getting it on. So he'd think about...

"I blew air into it so it would go on easier."

"You did *what*?" He raised up on his elbows and discovered that even in the dim light he could see she'd created a balloon out of the condom. "Tell me, have you *ever* seen a guy do that?"

"No, but it seemed logical. Men aren't always logical about these things. Besides, you weren't giving me any instructions, so I had to figure it out for myself."

"Let the air out."

"Okay. But I'll bet it will slide right on now that it's all expanded."

"Not really. That's why you're supposed to roll them on gradually. It's not like putting on a sock."

"Oh! It's like putting on nylons. I get it. I'll just scrunch it back up. Okay, I'm ready now. Hold still."

Clay could predict she was going to have trouble with the condom now that she'd handled it so much, and he knew the solution but was afraid to suggest it. Anticipation had him balancing on the very edge of an impending orgasm.

Sure enough, the condom didn't want to simply slide on the way it would have fresh out of the package. The more she struggled, effectively massaging the sensitive tip of his johnson, the more his control faded.

She made an impatient noise. "I can't seem to make it cooperate."

He couldn't see an alternative. He'd just have to be strong. "If you get the surface wet, it should go on easier."

"Oh. Oh! I should have thought of that." And she began to lick.

He clenched his teeth together and thought about the most boring job in the world, stringing fence. It didn't help. "That's enough," he muttered.

"I don't think so." She took all of him into her mouth.

"Emily!"

Slowly she released him. "I want to make sure you're wet enough."

A hint of laughter in her voice told him she knew he was in bad shape. Of course she'd know. He was breathing like a winded trail horse on an incline. "You're enjoying this, aren't you?"

"Uh-huh."

"Just remember what I warned you about."

"I'm not worried. You're all about discipline and order. You wouldn't let yourself come. And when you do, after all this torture, it'll be more intense. You'll see."

He dragged in a breath. "That's assuming I live long enough."

"Poor baby. Here you go." She put on the condom, and although it wasn't the most efficient application ever, she accomplished the task. "And since you're already on your back, I'm climbing aboard. After all, you know what they say on the bumper stickers."

"Save a horse, ride a cowboy?"

"Exactly." Positioning a knee on either side of his hips, she poised herself above him. "Ready?"

"I'm beyond ready." He braced himself for the sensation of her slick heat, and still he groaned as she lowered herself, taking him right up to the hilt. It would be so easy to let go, but she was right about him. He was all about self-discipline.

It took every ounce he had to keep from coming as she braced her hands on his shoulders and rode him hard. He bracketed her hips with both hands and urged her on as the blood roared in his ears. He felt her tighten around his cock, and only then did he begin to let loose.

At the moment of her climax, she slowed her movements and kissed him, yet the mouth-to-mouth contact wasn't enough to quiet her deep-throated moans of pleasure as she rocked back and forth. Heat poured through him, demanding release. With one mighty upward thrust, he found it, and his world shattered.

As he whirled in the carnival ride of an incredible orgasm, he wondered if he'd come back to earth and discover his world was still in pieces. If so, only one woman could put it back together. That made him vulnerable, very vulnerable, indeed.

11

EMILY LONGED TO spend the rest of the night wrapped in Clay's strong arms, but that was a risk neither of them could afford. Life began early on the ranch, especially during the summer months, and Clay needed to be back in his bunk long before dawn. So she didn't stop him this time when he came back from the bathroom and started gathering his clothes.

She slipped back into her boxers and tank top, as if to help signal that the rendezvous was over. "Did you hear the plan for tomorrow...I mean today?" she asked as he pulled on his jeans and tucked his shirt into the waistband.

"No. All I know is I have another semen collection in the morning."

"From the same horse?"

"No. Different horse. We don't want to collect Bandit's semen too often because that lowers the value." He sat on the edge of the bed to put on his boots.

"Darn it. I wanted to watch that process, but I'm supposed to help Dad work with Calamity Sam on the plastic bag thing."

"They're making Emmett do that on his birthday?"

"It's a tactic, so he won't notice all the nonperishables being trucked out to the picnic site."

"Oh." He stood. "Usually with a desensitizing session, the horse gets a break now and then to run around the corral and let off steam. You might be able to come over and watch the collection process during one of those breaks."

"I'd like that. I have to admit I'm fascinated. How do you get the stallion...excited?"

His smile flashed in the dim light. "I can only imagine what you're picturing. And some people actually do use manual stimulation."

"Oh my God."

"It's strictly a clinical process."

"Yeah, right."

"It is, I swear. This is business, like milking a cow." She laughed. "I don't *think* so."

"Well, anyway, I prefer using a teaser mare."

"So how does that work? Do you dress her up in fishnet stockings and a bustier?"

"We only did that once, and nobody thought to take pictures."

She stared at him. "You're not serious."

"No." He smiled and reached for her, drawing her into his arms. "Unlike the human male, all a stallion needs is a whiff of a mare in season, and he's ready to roll. We just have to make sure he never gets to her."

She nestled against him, relishing the solid feel of his body. "You intercept the goods, in other words."

"Yes, ma'am, that's exactly right." He massaged the small of her back.

"I think I've figured out what an AV is, too, and it's not an artificial vacuum, is it?"

"It didn't seem like the sort of subject you wanted to discuss with your dad, so I made that up."

"Instead it's an artificial hoo-ha, right?"

"Yes."

"Clay, do you think I could watch? I've heard about artificial insemination. Who hasn't? And the insemination part was never a mystery. But I never thought about how the semen was collected. For animals, I mean. I know perfectly well how sperm banks operate."

"This is…different."

"I can tell! And when you're working with such a large animal, the logistics boggle my mind."

"Tell you what. I'll stop by the corral and let you know when it'll happen. Oh, and if I carry the canister out on my shoulder again, does that mean you'll be hot for me tomorrow night, too?"

She looped her arms around his neck. "After what happened here tonight, you won't even need the canister, cowboy."

"That's good to know, but I'll probably saunter by the corral with it on my shoulder, just for good measure."

"I'll look forward to that." She stood on her tiptoes, sliding her body against his, and kissed him lightly on the mouth. "You should get going."

"I know. But I need one for the road." He lowered his head.

His kiss was so thorough that she was achy again when he finished. "No fair. How am I supposed to sleep after that?"

"You're not." He kissed the tip of her nose. "You're supposed to lie here and miss me. You're supposed to miss me so much that you can hardly wait until I'm back in your bed tomorrow night after the party. Back in your bed and deep inside your sweet—"

"How about you?" She rubbed her pelvis over his crotch. "Will you be lying awake missing me?"

"What do you think?"

Reaching down, she caressed the bulge pushing against his fly. "I think you will."

"I will." After one quick, hard kiss, he walked over to the window and raised it. Then he leaned down, picked up the ladder and hooked it to the sill before letting it drop. "Here's hoping my hat's still down there. I don't see it, but it could be there in the shadows."

"Do you only have one?"

"No, I have another one, but that's my best hat, and I'm partial to it."

"Then I hope it's there." Emily held on to the top part of the ladder as Clay climbed out of the window and started down.

When his face was even with hers, he leaned forward. "One more."

She kissed him quickly. "That's all. You're making me nervous."

"It'll be fine. See you in the morning, sweet cheeks." With a cocky grin, he climbed to the ground.

She started pulling the ladder up, but paused when she heard him swear softly. "What's the matter?"

"Can't find my damned hat."

"You need a flashlight."

"I know, but I don't dare get one and prowl around with it. Someone might think I'm a burglar."

She peered downward. "What color is it?"

"Brown. Which doesn't help much in the dark."

"I can't see anything from here, either."

He glanced up at her. "Go ahead and pull the ladder up and close the window. If I don't find it soon, I'll come back tomorrow and look for it."

"Okay. Night." As she finished pulling up the ladder, he continued to search. She kept hoping to hear him call out that he'd found it. When he didn't, she closed the window. She sure as hell didn't want to add a bat to the night's excitement.

On the other hand, she was having more fun than she'd had in a long time, and that wasn't even counting all the great sex with Clay. She tried to picture her mother riding out to the picnic site in an old truck and helping to dig fire pits. Jeri would be worried about ruining her manicure.

Emily hadn't thought about her manicure once today, and she wasn't about to turn on a light and look at it now. No, she would stretch out on this lovely bed that still held Clay's scent and relive the time they'd spent together there. She'd think about the fun they'd had today and how quickly the time passed when she was with him.

All that added up to more than a purely sexual affair, and she doubted he believed that's what they were having, either. She really liked Clay, liked him more than maybe any guy she'd dated. She wasn't sure if she liked cowboys in general or this particular one, but the boots and hat were part of who he was, and she was into it.

Her mother was right about the life of a rancher, though. Emily wasn't sure how she'd feel about spending all her days working outside and dealing with animals, both domestic and wild. Besides that, there wasn't a beach even remotely close to Jackson Hole. Lakes, yes, but lake surfing just hadn't caught on for some reason.

Surfing was her ultimate stress-buster. Catching a wave required split-second timing, and once she was up, the rush of riding that wave swept away all her worries. Californians loved their therapy, but she thought surfing beat sessions on the couch any day.

On the other hand, the beach where she loved to surf had nary a cowboy on it, let alone someone as yummy as Clay. Her dad had once told her that life was about choices, and for every choice you make, there's something else you're giving up. She'd never thought about that statement much until now.

She must have been more tired than she thought, because in spite of desperately wanting Clay beside her, she drifted off to sleep. She dreamed of a cowboy riding a surfboard wearing a brown Stetson. She woke up to sunshine and the fervent hope that Clay had found his hat.

CLAY DIDN'T FIND his hat, not that night, and not early in the morning when he gave the guys some lame excuse for why he needed to go wandering over behind the ranch house. Worse yet, the mangled screen he'd shoved behind the bushes was also gone. He could blame the missing hat on raccoons. They loved carrying things off, for some reason.

But he couldn't picture a raccoon carting off that screen. It was too big and not the sort of thing they'd be willing to drag to their den. Someone had found it, and now he had to sweat out who it might be and whether they'd draw any conclusions about why a screen that had obviously fallen from Emily's window was tucked into the bushes.

He reminded himself that nobody knew how close he and Emily had become yesterday. But she had opened her mouth last night about inviting him to the family dinner table. That could be a tip-off. All he could do was go about his business and see how everything played out.

Breakfast at the bunkhouse had been a raucous affair because it seemed Watkins hadn't slept in his bunk last night, either. It was a testament to how preoccupied Clay had been that he hadn't noticed that Watkins left the bunkhouse late in the evening and never came back, not even for breakfast.

Everyone speculated that Watkins had finally talked his way back into Mary Lou's bed, but if he'd struck out, he might have been too embarrassed to come back and had spent the night under the stars. Clay was glad Watkins's love life provided such a distraction.

If he could be lucky enough to have Watkins find his hat, things might be okay. Watkins would just return it without asking questions.

After breakfast down at the bunkhouse, Clay put on the hat he'd worn the day before, the one he didn't mind sweating in. The brown Stetson had been his dress hat, and he'd been a vain fool to wear it in an attempt to impress Emily. No hat at all would have been the smart choice.

He wondered what would have happened if he'd shown up under her window with no hat. Would she still have agreed to let him climb that ladder? He'd never know, but he'd gone all out in an attempt to get into her bed, and for all he knew, his good brown hat had tipped the balance in his favor. But he wished it hadn't gone missing.

He'd taken Patches, a brown-and-white paint scheduled for collection this morning, to the wash rack. As he hosed down the horse, Emmett walked by and Clay called out a birthday greeting. He'd bought the foreman a new pair of work gloves, really nice leather ones, but he wouldn't bring those out until tonight's party.

Emmett raised a hand in greeting. "Thanks!" he called, as he continued toward the ranch house.

Clay shouldn't assign any special meaning to the fact Emmett hadn't stopped for a chat. His daughter was at the house, and they had a project planned for this morning. Emmett must be going to get her and didn't want to waste time.

Clay understood that. But if he'd stopped for a word or two, even about the weather—which continued to be hot for Jackson Hole—then Clay could have gauged whether there was anything different about Emmett's attitude toward him.

As it was, Clay had to comfort himself with the thought that if Emmett had found that brown hat under Emily's window, he would have raised holy hell about it. Emmett had been the foreman when the Chance boys used those ladders to sneak out at night for keggers in the meadow. He had to know about those fire ladders. Clay tried to calm the churning in his gut.

From the wash rack, Clay saw Nick's truck pull into the circular gravel drive in front of the ranch house. Dominique got out and walked up the steps to the house, while Nick headed over to join Clay.

"Big doings today," Nick said as he approached. "Dominique came over with me so she could help Sarah get some of the supplies out there this morning. We, of course, are supposed to carry on as if nothing is different."

Clay wondered what Nick would think if he knew how absolutely different everything was today, at least for two people on this ranch. "I think Emmett suspects something's going on with his birthday. It's hard to put anything over on him." And although Clay didn't regret a single second he'd spent with Emily, he'd been ignoring that salient point the whole time.

"He probably does suspect something. Oh, well." Nick glanced over at Patches. "Don't you suppose that's enough hose time on his rump?"

"Absolutely!" Clay turned the spray on the horse's withers. He'd been caught daydreaming and paying no attention to his job. That was likely to draw attention because he wasn't known as a woolgatherer.

"Have you washed his penis and foreskin?"

"Yep." Clay had taken care of that first thing, because he had a feeling he'd be absentminded today between his lack of sleep and his preoccupation with Emily.

"Then I'll go fetch Cookies and Cream so we can get this show on the road." He started in through the back door of the barn.

"Uh, Nick?"

He turned. "Yeah?"

"Any objection if Emily pokes her head in during the procedure? She wants to see how this works."

"I don't care, as long as she's quiet and doesn't distract Patches. But...did Emmett make a special request to let her watch?"

"No, why?"

Nick pushed back the brim of his hat and stuck his thumbs in his belt loops. "Well, because I thought we didn't much like her, Clay."

"I know that's how everybody feels, but—"

"I mean, she's taking Emmett's money and has the gall to sneer at how he makes it. So I'm confused as to why we should accommodate her request unless Emmett wants us to."

Clay wasn't prepared for his visceral response to having someone attack Emily. His words came out harsher than he'd meant them to. "She's not like that."

"Oh, really? What makes you think so?"

In the afterglow of last night's lovemaking, Clay had forgotten that everyone on the ranch, with the exception of Emmett and now himself, thought Emily was an ungrateful brat. But Clay wasn't at liberty to talk about the inheritance lie Emmett had been telling his daughter, or even that she'd saved every penny Emmett had sent her.

He thought about what he could say without betraying her trust. "I spent some time with her yesterday, and I just think we might be misjudging her."

Nick studied him. "I see."

"Look, I'm just saying—"

"Am I remembering right that you had a major crush on her the summer you came to live here and she visited for a week or so?"

Clay shrugged. "I might have. Don't remember for sure."

"I do." Nick pointed a finger at him. "And you did. She was sashaying around in those Daisy Dukes and your tongue was dragging in the dust."

"Your memory is better than mine, then."

Nick gazed at him, his expression thoughtful. "She can watch, I guess. But be careful, buddy. According to all I've heard, she's a scheming little—"

"No, she's not. I've talked to her, and she's not like that."

"If you say so. I'm reserving judgment. Once she stops

accepting those checks, I might be convinced that she's a nice person, but from where I sit, she's taking advantage of a guy I happen to care about, and that doesn't sit well with me."

"Nobody's forcing Emmett to mail those checks."

"No, but all Emily has to do is bat those big green eyes at him and whine about how much she's missed having a father around. She plays on his guilt and he writes checks. Simple as that. Oh, and you're creating quite a mud puddle there. I think Patches is clean enough."

As Nick headed into the barn, Clay turned off the hose and swore under his breath. That had not gone well. When Emily made her innocent request to watch the semen collection process, she'd probably also forgotten that she wasn't a popular visitor around here.

Clay hated that for her because she didn't deserve such a bad reputation. But he'd promised to keep their conversation to himself, and that meant he was helpless to protect her from any snubs that might come her way. He understood why she didn't want to confront Emmett today, on his sixtieth. But tabling that discussion would make her life a lot tougher.

Damn, he wished he knew where his hat was.

12

EMILY COULD HAVE waited for her dad in the living room, but Sarah and Dominique were in there making lists of supplies to take out to the picnic site. So she figured she had a better chance of catching a moment alone with her father if she stayed in the kitchen.

Mary Lou was busy, as usual, and kept going back and forth from the kitchen to her apartment, which was adjacent to it. At one point Emily thought she heard a male voice in there, but it could have been the TV. Maybe Mary Lou had a show she liked to watch while she attended to her morning duties.

So Emily sat in the kitchen drinking coffee, a wrapped present at her elbow, and waited for Emmett to show up. She hadn't celebrated a birthday with her dad in ten years, and she regretted that. He hadn't celebrated her birthday with her very often, either, come to think of it.

Her birthday was February first, and traveling to Jackson Hole in the middle of winter had made no sense—especially since she'd never developed an interest in winter sports. Her dad had made it to Santa Barbara twice for her birthday. Once when she was six and when she turned twelve.

Both occasions had been awkward because he didn't fit into her suburban lifestyle. He'd stayed in a motel and had come over for the parties; they had involved a jumping castle when she was six and a gaggle of girls going to the movies when she was twelve. Emily had ended up hoping he wouldn't come for her birthday anymore.

What a shame that they couldn't have found more middle ground. But at least she was here today and could wish him a happy birthday first thing in the morning. And give him one of her presents, because she believed birthdays should involve presents all day long.

He walked in, smiling and looking very dashing in his blue striped Western shirt and worn jeans. He was holding his hat. Even though cowboys sometimes kept their hats on indoors, her dad was old school about that and always took his off.

He'd aged well, she thought with pride. He was still lean, and his dark hair, though graying, was as thick as ever. The mustache he'd had ever since she could remember suited him perfectly.

She jumped up and hurried over to give him a kiss on the cheek. His pine-scented shaving lotion was achingly familiar. "Happy birthday, Dad."

"Thanks, Em." His smile remained, but there was a look in his blue eyes she couldn't quite place. She wondered if he worried about growing older. Birthdays affected people differently. Some people loved marking the passage of years and others didn't. Sad to say, she didn't know into which category he fell.

"Here's your first present." She grabbed her package off the table. She'd found wrapping paper with horses on it and was very proud of that. Although she could make fancy bows, she'd tied a simple green ribbon around the package because she didn't want her dad to think it was too frilly and fussy.

"Why, thank you."

"Here's the man of the day!" Mary Lou bustled into the kitchen. "Can I pour the birthday boy some hot coffee?"

"Half a cup," Emmett said. "I'll sit down a minute and open my present. But then Emily and I have to get down to the corral. Oh, and we'll need a plastic bag, Mary Lou, if you have one handy."

Mary Lou poured a mug full of coffee, ignoring Emmett's suggestion of only half, and handed it to him. "Here you go."

"Thanks." He took it without commenting on the extra portion and took a sip. "You make great coffee, Mary Lou."

"And you've never been satisfied with half a cup, so you might as well stop telling me that's what you want. Now open your present. Let's see what Emily brought you."

Emily ducked her head to hide her smile. Not many people got away with bossing her father around, but Mary Lou had been on the ranch about as long as Emmett and obviously wasn't intimidated by any man, let alone her dad.

"I believe I will." Emmett sat down at the kitchen table that served as a gathering place for anyone wanting coffee and conversation during the day. After setting his mug and hat on the table, he carefully untied the green ribbon.

To Emily's surprise, she was nervous about whether he'd like her gift. Because she didn't spend much time with her dad, she wasn't sure what he might want. She'd also been feeling a little sentimental when she'd decided on this one.

After untying the ribbon, Emmett wound it up and set it on the table before peeling off the tape. His care in unwrapping her gift brought a lump to her throat. She'd sent him presents over the years, but too often she'd treated it as an obligation to get out of the way. Now she realized he must have devoted this much attention to opening each one, and she wished she'd put more thought into her other gifts.

Mary Lou blew out an impatient breath. "You are *the* slowest present opener in the whole world, Emmett Sterling."

Emmett glanced up at her. "If someone takes the time to buy me a present and wrap it, I like to appreciate the effort."

"Then I'm going to tell everyone coming tonight to bring their presents in a paper sack. Otherwise we'll be there till dawn while you open them."

"What's this about presents in paper sacks?" Watkins sauntered out of Mary Lou's apartment. His hair and handlebar mustache were still slightly damp, as if he'd recently shaved and showered.

Emmett's eyebrows lifted as he gazed at Watkins. "Morning, Watkins."

"Same to you, Emmett. And happy birthday."

"Thanks." Emmett continued to stare at the ranch hand. "Sleep well?"

"I surely did. And you?"

Emily watched the two men, fascinated by what wasn't being said. Obviously Watkins had spent the night with Mary Lou and that had been the male voice Emily had heard a few minutes ago. If Emily had to guess from her dad's reaction, that wasn't part of the normal routine.

"Oh, for heaven's sake!" Mary Lou stepped forward and handed Watkins a mug of coffee. "Stop dancing around the issue, both of you. Watkins and I spent the night together, Emmett. If he behaves himself, we may continue to do that now and then. I told Sarah and she's fine with it."

Emmett took a sip of his coffee. "And I never said I wasn't."

"No, but you should have seen the look on your face when Watkins walked out of my apartment."

"I was surprised, is all."

"You shouldn't be. Watkins has been sweet on me for years."

"And she finally took pity on me," Watkins said. "I promise you, Emmett, that it won't interfere with my work."

"I wouldn't expect it to," Emmett said.

Emily could hardly wait for a moment alone with Clay so she could tell him about this. She and Clay weren't the only ones who'd enjoyed a rendezvous last night. They might not have to worry about Mary Lou interfering with their plans for tonight, either.

"And that's enough on that topic," Mary Lou said. "Are you finally going to finish opening that present, or do you need someone to do it for you?"

"I've got it." Emmett folded back the wrapping paper and picked up a framed five-by-seven picture. Emily had found the snapshot when she was going through some old boxes. The original was faded and bent, but she'd taken it to a shop where they'd created a new and improved version.

Fifteen years ago, she'd had one of the ranch hands take the picture with her camera when she'd spent a week at the ranch. She and her dad were both sitting on horses, and at twelve she'd insisted on wearing sandals, shorts, a halter top and sunglasses. Definitely no cowgirl.

In the picture, her dad looked like the quintessential cowboy. And even though she winced now to think of how stubborn she'd been about proper riding attire, she still loved this picture. She hoped he did, too.

Mary Lou came over to take a look. "Oh, now that's sweet. Don't you think so, Watkins?"

The barrel-chested cowboy walked over to check out the picture. "Very nice. I think I remember when that was taken."

Emily appreciated their comments, but the man she needed to hear from hadn't said a word. Maybe she'd made a terrible mistake and he'd just shove it in a drawer. He might not care about an old picture like this, after all.

"You don't have to keep it if you don't want to, Dad," she said.

"Of course I'll keep it." His voice sounded rusty and he coughed. "Thank you, Emily. I thought I'd never see this again."

"I wondered if you still had a copy somewhere."

"I used to. Kept meaning to frame it and never did. Had it propped against a lamp beside my bed for the longest time, and then one morning I had it in my hand while I was drinking coffee and walking around the cabin, which wasn't very smart of me. I tripped and doused it with coffee. Ruined it."

Emily sighed with relief. "I was afraid you didn't like it." Instead he'd loved it more than she had. "I made a new copy for myself, too."

"Good." Emmett blinked and cleared his throat. He still hadn't looked at her.

She understood. A man like Emmett would be embarrassed to let anyone know that he could get misty-eyed and choked up over a simple picture. "I guess we need to get down to the corral, though." Until her dad was thoroughly absorbed in the Calamity Sam project, Sarah and Dominique couldn't begin ferrying supplies out to the picnic site.

"Yes, we do." Emmett polished off his coffee in several long gulps. The man had to have a cast-iron throat. Then he folded the wrapping paper back around the picture and laid the ribbon on top before picking up everything along with his hat. "You can meet me down at the corral, Em. I'm going to run this home so nothing happens to it."

Emily hadn't thought about what he'd do with the picture once he'd unwrapped it. "I could put it in my room for the day, if you want."

"Nope. This is special and I'd rather make sure it's safe and sound in my house. Finish your coffee and get that plastic bag from Mary Lou before you come down. I'll see you in a few minutes."

Watkins had ducked back into Mary Lou's apartment and returned clutching his hat. "I'll walk out with you, Emmett." He gave Mary Lou a quick kiss. "Thanks, Lou-Lou." Then he followed Emmett out of the kitchen.

After the two men left, Mary Lou let out a sigh. "I hope I'm not going to regret letting that cowboy back into my bed. I should have known he'd make a grand entrance to solidify his position."

Emily was gratified that Mary Lou would share such a

personal statement with her. It made her feel more a part of ranch life. "Sounds like he really likes you, though."

"He does, but I've been sleeping solo for a lot of years. And I've warned him not to bring up marriage like he did last time."

"You don't want to get married?"

"No, I don't. At my age, there's no point to it. It's not like we have to worry about which last name to give the kids."

"I see what you mean."

Mary Lou smiled at Emily. "That picture was a brainstorm on your part. Did you see how emotional he got over it?"

"Yeah." Emily smiled back. "That was nice. I think I need to be around for his birthday every year."

"He pretends like he doesn't want a fuss made over him, but I know he'd love that."

"He would." Emily's heart squeezed as she thought of all the birthdays her dad had celebrated without her. "As a matter of fact, so would I."

As Clay came out of the barn leading a well-scrubbed Patches, Emily bounded down the ranch house steps, a plastic bag in one hand. Dear God, she was gorgeous. Her blond hair shimmered in the sun, making her look angelic. He knew she wasn't, but he was struck speechless by the sight of her.

Once again she was dressed in shorts and a scoop-necked T-shirt. She carried the hat she'd borrowed from Sarah in her other hand and put it on once she'd cleared the steps. He wondered if she'd find a way to get her jeans washed for the ride to the picnic site tonight. She wouldn't want to make that ride in shorts.

She spotted him and waved. Because she was coming in his direction, he waited for her. Nick was already in the shed with Cookies and Cream, so he couldn't stay long, but he also couldn't resist a chance to talk with Emily.

He needed to alert her that the screen had been taken from behind the bushes, which meant someone had a pretty good idea what went on last night. Nothing was going according to plan this morning. He would have expected Emmett to be working with Calamity Sam by now, but something must have held up the program because the corral was still empty and Emmett was nowhere around.

Emily hurried up to him. "Did you find your hat?"

"No." The missing hat would be expensive to replace, but that wasn't even his biggest concern. Now that nobody had shown up with it, he hoped to hell it had been carried off by a raccoon.

He'd just seen Watkins, and he didn't have it, obviously. If some other cowboy had found it, then the guys could be planning to embarrass Clay. Cowboys loved to pull pranks, and unfortunately Clay could imagine someone announcing at the cookout that they'd found Clay's hat under Emily's window. Then things could get ugly.

"I'm sorry it's still missing," Emily said. "I wonder where it is."

"Yep, that's the big question."

"I have some other news. Watkins spent the night with Mary Lou."

"That's what the hands figured when he stayed out all night." Patches tossed his head and Clay tightened his hold on the lead rope.

"So you knew already?"

Clay lowered his voice. "Actually I missed the fact that he left the bunkhouse late in the evening and never made it back. The guys didn't miss it. This morning when his bunk hadn't been slept in, they all began to speculate whether he got lucky."

"I can see why you had to get back, then. They notice."

"Yep." Patches bumped Clay's shoulder with his nose. "Listen, Nick and I are about to do the collection, but it looks like you and Emmett haven't started with Calamity Sam yet."

"No. I gave him a birthday present and he wanted to take it back to his house."

"But everything's fine with him, right? He isn't acting strange or anything?"

"He's fine." She paused. "Well, when he first came into the kitchen, he had a funny look in his eye. Or maybe I was just imagining it. Are you worried he might know?"

"I'm worried that somebody knows. The bent screen is also gone."

"Oh!"

"Yeah, not good." Clay saw movement in the corral. "Emmett's back and he's turned out Sam, so you'd better get over there to help him."

"And you're doing the collection right now?"

"Yes. Nick's already in there."

"Let me ask my dad if he can spare me for a few minutes."

"You know, maybe you shouldn't. I know you want to watch this, but I have another collection scheduled for tomorrow morning. Let's see how everything looks then."

"You're worried, aren't you?"

He hated that he was responsible for the anxiety in her green eyes. And all the blame was his. He was the genius who'd decided to pay her a visit last night. He was the smart-ass who'd decided he needed to wear his best hat. And if he'd been more alert, he could have caught that screen instead of letting it bounce on the ground.

"I'm sorry, Emily. I hope I haven't put you in an impossible situation."

She smiled at him. "I'm not sorry. No matter what happens, it was worth it."

He let out a long breath. "Thanks for that. Now go help your dad."

"I will. Have fun with the AV, cowboy." With a wink, she turned and started off for the corral.

He watched her go way longer than he should have. If Patches hadn't jerked the lead rope, he might have watched even longer. If Emmett noticed him staring after Emily, Clay would be in deep trouble.

But she'd told him it was worth it. He'd hang on to that statement for dear life.

13

EMILY HALFWAY EXPECTED her dad to ask why she'd been talking to Clay, but he didn't. Instead he began instructing her on how they'd go about desensitizing Calamity Sam to the noise of a rustling plastic bag.

The yearling was a good-sized, gray-and-white paint, but he still looked gangly, like a teenager who needed to grow into his long legs. He had a gray patch over one eye that Emily found adorable. She would have liked to walk over and rub his silky-looking neck, but he was already eyeing the plastic bag warily, so she stayed back.

The routine was simple. Emily walked around the corral and shook the bag every so often. First she'd do it in front of the horse, then to one side, then the other, then in back. Meanwhile her dad held Sam's halter and talked soothingly to him. Whenever the colt was calm, Emmett gave him pieces of carrot as a reward.

They worked the program for fifteen-minute stretches, and then turned Sam loose to run around in the corral for a while and blow off steam. After that Emmett would snap the lead rope onto his halter and they'd repeat the process for another fifteen minutes.

By rights, Emily should have been bored. But she discovered that watching her father patiently coaxing Sam to accept the rattling plastic was fun. The horse was like a little kid, and she found herself laughing when he tried to get carrots he hadn't earned.

True, this was tame stuff compared to the noisy goings-on in the shed where Nick and Clay worked. Even though the shed stood quite a distance from the barn and the corral, the stallion's cries carried to where Emily and Emmett toiled with Sam. Emmett made no reference to it, acting as if he didn't hear the stallion.

After a while, the noise stopped. That probably meant Clay was using the AV on the stallion, and Emily really was curious as to how that all happened. Her curiosity would have to wait to be satisfied, though.

No doubt because she had sex on the brain lately, she worried about the stallion's satisfaction level. He'd been led to believe he could have the teaser mare, and she hoped the poor stud would get some fun out of the AV. She wondered if they warmed it somehow. If she got the opportunity, she'd ask Clay about that.

"Emily?"

"Yes?" She glanced at her father.

"You stopped rattling the bag."

"Sorry." Whoops. She'd have to be careful about staring off into space like that. She dutifully began rattling the plastic bag.

But as she moved around the corral, she caught sight of Clay walking out of the shed. Sure enough, he was carrying the canister of semen on his shoulder as promised. He was like a walking advertisement for virility—*have semen, will travel.*

"Emily?"

"Oh! Sorry, Dad!" She was seriously causing problems for herself. Her father might not have guessed that she was daydreaming about Clay earlier, but just now she'd been staring at the guy, so how much more obvious could she be?

She poured all her concentration into rattling that bag and somehow managed to ignore the tall cowboy walking across from the shed to the tractor barn on the other side of the corral. But still she knew, by keeping track from the corner of her eye, when he went inside.

"Break time," Emmett said. He unhooked the lead rope and Sam galloped around the corral, kicking up his heels.

On one circle he veered so close to Emily that she felt the wind of his passing. She rolled the plastic into a tight ball and jammed it down into her shorts pocket so that it was completely out of sight. Next time Sam came by, she called his name softly.

To her surprise, he wheeled and pranced toward her, his nostrils flared.

"Can I have a piece of carrot, Dad?" she asked. "I want to make a friend."

"Sure thing, Em." He walked over and gave her a couple of pieces.

Sam perked right up and ambled closer, sniffing loudly. Emily held one carrot back and put the other in her outstretched hand. The yearling's lips moved gently over her palm as he picked up the piece of carrot.

He turned his head to gaze at her while he crunched on it, and she could see herself reflected in his large brown eye. It was the eye with the gray patch, and it made him look like a war pony to her.

"Dad, I'm falling in love."

"What?" Concern echoed in that one-word question. "God, I hope not. You—"

"With Calamity Sam," she said before he could get any further into that response.

"Oh. That's different. But I'm afraid I can't buy him for you. He's worth a ton of money."

"I'm sure. He's beautiful." She didn't ask what her father had thought she'd meant. It was all too obvious, and she didn't want to discuss it.

"He's a good-looking colt, all right. Listen, sweetheart, since you have him eating out of your hand, I'm going to duck into the barn for a minute. Too much coffee this morning."

"Go ahead. I'll watch over this guy." After her dad left the corral, she gave Sam the other piece of carrot and finally got her wish of being able to stroke his soft neck. As she did, she talked softly to him and watched his ears flick back and forth as he listened to her, and then to other noises surrounding them.

"Looks like you've made a conquest."

She turned to discover Clay leaning against the rail. He'd stripped off his shirt again and looked like a fantasy cowboy with his snug jeans and his hat brim shading his dark eyes. Her heart thudded faster, both because he was so yummy and because he was tempting fate to even be here talking to her.

"You shouldn't stay," she said. "Dad will be back any minute."

"I'm sure he will. He doesn't walk off a job. But I saw you here alone and wanted to—"

"I know what you wanted. But it's dangerous to spend much time talking to each other, when *somebody* around here knows what's going on with us."

"You're right." He pushed away from the railing and his biceps flexed. "I'll leave."

"Did you get the semen?"

"Yeah."

"Is that AV heated?"

"A little. There's a surrounding cylinder for warm water. Why? Worried about the stallion's comfort?"

"It crossed my mind. I mean, how would you like somebody to shove your penis into a chilly artificial—"

"Emmett's coming back. See you later."

"Okay. And put on a shirt, will you? That's unfair."

"You're one to talk, standing there in shorts and a tight T-shirt."

"Bite me."

He kept his voice low. "If only I could. Later, sweet cheeks." Clay waved to Emmett. "Looks like Sam's coming along, Emmett."

"I think he is," Emmett called back.

Emily focused all her attention on Sam, rubbing his neck, scratching along the line of his mane, stroking his nose. "I think he likes me," she said as her father approached.

"I think he likes you a little bit too much, and I'm not talking about the horse."

"I know." She didn't look at him.

"I've said it before, but I'll say it again. The mistake your mother and I made was stupid, although I can't regret it because it gave us you. But to see you make the same mistake…"

"I won't, Dad."

"I wish I could be sure of that."

She took a deep breath and faced him. "I know you worry about Clay because he's an orphan and had such a difficult childhood, but he's not as fragile as you might think."

Emmett gazed at her, his expression troubled. "Of course I'm worried about him. I think the world of Clay, but he's not my kid. You are, and I don't want you tangled up in a messy situation."

And all this time she'd thought he might take sides against her because Clay was the son he'd never had, the cowhand he wished his daughter would be. Her chest tightened as she realized that he really did love her unconditionally. She didn't have to do anything special, or be anything special, to earn his love. She could make mistakes, and he'd still love her.

Gratitude flooded through her. "Thanks, Dad."

"Please be careful, sweetheart." He held her gaze for a moment longer, and then he turned to Sam. "And this squirt needs a lot more work. We'd better get to it."

Emily was happy to return to Sam's training. It was a blissfully simple job. Meanwhile her life was becoming so complicated it made her head hurt.

CLAY HAD A really bad feeling about how this day would end up, but he couldn't do a damned thing to prevent the disaster he sensed was coming. So he tried not to make it any worse and stayed as far away from Emily as possible for the rest of the morning. He even made a point of sitting at a different table during lunch.

But Emmett was called away after lunch to fix a plumbing problem for Pam over at the Bunk and Grub— another piece of the birthday plan falling into place. And Clay's determination to keep away from Emily was considerably weakened once her primary watchdog was no longer on the premises.

Because both Clay's hat and the screen had disappeared, he doubted that he'd be able to return to her room tonight. If he did, Emmett might be waiting with a shotgun. Maybe not literally, but the odds were good Clay would be shut out in some way.

Tomorrow Emmett would be on the ranch all day... and all night. The following day Emily would leave for Santa Barbara. The way Clay had it figured, he might have a window of opportunity this afternoon while Emmett was gone, and that would be it.

But he couldn't for the life of him figure out how to get her alone, even for twenty minutes. Now that Emmett was gone, the ranch had turned into Operation Central for getting this cookout show on the road.

Clay had been sent to the barn to organize saddles and make a list of who would ride which horse so mounting up would go like clockwork. Sarah didn't want to have any confusion that would give Emmett an excuse to try and call the whole thing off. Meanwhile Emily was up at the house working on the food angle and helping load boxes and coolers.

Fate seemed to be keeping them apart, and then, out of the blue, good fortune smiled on him. Emily appeared as he was counting saddles and making his list of guests and available horses.

"Sarah has decided that we need tiki torches to keep away the mosquitoes," she said. "We're running out of time, so she's commissioned you and me to drive quickly into town, pick up about ten from the feed store, and then go straight from there out to the picnic site and put them in the ground in a circle around the picnic area."

"Okay."

"She told me to make sure you didn't get picked up

for speeding, though." Emily gazed at him. "Is that a problem with you?"

"Sometimes. A lookout would be a help." Clay calculated how fast he could drive and how much extra time he could buy them with this errand.

Emily held out a roll of bills. "I have the money, and we're supposed to leave right now."

"Give me five minutes."

"What, you need to finish your list?"

"No, I need to get something from the bunkhouse." He decided not to tell her what because she might protest that they didn't have time, but he'd make time. He could feel it running out, and he was a desperate man.

"Okay, I'll be in the truck. Hurry."

She didn't have to tell him that. In this case, every minute counted. Throwing down his pen, he left the barn and jogged the distance to the bunkhouse. He passed Watkins on the way.

"Could you finish up the list of which guest is riding which horse?"

"I can." Watkins smoothed his moustache. "Where are you off to in such a hurry?"

"Getting tiki torches to make a ring around the picnic site. For mosquitoes."

"I was wondering if anybody had thought of that. They could be bad out there."

"Sarah just did think of it." And he mentally thanked her for that, plus her decision to send Emily with him to watch for cops. She hadn't changed into jeans and boots yet, and that was all to the good.

In the bunkhouse, each ranch hand had a small dresser for his clothes and personal items. Clay pulled out a drawer and grabbed one condom. That's all he needed, all he had time for. He told himself to be grateful for this gift and not be greedy for more.

Somehow, in the next few hours, he had a hunch everything would come to light and he wasn't sure how he'd handle that with Emmett. But, as the old saying went, he might as well be hanged for a sheep as a lamb. Maybe he was wrong and he'd find himself able to climb that ladder to Emily's room tonight, after all.

But his instincts were good, honed from years of making sure he survived in any environment. Those instincts told him that the shit was about to hit the fan. Before it did, he wanted one last moment with Emily.

She was waiting in the truck when he hopped in and started the engine. "I think I know what you went for," she said.

"You probably do." He backed the truck around and headed for the dirt road.

"We don't have time for that. We'll do well to get the torches in the ground and return before Dad does."

He didn't say anything, and kept his speed down until he was about a half mile down the road, because he didn't want to send dust billowing around the ranch house. But when he was far enough away that it wouldn't be a problem, he hit the gas and sent up a rooster tail of dust.

"Clay! What in God's name are you doing?"

He glanced over at her and couldn't keep the grin off his face. "I'm hauling ass, sweet cheeks. Because we are going to use the condom in my pocket, or my name isn't Clay Whitaker."

She gripped the door handle and pushed down the lock. "You're going to end up in a ditch and break an axle, and then your name will be mud."

"No worries. When I first came to this ranch, there

was a teenager living here by the name of Roni Kenway. She's a mechanic on the NASCAR circuit now, but while she was here, she loved souping up the ranch trucks and challenging any takers to a race. She taught a bunch of us how to drive fast."

"Good grief. I had no idea you were Dale Earnhardt Jr. in disguise."

"That's why Sarah sent me, but having me get a ticket wouldn't help, so when we get on the main road, you'll need to keep your eyes peeled."

"Okay, but after we get those tiki torches, you're not going to be able to drive like a bat out of hell. You can't have them bouncing around and maybe breaking."

"Leave that to me. I'll tie them down. Cowboys are good with rope."

"I still don't see how we'll have time to fool around, Clay. We have to fill the torches and plant them in the ground, you know."

He had that figured out, too. "We'll have an assembly line. You fill and I'll ram them in the dirt. There's sort of a sexual rightness to that, don't you think?"

She shook her head. "I think you're fixated on sex, so anything would be sexual to you."

"You're probably right about that, but I have my reasons why I'm fixated."

"Yes, and they're all located below your belt."

He swerved around a curve, sending a plume of dust ten feet in the air. "That's also true." He took a deep breath. "Emily, there's no point in kidding ourselves. I'm afraid our happy little arrangement is going to be over very soon."

"That's a given. I'm leaving on Saturday."

"That's not what I mean. I'm talking about hours, not days."

"And what makes you say that?"

"It's just a feeling I have, that all hell is going to break loose. Your dad's going to find out about us. I don't know why I thought he wouldn't. Just cocky, I guess. I'm not sure how the truth will come out, but I think it will. And once it does…"

"I hope you're wrong. I mean, it's his birthday."

"I know. And you want it to be all sweetness and light." Clay hit a straightaway and took it as fast as he dared, given that he was constantly on alert for critters crossing the road. Usually the loud roar of a racing engine sent them scurrying.

He raised his voice above the noise of the engine. "Did your dad say anything to you about me today?"

"Yes!" She had to yell to be heard. "He told me not to make the same stupid mistake he and my mother made!"

As the road began to curve, Clay slowed the truck again. "See, he knows. Whether he knows everything, I'm not sure. But somebody on the ranch has enough information to bring us down. It could happen any time."

"You're certainly a cheerful companion for this shopping trip."

"I'm just trying to make my case. I want to guarantee that I will hold you one more time. That's why I brought the condom."

"And where do you think you'll be able to accomplish this?"

"I don't know that yet. Not the picnic site. Even if no one's delivering stuff or arranging it, they would have left one of the hands to guard the place from critters. But

I plan to make it happen. You can count on that. So, are you with me?"

"Yes, but—"

"That's all I need to know." Desire surged through him. "Now, hang on."

14

EMILY HUNG ON. When they turned onto the asphalt road leading to Shoshone, she watched for any vehicle with lights mounted on the roof. Maybe because it was a Thursday instead of the weekend, they didn't see a single patrol car as Clay proceeded to demolish the speed limit.

Emily had always thought of the little town—located far enough from Jackson that it missed most of the tourist traffic—as boring because it didn't change much. Today she realized that having local families running the same businesses year after year gave the town a neighborly atmosphere.

She had no time to enjoy that, though, because Clay had the tiki torches tied down in the back of the truck before she'd finished paying for them.

"Ready?" he called from the doorway of the feed store.

She grabbed her change and thanked the man behind the counter.

"Welcome! I'll see you folks out there tonight!"

"Right!" Emily should have figured that most of the town was invited to the cookout. That's the way things worked around here. She dashed to the truck where Clay was holding the passenger door open for her. "I thought you'd be in the driver's seat ready to take off," she said as she hopped in.

"Just because I'm in a hurry doesn't mean I've forgotten my manners." He closed the door and jogged around the cab.

Emily smiled. *Cowboys. Gotta love 'em.* Then she blinked. Had that thought really gone through her mind? Yes, it certainly had, and she felt something give way inside her as years of dammed-up feelings began to surface.

She didn't hate cowboys, or the cowboy way of life. She didn't hate ranching or horses or dirt. That was her mother who disliked all those things. Emily had grown up hearing it, and somewhere along the way, she'd adopted her mother's prejudices as her own. Understandable, but still very sad.

"Are you watching for cops?"

She turned to him, joy washing through her as she recognized that she could love this man. She'd been battling the urge to do that because of who he was and where he lived. She didn't have to battle anymore. "No."

"Why not? And why are you grinning at me like that?"

"Because I just had an epiphany, which is amazing because I'm not standing on that sacred site you told me about."

"I'm happy for you, but if you don't help me look for the fuzz, we'll have a citation to go along with that epiphany."

"Okay. I can do that." But she couldn't wipe the smile off her face as she began scouring the side of the road for patrol cars lying in wait for the likes of Clay Whitaker.

"What's your epiphany?"

"I can't tell you yet." She wasn't about to blurt out that

she was falling in love with him while he was barreling down the road and had to concentrate. "But I can tell you that I had a blast working with Calamity Sam this morning. I had no idea that my dad's job was that much fun."

"Just so you know, it's not all fun."

"So tell me all the down sides to working with horses." She probably needed a reality check to go along with her epiphany.

"Summers are great, but we still have to take care of the horses in the winter. We usually run ropes between the main buildings down to the barn, so if we get caught in a snowstorm, we won't get disoriented and freeze to death."

"Wow. Sounds like a challenge. Do you hate the winters, then?" She'd never been here during the winter. Maybe she'd hate that part.

"I don't, actually. The barn's heated, and working in there when the wind's howling outside is kind of cozy. In fact, being anywhere inside is cozy. We have a pot-bellied stove in the bunkhouse, and of course there's the big fireplace in the main house. Christmas is great. The Chances always have a huge tree, and the hands put one up in the bunkhouse, too."

"So you're pretty much guaranteed a white Christmas every year."

"Yep." He was quiet for a moment. "Thinking of coming back for Christmas?"

"Yes. Yes, I am." She was thinking of doing far more than that, but it was a huge decision. She wanted to rush headlong into it, but she was trying to be more practical. "How do you feel about the riding part of your job?"

"Love it, especially when I have the chance to take a

horse on a good run across the meadow. I feel like the king of the world when I can do that. Why?"

Excitement skittered down her spine. "I've never had the chance to ride like that. Dad was always worried about me falling, plus I refused to wear practical riding clothes and boots. But I'd like to try riding fast." Judging from the times she'd been on horseback, she could easily imagine substituting a galloping horse for a powerful wave. Everything was falling into place.

"Maybe tomorrow."

"That would be great." Riding with him would fit perfectly with her epiphany. "So what do you dislike about your work? Tell me all the bad stuff."

"Some people complain about shoveling manure, but I don't mind that. Others complain about getting up early, but I don't mind that, either. It's not a nine-to-five job, either. You never quite leave it."

"But if you're doing something you love, no matter what it is, you never quite leave it anyway, do you?"

He thought about that. "I suppose not."

"But I'm sure there's at least one really bad downside to your job."

"There is. Horses are more delicate than you'd think. They get sick. They die."

"Okay, that would be tough." She thought of Calamity Sam as he cavorted around the corral and tried to steal carrots. Yes, that would be a downside, for sure.

"It's hard both emotionally and financially," Clay said. "That's why I'm glad the Chances agreed to start collecting and shipping semen. When you depend entirely on the sale of horses, you're too vulnerable to illness and death. But semen is an asset that's not so likely to go south on you."

"Would you call it a liquid asset?" She was trying so hard not to laugh.

"Not always. Sometimes it's a frozen asset."

She couldn't tell from his tone whether he was kidding her or not, but she couldn't hold back her laughter another second. "Sorry," she managed through her giggles. "I know it's a serious subject, but—"

"No, it's not." He looked over at her and grinned. "Politics and religion are serious subjects. This is a conversation about horse ejaculate. How serious can that be?"

"I didn't want to mock what you do for a living."

"No mock taken. Still watching for cops?"

"I am, I promise, because you're still speeding."

"Yes, ma'am, I am." He hesitated. "Mind if I ask why all the questions about my job?"

"Just collecting data for my new project."

"Which is?"

"I'll tell you later. Oh, slow down, slow down! There's a patrol car off to the right side of the road."

"I see it." He let up on the gas.

Emily held her breath as they drove past the cop. When the patrol car stayed on the side of the road and didn't pull out after them, she sighed in relief. "I *really* don't want us to get a ticket."

"Us?"

"Well, you would get the ticket, of course, but—"

"It's okay. You don't have to explain. I liked that you said *us*."

"Me, too."

CLAY DIDN'T KNOW what to think. All this talk about an epiphany followed by a bunch of questions about raising horses for a living told him that something was going on in that beautiful head of hers. She might be thinking that life on a ranch wasn't so bad, after all.

He could thank himself for that, because good sex could have a powerful effect on a person. From what he'd gathered from Emmett, good sex had been part of why Emmett and Jeri had decided to get married, even though Jeri wasn't the ranching type. Emmett had been so worried about history repeating itself, and now it seemed like a legitimate concern.

Clay had never consciously set out to change Emily's mind about ranch life, but motivations were tricky things. Deep down, he might have hoped that she'd start thinking more kindly about cowboys in general and him in particular. He might have gotten his wish, and now he had to deal with the potential problem he'd caused for both of them.

He couldn't pretend anymore that this was all about sex. He was falling for her. Her use of the word *us* had demonstrated how fast he was falling, because he'd loved hearing her say it. He wanted to hear her say it some more.

But whatever this supposed epiphany was, she couldn't trust it. Her hormones were in control, not her brain, and at some point he'd have to tell her that. Depressing as that thought was, it was followed by one even more depressing. All things considered, he shouldn't have sex with her again.

He shouldn't have surrendered to temptation in the first place, but that was water under the bridge. No sense in beating himself up for something that he couldn't change. He could change his current plan, though, so he wouldn't add fuel to the fire.

"You're quiet all of a sudden," she said.

"Just thinking."

"Anything I need to know about?"

"Not yet."

"That's enigmatic."

"Oh, you know cowboys. We're the strong, silent type." He turned right onto the dirt road leading to the ranch. The entrance, with its poles on either side of the road and another over the top to hold the Last Chance Ranch sign, always gave his heart a lift as he drove through it.

He hoped maybe Emily could feel the same someday. But she had to love the ranch for itself, and not because she'd fallen for him and wanted to find a way they could be together.

"Hold on," he said. "I'm going to speed up."

"Go for it." Her green eyes sparkled under the shade of her straw hat.

If only he could. He gripped the wheel and stepped on the gas. He concentrated on his driving and tried not to think about Emily sitting there beside him.

He'd promised her they'd have sex, but it was a promise he'd have to break, for her sake and maybe for his, too. After bragging about how easily he could protect himself emotionally, he'd done a piss-poor job of it. He'd known she'd be sexy, but he hadn't counted on her being fun and endearing. Bottom line, he was already dreading the day she drove away.

The trip to the picnic site was a wild ride, but not for the reason he'd originally given Emily. He wanted to be finished with this job so he could take her back to the house and put some distance between them. Nobility would be far easier when she wasn't close enough to touch.

But he wouldn't leave her hanging, either. She shouldn't have to wonder why he'd changed his mind. He didn't play those kinds of games. So instead of making love to her, he'd explain exactly why he wasn't doing that.

"Wow, it looks different out here," she said as they pulled up behind one of the ranch trucks.

"It better look different. The party's in a few hours." He got out and waved at Jeb, a young ranch hand with red hair and freckles. Jeb must have been assigned to guard duty because he was sitting on a bench talking on his cell phone.

By the time he came around the truck to let Emily out, she'd opened the door and was ready to hop down. "Your manners are wonderful." She jumped to the grassy edge of the road. "But we need to get this done."

"Hey, I can help." Jeb walked toward the truck, tucking his cell phone in his jeans pocket as he approached. "Sarah just called and said you'd be coming with tiki torches. In fact, I can take care of the whole job if you want. There's nothing much else to do out here and I'm supposed to stay until everyone rides out."

Clay took a look around. Wood was piled in both fire pits, and every table was decorated with a red checkered oilcloth attached to it with metal clamps. One table held boxes of nonperishables, and the coolers were stacked in the back of the ranch truck with a tarp over them.

Jeb shrugged. "It's all done. I may drag some fallen tree branches out here from the woods and chop them up for extra firewood, but other than that, we're good to go." He glanced at Emily. "It's sure nice that you could make it for your dad's birthday, Emily."

She smiled at him. "I'm glad I could, too. It's Jeb, right?"

"Yes, ma'am." His face was shaded by his hat, but that didn't completely disguise the blush that made his freckles disappear. "Saw you working with Calamity Sam this morning."

"I had fun."

"Yes, ma'am. That yearling is lots of fun. I remember one time he managed to let himself out of the corral. I had to chase him all over the yard, but I finally caught him. And then there was this other time when he—"

"Sorry to interrupt, but we'd better get going." Clay knew that if he didn't say something, Jeb would keep talking forever, just to maintain a connection with Emily. Clay had been like Jeb ten years ago—totally infatuated. "So if you'll help unload the torches and set them up for us, that would be great. Sarah wants them in a circle surrounding the picnic tables."

"I know." Jeb nodded. "For the mosquitoes. That's a really good idea. Emily, I don't know if you've experienced Wyoming mosquitoes, but they—"

"With luck we won't experience them tonight," Clay said. "Let's get those torches unloaded so you can start putting them up."

"You bet." Jeb seemed to take the hint and headed for the back of the truck. When Emily followed him, he paused. "You don't need to be hauling torches, Emily. Clay and I can handle this."

Emily exchanged an amused glance with Clay. "Thanks, Jeb. I'll go relax in the truck."

"You do that." Jeb proceeded to unload the torches with as much swagger as possible, carrying one on each shoulder over to the picnic tables.

Clay sighed, understanding the impulse far too well. He wasn't so different from Jeb, after all. This morning he'd paraded across Emily's line of vision carrying the collection canister on his shoulder because she'd commented on how manly he'd looked doing it the day before.

Once the torches were unloaded, Clay shook hands with Jeb and climbed back in the truck. "That's done."

"Yes." She gave him a sideways glance filled with meaning. "That's done. Now what?"

He started the truck and made a U-turn so they were headed back toward the ranch house. "Now we find a private place to talk."

She laughed. "Talk? That isn't the way you presented it before."

"I know. But we do need to talk."

"Actually, I agree. But we have extra time now that Jeb's setting up the torches. We should have time to talk, and...do other things."

He stifled a groan.

"Unless you don't want to do those other things anymore?"

"I do. You have no idea how much. It's just...let's wait until I can pull off the road. I want to be far enough away that Jeb doesn't realize what we're doing."

"I'm for that."

The meadows were crisscrossed with various temporary roads that were nothing more than two indistinct tire tracks. Clay found one off to the right and took it. As he recalled, this one curved around behind a line of pine trees, so the truck would be out of sight.

The road turned as he'd remembered, and he drove until he was satisfied with the level of privacy. Then he switched off the engine and unfastened his seat belt. "Let's get out and walk a bit." He laid his hat on the dash.

"Walk? I thought cowboys hated to walk."

"Humor me."

"Sure." She unfastened her seat belt and followed his example, putting her hat on her side of the dashboard.

"And let me help you out."

"I can do that, too."

He thought about what to say and how to say it as he rounded the truck and opened her door. But once she placed her hand in his and he helped her down, all thoughts went out of his head, and he pulled her close with a groan, cradling her head against his chest while he fought the need to kiss her.

She wrapped her arms around him. "What's wrong, Clay? Is it that you're worried about my dad? Because I would never let him take this out on you. And, anyway, I don't think we have to worry about that."

"It's not your dad."

She lifted her head and gazed up at him. "Then what is it? You seem very upset."

He looked into those glorious green eyes. "It's you I'm worried about, Emily. I think I know what your epiphany is all about, and I'm afraid you're not thinking very clearly right now."

Her lips firmed. "Since you seem to be able to read my mind, would you care to tell me what's muddled about my thinking?"

"I don't mean to insult you. I'm just trying to help."

"Help me think?"

"Help you realize that our lovemaking has cast a rosy glow over your whole ranch experience, making you see things through that filter. That's no way to make a decision that could affect the rest of your life."

"What decision?"

"About moving here. About being with me."

She stiffened in his arms. "Forgive me for assuming you might welcome that idea."

"God, I'm saying this all wrong. I would love to have you here. You have to know that."

She backed out of his arms. "I'm having a little trouble believing it while you're harping on the rosy glow that's skewed my thinking all to hell and gone."

"But isn't that what happened to your mother?"

She stared at him. "My mother had never been to Wyoming in her life. She came out on vacation, met my dad, and on the basis of great sex she decided to marry him and live here."

"Exactly."

"Clay, that is *nothing* like my situation. I've been coming to this ranch ever since I was old enough to travel by myself on a plane. My dad is a cowboy."

"But—"

"Let me finish. I have ranching in my blood, whether I wanted to acknowledge that before or not. My mother has been telling me for years that I don't want this life, and her brainwashing has worked until now, when I've finally begun to think for myself. You—" she paused to point a finger at him "—are the icing on the cake, but you're not the cake! This ranch and my ties to it are the cake. Got that?"

"Yeah, but if we hadn't made love, I wonder if you would feel the same."

She threw her hands in the air. "Maybe not! Maybe I like icing on my cake! So is that why you're reconsidering having sex with me right now? You're worried there's too much icing?"

He rubbed the back of his neck, more confused than ever. "I don't know. Maybe."

"Well, heaven forbid that could happen. Take me back to the ranch house. I have a party to get ready for."

He reached for her. "Emily, I didn't mean to imply that you aren't capable of making a good decision. I just—"

"Oh, you didn't imply anything." She backed out of reach. "You flat-out said it. And because I don't relish having sex with someone who thinks my brain's so addled with hormones that I can't think straight, I'm glad you decided against using that condom. Let's go." She turned and climbed back into the truck and closed the door with a loud bang.

Uncertain what to say or do, he had no choice but to walk back around to the driver's side, get in and start the engine. He hadn't expected this conversation to be a lot of fun, but he'd hoped they'd be able to discuss things rationally.

He put on his hat, and she grabbed hers and crammed it down over her shiny hair.

"Emily, I just think you need to take more time before you come to any conclusions. That's all I'm saying."

She stared out the windshield. "Just drive, Whitaker. And make it fast. I know you're good at that."

Cursing under his breath, he backed the truck around and headed toward the ranch road. Once on it, he drove as fast as he dared. He could hardly wait for this ride to end. Being noble truly sucked.

15

EMILY CHOSE NOT to say anything more on the ride back to the ranch, and she hopped out of the truck before Clay had shut off the motor. She left with a curt goodbye and thank you. Clay had tarnished her shiny new epiphany, and she was furious with him for doing that.

She wondered how she ever could have thought she was falling in love with a guy who had such a low opinion of her reasoning ability. The argument had clarified her thinking nicely, though. She'd discovered an affinity for horses and for ranch life in general.

For the first time in her life she felt excited about a career option, and she had a built-in mentor. She would ask her dad if she could move here and apprentice herself to him. She figured he'd be thrilled.

Because of all the money she'd saved, she wouldn't need a salary for quite a while. Her living quarters might be an issue, but maybe she could rent one of the vacant rooms in the main house from Sarah. As for Clay, she'd learn to enjoy her cake without icing, thank you very much.

Fortunately nobody was in the living room when she

walked into the house, because she was in no mood to talk to anyone. Mary Lou had run Emily's jeans through the washer and dryer this morning while she was working with Calamity Sam, so she'd take a hot shower and get dressed for the party. She wouldn't mention her idea to her father until tomorrow, when they could find some quiet time to sit down and make plans.

Maybe she wouldn't have to confront him about the fake inheritance, after all. She could simply say she'd saved a lot of money over the years, which would fund her apprenticeship. And once she was working here, he wouldn't need to send her any more. That way she could save his pride.

Being on the premises would make it easier for her to encourage his romance with Pam, too. But Emily didn't intend to mention Pam to her mother. Jeri would be unhappy enough about the move without the added news about her ex's new girlfriend.

Emily could soften the blow of leaving Santa Barbara with frequent trips back there, but she'd spent the first twenty-seven years of her life within a short distance of her mom's front door. She'd thought her mother needed her, and perhaps she did, but so did her father. And Emily's future was here at the Last Chance.

Climbing the curved staircase, she walked down the hallway to her bedroom. Before she reached it, she knew someone was in there fiddling with her window. She recognized the sounds after all the action that window'd had the night before. No doubt the person in her room was replacing the screen.

She knew for a fact it wasn't Clay. She paused, not sure if she wanted to find out who it was. She could always go back downstairs and…and what? Lurk around watching to see who came down the staircase?

No, that was cowardly. If she hoped to work at the Last Chance, she might as well own up to damaging the screen and get that behind her. She'd rather not admit exactly *how* it was damaged, but maybe she wouldn't have to.

Then again, maybe she'd have to confess all… When she walked into the room, she found her father fastening a new screen into place. His hat was lying on the bed. Next to it was a brown Stetson.

She cleared her throat, in case he hadn't heard her footsteps. "Hi, Dad."

"Hello, Emily." He finished adjusting the screen and turned around.

"Thanks for doing that." How lame that sounded, but she wasn't sure where to start.

"It needed doing. I had to go help Pam with a plumbing issue, so while I was buying an elbow joint for her bathroom sink, I picked up a new screen for the window."

"You're probably disappointed in me."

"Actually I'm more disappointed in myself. If I'd been more involved in your life, you might be more inclined to listen to my advice. As it stands, I can't really blame you for ignoring me. Why should you pay attention to a guy who's spent maybe thirty days with you all told since you were a toddler?"

"Dad, I've just figured something out. If you have a minute, I'd like to tell you about it."

"I have as long as it takes."

Her throat tightened with love for this man. He'd loved her so much from afar, and he hadn't been willing to make her the battleground between him and Jeri. He'd simply abandoned the field.

"I need to start by saying that what I'm about to ask has nothing whatsoever to do with Clay."

"Okay."

From the way he said it, she knew he didn't believe that. But she plowed ahead anyway, explaining how she felt about the ranch and why she wanted to become his apprentice. "And I have a fair amount of money saved, so I wouldn't need a salary for at least the first year."

His eyes widened. "A year? Really?"

"I haven't spent all you gave me. I've been investing." She decided to substitute *all* for *any* and hope he wouldn't question that.

Fortunately he didn't. "You must be one hell of an investor."

"I am, actually. But I don't want to go into that field, if that's what you might be thinking. It's fun to do it for myself, and I'd be happy to help you if you want, but I know now that I need an outdoor job. I basically want to do what you're doing."

"You might need to get in line. At one time Jack said he wanted my job when I'm done with it. That might have changed now that he's settled in with Josie, but that's what he said once."

Emily shrugged. "Then I'll be one of the hands for as long as they'll have me. I really don't care. But I've discovered I love it here. I love not having to dress in business clothes and sit behind a desk. I love that I could walk out my front door and be at work."

"The weather's not always so balmy, you know."

"That's what Clay said." Instantly she regretted bringing Clay's name back into the conversation.

"So he knows about your plan?"

"Not really. He got an inkling of what I had in mind and told me I didn't know what I was talking about."

Emmett sighed. "I'm afraid he's right. Look, I know you're involved with him, and you think that you can just change your life around to accommodate that, but—"

"No, Dad! That's why I said right away that he has nothing to do with this. As far as I'm concerned, Clay and I are finished."

"Finished? You barely got started!"

"We shouldn't have started at all. Now he's convinced that the only reason I want to move here is because of him. How's that for an ego?"

Emmett folded his arms. "Can you honestly tell me that you would have come to this conclusion if Clay hadn't been part of the picture?"

"Obviously I can't. He's been part of my experience, so of course that had to have some bearing. But he's not *the* reason I want to move here. This is not a replay of you and Mom. I wouldn't care if he moved to…I don't know…Texas."

"Emily, he won't do that, and you know it. This is the place that became his first home, and that's why he came back after he finished school. You couldn't pry him away from this ranch with a crowbar. So if you move to the Last Chance, you'll be running into Clay all the time. And I think that's what you have in mind."

Now it was her turn to cross her arms. "No, it isn't."

Sarah's voice drifted up the stairs. "Emily, are you up there? I talked to Clay, and he said you two delivered the tiki torches."

"We did!" Emily glanced at her dad and lowered her voice. "Does she know you're up here replacing the screen?"

"No. I made sure the coast was clear."

"Well, I'm here, now, so we can make it look like you came to see me." She walked out into the hall and over to the top of the stairs to peer down at Sarah. "My dad and I were up here having a father-daughter chat, but if you need me for something, let me know."

Sarah beamed at her. "Good girl," she said softly. "Keep him occupied for a little longer. We're lining the horses up on the far side of the house so he won't see them until the last minute." Sarah made a circle of her thumb and forefinger, winked at Emily, and walked out the front door.

Emily walked back into the bedroom. She might not get that hot shower, after all.

"Something's cooking, isn't it?" Emmett gazed at her.

"What makes you think that?"

"The way everyone's concerned with keeping me busy all of a sudden."

"Well, I'm not. I just want to know if you'll hire me, at no pay, as your apprentice."

"Emily, I think you're making a big—"

"What have you got to lose? You'll get to see a lot of me, you'll get some free help around here—even if I'm not very good at first—and if I find out after a few months that I don't like it, you're out nothing and I've spent a little money and time finding out it doesn't work for me."

"But you will have quit your job and, I assume, given up your apartment."

"So what? I don't much like the job or the apartment. I can easily find another one of each if I really can't stand it here."

"Let me think about it. I need to get out of here while Sarah's otherwise occupied." He started toward the door.

"Wait."

"For what?"

"You forgot your hat." She picked it up and held it out. "And what about the other one?"

"I thought you should give it to him. Less awkward that way."

She held out both hands, palms up. "No, thanks."

"Oh, for crying out loud, Emily. You could give him back the hat."

"I won't be rude to him in public, but I really can't see myself returning his hat. I'd appreciate it if you would."

"He's not going to like getting this hat from me."

"He won't be as surprised as you think. He knows somebody found it, and that somebody also made off with the damaged screen. He's worried that it'll all come out publicly at the party tonight."

"Good God!" Emmett stared at her in shock. "I would never embarrass you two like that!"

She dredged up a smile. "Thanks for that. But I really think you need to return the hat and talk to him. That way, you'll find out I'm right. Hope for a relationship with Clay is not my motivation for coming to the Last Chance. I'm sure he knows that now." She picked up Clay's hat and extended it toward her father.

"Maybe you're right." He took the hat and tucked it under his arm. "I suppose while I'm at it I should also ask him his intentions toward my daughter. That's what dads are supposed to do."

"Well, I'm not sure you want to ask him *that*." She didn't think Emmett wanted to know what Clay's intentions were, or what they had been, before he'd decided sex was rotting her brain.

"I'll talk with him," he said. "I'll find out his stand on all this." He paused. "Do you want me to give him any message?"

"No." That sounded too abrupt. "No, thank you."

"Okay, then. Guess I'll be riding with someone else instead of driving myself to the Spirits and Spurs, so let's try to get in the same vehicle."

"You bet." She was astounded that her dad, who had been alert enough to discover that Clay had climbed through her bedroom window last night, hadn't figured out that the Spirits and Spurs plan was a decoy. Maybe that was her doing, hers and Clay's. Emmett was so worried about his daughter and Clay making a mess of their lives that he'd missed the cues that his birthday would be in a whole other venue. She walked over and gave him a quick hug. "See you soon, Dad."

Maybe it was mean of her to send him off with that hat, but he and Clay had their own relationship to work out. They needed to come to terms with what had happened and get beyond it. That was her goal, and it should be theirs, too.

CLAY SAT IN the driveway for a while after Emily made her chilly exit and wondered if he could have done anything better. Maybe not. He still thought she was making a snap decision based partly, if not completely, on what they'd shared.

He might be a fool for not embracing her cockeyed plan. If he'd been enthusiastic instead of discouraging, things would be a whole lot more pleasant—at least for the short term.

But the fun wouldn't have lasted long. Emmett was bound to be suspicious of her sudden change of heart, especially given her poorly disguised interest in Clay. Plain and simple, Clay felt responsible for Emily's supposed epiphany. He'd owed Emmett the courtesy of trying to talk her out of it.

Thinking about Emmett reminded him that the foreman's birthday party would start soon. Clay wasn't in the mood for a party, but he could fake it. He should also check how Watkins had made out with the lists.

After parking the truck, Clay went looking for Watkins in the horse barn. He found the place virtually deserted. Apparently the horses had already been saddled and taken to the agreed-upon gathering spot at the far end of the house, a place Emmett wasn't likely to look.

Scanning the yard for any sign of Emmett, Clay walked quickly from the barn to the house and hurried around to the east side. Sure enough, a string of saddled horses was there, with a couple of the guys keeping track of them until the appointed hour.

Since everything seemed to be under control, Clay gave them a wave and started back toward the bunkhouse. But skidded to a stop when he saw Emmett coming down the steps of the ranch house. The foreman was carrying Clay's brown Stetson. Shit.

He decided to stay where he was and see what Emmett did. Emmett was headed in the direction of the bunkhouse. If he walked in and didn't come back out right away, Clay would follow. Although, with the party coming up so soon this didn't seem like the best time to discuss Clay's relationship with Emily.

Emmett disappeared into the bunkhouse with the hat. He came out seconds later without it. Clay sighed in relief. They'd have to talk about Emily sometime, but not right now.

Clay had known in his gut that Emmett had found the hat, and likely the screen, too. He wondered if the foreman had already talked to Emily. She'd probably run into him on the way to her room.

Clay wanted to know how that conversation had gone, but he'd have to wait to find out. He needed a quick shower and a change of clothes. At least he could wear his best hat to the party.

16

By the light of a roaring bonfire, Emily watched her dad open his presents. He took his own sweet time with each one and tolerated the heckling with a good-natured smile. For a guy who tended to avoid being the center of attention, he seemed to be thoroughly enjoying himself.

One of the hands had bought him the expected whoopee cushion, and he'd been sitting on it ever since. Every time he shifted his weight, the cushion bleated, causing a roar of laugher from the hands. It was silly and fun, exactly as a sixtieth should be.

Sarah approached, a wine bottle in one hand and her own plastic goblet in the other. The guys mostly had beer, but Sarah had provided wine for those who preferred it. "Need me to top that off, Emily?"

"Thanks, but I'm fine. Listen, I can take that bottle and go around checking on the wine drinkers. You should relax after all the work you've done."

"It's okay. I love being the hostess. But thanks for offering. It's gone well, don't you think?"

"Beautifully. I can't believe how surprised he was when you took him around the house and he saw the horses all saddled and ready to go." Emily held up her pocket-size camera. "I know Dominique's the official photographer, but I wanted some, too. I got that one, for sure."

"Good. It never hurts to have more than one camera in the mix."

"That's why I brought mine," Pam said, coming over to stand beside Sarah. "I'm following you, wine lady. I need a refill."

"My pleasure." Sarah poured wine into Pam's glass. "I was just telling Emily that I think this turned out great."

"It sure did. It took more advance planning than the Normandy Invasion, but the results are outstanding." She glanced over at Emily. "Having you here is the crowning touch. I don't want to lay a guilt trip on you, but I know he'd love to have you visit more often."

"Funny you should mention that." During the party Emily had realized that the person with the power around here was Sarah Chance. If Sarah agreed that Emily could become an unpaid employee, then everyone else would have to fall in line. Emily had been talking to the wrong people.

"Oh, good," Pam said. "Are you saying you'll be here next summer? Or how about Christmas? It's beautiful here during the holidays."

"Actually," she turned to the woman who could give them both the answer they wanted to hear, "I was wondering if I could rent a room from you, Sarah, and start learning the horse business."

Sarah didn't look as surprised as Emily might have thought she would. Instead she exchanged a glance with Pam. "See? I told you she'd started to like it here."

"I love it here. I probably always have, but I've been

hearing all my life that ranching was wrong for me and I wouldn't let myself see the truth." She paused for a breath. "And before we get any further in the discussion, this isn't about Clay."

Sarah gave her an understanding smile. "Not even a little bit?"

"All right, it was a little bit at first, but he said I don't know my own mind, so he's not my favorite person right now."

Pam chuckled. "No woman likes a man telling her she's not thinking straight. I'm still trying to teach Emmett that lesson."

"I dearly hope you succeed, Pam." Emily turned back to Sarah. "I have money for rent and food, so I wouldn't need a salary for at least a year, maybe longer. I've saved…most of what my dad's been sending me, and I've invested it. So I'd be free help for as long as it takes me to learn the job."

Sarah gave her a long look. "You realize a lot of people on the ranch think you've been soaking your dad for years and squandering his hard-earned cash."

"Clay told me. But I'm not that kind of person."

"I've known that from the moment I found out you drove seventeen hours to get here so you wouldn't have to spend money on a motel." Sarah grinned. "That's your dad all over."

"This afternoon at my house," Pam said, "he couldn't say enough about the way you worked with Calamity Sam. But he's worried about you and Clay. He thinks you'll make the same mistake your mother made. You'll hook up with a cowboy and then find out this life isn't for you."

"But I don't see that happening," Sarah said. "Do you, Pam?"

"No, I don't. I saw you helping Mary Lou grill those steaks tonight. Then you ran around making sure everybody had bread and coleslaw. I've watched your face tonight, Emily. You're in your element, aren't you?"

"Exactly!" Joy bubbled in her at finding someone who understood. "I've never been able to figure out my place in this world because I refused to consider that the ranch was it. But it is…if Sarah will have me."

"I would be delighted. When do you want to start?"

"Is tomorrow okay?"

Sarah laughed. "I thought you'd want to go home and take care of things there first."

"But this is home."

"That's nice to hear, but I only meant—"

"I know, and I'll make some calls tomorrow. The most important one will be to my mother."

Sarah took a swallow of wine. "She won't like this."

"No, but I'll visit. Once she understands how happy I am here, she'll be okay with it. I hope so, anyway." Emily couldn't let herself be sidetracked by what her mother wanted. She'd done that all her life.

"Well, I think this deserves a toast." Pam raised her glass. "Here's to going after what you want."

"I'll drink to that." Sarah touched her glass to Pam's and winked.

"Me, too." Emily clicked her glass against each of theirs. "Thank you. Thank you both for all the support. And by the way, Pam, I intend to help you get what you want, too."

Pam held her gaze. "Thank you. He's a stubborn one."

"Who thinks you don't know your own mind," Emily added.

"Yes. But if you and I put our minds together…"

Emily smiled. "He'll be a goner."

"This is going to be fun to watch," Sarah said. "And speaking of watching, Clay hasn't taken his eyes off you all night, Emily."

"Maybe he's waiting for me to do something stupid."

Sarah glanced in Clay's direction. "So do something smart. Go over there and tell him you're staying, whether he thinks it's a good idea or not. Let him know you don't need his approval."

Pam grinned. "Sarah Chance, you are a troublemaker."

"But she's right," Emily said. "Instead of getting angry when he said my plan was bad, I should have laughed and said I was doing it anyway." She drained her wine-glass and tossed it in a nearby trash barrel. "But it's not too late. I can still say that. Excuse me, ladies. I have a man to put in his place."

CLAY HAD TRIED to ignore Emily. He'd really tried. Turned out it was humanly impossible. He loved watching her move through the crowd, her borrowed straw cowboy hat at a jaunty angle, her smile charming everyone she met.

He'd noticed each time she laughed, and the reflection of the firelight in her long blond hair. She'd seemed thrilled when Watkins had tuned up his guitar, and she'd participated with gusto in the sing-alongs. Many of the tunes were old cowboy songs, and she didn't know all the words, but she'd chimed in happily when the chorus arrived.

If he'd expected her to retreat into a shell because he'd shot down her plan, she didn't seem willing to oblige.

He'd noticed Emmett watching her, too, a fond expression in his eyes. Emmett hadn't looked quite so happy when he'd glanced at Clay, though. The foreman was worried, and Clay regretted that.

Emmett had thanked him after unwrapping the leather gloves, but other than that, he hadn't said much. Clay didn't blame him. He'd complicated Emmett's life, and at some point he needed to ask for forgiveness. But bringing up problems wasn't what tonight was about.

That's why he couldn't figure out what Emily had in mind when she tossed away her wineglass and started in his direction. Surely she wasn't coming over to apologize for her angry response this afternoon. Was it possible she'd decided he was right and wanted to tell him so?

Funny, but that thought didn't make him feel very good. If he'd been right in his assessment, then she'd leave and might not be back for quite a while. Years, even… Suddenly he didn't want to be right. He wanted to be dead wrong.

She walked up to him and tilted her hat back so she could look him straight in the eye. "I'm staying," she said.

"Staying?" He wasn't sure what she meant. "You mean through the weekend?"

"No, I mean for good. I've talked to Sarah and she's fine with it. I'll rent the room I'm in and start learning how to train cutting horses. I start tomorrow."

His heart raced out of control. This was exciting, but so full of pitfalls, too. "Does Emmett know about this?"

"He knows that's what I want to do, but not that I've made a decision to do it and confirmed it with Sarah."

Clay hesitated. There were minefields all around him. "Uh, shouldn't you have checked with him first?"

"You know what? No. I asked him about it this afternoon, basically giving him the right to say whether I could or not, and he said he'd think about it."

"Sounds reasonable."

"It's a delaying tactic, and I'm tired of having my life on hold. Now that I know what I want, I'm impatient to get going. Tonight I realized that the person who ultimately gets to decide is not my dad, but Sarah. She's the boss lady, and it's her house I'd like to rent space in. So I asked her."

"That takes *cojones,* Emily."

"I'll tell you what it takes." She shoved her hands in the back pockets of her jeans and squared her shoulders. "It takes a woman who knows her own mind. And I do, Clay Whitaker. I most certainly do."

"I love you." The words spilled out before he knew they were coming.

Her eyes widened. "Did you just say what I think you said?"

"Yeah." He let out a breath and his whole body relaxed. There it was, out in the open. Just as well have it that way. "I love you. That may seem quick, but it's not. I've been half in love with you since I was eighteen, but then I really got to know you, and…I'm crazy about you, Emily."

A slow smile tilted the corners of her mouth. "And you couldn't have told me that this afternoon?"

"Are you kidding? That would have been the worst thing I could have done. Talk about stacking the deck! But now that you've planted yourself on this ranch, whether I like it or not, I'm free to say…I like it, Emily."

She glanced over her shoulder at the rowdy group gathering around Watkins as he tuned up his guitar. "They're starting another sing-along."

"You seemed to really enjoy that."

She turned back to him. "I did, but I think I'll skip this one. What do you say we step into the shadows for a few minutes?"

He knew he was grinning like a fool and couldn't help it. "You are getting assertive, Miss Sterling."

"I've discovered that's the only way for a girl to get what she wants." She gave him a little shove on the chest.

He stepped back out of the light given off by the bonfire and the tiki torches. "And what is it you want, Emily?"

"You, cowboy." And she grabbed him around the neck and put him in a lip-lock.

Judging from the way she was kissing him, he thought he was going to love this new, more aggressive Emily even more than he had the California surfer girl who hadn't known quite who she was or where she belonged. But he needed to get a few things straight, so he reluctantly lifted his mouth from hers.

She tried to pull his head down again.

"Wait. I want to ask you something. Is this all about sex?"

"It's partly about sex."

"I need more than that, Emily."

She chuckled. "Isn't that supposed to be my line?"

"Yes, and for some reason you're not saying it. I've laid my heart at your feet. So far yours is still safely tucked away. That won't work."

She cupped his face in both hands and her voice gentled. "I was going to tell you this afternoon, but then you insulted my intelligence."

"I'm sorry. I didn't give you credit for—"

"For being smart enough to know what's good for me?"

"Basically."

"That's right, you didn't. But before you made those patronizing remarks, I'd planned to tell you that a significant part of my epiphany…was you."

He couldn't believe how his soul thirsted for the words, the three little words that would make all the difference. "And what about me?"

"I haven't been dreaming about you for ten years, so I can't say that, but I have been hearing about you from my dad for a long time. Sure I was jealous, but I admired you and all you'd accomplished. And then I discovered you are awesome in bed, and you have a great sense of humor, and you carry a canister of horse semen better than anyone I know."

"Okay, so my résumé looks pretty good." *Say it, Emily!* "Anything to add to that?"

"Only that I love you desperately and can hardly wait to see how everything turns out between us now that I'll be staying here right under your nose. Is that what you were angling for?"

"Uh-huh." He tightened his arms around her and thanked his lucky stars for Emily. "But instead of being under my nose, I'd rather have you just under me, period. Do you think we could arrange that?"

"I have to find out from Sarah if I'm allowed to entertain men in my room. I can't have you climbing up and down that rope ladder anymore. It's hard on the screens."

He gazed down at her. "So I'm not dreaming this? You're really staying?"

"Yes."

"Then don't just ask if you can entertain a man in your room, like I'll be a guest." His mouth hovered over hers.

"Why not?"

"Because I want my own key." And then he kissed her as the birthday party crowd sang "Home on the Range." He'd thought that the Last Chance was his home, but now he knew where his home truly was—here in Emily's arms.

Epilogue

The following week

EMILY HELD THE LEAD ROPE as a black-and-white stallion named Rorschach mounted the dummy. Clay moved in with the collection canister with its warm AV, and Rorschach filled it. Emily still planned to learn how to train cutting horses, but because she'd been so fascinated with the semen collection process, Clay had suggested she might want to be his assistant now and then.

That worked for her. It seemed as if the mornings she helped him fill that canister affected them that night, making them more crazy for each other than usual. She'd decided not to point that out because this was supposed to be a clinical operation with no sexual overtones. But she knew better, and she thought Clay did, too.

Rorschach finished up and they let him rest on the dummy. Clay had set up a couple of sawhorses nearby where he could set the canister temporarily so he didn't have to hold it while they waited for Rorschach to recover. Emily wasn't quite ready to have Clay leave her alone to deal with a valuable stallion and a teaser mare.

"My mom's sending a box of my clothes over," she said. "I don't know how much of it I can wear around here, but it'll be good to get some of my underwear, at least."

Clay wiggled his eyebrows. "I love it when you talk dirty."

She smiled. "Actually there might be a few items you'll enjoy seeing on me. Obviously I didn't pack my sexy stuff for a trip to the ranch."

"Considering how I've reacted to the underwear you already have, I'm not sure my heart can take the racier type."

"We'll do some test runs and see how you hold up. Anyway, knowing my mom, she'll send mostly party dresses to remind me of all I'm giving up." She glanced at him. "Which is nothing, so don't look worried."

"You'll need a party dress for Alex and Tyler's wedding, though."

"I will, won't I? I can hardly wait for them to get back so I can meet them. I like Josie so much that I'm sure I'll like Alex. Morgan keeps saying her sister, Tyler, is way different from her, but still, they're sisters, so I'm sure I'll also like Tyler."

"If Alex loves her, then she has to be great. So did you hear about the best man? Alex's friend from Chicago, the baseball player?"

"I guess not. I've been too focused on the semen expert." She winked at him.

"And I want to keep it that way. Baseball players aren't nearly as sexy as cowboys, right?"

"Right." She laughed. "Unless they're in the major leagues."

"That lets out Logan Carswell, then. He just got

dropped by the Cubs. He suffered a career-ending injury of some kind."

"That's too bad."

"It is, but it puts him out of the running for you, which is all to the good." He glanced at Rorschach. "I think the big guy is ready to dismount and meander back to his stall."

"This really feels like a cheat, you know?" She made sure Rorschach climbed down safely and then led him toward the door.

"It's less of a cheat than making love with a condom." He hoisted the canister to his shoulder. "At least these little swimmers have a chance of hitting the big time."

She glanced at him. "Do you think about that much?"

"More, lately."

"This situation between us is getting serious, isn't it?"

He nodded. "'Fraid so."

She met his gaze. "I like that."

His warm smile wrapped her in a cozy blanket of love. "Yeah. Me, too."

* * * * *

We hope you enjoyed reading this
special collection from Harlequin® books.

If you liked reading these stories,
then you will love
Harlequin® Blaze® books!

You like it hot!
Harlequin Blaze stories sizzle with strong
heroines and irresistible heroes playing the
game of modern love and lust. They're fun,
sexy and always steamy.

Enjoy four *new* stories from
Harlequin Blaze every month!

Available wherever books and
ebooks are sold.

◆ HARLEQUIN®

Blaze®

Red-Hot Reads

www.Harlequin.com

STEPHB

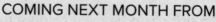
#839 WICKED SECRETS
Uniformly Hot!
by Anne Marsh
When Navy rescue swimmer Tag Johnson commands their one-night stand turn into a fake engagement, former Master Sergeant Mia Brandt doesn't know whether to refuse...or follow orders!

#840 THE MIGHTY QUINNS: ELI
The Mighty Quinns
by Kate Hoffmann
For a reality TV show, Lucy Parker must live in a remote cabin with no help. Search and rescue expert Eli Montgomery tempts Lucy with his wilderness skills—and his body. Accepting jeopardizes her job...and her defenses.

#841 GOOD WITH HIS HANDS
The Wrong Bed
by Tanya Michaels
Danica Yates just wants a hot night with the sexy architect in her building to help her forget her would-be wedding. She's shocked when she finds out she went home with his twin!

#842 DEEP FOCUS
From Every Angle
by Erin McCarthy
Recently dumped and none-too-happy, Melanie Ambrose is stuck at a resort with Hunter Ryan, a bodyguard hired by her ex. Could a sexy fling with this virtual stranger cure her blues?

YOU CAN FIND MORE INFORMATION ON UPCOMING HARLEQUIN® TITLES, FREE EXCERPTS AND MORE AT WWW.HARLEQUIN.COM.

HBCNM0315

SPECIAL EXCERPT FROM

HARLEQUIN

Blaze

*Military veteran Mia Brandt agrees to a fake
engagement to help sexy rescue swimmer Tag Johnson
out of a jam. But could their fun, temporary liaison lead
to something more?*

*Read on for a sneak preview at
WICKED SECRETS by Anne Marsh,
part of our UNIFORMLY HOT! miniseries.*

Sailor boy didn't look up. Not because he didn't notice
the other woman's departure—something about the way
he held himself warned her he was aware of everyone
and everything around him—but because polite clearly
wasn't part of his daily repertoire.

Fine. She wasn't all that civilized herself.

The blonde made a face, her ponytail bobbing as she
started hoofing it along the beach. "Good luck with that
one," she muttered as she passed Mia.

Oookay. Maybe this *was* mission impossible. Still,
she'd never failed when she'd been out in the field, and
all her gals wanted was intel. She padded into the water,
grateful for the cool soaking into her burning soles. The
little things mattered so much more now.

"I'm not interested." Sailor boy didn't look up from
the motor when she approached, a look of fierce concentration creasing his forehead. Having worked on more
than one Apache helicopter during her two tours of duty,
she knew the repair work wasn't rocket science.

She also knew the mechanic and…holy hotness.

Mentally, she ran through every curse word she'[v]e learned. Tag Johnson hadn't changed much in five year[s]. He'd acquired a few more fine lines around the corne[rs] of his eyes, possibly from laughing. Or from squintin[g] into the sun since rescue swimmers spent plenty of tim[e] out at sea. The white scar on his forearm was as new a[s] the lines, but otherwise he was just as gorgeous and ever[y] bit as annoying as he'd been the night she'd picked hi[m] up at the Star Bar in San Diego. He was also still out o[f] her league, a military bad boy who was strong, silen[t] deadly…and always headed out the door.

For a brief second, she considered retreating. Unfortu[-] nately, the bridal party was watching her intently, clearl[y] hoping she was about to score on their behalf. Disap[-] pointing them would be a shame.

"Funny," she drawled. "You could have fooled me."

Tag's head turned slowly toward her. Mia had hope[d] for drama. Possibly even his butt planting in the ocea[n] from the surprise of her reappearance. No such luck.

"Sergeant Dominatrix," he drawled back.

Don't miss
WICKED SECRETS
by New York Times *bestselling author Anne Marsh,*
available April 2015 wherever
Harlequin® Blaze® books and ebooks are sold.

www.Harlequin.com

Copyright © 2015 by Anne Marsh

HBEXP03

Love the Harlequin book you just read?

Your opinion matters.

Review this book on your favorite book site, review site, blog or your own social media properties and share your opinion with other readers!

Be sure to connect with us at:
Harlequin.com/Newsletters
Facebook.com/HarlequinBooks
Twitter.com/HarlequinBooks

HARLEQUIN®

A *Romance* FOR EVERY MOOD™

JUST CAN'T GET ENOUGH?

Join our social communities
and talk to us online.

You will have access to the latest
news on upcoming titles and special
promotions, but most importantly,
you can talk to other fans about your
favorite Harlequin reads.

Harlequin.com/Community

Facebook.com/HarlequinBooks

Twitter.com/HarlequinBooks

Pinterest.com/HarlequinBooks

HSOCIAL